THE WASHINGTON SQUARE ENSEMBLE

THE Madison Smartt Bell
WASHINGTON
SQUARE
ENSEMBLE

The Viking Press New York

LIBRARY OF CONGRESS CATALOGING IN PUBLICATION DATA
Bell, Madison Smartt.
The Washington Square ensemble.
    I. Title.
PS3552.E517W37   1983   813'.54   82-40372
ISBN 0-670-75005-0

Grateful acknowledgment is made to the following for permission to reprint from copyrighted material:

Bruce Springsteen and Laurel Canyon Music Ltd.: Excerpt from "Does This Bus Stop at 82nd Street" by Bruce Springsteen. Copyright © 1972 by Bruce Springsteen and Laurel Canyon Music Ltd. Used by permission.

Farrar, Straus & Giroux, Inc., and Faber and Faber Ltd.: Excerpt from "Last Days of Alice" from *Collected Poems 1919–1976* by Allen Tate. Copyright 1931, 1932, 1937, 1948 by Charles Scribner's Sons. Copyright renewed © 1959, 1960, 1965 by Allen Tate. Reprinted by permission of Farrar, Straus & Giroux, Inc., and Faber and Faber Ltd.

Fifth Floor Music, Inc.: Excerpt from "Step Right Up" by Tom Waits. Copyright © 1976 by Fifth Floor Music, Inc. Reprinted by permission.

Macmillan Publishing Co., Inc., and George Allen and Unwin Ltd.: Excerpts from *The Koran Interpreted,* translated by Arthur J. Arberry. Copyright © 1955 by George Allen & Unwin Ltd. Reprinted by permission of Macmillan Publishing Co., Inc., and George Allen & Unwin Ltd.

The University of Chicago Press: Excerpts from *The Mystical Poems of Rumi: First Selection Poems 1–200,* translated by A. J. Arberry. Copyright © 1968 by A. J. Arberry. Reprinted by permission of The University of Chicago Press.

*This book is dedicated to the long patience of my parents,
with a tip of the trick hat to George Garrett.*

Acknowledgments

My deepest gratitude to Richard Dillard, Rosanne Coggeshall, Stephen Koch, and William Goyen, for good advice freely given. To Jane Gelfman and Margaret Blackstone, for indispensable practical help and encouragement. To Cork Smith, for faithful attention to every detail of this book. To the editorial staff of The Franklin Library, for keeping my body and soul together during much of the writing of it. To Alex Roshuk, Rick Feist, and Neil Cartan, for teaching me many survival skills, and providing the community which has sustained us all.

. . . I tell you that, if these should hold their peace, the stones would immediately cry out.

—Luke 19:40

Part One

THE STORYTELLING STONE

. . . and it walks your dog doubles on sax
doubles on sax you can jump back jack
see ya later alligator see ya later
alligator and it steals your car Gets
rid of your gambling debts it quits smoking
it's a friend it's a companion it's the
only product you will ever need . . .
—Tom Waits

Johnny B.

It's Saturday night and I'm coming into the park from the foot of Fifth and what do I see? Alex the fuzzbox guitar player has taken the prime spot under the arch, the Washington Square arch so newly purged of ugly graffiti by the good people in this world, and Alex the fuzzbox guitar player is actually singing in public, for the first time ever, to my knowledge. It would seem that Alex has raked enough quarters out of his scummy guitar case to spring for a Mighty Mouse amp with matching microphone for his voice. A big yellow man with a raggedy Afro, Alex is, and he plays very nicely on his fuzzbox guitar, always has, and he probably thinks he looks like Jimi Hendrix, but what is he singing into the new amp bought and paid for with the quarters of NYU students and tourists from Iowa? "The Nights of Broadway," by the Bee Gees. And the vocal tones coming forth from the Mighty Mouse amp sound like not one of the Bee Gees but all three of them, and Alex is attracting a big big crowd, with lots of chic white people in it for this park on the short end of Saturday night. Which must be why Alex is in the arch instead of at his usual post by the fountain, for here within screaming distance of the lights of Fifth Avenue these well-dressed white people with pockets of money feel safe and secure. And Alex has brought two walking muscles down from Harlem to protect the nickels and dimes they will give him, so he can buy another Bee Gees album and practice for the Carson show.

But I have no time to stand on the edge of a crowd and listen to Alex spit smarmy pop-tones into his gleaming new microphone. I am a businessman, and I am not in the entertainment business. I sell pharmaceuticals, and I have four retailers working nights in the park, and I would like to know why at least one of them is not working this nice crowd got together by Alex the fuzzbox guitar player and his classy new act. So I proceed onward, over to what used to be a volleyball court and is now the disco skaters' track, where my little Rican Santa Barbara should be stationed right now. Because pharmaceuticals make for zippier, happier skating.

But Santa Barbara is nowhere to be seen, and there are not even any disco skaters, except for Eva the Swede. Though I don't know if that is really her name, because we have never exchanged word one, because she comes to the park for the sole and only purpose of picking up black dudes. I gave her that name because of her looks— she isn't so gorgeous but she has ice-white skin and chrome-blond hair hanging down her back in a Nordic plait. And a dynamite skater too, if you care. Spends all her time skating from one big sulky black dude to another, rotating on her plastic wheels to pro- vide a round-the-clock view of her pale charms, and leaves with a different one every night. Poor Eva, she doesn't discriminate Ras- tas or Haitians or hard Harlemites, she just takes the blackest one she can get. I think she must have once flunked out of art school, and it's some kind of aesthetic turn-on for her to get that white skin against something real dark. And maybe it's a big kick for her, but I think it's a lousy reason to die, poor Eva the Swede, I get so tired wondering whether it will be the Rastas who claim her flaxen head for a soccer ball or the Haitians who will shrink it down to one- quarter size to add to their voodoo relic collections that I have thought of knocking her off myself. Just to save myself the sus- pense. Or maybe I could concoct some sort of ultra-aphrodisiacal pharmaceutical (with color blindness as a side effect) and afterward put her out with Lopez's string on Twenty-first and Park, where she could get professional protection from herself and from others. But then she's not my type, and that's not my type of business.

And I have no more time to devote to thinking of Eva the Swede, for I have now covered three quadrants of the park and I have not seen any of my retailers, which means that something is very very wrong. Because according to the system which I have devised, every member of my staff must stick to his sector, supplying prompt and courteous customer service and at the same time staying in touch with the others in case any trouble should arise. And perhaps trouble has arisen. Because now that I have cruised the southeast and northeast and northwest sectors, my staff can only be in the southwest quadrant, down there where the little chess tables are, unless they have split without reporting, an unthinkable thought.

So I am now approaching these little chess tables, and yes, all four of them are there, all sitting around a concrete chessboard— Santa Barbara and Yusuf Ali, Carlo from Santa Domingo and Holy Mother from my old neighborhood, which shall remain nameless. I take a sigh of relief to see that they all appear to be well and happy, and then a deep breath to prepare to scream at them for not being on post. And then I see a fifth head protruding from this little cluster, and I get very angry inside, because it is against the rules and ethics to sit down with strangers at this late hour, because it endangers the take.

Yet when I draw nearer I see that the fifth wheel is not precisely a stranger, it is Porco Miserio, Porco for short. Porco looks nothing at all like a pig, being worn and emaciated to the very bone, like a speed freak, though he isn't that either. I gave him the name for reasons which I will develop in due time, the same reasons, in fact, that I do not want him to fraternize with my retailers, who also got their names from me. I give everything a name, and perhaps it is time that I gave you my own.

My true christened name is Enrico Spaghetti, or something like that, but I am known to my colleagues and business acquaintances as Johnny B. Goode. Because I love black people and their music and money, and because I do be good. I carry no I.D., my pockets are perennially empty of pharmaceuticals or anything else that you might want to find, and I do not do business with my relatives. Absolutely no way, not for years and years. I buy my pharmaceuticals from the Latinos in Alphabet Town, and what do I care if the Gambino family brings it all in from Turkey? Nothing, that's what I care, I care so little that most of the time I don't even know it. And I can afford the markup, because here in Washington Square Park we cater to a classy clientele.

There's just one other reason for this name I gave myself. When the narco squad comes down looking for Johnny B. Goode, they are not looking for a white Italian. But enough of all this personal stuff.

I am not happy to see Porco here, partly because he is in and of himself a bad influence, but chiefly because I told him very firmly at the start of the summer to stay the hell out of the park, and to be disobeyed in this frivolous way knocks a chip off my precious authority. But before I toss him out on his backside, I would like to find out why he is here.

"Well, well, my happy family," say I. "Why are we sitting down on the job without the permission of our supervisor? If I may inquire. And what has brought our prodigal brother home from exile?" And I rap my knuckles on the black and white squares and look around at all their beaming faces. It is Yusuf Ali who answers my question.

"Porco has come up to see you especial, Johnny B. He says he has a talking rock."

"My son, you are confused," I say. "Porco is himself a talking rock." But behind this air of casual unconcern I am in truth a little worried. The problem with Porco, in brief, is that he's crazy. Otherwise he's a very nice guy. Tough for his weight—I think he has done time, probably in hospitals more often than jails. He has a fighting style which suggests experience with jujitsu-trained orderlies, including a reflex hip wriggle designed to take the buttocks out of range of that soporific syringe.

Past that he's hard to classify. Porco drinks, and when he drinks he talks. A fascinating conversationalist, up to the point where he bugs out altogether. I ran across him first at the Spring Street Lounge, where I understand he is a habitué. I'm not. It's too close to my old neighborhood. I understand he spends his down-and-out periods on the Bowery with the winos, but he's not particularly one of them either. Now he's sitting in my park, and in the little bit of light trickling over from the MacDougal Street streetlamp, I can see that he does have some sort of an object clamped in his right fist. Yusuf Ali says it's a talking rock, but knowing Porco it could just as easily be a grenade. So I sit down on the bench across from him.

"So, Porco," I say. "Tell me all about your talking rock. Take ten minutes, then farewell forever, at least as far as these premises are concerned. You must have forgotten all the things I said before."

"Feel it," Porco says. He drops his fist into my hand, and I am truly impressed. Porco's hollow finger bones never had a tenth that heft, I feel as if I'm holding a cannonball. Then the weight is lifted and it lands next on the outstretched palm of Santa Barbara, which then gets mashed flat on the chess table.

"Heavy, mon," says Santa. He's a tiny guy, no bigger than Porco, and his whole face is composed of points, right down to his little goat's beard. He commutes from Hoboken, and he used to be in business for himself. Want to hear how he got his name? I used to know the witch in his neighborhood out there. And I found out that his patron was Saint Barbara. The one that holds a tower up, because she died in one just like it. And I knew that when Santa smears chicken blood on Saint Barbara's statue, it is Chango the Yoruba god of lightning that comes to lick it off. I called him Santa Barbara in the park one day and he knew that only the devil himself would have the knowledge and the nerve to call him that. I named him and I had him by the short hairs of the soul.

"If it's words your rock is full of, mon," says Santa, "it will still be talking at sunrise."

"Let's have a look at your talking rock," I say. In spite of myself I'm curious. But Porco won't let go of it. He just stretches out his fist and lets one end of whatever it is peep out between his thumb and forefinger. It's too dark to see so I take out my little penlight that I always carry for inspecting pharmaceuticals during the night-time. (And at the other end, tear gas. In case Santa stops believing in my magic powers, or if something else goes wrong.) Under the light I can only see that this rock is as black as the guts of the universe. And deep down inside it I think I see some silver sparkles but they keep moving around, and maybe it is only a trick of reflections and my weary eyes. My retailers bend over too to take a look and Porco covers the rock with his hand.

"Yah," says Yusuf Ali. "A talking rock. Where is its mouth?"

I picked up Yusuf Ali about a month after Santa. It took more daring but I had to have him. He has the height of Kareem Abdul-Jabbar and the build of a world-class weightlifter, and I needed him for visible protection, show of force. For that very reason it was scary when it came time to choose him a name. I thought of Blue Gum Nigger, but after I had watched him for a while I figured out that he was a Muslim. The original Yusuf Ali translated the Koran and printed it in parallel lines with the Arabic. I called my man that name and he came to me. My Yusuf Ali is also a scholar. He is learning Arabic and he doesn't believe in talking rocks. Also he can be mean. But Porco, a cockroach by comparison, is not afraid of him.

"It is not a talking rock." Porco's voice drops two octaves. "It is The Storytelling Stone." And I know that I will listen to him now even if he runs all over the ten minutes I allotted. Porco's voice, when it goes deep, makes you feel like you have fallen out of your own little life into a very deep well, at the bottom of which is a large and beautiful cathedral. Or it makes you feel like you have been shot in the heart. He should have been a politician or a priest. Too bad he's crazy.

"The Storytelling Stone," says Porco. "I hold it in my hand and I have knowledge and power."

"Oh, Mister Knowledge and Power," Carlo says. "So make it talk." Carlo is a very handsome guy from the Dominican Republic, a quadroon, a picture-book Kool Kat. What interests him above all other things in life is his clothes. Carlo is his real name as far as I know. I never bothered to name him because he has no power worth tapping into. I keep him around simply because certain customers are impressed by his style.

And while I'm on the subject of names and personnel, I should cover Holy Mother too. From my old neighborhood, I've known him all the way up from my beautiful childhood. Nowadays he's so depressed all the time that he really can't even talk. He actually takes pharmaceuticals, poor bastard. I call him Holy Mother because as a little kid he had a thing about the Virgin. But I don't want to hurt the guy; I take care of him the best I can. (Also he's my knife.) And at least with me he'll die of a clean OD or a straightforward stabbing; he won't end up with his brains splattered across a plate of linguine with pesto. My relatives, they like to shoot you while you're eating out. Sets an example, so they say.

"Shut up," I tell Carlo. He always does just what I tell him to because if he ever doesn't I will have Yusuf Ali put a knot in his nose, and he loves his nose even more than his silk shirts.

"I can't make it talk," Porco says. "It can make me talk. It can even make you talk, Johnny B. But we are not to know the day or the hour. But I didn't come up here to talk to two-bit pushers. I came up here to tell you, Johnny B. Goode, that I have The Story-telling Stone and that I am holding it here in my hand. Because you have every right to know. Because of the names."

And with that Porco demonstrates the eerie power that he has to make me think. In happier days gone by, Porco and I used to be what you might call friends, perhaps because of his thing for talking and mine for names. I used to actually go down to Spring Street, where I am not popular, just to talk to him. And he would come up to the park to talk to me. And everything was very nice. Then one day Porco bought some pharmaceuticals from Santa. I believe I mentioned that what he usually does is drink, but he was of age and he paid Santa with perfectly good American money. With his head full of pharmaceuticals, Porco began to preach. The theme of his sermon was, in brief, that the world is hell. Now a very good case can be made for that, and plenty of people make it in the park every day, but personally I have no time to listen. *Don't think about what you can't do about* is and ever shall be my primary motto. And my secondary motto, for those who are interested, is *Let other people do what they want (within reason)*. But Porco's sermon turned into a screaming freakout, and freakouts bring the man and drive away your business.

I told Santa to try to calm him down while I blew red alert for Holy Mother and Carlo. Carlo's not a lot of use for this kind of work, because he doesn't like to get himself mussed up. But I thought Santa and Holy Mother would be plenty of calming influence for a little cat like Porco. I was wrong. Half the time Porco had them wrestling each other by mistake. That was the day I got to analyze his fighting style. I dispatched Carlo for Yusuf Ali but he was at the far end of the northwest quadrant, and the man had arrived before he could get back, and we all had to blow out of the park very quickly indeed.

We were fingered for that one, and we had to go under for a couple of weeks. I lost thousands of dollars in retail sales and naturally I got very upset. When they turned Porco out of his straitjacket I went and paid him a personal visit. I gave him my sympathy, quite sincerely, and a warning to stay out of the park. I explained to him why. And I gave him his name. He's not Italian so he probably didn't know what it meant at first. But maybe he looked it up somewhere. Now he's back and he's talking again.

"I can't make it tell the stories," Porco is saying. "I can feel them here in my hand but I can't bring them out. But since we used to talk together I will now tell you the story of how I got the Stone.

"I spent today at 219 Bowery. I was shooting pool."

"Good, Porco," says Carlo. "You have a funny-looking rock. You hustle dollar bills from winos. What else is new in your wonderful life." A long speech for Carlo, that.

"One more time, Carlo," I say. Carlo shuts up.

"I was sitting at my table drinking my wine. A man sitting across from me didn't look right. For an hour I was sneaking looks at him trying to understand why. After an hour he got up to go to the can and I saw it. You know the clientele. They aren't just broken. They are dissolved. This one, no. His back was as straight as the World Trade Center. When he came back I looked at his face. He had a Roman nose and high cheekbones and eyes like obsidian. Those eyes were the other thing about him that wasn't right. Those eyes were still alive for sure. I decided he had to be an Indian. I wanted to find out if I was right or not so I bought him a glass of wine.

"He told me he was a Comanche. He had come in from Arizona at the start of the summer. He had come on the freights. He didn't say what for. I asked him if he knew anyone in the city. He told me no. We shot pool and drank more wine. I wanted to ask him some more questions. I wanted to find out what it felt like to a Comanche to be in this place.

"I asked him a few and he told me to walk out on the street. We went down to the vacant lot on Stanton. 'I'd like to tell you all these things you want to know,' he said then. 'I'd like to but I'm too tired. I've come a long way and I'm tired.' Then he put his hand in his pocket and gave me The Storytelling Stone. He didn't tell me that he wanted me to have it. He told me that It wanted me to have it."

Porco stops talking. He's bent over looking at the fist with the rock in it. Ten minutes is long gone but I don't break the silence.

"What did you give him in return?" Santa wants to know.

Porco laughs, a nasty laugh, and his voice climbs back up out of that well, up to those familiar whining Porco tones.

"I told him I would give him anything he wanted," Porco says. "He said he would like a good quart of tequila. We went to the liquor store on Grand and I bought a bottle of mescal. Then we went to sit down in Roosevelt Park, but I never tasted that liquor. The Comanche pulled it straight down like he thought it was a bottle of apple wine. He didn't even leave a worm in the bottom of the bottle."

"Then what happened," says Yusuf Ali.

"What do you think happened," says Porco. "He lived about ten minutes."

"My man, Porco," says Yusuf Ali. "You killed a wino for a rock."

Porco sits back and raises his right fist with the rock in it.

"You're a cotton-chopper walking around with a skullcap on, trying to impress people with black squiggles on paper," Porco says. "What do you know about the world?"

Yusuf reaches out his monster hand to pinch Porco's head off, but Porco is there first with the right fist, boffo. Now there's a *practical* reason to walk around with a rock in your claw. Knock somebody's head off. Yusuf is flopped out on the pavement like a butchered ox. From the corner of my eye I can see that Holy Mother and Santa have pinned Porco and his talking rock to the bench, eager no doubt to make up for last time, but the first thing I want to find out about is whether my man Yusuf Ali is dead or alive. I can feel air going out of his big flat nostrils, good. Feel the lump rising on the side of his head, no bone fragments, good. Examine eyes with penlight, okay. Count pulse against my LED wristwatch, it's steady. Yusuf will probably wake up without even a headache; for now let him sleep.

I sit up and look across the chessboard. Santa and Holy Mother are trying to pry Porco's fingers off the rock but he still won't let it go. Even Carlo is in on the act, but I know that Porco isn't going to hit anyone else with that rock, as surely as if the rock had said so itself.

"Forget about the rock," I say. "We aren't going to worry about the rock." Holy Mother misinterprets and goes for his boot sheath, brings up the shiv, and waits for the word to cut Porco's throat.

"No. No. No," I say. "All wrong. This is personal." Even in my mickeymouse organization there's a rule for everything. If it's a business problem, we all help cut Porco's head off. As it is, Yusuf can hunt Porco down on his own time.

So they're still holding Porco and waiting for instruction. Maybe the strong arm seems in order, but I myself never lay on a finger, and I hardly ever have it done by personnel. It's scarier somehow if you can and don't. Besides, Porco doesn't scare, whatever his other little weaknesses may be.

"So let him go," say I, and Porco's hands are free. Talking rock and everything. Here's me and Porco staring at each other across this freaking concrete chess table. *Porco miserio*, I forgot to tell you, means pig misery, the lowest of the low. It's what you get when you think about what you can't do about.

"I don't suppose I have to tell you to stay out of this park if you want to live," I tell Porco. "Of course I don't know if you want to live or not."

"I don't suppose I have to tell you that your soul will shrivel up and die if you don't listen," says Porco, spitting it at me like an ugly little alley cat. "Of course I don't know if you want your soul or not." And really I can't believe it; even for a maniac Porco is being very ungrateful. I give him his head back for free and he's upset because I insulted his rock.

"Take your life and get out of here," I say. "I wash my hands of you forever, Porco Miserio." He stands up and faces me. He's still holding his rock like it had grown onto his hand.

"Tonight it's only me talking like always," Porco says. "When the Stone speaks to you, you won't have any choice, Mr. Johnny B. Goode." And he steps over Yusuf, he crosses the corner, and he's gone in the dark. I'm supposed to sit here in Washington Square and wait for a rock that isn't even here anymore to start talking to me. What a lousy night. My staff all want to know what they should do now.

"What do you do now, my pretty children?" say I. "You push crystal meth up Yusuf's nose till he wakes up and we all go over to Second Avenue and do the accounts." Since I left my old neighborhood I have cultivated a taste for Russian food, and there's a good deli on Second Avenue staffed entirely by illegal aliens, who aren't very fussy about what other people do for a living. On weekend nights we go there to eat pirogi and split up the assets. Sunday we work again, Monday we're off. Very little action Mondays, not worth it. So you see, it's all in a day's work. And I have an appetite after my hard day.

But no, I think, while my staff is working on Yusuf Ali, I don't really feel so fine after all. In fact, I feel like I've got rocks in my throat, and why should that be? Is it that I almost surely lost money tonight? Is it because my main man is KOed at my feet, taken out by a flea-sized maniac with a rock and crazy ideas? No and no. I'm standing here with tears in my eyes because I think I'm going to miss Porco Miserio, that rat—me, Johnny B. Goode, I'm so careful that I don't even know my real name, and I'm sure I never cried since the day I was born.

Something like an hour later Yusuf is up again, not exactly with it but at least on his feet, resuscitated in part by our own special smelling salts. My willing helpers get him standing and then they pack him into the back of the company car, no small feat this, since the car is a Volkswagen. And Yusuf takes up so much room in the car that I must dispatch the rest of my staff to Second Avenue on foot, excepting Holy Mother, who rides shotgun.

A short run and we have arrived and Holy Mother leads Yusuf into the deli, Yusuf lumbering like a blind and drunk elephant, but awake enough now to resent handling, I observe. I follow him into the yellow glow of the interior, where I can see the owner leaning into the counter like always, with his white hair standing out from his head like a halo and an expression which seems to convey the peace of infinite resignation. And as I pass him I listen very closely to see if I can hear what he is thinking.

Were I him I would likely be thinking that things are not so very bad in his particular corner of this vale of tears, though he may regret the cigars which I notice he has forsaken in the last three weeks or so, for health reasons, no doubt. But in general things are smooth for him. Although he will never have as many diners as Kiev across the street, in spite of the fact that his prices are lower and his food as good, he will always have enough. He owns this place outright and it is decorated to what is presumably his taste, the walls painted a dull bloody shade and colored light fixtures and even Muzak radio to make people feel happy while they eat.

Also tonight he has a brand-new waitress in here, who we will assume for the sake of argument is called Masha. This Masha is quite young, though not beautiful in the slightest, and is wearing a dress which is not at all flattering, being cut like a sack and too short in the bargain. Her legs stick out of the bottom of it like some kind of white tubers dug up too soon, and meanwhile she seems to be trying to keep her hair in a knot on the top of her head, but it keeps falling down, and poor Masha appears to be so confused that I am expecting her to blow her nose on this hair at any moment.

So this is Masha, who will have been in America for maybe a month, who speaks perhaps ten words of English, and certainly has no green card. Therefore the old man can congratulate himself on his charity in giving her work; and in fact I notice that he does this kind of thing rather frequently, so that there is an endless parade of Mashas through his place, and sometimes Borises too. As soon as they learn the language they are sucked back out of his door into the rest of the city, but surely the old man will be thinking that the current Masha is a long way from being ready for that.

Because first she will have to learn what to be afraid of and what not, because this wicked city is simply an undifferentiated wall of menace for anyone so recently arrived. The old man will teach her that the crazy young people in leather and chains and pink hair who walk up and down Second Avenue on the other side of his plate-glass window are really only harmless fools who don't even know anything about the real evils in this world. And perhaps he also knows enough to tell her that the five men now settling down at their accustomed table in the back (that's me and my family, in fact) are more worth worrying over than the punks. Certainly he will teach her the minimum about this group—that the black giant must always be given a special plate which has never touched pork, that the brown man in the dressy clothes will often be rude, that the short man in the shiny black shirt (that's me) is the one that has the money and will be leaving more of it here than most people do. Of course, Masha will learn all this and more, and she will grow eyes in the back of her head in the process of discovering all the other things one must know to live here. But for the moment it will be enough for him to tell her to come over and try to ask us in good English what we want to eat.

But of course all this is entirely speculative, and the old man may really be thinking about Plotinus, or New Jersey, or the dark side of the moon. All I really know about him is that he has a nice personality as far as I can tell and is a good cook and has a near perfect memory for figures. He remembers what he saw on your plate and can tell you the total without touching a pencil, and this is a talent which I have some reason to admire. Every so often he gets a really spectacular tip from me, as a token of my special esteem and also to remind him not to give us too much of his attention. Most nights he could set his clock by the time we walk in here if he wanted to, but not tonight, we're all off schedule. Yusuf has been slow in responding to treatment, and everyone has been under strain. And right now I can't take time to imagine myself behind someone else's eyes, so I will just have to look at the world through my own. I wake up from my daydream to attend to this pitiful mess of a girl just off the boat, who is standing by the table trying to find a way to communicate the idea that she is here to take our orders for food.

"What is this noise you're making?" I hear Carlo say. "What we want is something to eat." What would I ever do without Carlo? He always irritates me just when I need irritation to keep me awake.

"You should be nice with the unfortunate immigrant lady," I tell Carlo. "A stranger in the world like you and me. If not you're eating bananas for dinner to remind you all about the banana boat." Though of course Carlo never came in on a boat. He flew in on a double-decker jet with a passport and everything, and didn't run out of money for two months. He got used to money, and the next thing you know he was working for me. Even though he doesn't like me and he disapproves of drugs, with the possible exception of amyl nitrate, which I suspect he takes when he goes to the disco.

That's just fine, because doping on the job is strictly forbidden. And Carlo is welcome to hate me if he wants to. Sometimes I hate him.

Everyone is talking at once and Masha is getting all upset, and we aren't getting anywhere. To make things more simple I walk over to the counter and tell the old man that we are having a big dish of cheese and meat and potato pirogi, black bread and coffee for all, plus the usual vegetarian platter for Yusuf, who won't eat any kind of meat in a restaurant. I had big trouble getting him to eat in here at all. Yusuf Ali is still looking punchy and I ask also for cold borscht all around. He makes it in a lovely shade of violet and serves it up with lots of little chunks of radish and sections of hard-boiled egg. On a hot summer night this borscht is more refreshing than a swim in a cold mountain stream. When the first spoonful hits my mouth I can feel my body temperature drop a good ten degrees. Maybe it will snap Yusuf out of his trance and if not, at least I will have fun eating it. I exchange a few compliments with this nice old man whose name I don't know and go back to my seat. He calls out a mouthful of Russian and Masha leaves us and goes into the kitchen. Everyone is sitting around the table staring off into space. I don't think we're going to have a lot of brilliant conversation tonight.

"I don't see why we didn't knock him over on the spot," Carlo says. He's not looking at me, but I think I know who he's talking to.

"You don't see," say I. "Look, my son, in case you didn't notice yet, you don't just drop bodies in Washington Square. What if we do whack him out, then I tell you, Carlo, to get rid of the pieces some way? It's a long way to the river—what are you going to do? You're going to walk up Greenwich Avenue with a corpse slung over your shoulder?" This is laying it on thick, but I am hoping to shut Carlo up for the night because I would rather listen to someone with a brain. Or even perhaps to the sweet silence. However, tonight I do not even have that much good fortune.

"A dirty little wino," Carlo says, still addressing the air, or possibly the ceiling. "He could lie dead for three days and nobody would notice. Probably not even from the smell."

At this remark I feel a terrible cold sensation just underneath my sternum. It's not from the borscht this time at all; what it means is that I just lost my temper. I lean forward across the table so that my nose is almost touching Carlo's nose, and I speak to him in my gentlest tones, because I don't want to make a lot of noise and upset the management.

"Carlo, my boy," I say, "you aren't a man, you're a dressmaker's dummy. God made a mistake when he gave you a mouth. Without it you would be perfect. As it is you've just committed three offenses against decency, and all in the very same evening."

"What are you talking about?" Carlo says, but he's looking a little alarmed.

"You can keep whatever you're holding tonight," I say. "Cheap at the price to get rid of you. Just don't let me see you again in the Square."

Carlo's eyes start shifting around the table, looking for help somewhere. I reach with my left hand and sink five fingers into the base of his ear, which brings his attention straight back to me. Carlo's eyes are getting watery now, but that isn't just because he's a yellow dog; he's really in quite a lot of pain. I know, I remember this trick from the nuns in my grade school.

"I make the decisions," I whisper to Carlo. "Me. All the decisions. This is not a democratic community. Anything does not go. I don't think you've ever really understood that, Carlo. What do you think?"

"I think I'd like to leave now," Carlo says with a blink.

"What a brilliant idea," I tell him. "Your best in some time." I let go of him and lean back in my chair. Carlo stands up with one hand on his ear.

"You're free to go, Carlo," I say. "The dinner is on me anyway. Good-bye, good-bye, sorry it had to end like this. And please make sure you never come back, because there's no second chances for you, not one."

By this time Carlo is well on his way to the door.

"I'm sorry I don't carry unemployment insurance," I say as he opens it. "But if you're really hard up you can always go stand in the window at Saks."

The door bangs shut on my words, no answer. I look around the table, and no one is even cracking a smile at this witty remark I just made. Everybody looks so depressed that I'm afraid they must be thinking about the meaning of life, which is not allowed during work time. They're not going to chuckle, so then I am going to give them a lecture.

"Don't anybody worry about Carlo," I say. "You probably won't even notice he's gone. Carlo is actually made out of plastic. He is a disposable item, forget him. The real issue of the evening is something quite different." I tilt back in my chair and put my fingertips together like Alistair Cooke.

"Here we are in the modern world," I tell them. "In only twenty little years we will be having the third millennium. This modern world is ruled and controlled by the laws of science, discovered by scientists at MIT. Under these laws of science, talking rocks cannot and do not exist. So don't be thinking about talking rocks. You will only get a headache for your trouble.

"So we come to the subject of headaches. Our brother Yusuf Ali has one now, we see, which only goes to show that the world is full of surprises, nasty ones more often than not. You underestimate someone, and maybe you get hit on the head with a hard object and feel pain. This is simple and easy to understand."

Now I drop the front legs of my chair back down, kaboom, because this is the part I want people to listen to. "So we come to the subject of Porco Miserio, a little man with a big rock. Under the laws of science, Porco doesn't exist any more than talking rocks do. I'm now looking all around this room, and I don't see any Porcos anywhere. Tomorrow I'm looking all around the park and I don't see him there either. If I do see him it won't be for long, because even if Yusuf has lost a few brain cells tonight he has plenty to spare, and I don't think he's going to be conned twice by the same person. I don't believe in things I don't see, so Porco doesn't exist, finito. And as far as my soul goes, I keep it at home in a jar on the mantelpiece." This last line is for Santa. He believes it.

But no one has blinked an eye at any part of this long speech, so maybe I'm just talking to myself. I was really hoping to catch the attention of Yusuf Ali, who has a mind like Thomas Aquinas and usually loves to pick holes in other people's shaky arguments. But Yusuf is sitting on his chair like someone hypnotized, with one eye on the floor and the other on the ceiling. I hope he's not hurt worse than I think he is. Why do I keep thinking about depressing things?

Luckily Masha breaks into the silence by bringing the bread and the soup. I take a mouthful of borscht and I feel like I just dove into a swimming pool.

For the next little while the food is still coming and we're all eating it, except for Yusuf Ali. When I have finished my soup I look over at him. His mouth is open a little and back inside somewhere I think I see his tongue. I pick up Yusuf's fork and spear a cheese pirogi off his special plate and put it into his mouth.

"Eat and be strong, my son," I say. "Build up your body and mind for the days to come." Yusuf Ali puts his hand on the fork, so I assume he gets the idea. But when the fork comes back out of his mouth the pirogi is still on it undamaged. Yusuf puts the pirogi back on his plate and starts braiding the tines of the fork together. I've always wondered how people with big meaty hands can do little picky jobs like that.

"I am not hungry, Johnny B.," Yusuf tells me. His eyes seem to be focusing now, somewhere around my left ear. "I am thinking."

"Well, all right, Yusuf," I say. "If you're not hungry then don't eat. Basically I was only wondering whether or not you were okay."

"I feel fine, Johnny B.," he says. "Never better."

"Good," say I. "So if you're not eating you can start telling me some numbers."

We use the honor system in reporting the nightly receipts. Everyone tells me what they grossed and I figure up the percentages on the tiny calculator that the Japanese were so thoughtful as to build into my wristwatch. I read a second number back, and everybody gives me a little folder full of money before they leave for the night. Obviously I don't want to throw stacks of cash out on the table of a public restaurant, and neither do I want to invite these awful drug pushers into my home, hence the status quo.

Naturally, I have some checks and balances hidden in the system. First and foremost, I am not a greedy man. I do not take a larger cut than is reasonable, and my retailers make enough to keep them happy. There is even an incentive program with bonuses and such. Second, one of the important advantages of hiring employees of mixed ethnic backgrounds is that no one is going to trust anyone else quite enough to set up any fancy deals. Third, on Mondays, the big day off, I compare receipts against surplus stock. If anything strange is starting to occur—price-fixing for instance, or favors for friends—I am going to find out about it. So we see the honor system only goes so far.

The final fail-safe is Holy Mother. Behind closed doors, I throw him a percentage of my percentage, which he generally takes in pharmaceuticals. I give him this little break since he's probably my cousin and since his life has been very lousy so far. I am not about to give him pharmaceuticals for free, not because I am mean, but because I hope that he will just be maintaining as long as the stuff is costing him money. And I hope Holy Mother is going to live for at least a few more years. He doesn't love me, but he does owe me big favors, and I think that if the roof is about to fall on my head, he will at least try to give me fair warning.

So when everyone has reported tonight, the numbers look better than I was expecting under the circumstances. I do feel bad that no one was covering that crowd at the arch, because I could smell money when I walked through it. Still, with Porco showing up unexpected like that, he had to be watched and restrained if need be, and I feel like everyone did the right thing.

"Everybody done good," I tell them. "Four cool heads in a crisis, just as I would wish. My sincerest compliments to all involved." Once again, the reaction is slight to nonexistent.

It looks like it's time to break up the party. Santa is beginning to squirm in his seat. "I going now too, Yanni-B, okay?" Like many P.R.'s, Santa tends to swallow his *j*'s.

"Off you go, Santa," I consent. "*Mañana*, one o'clock." He nods, and I'm watching him go through the door. He turns right instead of left; he's going downtown, which is odd. The PATH train is what takes you to Hoboken, and it isn't in that direction. The closest stop is on Ninth Street, west of the park. So maybe Santa has something to do in Loisaida. Should I take an interest in that? No. I'm getting paranoid.

Now there are three little Indians. Yusuf Ali should go home too, I think.

"Yusuf," I'm calling, "Yusuf Ali." Finally he looks up. What's wrong with my people tonight?

"Yusuf, man, stop thinking so hard; you got problems enough with a lump on the outside of your head. Go home, get some rest.

You don't feel good tomorrow, you take time off and see a doctor. But if you aren't going to show, have somebody call Telephone 2 at one-thirty, right?" Telephone 2 is in the basement of the Loeb Center, across Fourth Street from the park. It's on a long line of pay phones, and if a call is expected someone goes down there and sits holding the receiver with his thumb on the hook. I've numbered this phone and the others we use so we don't end up on the same one too many times in a row.

Yusuf is now getting up and saying good-bye. His shoulders almost take the doorframe along as he leaves. I hope he will be in good shape tomorrow. He's a very important person to have around, and if he can't make it I will have to spend time smelling the air and trying to decide if it's safe for the others to work or not. Is it possible I'll live to regret getting rid of Carlo so suddenly? No, I think not. Carlo has always been as much trouble as he's worth, and recently more. And for sure it's too late to worry about it now.

Two little Indians. I'm looking at my wristwatch and it's 0358 EST. Holy Mother and I still have to dump the car somewhere. Now I'm getting up to go pay the tab. These late-night snacks are always on me, another fringe benefit for those in my employ. I'm giving money to this white-haired Russian and he's making me change.

"Keep it," I tell him. "You make soup like no one else in Russia."

He's smiling at me across the counter. He's happy. I like to cook myself. I make some good Italian platters. I could almost afford to open up my own café, but then people would start to know where I am all the time. I'm looking at Holy Mother sitting at the table all by himself. Masha is picking up plates from under his nose, but he has no idea she is there. I don't think I'm quite ready to go outside in the dark.

"Why don't you give me two more coffees," I say. "Milk and no sugar." He makes them and I take them to the table. I sit down and push a coffee over to Holy Mother. He finds it without looking down and takes a sip.

I'm looking at Holy Mother. He's about my size, but lighter. He lost a lot of weight while he was gone and never gained most of it back. His complexion is fairer than mine is and he's got brown hair, not cut in any particular way. Doesn't care much about his appearance these days, though he used to be very snappy and up to the mark. He's got a face that looks something like a bird's, which is one of the reasons he used to be called Crow, years back before he went away. The other reason was that when he appeared it was often as an omen of bad things about to happen to you. Now the total effect of his features is all messed up by the scar that runs through his right eyebrow and down the side of his nose. The stitches got left in too long and they left marks. Plus the gloomy expression he wears all the time; this is a face that scares people, and so it's valuable to me. People who are too subtle to be impressed by Yusuf Ali will think twice when they look at Holy Mother. Most people are not that subtle, of course.

I'm trying to figure out if Holy Mother is more out of it than usual. It hasn't been such a great night for anyone. Is he worrying over this thing with Porco like everybody else seems to be? I think not. He has lots of other things to be depressed about. Perhaps I'm the one that has the problem. But I feel like I'm not exactly sure what's going on, and that's a very uncomfortable feeling for a man in my position.

The nine millionth Muzak cover of "Yesterday" is coming in over the speakers and it's beginning to get on my nerves. I would like some talk, maybe, but Holy Mother is just not much of a talker anymore. What do you say to him, anyway? I reach over and touch him on the elbow.

"Don't take it hard, Crow," I say. I still call him that name when I'm sure no one is listening. "*Questo è la strada.*"

Porco

Yes. I'm across the street. I'm walking, one-two, one-two. I'm still alive. I'm still alive. Isn't that amazing?

It passed the test. Didn't It?

I think I'm shaking. No, I'm not. Yes, I am shaking. But only on my left side. My left arm jerking through parabolas, hyperbolas, cardioid curves, like Arthur Fiedler, maybe, in his last stroke. My legs are doing a sine wave on the sidewalk. My left ear is wiggling itself. Now it's over, I think I'm scared. But then my right arm is as steady and cold as a glacier on the North Pole. Bent toward It in my right coat pocket. With my hand around It. It is a coat hanger on which the rest of my body is hung.

We did it. We said what we were going to say. We took the big sucker down. For a bonus. Feel like I just pushed over the Chrysler Building. And after that we walked out of it too. I think I deserve a, a . . . uh-uh. No. Think about something else for a minute.

Here we are walking down MacDougal Street. Not too many people out now. But some. Enough. Nice people. Well-dressed people. Pretty, happy people. Hi. Hi. Hi. I smell refried beans. Taco Rico is open. Also garlic sauce and 98¢ felafel. Haji Baba is open. Still playing bazouki music. Did I use to know a waitress there? I think I did.

We're crossing Bleecker Street. Come out of the pocket, wave bye-bye to high-priced clubs and sidewalk cafés. Bye-bye, bright warm lights and people all dressed up. We're crossing Houston Street now; it's wide as a river.

Now we're looking at a church. Outside there's statues of God and His Saints. Hello, Mother of God. See how sad she looks? With her face turned down? Doesn't want to look at things. That looks like moonlight on her face. It's not. It's cold white Houston Street street light. No moonlight ever pushed down this far. You got to climb fifty stories to see over the lip of the pit.

But here is a place to seek asylum. Where the lost and desperate have found it in all the days from the beginning. Let's get down here behind this statue. Roll up in a ball behind this bush, secret from anyone who might possibly be following. I tuck my head into my elbows, the familiar old ostrich technique. And can hear nothing but my own heart beating, blood counting time.

A lot of time, I would imagine. I get up to a crouch and look. It's later, definitely later, Houston Street is empty. I rise to my feet. With an assist from Mother Mary's concrete elbow.

Good-bye, Mother, we're taking a left. We're going east on Houston Street. Just one lonely hack on the asphalt river. Waiting for a traffic light. We're looking down West Broadway. Artists and things live down there. Did I leave a horn down there? I think I did. An artist or something is looking after it for me. Come on. Right now the very thought of artists makes me sick.

Now we're taking a right on Mercer Street. No street lights down this way this late. There's big old dark heavy warehouse buildings tilting toward each other across this narrow street. Narrow enough? Look up. Yes. Stars. A fine line of stars between the tops of buildings. We're waving at them. You have to be crafty to find stars in these parts.

Stars in my coat pocket. Keep going, one-two. In the dark I've stopped shaking. Footsteps as steady as a heartbeat, iambic infintameter taking us down to the corner of Spring Street.

Drunk wrapped around a parking meter. Not dead. Snoring. Broke his bottle when he fell. I can smell that. See the pieces. The odor is drifting through my sinus and condensing into tiny drops of wine on the roof of my mouth.

I'm thirsty. Thirsty. Shouldn't do it. Know I shouldn't do it. Why shouldn't I do it? What happens happens. So it is written, said, and sung. All right, then. We're taking another left.

Holy Mother

"Questo è la strada."

Do I need anybody to tell me that? No way. I need to hear that about as much as I need to sit here and drink another stale coffee. All right, Johnny B., we know each other, but I still don't need your fingers digging into my arm.

Funny how I don't even think of him by his real name anymore. Though I know it as well as my own. And for almost as long.

I move my arm away, pick up the coffee, and drain it. It's three-quarters full, so of course it burns my tongue. But it's gone, and there's no reason to spend any more time sitting here.

"I don't feel like hanging out," I tell him. "Let's get rid of the car and go home."

"Whatever," he says. "I thought perhaps a little cooling-out period might be worthwhile. After all that fast action and everything."

"Yeah," I say, "but it's late. We're running late, you know?" I catch his eye to remind him. Not that I want to remind him. I don't want to remind myself. But my muscles are tightening up already and I've *got to get home* fairly soon.

"Whatever," he says. "You want to go now, we'll go now." He stands up and takes the throwaway coffee cone out of the plastic holder. He's taking his coffee along for the ride. I should have done that myself.

On the street I feel better. It's good to be moving in the right direction. It's better to walk than to sit down and think. And I'm lucky to be walking at all. I could make a novena for that one every day in the week.

We find the car where we left it, a couple of blocks down Second Avenue. It's a real piece of junk. A Volkswagen Beetle. Used to be red, but almost all of the paint is gone. Now it's rust-colored with red paint flecks. Both rear fenders are missing too. You wouldn't even think the thing would run. The only thing that's in good shape is the storage compartment up under the hood. That mother is built. It has a Fox lock on it with the T-bars modified to fit the curve, and a Medeco cylinder. Johnny and I did the job ourselves. It would take somebody an hour to crack into it, even with tools and free time.

Me, I have some taste in cars. I used to drive a Maserati, back in the Colombo days. Johnny used to crab at me then for being too flash. Even that early in the game he was getting real cautious, keeping his nose extra clean, pretending to be invisible. I used to laugh in his face outright. At the time I was sure I had nothing to worry about. Later I began to see he had a point. In those days Johnny used to drive Volvos. A Volvo is a plenty good car, but nobody is going to hate you for having one.

The point of the bug is easy to see. It's a car that nobody would ever look at twice. No one would ever try to rip off this car. No one would even try to strip it for parts. You can tell at a glance there's hardly anything on it to strip.

"You driving?" he says.

"I don't care," I say. Because of these little twitches I'm getting in my arms, I'd really rather not. But he tosses me the ignition key. We both carry keys to the hood.

"Why don't you drive," he says. "I got this coffee in a cup I can't put down."

"Okay." I open the driver's door and get in and pull the lock up for him on the other side. He shines his penlight over the back seat before he opens the door. Johnny's getting to be a nervous sort of guy in little ways like this. Of course, we've all got our reasons.

Then again in other ways he won't even let a person take normal precautions. I still remember the big argument we had over whether or not I was going to carry a piece. I wanted one. I'm used to it, and with everything that had been going on I would have felt a lot better with one on hand. Johnny said no. He said, of all things, that he was worried I'd get caught with it, get pulled back in.

"Big deal," I said. "Big problem. You got me selling dope in the park and you're worried I'm going to get shook down for a piece."

"You're right it's a big problem," he says. "Maybe you haven't seen a newspaper lately? Unlicensed guns are getting too hot to handle. That new law goes through, they're going to start sending people away for that and that alone. Even good solid citizens, people with no sheet. You know?"

"Sure I know," I said. "I've read some law." I have. Johnny took night school at City College and he's got a degree and a smart mouth to show for it. I got a degree too. From a different institution.

"Yeah," he says. "Remember what you went up for? Somebody finds a gun on you, you're going straight back."

"I remember," I told him. "I remember a lot of things that you don't even know." That froze that end of the conversation.

"Okay," Johnny said. "Maybe it sounds unreasonable to be making a big thing over a gun or no gun when you're dealing with dope. But who needs double jeopardy? You've got dope around anyway. If you were going to get separate from that then maybe you'd have an argument. As things are now you don't."

And that iced the whole conversation. Me and Johnny don't go too far in any direction without hitting something one of us can't talk about. It's a tight little box we live in. I went out and bought myself a double-edged Gerber steel stabbing knife. Couple of weeks brushing up with that and I felt okay. Not great, but okay. I never heard any complaints from Johnny about my having that. It's come in useful once or twice already. I thought for sure it was going to tonight.

And with all that hot air that got blown around, I think Johnny's carrying something himself. Not a gun. He never did like guns. Got no feeling for them. But something. Sometimes when I got time on my hands I wonder what it could be.

Finally he gets in the car. I try to start it but it's slow to turn over. I try a couple of times. Johnny lights up a Kool. Smoking Kools is part of his program to try to turn himself into some kind of nigger.

"Try the choke," he says. There's a manual choke on this dog of a car. I forgot about it. I pump the choke and the car starts. It runs like a meat grinder full of nails. I light myself a Lucky, just to clear the menthol stink out of my area. After I burned my mouth with the coffee it don't taste too good. I aim the car down Second Avenue. We'll swing across Houston and pick any avenue going uptown.

"Put on the radio," I say, and Johnny reaches over and snaps it on. It's just AM and barely works anyway. You can only get ABC, and ABC only plays disco these days. But I still feel like listening to something. I make the turn onto Houston Street okay. The steering on this bug isn't so sensitive that my hands shaking is going to matter much. But I think I saw something out of the corner of my eye.

"Hey," Johnny says, "watch the street. You're spilling my coffee. Hot coffee."

"Did you see that?" I say.

"See what? No."

"The spic, Santa. Over on the edge of Roosevelt Park."

"I didn't see him."

"I think it was him. Looked like he was talking to himself or something."

"I didn't see anything. It's on your side, I can't see through your head." But Johnny is thinking about it.

"He was headed down this way," he says. "I noticed when he left the deli."

"Santa?" I say. "He don't live down here, does he?"

"No, he doesn't." We listen to the radio for a minute.

"Talking to himself," Johnny says. "He was talking to himself?"

"I saw him for maybe a second," I say. "Maybe it wasn't even him."

"Maybe not. Maybe it was a giant tarantula. Maybe it was a rhinoceros with wings."

"Look." I squeeze the wheel. Some things I'm not taking even now. Let him crack jokes on the rest of the niggers. Not me.

"Sorry. Cool out, all right, it's been a bad night. Everybody's crazy."

A bad night. To me it's no different from the last one. Except I had a chance to stick my knife in that bigmouth little dirtbag, and Johnny wouldn't let me take it.

"You think you're going to cool me out by talking crazy yourself?" What he told Carlo wasn't completely true. It was true as far as it went, of course, but all the same, Porco could be lying dead somewhere right now, and I don't quite know why he's not. And what did we dump Carlo for? He's a punk, all right, but he's been worse before. If everybody's crazy, I think Johnny is right up there with the rest of them.

"I apologized." Johnny's getting an edge on his voice. "The quarrel is over, *capisce?*"

"*Si, si.*" I relax, as much as it's possible. Really, we've got nothing to fight about. In the long run we owe each other too much for that.

So maybe he did handle it right tonight. The idea that you don't bring your private trouble to work is a good one, though Johnny didn't make it up, of course. Still, if the two things just happen to coincide there's no law that says you can't slam the knife in a little harder and give it an extra twist. I've had the hots for Porco ever since he made a fool out of us all at the start of the summer. I know it's not good to think that way, but then I don't have much else to keep me interested in life.

I think Johnny still likes the little bastard, God knows why. Who is he, anyway? A little rat of a horn player that drinks too much and talks too much. But Johnny must have a soft spot for him, because otherwise we had every reason to whack him out. His second offense, and that people have to stay told is basic. And I know it had to have shaken Johnny up to see his big nigger go down. Not that I care. I was almost glad. The guy is full of himself and has a big head. Islam, oh yeah. To me it's just an excuse to run around killing white people.

No, but I can't even think that to myself. I've seen with my own eyes it's not true.

Yusuf Ali, or whatever his name really is, is nothing to me, but he's plenty to Johnny. Even I'll admit that he's useful to have around, if only to keep us straight with the rest of them. So Porco messes with him, he should die, no? But Johnny says he lives till next time. Which is a lot like what he said the last time. Maybe the answer is that Porco just doesn't make that much difference either way. Either way it's not worth thinking about. What we did, we did already.

"West Side tonight?" I say. "I want to get home."

"No problem," he says. "Make it Twenty-second Street." I turn on Sixth Avenue and start driving uptown. This late there's practically no traffic. Maybe I can take a few red lights.

The deal with the car is as follows. The car is a rolling vault. It doesn't have any registration, and the stickers on it are fake. It's got Jersey plates, looks like some kind of Jersey hippie's car. No one is going to guess what's under the hood and if anyone did they would never find out who it belonged to. We leave it parked around somewhere out of the way when we're working in Washington Square. Everybody carries a key to the hood. Johnny thinks, and he's probably right, that if anything turns up missing he's going to know who's responsible inside of the next two minutes.

That leaves the problem of where to put the car when we're not in the park. The solution is simple, although it takes time. We just drop the car in a garage somewhere. One of the ones where you just take a claim check and don't leave a name. That would be easy enough except that Johnny has got so nervous that he won't use the same garage twice. There's a million garages like that in Manhattan and some nights we might kill an hour driving around looking over new ones. Johnny won't do it alone and I get elected to come along because he thinks I'm the least likely to try to snatch it out from under him.

It's not such a bad system. He's taking a chance on losing the stock, but the chance is as small as he can make it. And even changing garages may be worth it, because it does make it harder for anyone to set us up. We end up spending too long sitting in the car, but what can you do? Nobody's perfect. We used to use dead drops but that turned out to be a big headache. People would find them and we'd be in all kinds of trouble.

It's a small-time operation with small-time problems attached. To me it's almost embarrassing. It could be embarrassing to Johnny too. But being small-time is part of his program to not be worth killing. I'll buy that with everything I've got.

The only place I see open is the Blimpie on Twelfth Street. ABC is putting across another Donna Summer song. Not bad, this one, it's about losing sleep to your troubles. Catchy. I'll light another cigarette for that one. Johnny pulls out two paper wallets and starts counting money from one into the other. He carries three or four of them on him all the time now, to keep the petty cash in order. Buys the wallets in Chinatown. Seems like he's going down there a lot recently, sometimes I wonder what for. He's not the type to get involved with the Chinese gangs, so it can't be business. People talk about meat hooks. You get little yellow men upset, you end up being pork-fried rice.

I swing the car left on Twenty-third Street and drive over to Ninth Avenue. The streets are dead all over. Just a few lights on in the Chelsea Hotel.

"We're going to Twenty-second Street, no?" says Johnny. Now he's putting money in an envelope.

"Sure," I say. "I'm just making the block." I turn down Ninth and over on Twenty-second. Johnny seals the envelope and pushes it across the dash toward me.

"Thanks." He's giving it to me now while there's still time to stop and open the hood, in case I want to buy something. Sweet of him. But I don't need to buy tonight. I turn the car into the lighted ramp of the garage and pull it over to the booth. A punk kid with a green hat on comes out and reaches for the key. I pick up my envelope and we get out of the car and the kid gets in. Johnny takes a claim check from him.

"Be careful you don't scratch the paint," he says. Kid don't know what to make of that. He guns the car and drives it around a pole out of sight. Johnny hands me the ticket.

"You're picking up," he says. We listen to the engine echoing back down the ramp.

There's oil spilled on the sidewalk; I can smell it. Dark on the street. I shoot my butt into the pool of oil but it doesn't explode.

"Want to go dancing?" Johnny says. He's lighting up another Kool.

"No."

"What a long rotten night," he says, blowing out menthol smoke. Yeah, I'm thinking, and we're a long way behind time. Can't he see I don't feel like hanging around?

"Which way you going?" I say.

"East," he says. "Try to find a cab."

"I'm going home, then," I say. "See you later."

"*Domani*," he says. "Pleasant dreams."

I turn my back and start west along the sidewalk. I've got an apartment on Twenty-third Street, across Tenth Avenue, near the abandoned El track. It's a little inconvenient living that far over, but then I'm not likely to run into any old friends over there. It's two long crosstown blocks away from here, and I am hurrying. Now that I'm this close my head is starting to jerk itself around. I cross Ninth Avenue, and I see the lights of the Empire Diner up ahead.

Half a block. I'm making it. In a minute I will be there. I take my key ring off my belt to get ready to open the door. Now I'm this close I'm almost ready to forgive all the people who ever made me trouble. Maybe I should have tried to talk to Johnny, maybe. But we've got too different from each other, over the years. He worked for me, he stayed with my case. If not for him I might not be around anymore at all. It's partly owing to him that I came out when I did. But even by then we didn't have a lot left to say to each other.

It was a cold spring when I came out, and I was still walking with a cane. It wasn't too easy to get around and I didn't feel so good. I'd been gone for a long time and forgotten the city, and the people I used to know weren't supposed to talk to me anymore, the way things got worked out.

Except for Johnny. And there wasn't such a lot the two of us could do. We'd hang around each other's house and eat pasta and watch TV. Or we might go to a club and sit staring at each other over a couple of drinks.

I remember one day Johnny got sick of it too.

"Up this," he said. "Let's go to the beach."

I told him he was crazy. It was a cold day. But since it was his idea, we had to go. Neither one of us had a car at the time so we end up sitting on the F train for two hours. Finally we get out at Coney Island. Of course there's nothing to do. Who goes to Coney Island in March? We're the only two people on a boardwalk that stretches

Holy Mother | 33

out in both directions as far as you can see. It's cold and windy and me with only a light jacket.

We go to the aquarium to get out of the wind. Johnny wants to look at these little white whales they got down there. You can look at them from above and then you can go down and watch them through a glass wall in the tank. Great. We get tired of the whales and go back up on the boardwalk to watch year-old newspapers blowing around. Finally we find a place where we can get a piece of stale pizza to eat. Johnny's still not satisfied.

"Let's go down by the water," he says. "You come to the beach, you should walk on the sand." So we walk on the sand. It's hard for me with my stick. There's nobody down there either except for a couple of niggers fishing for crabs off the pier. The water looks as flat and empty as pavement.

"Let's build a sand castle," Johnny says. "You want to?" Jeez, why not? We get down on our knees and start piling up sand. I can hardly believe we're doing it, but in a way it's almost fun. I'm working away on my part. After a while Johnny gets up and looks.

"What the hell," he says. "You're not making a sand castle. You're making a sand penitentiary."

I get up too and look over what I've been doing. I thought it was a basic sand castle. Big square of walls with two little walls making a cross in the middle. But Johnny was right. Only they don't call it a penitentiary anymore. They've changed all the terms around, and since 1970 it's been called the Attica Correctional Facility. There's no more prisons in New York State, technically speaking.

We stomped the sand castle flat to the ground. Then we went back to the city.

Porco

I'm plowing across Spring Street with all the pores of my tongue wide open and I'm rummaging in my left hip pocket for my petty cash. Here's the little wad; I'm taking it out and looking at it. What's this I see? There's only four singles here, and I'm sure I had at least a ten.

I back into a doorway and go through all my pockets twice. This can take time. I've got five coat pockets and four pants pockets and one shirt pocket, all full of extra screws and cork pads and pens and cigarette packs and slips of paper and empty matchbooks with telephone numbers written inside and keys to here and there, and It. At the end of the search I net only the same four singles, plus two quarters, four nickels, a dime, and twelve pennies.

I take my coat off and feel the lining all over. *Nada.* In all the names of all the gods, *What happened to my ten-dollar bill?* The gods are kind to me and I remember. I broke that ten on an expensive bottle of tequila and someone drank it and it's gone.

Porco Miserio, that's me. I haven't worked in a good two months and I got no fixed address and that ten was the absolute last of the proceeds of hocking the alto on Third Avenue, which action was a stupid mistake induced by galloping alcoholism. "Sax Player with horns—will travel" always did look better than "Sax Player with pawn tickets—will take money." And maybe my best friend died today too, though I don't really know, since I only just met him. But there's no use in getting upset over these little things. Anyway it's summer and it's not raining. Anyway, I have the tenor with the artist and the soprano in a locker and a sopranino with a girl somewhere, I think. Also if I go back west now I might be able to buy a five with what I have now and when I have a five there is a change scam that might work on someone.

Suiting the action to the word, I'm off backwards on Spring Street. Having a good practical mission steadies my pulse and opens my mind to the manifold possibilities of life. I think I'll try this at Terri's, where I think no one knows me. Also there's two other good bets near the same corner.

West Broadway, and Terri's it is, still full of people despite the lateness of the hour. Every last one of these people is a card-carrying artist, I betcha, registered with the New York State Council, or claiming to be, or trying to pick up someone who is. They're all dressed to kill and drinking Kahlua and coffee and milk. I brush down my coat before I go in. It's an old black shiny suit coat I picked up out of a barrel on Broadway, but, God bless the punks, these things are in style. I am going to look like every other man in the bar, from the waist up, anyway.

I walk in and start trying to catch the eye of the bartender. He's a little cutie. Got silver-blond hair and he's wearing one of those V-necked hospital orderly shirts, dyed mauve. Here he comes. I put the money down on the counter.

"Excuse me," I say. "Could you make that a five?"

Major misfortune, he's counting the change. Slowly, stacking the pennies. And all these people waiting for their Black Russians, too. What a shame for everybody.

"Eight cents short, friend," he says.

"What are you talking about," I say, "it's five exact." I look down at the change. "I put down two dimes," I say, "you must have knocked one on the floor." After all you have to try. Owe it to yourself.

"Maybe some fresh air would clear your head," the barhop says. "The door is still where it was when you came in."

"Maybe you would like to eat some dirt, you maggot," I say in a nasty low whisper. "We both know you pocketed that dime."

"Hey, Mike," the barhop is calling. Down at the far end of the counter something very big turns its head to listen. Looks like some sort of dinosaur.

"Fine, maggot," I say. "Put the bouncer on me over a rotten dime. See if this establishment gets any more of my business." I sweep the money into my pocket and turn around to huff my way out and an awful accident occurs. I clip a Black Russian with my elbow and it splashes all over a successful artist in a white cashmere coat.

"Jesus, sir," I say, "I *am* terribly sorry." Really, it has made a grisly mess of the coat, which I'm sure is worth a good six hundred dollars, or was eight seconds ago. I begin brushing frantically at the lapels, making matters generally worse.

"Get me a bottle of Perrier, sonny," I call to the barhop. "On the double." He's impressed enough to bring me a glass of soda, which I toss at the gentleman's breast.

"Nothing like a little soda to lift out a stain, sir," I say. "Always use it on my carpets at home." In fact, it does work very nicely. I get the barhop to bring me towels to mop up the residue.

"Good as new, sir, practically," I say. I grasp his lapels again and peer into his face. Successful artist, about forty years old. You can see he's thinking about articles in *Artforum*.

"Say, don't I recognize you?" I say. "Aren't you well known for something?" I know he's a star, I can tell from the double chin he's got. He's giving me a discreet hint of a smile.

"I guess I'd better be off now," I say. "Terribly sorry about all this, really I am. But a pleasure to meet you indeed. In case there should be any further problem, just let me give you my card." And I slip him something from one of my pockets, God knows what. Probably a matchbook, and I hope there's nothing critical written inside.

I bow and smile my way through the door, take a breath of fresh air, and blow. One block on Spring, one down Wooster, one over on Broome, and a couple more for good measure. Then I lean on a mailbox to catch my breath.

I take one more tour of my pockets and discover that something funny has happened. It seems that during the confusion the gentleman's wallet fell into my coat pocket somehow. What an awkward situation. If I take it back now people will probably think I stole it. So I'll just drop it in the mailbox. But if there's money inside then the postman might steal it. I should take the money out and return it to the gentleman later.

I lift out the bills and drop the wallet in the mailbox. I count over the money—there's three twenties and a few singles. That's nice. I don't want to get it mixed up with my own money, so I bend over and shove it down in my sock.

Yusuf Ali

Allahu akbar
There is no God but God

And to he whom Allah assigns no light
no light has he.

I awake and I cannot see. I do not know what is happening. I am groping even to remember my name. I cannot find my legs, my arms, my head. Yet I am moving. How is this? I am going somewhere. Someone is holding my arms. I cannot see who it is. I see nothing, or only light, there is a light in front of my eyes like a star.

How should I know what is the night star?
The piercing star?
Over every soul there is a watcher.

I hear voices. Hands are turning my body, bending it, lowering it, I am sitting down. My knees are cramped against my chest. There is no room to move. Am I dead? I still cannot remember. I stare into the star, and it dissolves into a wheeling constellation. I close my eyes and feel my blood racing across my head.

Not just my blood. There is a drug in it. Then I am not dead, if I can feel a drug in my blood. Someone put it there, and I am angry. I do not take drugs. It is forbidden.

How then did the drug come into my body? There is a great pain near the front of my head, and I think that I almost remember. I am so near to the memory that it hurts, and the tide of blood carries it away again.

> . . . they are as shadows on a sea obscure
> covered by a billow
> above which is a billow
> above which are clouds
> shadows piled one on the other.

The wave passes over and I try once again for my name, finding nothing, nothing, a vacancy. I can see shadows now behind the constellation, two discrete shadows like tombstones or trees, and behind them more light yet. I understand. I am in the back seat of a car, and there are two people in front, and the car is moving. It is a very small car, because my knees are pressed into my collarbone, and I cannot move to the right or the left.

What car? How do I come to be in it? Again I reach the point of memory, and again it is lost in the wave. The car has stopped now and hands are reaching for me out of a triangle of light. I hear the voices again. There is cool air on my face and I am pulled through the triangle. The hands are holding me upright. Now I know my body again. I can stand without support. I shrug the hands away now, and the shadows are falling back to my sides, small people, they must be, their heads would not reach my shoulder. I look to see them but the constellation is in the way. I shake my head to clear it and again I get pain and the wave.

"So let's go," I hear a voice saying. "If you can shake us off like that then you can walk through that door." I know the voice, familiar to me as a recurring dream. I look for the shadows and now I see four of them; with distant voices murmuring, urging me to a lighted door. I follow them, and there is a new pain with the brightness, but inside this room I take a seat so easily that I know I must have done it many times before.

The constellation has now become a skein of flowing golden

dots, and I can see through it better than before. I see faces. They are faces that I know. My eyes scan two brown faces, one white, and then stop on the last, a tense face with black eyes and several conflicting expressions: confidence, cunning, wariness, fear, a trace of compassion, and behind all these a flicker of understanding, which the whole face shelters like a sputtering match. The voice I heard belongs to this face, I can hear it calling my name. Yusuf Ali. The flicker holds for an instant—Yusuf Ali. That happened a long time ago, in the park. The park. I reach to touch the swelling near my left temple. I remember. I was hit.

Al-'Alaq:
He created man from a clot of blood.

Al-Tariq:
So let man consider of what he was created
he was created of gushing water
Issuing between the loins and the breastbones
Surely He is able to bring him back
Upon the day when the secrets are tried
and he shall have no strength, no helper.

I consider. I am now Yusuf Ali. Once I was Leon Lenox of Hunts Point. I threw that name away and was nothing for a time. Then a stranger came and called me a new name. The voice was compelling, from what knowledge or for what reason, I don't know. I accepted it. Everything is written. *Allahu akbar. La ilaha ill' Allah.*

For God there are written names at least to the number of ninety-nine. *Al-Baqarah:* it is written that the Lord made Adam and taught him the names, all of them. He presented his parts to the angels, and the angels did not know the names of them. Then Adam recited the names, and the angels made obeisance to Adam, all but Iblis, who became the first of the unbelievers.

I look around the table now to see if I can name the faces. Santa, a Puerto Rican possessed by devils. Carlo, a Dominican with expensive clothes and barely enough intelligence to insult a Russian waitress. Holy Mother—that name is a joke, and he is a professional killer. Johnny B., him with the persuasive voice, saying now,

". . . a stranger in the world like you and me." I just catch this phrase. It is a joke he thinks he is making, to press some point onto Carlo. The Prophet said:

> Blessed are the Strangers, for they are the pious among
> the evil.

I know my name now, and the names of the people at the table, and I remember how we are associated, and roughly why we are here. I know by induction that I have been hit on the head, but I still do not remember who did it or why it happened, or anything much at all about the last few days. I am not going to start asking what happened. I will be silent until I can remember.

Carlo and Johnny B. are arguing. Johnny B. is talking about getting rid of bodies; there's been a question of killing someone. Who? Someone who hit me on the head, probably. From what Johnny B. is saying it appears that the someone is still alive.

Who is it? I try to push through my memory in chronological order, but I cannot get very far. All the events of the last couple of days are somehow scattered in my mind. I think the last thing I recall is standing in the dark end of the park, watching some people who were selling luminous plastic chokers, glowing green through the darkness. Tonight or another night? I am not certain.

Johnny B. is talking now about the world. He is trying to make it small for us, a compact package which we can carry around in our pockets. He is saying something about talking rocks, and that touches a memory. Strange as it seems, I feel sure that I have had some sort of dealings with a talking rock. Johnny B. is now telling something about Porco Miserio. Porco. The pieces of my memory roll together around the name and coalesce like beads of mercury.

I was going down to the southwest end. I passed the people with the glowing chokers, and I noticed Porco sitting on a bench. When I told him to get out he said he had to talk to Johnny B. He was very persistent. I did not want to pull his arms off because he used to be a friend of Johnny B., so maybe Johnny B. would not want him damaged. But he was saying such crazy things that I called the others in to help me watch him.

Johnny B. came. Porco began talking. I do not remember what

he talked about. There was an argument and I was angry. Then the lights went out. Porco hit me with a rock, apparently. I am still not sure exactly why.

I look up at the clock on the wall. It is three-fifteen. I can barely read the time through the swirl of golden dots. I must have been out for more than an hour. That would explain the holes in my memory. I was hit hard. The others must have given me speed to get me up again. That would explain the drug I feel, against the darkness and the wave.

Now. I have the beginning and the end and I want to know what happened in the middle. I try to think of it by going backward, but I get interrupted by someone pushing food into my mouth. I stare through the drifting dots and see that it is Johnny B. He is hand-feeding me as though I were a teething baby.

I am not in any mood to eat, or to be bothered. I feel angry again, but it is better not to be angry at Johnny B. I bend up the fork a little, until I feel more calm. Johnny B. has good intentions, I believe. But he is not my mother.

"I am not hungry." I tell him this as soon as I feel able. "I am thinking." Then I do not listen to anything more. My mouth can handle my part of the accounting without any assistance from me, and I let the voices of the others fade into a dull humming. I try again to bring back the details of what Porco was talking about and why I was angry and how I got hit with the rock.

Time has passed, and I realize I am now alone with Johnny B. and the killer, and I still have not found the answer. Johnny B. tells me to go home, and that sounds reasonable. We talk about tomorrow, then I get up and leave.

Second Avenue. The swirling dots are almost gone, I only see a few still glowing at the corners of my eyes. I feel my bruise again. It's just in front of my left temple. Perhaps I have a slight concussion and amnesia, and that is why I do not remember what has happened.

One thing is certain, I realize, it is very lucky that I am alive. An inch farther back and the talking rock or whatever it was would have gone straight through my temple and ended up in my brain. Was Porco thinking about that at all? Not likely. He swung wild, I imagine. I am beginning to feel angry at Porco again.

I am walking down toward the bottom of Second Avenue, past Indian restaurants, newsstands, bodegas, all locked down behind steel gates for the night. I do not want to go home just now, I have decided. First I want to get this thing sorted out. For a moment I almost want to go back and ask Johnny B. what exactly happened. But I do not want to let him see that I don't know. Who else could I ask? Porco. Porco is the other one who would be sure to know. He is the one I want to see. The only problem is to find him.

Where is Porco going to be? I don't know where he lives. I do not know much at all about him. I have heard that he is a horn player who drinks more than he works. All right. What do you do if you are Porco and you just hit me over the head with a rock? If you are Porco you probably go and have a drink if you can buy one. Porco drinks in the Spring Street Lounge sometimes. That is the one other thing I know about him; I found it out from Johnny B. Then I will go to the Spring Street Lounge now. If he is not there then maybe there will be someone there who knows his pattern.

I come to Houston Street and stop to think about directions. This is not really my area. It has only been a couple of years since I moved to Manhattan, and I live now on the West Side, far downtown. I have come a long distance from Hunts Point, where Leon Lenox used to live. Yusuf Ali lives in Independence Plaza, a solid housing tower which has a view of the river and is not going to be torched. Yusuf Ali makes quite a lot of money and keeps what he makes. Yusuf Ali has Islam, where Leon Lenox had nothing, and when Yusuf Ali has enough money, he will make the hajj.

Second Avenue ends here. It splits into Forsyth and Chrystie, on either side of Roosevelt Park. I want to walk down Chrystie Street. I can pick up Rivington Street from there and walk across to the bar.

I go over to catch the light and cross Houston Street. Crossing, I think I see someone that looks like Santa Barbara hanging out under the streetlight at the east corner of the park. My vision is still cloudy, but I think I recognize the ritual necklaces he wears. I turn my head away and keep walking on. I do not want to talk to Santa now, even though he could probably answer some of my questions. He does his job, but we have never been better friends than necessary. His machismo doesn't like the fact that he is little and I am big.

In Washington Square they used to call him Paco, before Johnny

B. came along. Perhaps that was not his real name either. He is one of the Hoboken santeros, now, and Johnny B. got to him, I suspect, because he knew something about santeria. I know something about it too. In Hunts Point there were witches, and when you were sick some people might send you to the witch instead of the doctor. I have known people who went and claimed that they were cured. There are still botánicas all through Loisaida and Harlem and the Bronx, small storefronts with statues of the saints in the windows and all sorts of herbs in the back, and if the cures sometimes work, you don't have to be a brujo to know something about herbal medicine. That is what Leon Lenox thought, and he knew the territory.

If you come up against the Ricans in Hunts Point, maybe the Young Lords will wrap a pipe around your skull, or maybe someone else would buy a spell and send it on you. To make you not eat or not sleep or get pain without cause or die for no obvious reason, so they claimed. Sometimes the magic might work, on those who believed. Leon Lenox did not believe, knowing that there was plenty of bad luck to go around Hunts Point without having anyone wish it on you. Yusuf Ali is not so sure.

Santa takes pride in the orishas because they are real. He can feel them come to him. He knows that they can make things happen in the world. I would not say for certain that they can't. I only wonder if the orishas are what he thinks they are. It is written how the jinn were created by Allah out of the scorching wind of the desert, long ago, before the first man was made. Now, so many years from the beginning, they have become something like a vapor, so that we cannot see them, although they still return to fire when they die, as man returns to dust. And meanwhile, they are still around. The jinn live in the insane, and in certain poets and soothsayers, and forever they are the servants of disobedience. Like Iblis, they are respited unto the last days of our world. Like Iblis, they are empowered to lead men astray from the way, and this too is the will of Allah. *Allahu akbar, la ilaha ill' Allah.*

Santa belongs to the devils, I think, and I belong to Islam, but both of us have to live in the world we can see. I turn onto Rivington Street and look back over my shoulder at Roosevelt Park, where I see an iron fence, old papers and trash, some grass and a few trees trying to keep themselves alive. There are no lights inside this park and so it usually empties out at night. Everyone is afraid and so no one is there to be afraid of. I do not understand why Santa would be hanging around there now. But now I think I remember that whatever Porco was talking about had something to do with that park. Yes, and it was something that Santa would be interested in. I think I got knocked on the head because of something that happened in Roosevelt Park. I can almost remember, not quite. Should I go back? No.

I will find Porco and get the answer from him. But it would be better if I knew before I find him whether I want to kill him or tell him salaam. I cross the Bowery and Elizabeth and Mott streets, and still I am not sure. I am coming up on Mulberry Street, and there is the Spring Street Lounge.

I do not know whether I want to go in there or not. My head is beginning to hurt again, and the dots are coming back. It might be a better idea to go home. Here on my left is an asphalt playground, set off from the street by a storm fence. There are benches inside, I will go in and sit down. From here I can see the door of the bar, and I will know if Porco comes or goes. I will rest here a little and try to think clearly.

I try to think, but my mind is drifting, floating out of this playground through the parks of Manhattan to the empty lots in Hunts Point, where Leon Lenox used to do his work. These are the vacant spaces, the hollowness where nothing is, our deserts. I may never see the Arabian deserts, but I could tell you all about the scorching wind. I have seen it tearing at every building on Fox Street, hungering for human life, funneling into the emptiness when all the life was gone. That is where Leon Lenox died. *Allahu akbar.* And for them await gardens, beneath which rivers flow.

The one thing Yusuf Ali has in common with Leon Lenox is that both of them sell drugs. So both of them are under the malediction of the Prophet. But the Prophet also said, "The first thing Allah, majestic be His name, created was the Pen, which He took in His right hands, though both His hands are right hands, and wrote this present world and all that there is to be in it." And the Prophet also said, to Abu Bakr, "O Abu Bakr, if Allah most high had not willed that there be disobedience, He would not have created the Devil."

Also, I am at least not selling the poison to my own people, which is what Leon Lenox used to do. The people coming to us in Washington Square are most of them unbelievers. It is not true, as the professional murderer thinks, that I want to kill all these people. That was an error eliminated from my thinking long ago.

But these people are welcome to kill themselves if that is what they want to do.

> The Prophet said:
>> There is no soul but Allah has written its entrance
>> and its exit and what it will meet.
> The people asked him:
>> Then what is the point in acting, O Messenger of Allah?
> The Prophet replied:
>> Go on acting, for everyone is inclined to that for
>> which he was created. If he is for Paradise, he
>> will be inclined to the works of the people of Paradise,
>> and if he is for the Fire, he will be inclined to the
>> works of the people of the Fire.

I like to think that I stand somewhere in between. And the Lord is known as *ar-Rahman*, the Merciful, as well as *al-'Adl*, the Just, as well as many other things.

> *Allahu akbar, la ilaha ill' Allah.*
> *And God knows everything.*

Porco

I start walking across whatever street this is till I hit Lafayette. I go up Lafayette to Spring Street and make a right. I go past the number 6 stop and I'm walking into the Spring Street Lounge, finally, at last. I don't even look around to see who's sitting here at the tables. I go straight to the bar and sit down on a stool. All the little aggravations of this evening have taken a terrible toll on my nerves. I want a drink and I want it *now*, man.

Bartender slides over, what do I want? There's three things I drink—bourbon, beer, wine, or failing that, anything I can get. I'm not failing that tonight. I got money so I'm going to drink bourbon. Do I want a shot, or one on the rocks? Or maybe I want a beer first to settle my nerves. Or maybe I want some shots first to blow my nerves out of the ball park. My fingernails are dancing a little salsa of indecision on the countertop.

"What's it going to be," says the bartender.

"A shot," say I.

"Shot of what?"

"Of what do you think? Bourbon, house brand."

He reaches behind him for a bottle and glass. No, no, I keep forgetting I have this money.

"Wait a second," I say. "Make it Jack Black."

"You in the money again?" says the bartender. "Haven't seen you around in a while."

I don't answer that. He pours the whiskey into the little glass in front of me and goes off to wait on somebody else. I look at the glass. It's brimming. It's actually standing an angstrom above the lip of the glass, held there by surface tension alone. Somebody sets down a glass at the other end of the bar and the top of my drink trembles like it was a living thing. If I try to pick it up now I know I'm going to spill half of it. My hands start shaking just thinking about it. The bastard, he filled it too full. No, I shouldn't think evil of a friend. He probably was trying to do me a favor.

I look at my hand curled toward the glass on the counter. It looks steady enough, just lying there. Now I stare into the shot of bourbon. What a pretty thing it is. I see light inside it, like I'm looking through a red agate. I lift my hand for a test flight. Just checking out the aerodynamics of my hand. I get it almost to the glass before it starts to flutter. So I pull the hand back and start combing my pockets for a cigarette pack with cigarettes in it. I pull out a few rejects and store them on the counter under my other hand. I don't dare lose them. There could be valuable information inside.

Eventually I seem to feel a pack with a couple of cigarettes in it. I pull it out for inspection. Delicados, all the way from Mexico. I'd just love to know how they got in my pocket. I stick one in my mouth and right away I can taste the heavy sweetness. Very syrupy tobacco they put in Delicados. Also they pack them so loose that half of it ends up in your teeth and tonsils.

I pick up matches from the counter. I am now going to attempt the one-handed match light. Useful thing to know how to do, in case one of your hands should get lost somewhere. It's largely done with the thumb. My thumb flicks the matchbook open and finds the head of a match and bends it up to ninety degrees. Now I rotate the matchbook over in my hand, at the same time bending the match down over the staple, thus bringing the match head into contact with the striker. Snap, and it lights, and the Delicado drops out of my mouth and falls on the floor.

So it's getting worse, is it? If this goes on I'm going to embarrass myself. I pick up the cigarette and light it with two hands and twirl around on my stool to see if there's anyone in here I dislike. If I could just hate somebody for a couple of minutes, it would steady my hands long enough for me to hook down my drink like anybody else, and the whole problem would go away. Unfortunately, I don't see anybody I know well enough to hate even a little bit. I twirl back toward the rear wall, where there's the jukebox and some guy playing Asteroids.

What's this music coming out of the jukebox. It's a new tune by Frank Sinatra. They put it in a couple of months ago and someone is always playing it. "New York, New York," it's called. I don't like this song. I hate this song. I don't want to listen to this song one minute longer.

I get off my stool and slide over where I can watch the guy playing Asteroids. There's this video rocket ship being attacked by video asteroids and sometimes by other video spaceships. You got to shoot them with your video death rays before they shoot you or bang into you or whatever. If you don't, there's a video explosion and you lose. If you don't lose, it all starts to come at you faster. This guy playing now must be pretty good because the asteroids are flying thick and fast. I jump when I notice he's got a gun on his belt, but then I look at his shirt and realize he's a court officer. Probably just off the swing shift at Criminal Court.

I'm listening very closely to this record, because I think I remember that it sometimes sticks. Yes, there it is. Right at the most boring part of it I step over and hit the box a good bash with my fist. The arm flies all the way across the record and goes into reject, just as I was hoping it would do. Then it proceeds to the next selection, which turns out to be "Spirit in the Night" by Bruce da Boss.

The bartender is over staring at me now.

"You trying to break something or what?" he says.

"The record was stuck, my friend," I say. "I fixed it." I look at him for a second and feel the strength of the Stone in my pocket. Then I walk back to my stool and lift the shot glass and pour every drop right down my throat. I put the glass back down and stand there, listening to the new tune. It is a great improvement. In thirty seconds I feel very fine. I call the bartender over.

"Bring me another shot," I say, "and one on the rocks and a Heineken. Make it a double on the rocks. And buy that man a drink."

Santa Barbara

Grand Pays, the big country. That how we call the dead, all of them, when we dont know they names. I learn it from Ti Jeanne, little black woman born in Haiti. People telling me she know few things even the santeros dont know. I go up to see her and it true what the people saying. Ti Jeanne living in East Harlem till she die, some time ago. She too now in Grand Pays. You look for her now under the water of the river or in the stones of the street. Always they more of the dead than they are the living.

When some man die, we say, Olofi take him into the cloud. It rain, and the man go in the river with the rainwater. Maybe after a long time he come to be a stone. We calling this stone, otan. It like that too with the orishas. We find them too sometimes in otanes. Since I making the asiento, some months ago, I keep now in my house the otanes of Chango. The god of fire and thunder and lightning and people calling him sometimes Takata, the god of stones. Chango, I touching now the eleke, six white beads, six red, six white, six red, and that is also Chango.

Ti Jeanne once telling me of an otan a man she know is having. A little stone with Oggun in it twenty times and it so heavy you cant pick it up. This stone that Porco got, maybe it is one like the same. I think for sure this thing Porco got must be an otan. Before I always thinking that Porco is a big nothing. Just the sound of empty talking, like the wind when it blow over the empty bottle. But now he having this thing and he talking like he put his hand on a god. If it true I know the god dont let him lie. I got to believe that what he saying. Anyway about the man from 219 Bowery. That man got to be a santero, maybe even babalawo. I never think Porco got power, not like Yanni-B. But I know the babalawo dont give him the otan for no reason. Not if he give it away and then he die. I looking now through the light of the streetlamp into the park where the babalawo lying dead now. I touching my elekes. I fearing the dark in there like I am again a little child.

Here Yusuf Ali coming down the street. Coming down and stopping here across from me looking like he dont know where he going to go next. Bignig Yusuf be knocked on the head like when I see them hitting cows with hammers when I four year old walking around Puerto Rico with no pants on. Cows they die but Yusuf Ali dont be no different. He whole head a muscle like he big body. Walking around the city trying to make people think he a Arab. He no more an Arab than I am.

Yusuf Ali turning he big bull head back and forth like a rock on a string. I turning my back to him so he not going to see me. I dont want nothing to do with Yusuf Ali. When Yanni-B tell me he going to take him in with us I tell him we dont need him. Dont need this bignig body. That not what power mean. Yusuf Ali making some trouble, I send a bilongo on him that fix him right. I make him fall in love with a telephone pole. I make him fight with he best friend. I make him sleep and not ever wake up, turn he whole life to ashes. Maybe I send a mort on him, how Ti Jeanne teaching me to do. I telling Yanni-B these thing and he say to me, Wait, Santa, you cant be doing that to everybody in this park. We use what you know when we need it. We dont waste it. We do how everybody does. Yanni-B explain me this two three time. After while I see he right like always.

I looking back over my shoulder, see if Yusuf Ali still be hanging on the corner. See him now crossing the street. See him going away on Chrystie Street. Going out of sight. What it matter if he dont know where he is? He dont even know who he is. He think he know allah, but he allah just a trick to make fear in the city again. Yusuf Ali happy like a pig in eating out of other people footprints. Tonight he dont even know when Porco saying something true, maybe for the first time in he dirty life. Yusuf asking to get hit on he big head.

But it not easy to know these thing if no one telling you. Too bad for Yusuf he reading quran and be so smart he wont listen. He never learn now that god having the same faces for him and me. He never learn to see the faces now.

My family coming from Puerto Rico when I five years old. My father die in the winter. He step on a shell and die of blood poison. My mother she dont want to stay in Puerto Rico anymore so she take me and my two little sister in U.S.A. In the spring we living with my mother sister on Willow Street in Hoboken. Me my mother my sisters and my mother sister and her husband and her children all living in some rooms in a big building of all Spanish people. Mostly they from Puerto Rico or else Dominican Republic. It cold that spring, colder than I ever know. Till summer come I dont go out of the house ever.

Summertime I going outside again. Walking in the street all my time just to be alone from the people of the house. Anytime I go in the street I got to put some shoes on. Too much glass lying around for bare feet. I go around the corner on Newark Street. Lot of thing there, some stores, some restaurant, Los Islas bar with a palm tree on it sign. One store I looking at I dont understand. It got glass window with saints inside, like at the church. But it not looking like any church I ever see. One time I pass by and see some kinds of birds flying there inside. I want to go in and look at them close up, but this store never open.

Every time I pass by this store I looking in through the gate like a kid at the zoo. Most times I dont see nothing. Sometime I see the birds again but I cant ever tell what kind birds they are. At night sometime candles lit inside. Sometime also some drums.

I find out they a man living in the store. See him few time at the door, middle-age man not too tall. Got beard and some gold tooths at the side he mouth. Everybody calling him Mr. Rivera. He the only Mr. anything on all of Newark Street so I know he some big man. I watch careful he dont catch me looking in his window but one day he catch me anyway.

It happen sometime later. I now maybe seven year old. We be in U.S.A. for longer than a year. My mother getting welfare for me to go in school but sometime we have to use it on the landlord so sometime I go and sometime I dont go. I wearing the same first shoes I have when we first come. They split open in places where my feet getting bigger so I got to put in newspaper to keep out the cold. I standing outside Mr. Rivera store and the wind making so much noise I dont hear him come.

I feel the hand on my arm and I look up and see who it is. I dont try to pull back my arm from him. I stand there while he opening up the gate. He pull me in the gate and lock it behind. Now it too late for me to go somewhere. He open the door with another key and bring me into the store. It dark and smell like things I never smelling before. Mr. Rivera go in back and light some candles. He ask me something in English and I shake my head I dont understand.

"Why you looking in my window?" he ask me in Spanish.

"I just walking by," I say.

"No, you not just walking by," he say. "You looking in my window now for longer than a year."

I dont say nothing. In all my life I never been so scared. Not even the time the dog try to eat my foot in Puerto Rico. It quiet for a minute. Then Mr. Rivera say, "You want to know something, you can ask."

We sitting down on some chairs. I dont know what I going to say. In a minute I ask him, "How you got this store and it not ever open?"

"Not a store," he tell me. "Is an ileocha. You know what it is?"

I shake my head no I dont. Mr. Rivera he smiling. I see his tooths shining in he mouth and I not too scared anymore. Mr. Rivera point me the crucifix on the wall. He say, "You know who it is?"

"I know," I say. "Jesu Cristo." But Mr. Rivera shaking he head.

"Not Jesu Cristo," he say. "Is Jesu Cristo and not Jesu Cristo too. You know who I am?"

"You Mr. Rivera," I say. Mr. Rivera start laughing.

"I Mr. Rivera and I not Mr. Rivera too. You know who you are?"

He laughing now so hard he start to choke and bend over. Must be I looking funny to him some way. After while he straighten up. He point me crucifix again.

"Olofi," he say. "He make the world."

"Jesu Cristo make the world," I say. "I know. Jesu Cristo is Dio."

Mr. Rivera lean over at me. I see his eyes black. I smell the smell stronger.

"Oludamare-Olofi make the world," he say. "He make everything. He make you and your brother and sister and mother and father. He make me and this ileocha. He make your shoes and the wind and the glass on the street. He make everything. Long time ago. Before Jesu Cristo. Before Dio. Before even time."

I looking all around now. Yusuf Ali gone. Nobody here but me and the winos sleeping on the benches east of Second Avenue. Olofi make them too. He make this summer night. I know this now. I knowing many thing more now than when I seven year old. But I still a child in this world.

Mr. Rivera telling me, Olofi having many children. The first of his children be the orishas. The orishas children be people like us. They living a long time in Africa. They call them the Yoruba people. The Yoruba people talking to Olofi and all the orishas.

Sometime later is the Spanish people. They sailing all around the world in ships. They sailing in Africa and taking the Yoruba people. Then they sailing in Puerto Rico and make the Yoruba people grow sugar cane. Make them listen to the Mass and pray to Dio. Take away the drums and the orishas.

But no one can take away the orishas, Mr. Rivera explain me. Orishas being everywhere, in everything. Finally someone understand. Jesu Cristo and the saints are other names and faces for the orishas.

I stop Mr. Rivera to ask him a question. I tell him how the dog was eating my foot in Puerto Rico. I take my shoe off to show him the marks and tell him how the doctor saying I be limping on this foot my whole life long. I tell him how my mother take me to the priest and the priest give me the body of Jesu Cristo to eat. The pain go away and I walking now like anybody.

"So," Mr. Rivera say. "Is many words for many things. Go now, it late. Your mother she dont know where to find you." He unlock the door and the gate for me to go out. "Come back tomorrow," he tell me. "You are a child of this house."

Mr. Rivera dead now too. He die when I am still a yaguo. Since I a yaguo and he my yubbona I can be there when they making it ready for him to leave the world. Santeros coming from all over when Mr. Rivera die. From all over Harlem and Brooklyn and the Bronx. I dont know before he that big a babalawo. All these people coming to see the right things be done.

I looking now again to see into Roosevelt Park where the babalawo lying dead. If what Porco say be true. Who going to send this man off from this world? Not Porco, that for sure. Probably Porco off drinking somewhere now.

I going back to see Mr. Rivera many time after this first day. Every day I pass by the ileocha. Mr. Rivera explain me answers to my questions if he can. I asking about the birds he keep. He say he make them food for the orishas. I ask him about the drums I hearing. He tell me the drums be bata drums. Use them to call the orishas. So they make the bata speak and the orisha come to the omo-orisha. "Subirse el santo a su caballo," Mr. Rivera say, the saint getting on his horse. This I dont yet understand.

"Too young to know these things," Mr. Rivera tell me. But still he like to talk to me. After while he begin teaching me to make the bata speak. He have good drums, skins coming from Africa. Mr. Rivera teaching me talking drum. It dont talk in sign or nothing. It sound just like the voice of a man. He teach me how to hear the drum speak in the street. Sometime it be just music and sometime something more. Maybe if a house catching fire you hear it on the drums before the telephone. Mr. Rivera give me a small drum for taking home in my house. After while my mother make me take it back.

My mother find out I going to see Mr. Rivera, and she dont like it at all. When she find out where the drum came from, she dont ask no more question. She grab me by my ear and snatch me behind the curtain onto the bed where she sleeps, so my sisters not going to see what we doing. No room in there except the bed, so we sitting on the bed. My mother still got hold my ear and it hurting me plenty. She jerk my head around to look at the crucifix she keeping over the head of the bed.

"Who that?" she say. "Tell me now."

"Jesu Cristo," I say. My mother she let go my ear.

"Who make you?" my mother say.

I dont say nothing. I not going to say Olofi to my mother.

"*Who make you?*" she say. "Tell me now."

I dont say nothing. I dont think I know the answer. My mother whop me across the side of the head with the back of her hand. She hitting me hard as she know how, and my mother she not a weak woman. It lay me out sideways on the bed but I dont say nothing. I dont cry. Last time I cry was in Puerto Rico when the dog got hold my foot. I crying then and the dog he just chewing harder. After while I stop crying then. I pick up a rock off the ground and beat the dog on the head till he let me go. After we come in U.S.A. I dont even cry one time. People in the street find out you going to cry, you might as well not be alive no more. If you can fight you fight. If you cant fight, you hold your mouth shut and wait for when you can.

My mother though, she crying good. Crying and praying and crossing herself and yelling out things about Mr. Rivera I never hear nobody say about nobody before. My mother yelling so loud my aunt come running in the room.

"Be quiet," she say. "People going to hear you all over the building."

"What I care if people hearing me," my mother say. "The devil from hell is taking the soul of my son."

"Be quiet, Anita," my aunt tell her. "You dont know what you saying." She take my mother into the kitchen. I hear them talking through the door, and after while my mother stop yelling but I hear her crying still. My uncle he go in the kitchen too and I hear them whispering in there a long time. I lying on the bed behind the curtain feeling my face where it starting to swell. It not so bad. I like to be lying there quiet behind the curtain. First time all that winter I be alone and not be cold. I hear my two sister playing on the floor outside the curtain. One of them five now, the other four. After while I crawl up to the head of the bed and kiss the crucifix. I dont want Jesu Cristo mad at me.

Some time later my aunt come looking for me and take me in the kitchen too. My mother sitting at the table and wiping out her eyes with a paper towel. My aunt making coffee, and we all going to get some. We sit drinking the coffee, thick and black with a lot of sugar. When I finish my cup I get it filled again like it was a saints day. But when my mother look at me she getting tears again.

"Stop, Anita," my uncle say. "Mr. Rivera never hurt nobody. Walk down the street one day and see if you find anybody dont give him respect."

"All these thing coming from the devil," my mother say. "I'm a Catholic, I dont want these thing."

"It santeria," my uncle say. "It not palo mayombe. It only the same saints like at the church."

"Im a good Catholic," my mother say. I see she got her rosary wrapped around her fist. "I come in America to get away from these thing."

"Maybe you like to get away from yourself too," my uncle say. "*Son cosas de la vida.* Stop crying and drink your coffee and we dont talk about this no more."

My aunt come over with a cold cloth and put it on my face where it red.

"You got a good son," she say to my mother. "He going to be strong. You should be happy he going to see Mr. Rivera and not stealing things out of the stores."

But the next day I got to take the drum back to Mr. Rivera anyway. Even my uncle dont want me hitting the drum in the house and driving all the people crazy. I tell Mr. Rivera what my uncle telling me to say, that I got to give it back because it making noise keeping people awake. But Mr. Rivera know all about it already some way. I scared maybe he going to do something to my mother. But he dont do nothing at all, just like my uncle saying. Next week Mr. Rivera sending my mother some sugar and one pound Colombian coffee. If he pass her on the street he bow to her so low he head almost touching the ground.

I ask Mr. Rivera how he know what happen with me and my mother.

"I am omo-orisha of Orunla," he tell me. "Orunla he knowing the past and the future."

Mr. Rivera take some shells and show to me. Looking like shells out of the ocean. Where they open they filed down so they got teeth and looking like a mouth.

"Is the Table of Ifa," Mr. Rivera tell me, "los caracoles."

He tell me how every shell be the mouth of a god. He throw the shells down on a mat and the orishas telling him what already been and what going to be. That what make the babalawo. It only for the children of Orunla.

Mr. Rivera take out a few stones and line them in a row. He asking me which one I like the best. I dont have no trouble picking. I like the red one, it so pretty. Looking more like glass than a stone, it shining from inside.

"Good," Mr. Rivera say. He come over and open my mouth and look inside with a candle.

"Good," he say, "you are the child of Chango. When you older you be omo-Chango like I omo-Orunla. Till then Chango going to be you guardian."

Mr. Rivera take up a little cloth bag and fill it with spices and leaves. He go in back and say some words in front the statue of Saint Barbara. He sew the bag shut tight. Then he take a little golden sword and sew it to the front of the bag. Mr. Rivera sewing good as a woman sew.

"This be your resguardo," Mr. Rivera say. "It going to keep you safe. You going to hide it where nobody find it but you. You look at one time each day. This little sword belong to Chango. If ever this little sword be broken you come to me next minute."

Then he give me too a small statue of Saint Barbara standing beside the tower with a cup and sword in her hand.

"This Chango too," Mr. Rivera explain me, "but nobody got to know that but you. You take it home, and when you mother see it she think it just the saint."

Mr. Rivera tell me how Saint Barbara living in the old world. Her father he dont like what she believe, so he keep her locked into this tower. After while she still dont change her mind, so her father take her on top the tower and cut off her head with he sword. Next minute he get killed by thunder and lightning. Chango living in a tower too, Mr. Rivera explain. Chango holding thunder and lightning too. Saint Barbara and Chango be the same, only most people dont know.

One man that do know is Yanni-B. He come up to me and call me Santa Barbara, and I know he know what he saying. How he know, I cant tell. He dont act like santero but he know something only the santeros know. Maybe he could be just a santo lavado but I think he got too much power for that.

Some time I thinking maybe he dont know nothing. Maybe somebody just tell him words to say and he dont know what they mean. But now I dont ever think that no more.

I come in the park early one day and Yanni-B call me over under the trees where the little fountain is where nobody going to see us. We sitting on a bench under the trees and Yanni-B got a little bottle in he hand. He shake the bottle out. It sit in he hand, little round ball look like shiny chrome but it moving, it moving just a little bit around the edge like it alive. Yanni-B give it touch with he fingernail and it break apart in little balls like the big one. He roll them in he hand and they coming back together in the one big ball. He holding it out for me to take. I take it in my hand, and I want to touch to my mouth because I know it strong. Yanni-B yelling, "Dont do that, Santa, it death to any man tongue." He tell me, "Keep it, Santa, but keep it secret. Keep it in a jar that wont never break." He tell me, "Santa, this is the god of changes." It true what he saying.

I learn many thing from many people. I learn some thing from Ti Jeanne. Most thing I learn from Mr. Rivera. When I twelve year old he start me playing bata for the guemilere, the birthday of the saints. When I eighteen he make me yaguo. I stay yaguo for long time, two years. When last spring come, Mr. Rivera going to help me make the asiento. Only instead he die.

Little time later I make the asiento anyway. I go to an ileocha in Loisaida, here on the Lower East Side. After it over, I a santero like all the rest. Only I got nobody left to answer my questions.

I looking again into Roosevelt Park. Going to have to go in there soon. Only going to be dark a few hours more. I know I got to go. Somebody got to see this man out of the world, and nobody even know about him but me. Only I not sure what it right to do. I only been santero a short time.

I holding my elekes, my hand over the bottle with the silver ball. We call the god of changes Eleggua. In one way he the strongest orisha. The other orishas not going to do anything Eleggua dont let them do. I keep Eleggua at home by my door and I carry him here on my neck. Eleggua carry the messages and open the doors. He at the beginning of everything happening. I going to have to call him now. I touch my elekes.

IBARAKOU MOLLUMBA ELEGGUA IBACO MYUMBA IBACO MOYUMBA. OMOTE CONICU IBACOO OMOTE AKO MOLLUMBA ELLEGGUA KULONA. IBARAKOU MOL-LUMBA AKO ELEGGUA KULONA ACHE IBAKOU MOL-LUMBA. ACHE ELEGGUA KULONA IBARAKOU MOLLUMBA OMOLE KO AKO ACHE.

I see the red car coming down Second Avenue and turning the corner. I know the car but already now it not me seeing it. It not me saying these words and I hear them coming from a long way away.

ARONGO LARO AKONGO LAROLLE ELEGGUA KUL-LONA A LAROLLE COMA. KOMIO AKONKO LARO AKONKO LAROLLE ELEGGUA COMA KOMIO ACHE. AKONKA LARO AKONKO LARO AKO ACHE IBA LA GUANA ELEGGUA. LAROLLE AKONKO E LAROLLE AKONKO E LAROLLE AKONKO AKONKO LAROLLE AKONKO LAROLLE AKONKO LA GUANA E LAROLLE.

Porco

Now I'm buying a drink for the Man with No Face. Of course, he's got a face of sorts. Doesn't everybody? No Face is just the impression he happens to make on me. My little idea of what he looks like.

"Take him a bourbon and a beer," I tell the bartender. "Tell him it's compliments of Mayor Koch." Bartender turns around for more glasses and I check out No Face once more. He's standing next to the Woman with Almost No Face, at the other end of the bar near the door. She's sitting on a high stool with her feet hooked on the rung and her knees touching neatly like the knees of a little girl. A little girl she's not. She's forty or so and has straight no-color hair and straight worry wrinkles in her forehead and a straight line for a mouth. The hair is long and looks like it could have been red at some time in the past. She's skinny and hard. Ten years ago she might have been a hooker and maybe now she's on the PONY retirement plan, prostitutes of New York pay for the glass of wine sitting in front of her, that she might decide to take a sip of in ten minutes or so. I see her in here just once in a while. Now that I think of it, it gets me depressed to look at her. I swivel back facing the bar and knock off my second shot and chase it with a slug of Heineken.

Bartender is serving No Face now. No Face looks at the two glasses and looks up at the bartender. If he had any expressions to use I guess he might look surprised.

"Mayor Koch just bought you a drink," says the bartender. But he jerks his thumb down the bar at me. Now why does he have to spoil my little joke? I know why. He's a kid twenty-two years old, and eight months ago he got out of bartender school, where he learned how to make margaritas and grasshoppers and Singapore slings. After all that, this was the only job he could get and he feels like his talents are being wasted, because the most complicated thing anybody orders in this place is liquor poured over ice cubes. So he's bitter against the world, and he doesn't like to see anybody else be happy. Bad characteristic in a bartender. One afternoon he actually tried to take a whole beer and a half a pack of cigarettes off my table when I went in the bathroom. Claimed later he was just tidying up.

No Face just popped off his shot. He takes a sip of beer and looks over my way. He's a little man. Got on a little white shirt with all the buttons buttoned right up to the very top one, so that his collar is tight on his leathery neck. Dark-skinned little man, with a fringe of hair around the rim of his head. Got a flat nose that goes first to the right and then to the left. Little button black eyes and a mouth that looks like it's been sewed shut with twine. A shrunken head, that's what he reminds me of. Never thought of that before. He takes a crab step along the bar toward me. I'm terrified he's going to thank me for the drink. Can't stand politeness. Maybe I should try to think up an insult for him before he gets over here.

The really odd thing about No Face is that he looks like someone else dressed him. Someone buttons him into his little shirt and trousers, ties up his pallbearer's black shoes, and pushes him down the street to have his beers in the bar. He's not quite the bar type, I realize now. Nor yet the type to lie on his nose in the street. He's an inbetweener, the guy you see sitting in a three-legged chair just off the steps of his tenement where nobody will trip on him, with his bottle propped up between his two feet. He sits there eighteen hours a day and looks across the street at the tenement on the other side. When someone passes that he knows, he lifts his hand and doesn't look at them.

No Face has made it to me now. He's going to say something. Looks like he's going to say it without opening his mouth. *"Jhvhphs yhkqh,"* he says, with his mouth shut. *"Eiaojjf lksjdfj jkhaithdw."*

Lips pressed together hard. Looks like maybe he's missing his teeth—the valet forgot to put them in this evening, or maybe he doesn't have any. Or maybe this is just his own private No Face language. The mystical utterances of the lost No Face tribe. I can live with that. To reply I put my fingers into the sides of my mouth and toot off a short run on the changes of "Spirit in the Night," still coming out of the jukebox.

That seems to make him happy. He ducks his bullet head toward his shoes and starts into a little double shuffle. I can tell by his feet he's thinking about Jimmy Cagney. It must be the whiskey. He usually sticks to bottled beer, if I recall. Now he twirls around and jerks Almost No Face off her stool, he's got to have a partner. He pushes her around in the narrow space between the bar and the tables, while Bruce winds up his little song about how things used to be on the Jersey shore. She dances like a cigar-store Indian. Doesn't resist, doesn't cooperate. Doesn't care. The song ends, and now we get "Far Away Eyes," last summer's Stones B-side. No Face is not going to dance to that.

He goes back to his place at the bar. She gets back on her stool and sets her knees back together. She pushes her hair back over her shoulder and takes a sip of her wine. No Face looks down in his beer. Does he remember what he just did? Did he just do anything? Is it the DTs I'm having here now?

I touch the Stone in my pocket; got to be careful I don't lose it. As far as I can tell everything is still real. Porco Miserio, this is your life. I take a sip of my drink, the one with the ice in it. Some people find it hard to remember things. Some people find it painful. People like Johnny B. don't do it at all. Personally, I remember that this is my third drink. It has reestablished my motor control and seems now to be bringing on the first wave of maudlin sentimental sadness. I should order my fourth drink now before I forget. I kill the last of this one with a silent toast—Lord have mercy on No Face and the lost No Face tribe; may God defend and cherish every silent screaming soul that hasn't got a voice it can speak with.

Holy Mother

I turn the corner onto Tenth Avenue and almost crash into one of the little white tables the Empire Diner leaves out on the sidewalk. The place stays open all night, but there's nobody sitting outside except for a ratty-looking white kid and a girl with red hair, falling asleep into their last drink. I go past them up to Twenty-third Street and walk into the avenue without looking. A teamster truck almost runs me down. The driver pulls his foghorn and I jump to the far corner.

This is my building, a four-story box with some kind of restaurant on the first floor. My key is in the street-door lock. I go in and climb two narrow flights of stairs and I'm facing my own door, under the yellow light bulb in the hall. My door is sheet steel, with the cylinder set in the center. I find my other key and put it in the lock. It's stiff and I have to twist the key over with both hands. The lock bars roll back from all four sides, and I hear them grinding together. How many times have I heard that before. I push on the door and it opens.

Hi, honey, I'm home.

I go inside and push the door closed. I lock it. I could forget to do that if I wait. It's another Fox lock. Four bars are geared to the central knob and when I turn it the bars slam into the ceiling and floor and the wall on both sides. Nobody is going to come through this door. It would be much easier to break down the wall.

I turn into my apartment and walk through the door into the back room. There's an army trunk pushed against the wall and I shove it out of my way. I kneel down and find the edge of the loose board and lift it out of the floor. In the space between my floor and the ceiling downstairs I keep my box. It sits on a folded blanket, so the people downstairs won't hear me lifting it in and out. I take hold of my box and pull it up and set it on my knees. It's a heavy affair, scraps of thick metal butt-welded together. I made it myself. It has a hasp and a good combination lock. I keep my stuff safe. I get up and take my box to my table and sit down in my chair.

It's too dark in here for me to read the dial on the lock. I came in in such a hurry I forgot to hit the light switch. There's just a little light coming in off the street. I look up at my window. It has a steel gate on it. The gate is not there to keep me in this time. It is there to keep the other people out. But it throws shadows on the wall at night and in the daytime it's still there between me and the outside.

I go to the wall and snap on the overhead. Then I cross back to the table and open the box and look inside.

Inside is everything in this world I really want.

I start taking the things out and putting them on the table: an alcohol lamp, a ring stand, a glass cup, a rubber tube, a bulb syringe, the bag. I do it the nice way. I don't want hepatitis. I light the lamp and swing the ring stand over it. I mix the stuff in the glass and put it on the stand to dissolve in the heat. Like a science experiment or something.

Now I take the piece of hose and knot it around my right upper arm. It's hard to make a slipknot with my left hand but the veins in my left arm have collapsed and I can't use them anymore. My right arm is still good, and I try to stay away from it as much as possible. I stick it in here and there, a little bit at a time. But tonight I've had to wait so long I want this shot to go straight home.

The cup is hot. I run the needle through the burner and wipe it off a time or two with alcohol. I pinch the bulb and put the needle in the cup and let it draw the dope in the syringe.

The syringe is in my left hand and I bend over and catch the end of the tube in my teeth. I pull my head up and pump my arm and in a few seconds my vein is standing up pretty; it's a good vein. I bite down on the tube and sink the needle in the vein, about three inches up from the bend in my elbow. My blood jumps in the syringe and I watch it mixing with my dope. I open my mouth and the hose drops loose. My blood flows again and it sucks the syringe empty. I jerk the needle out while I still can, for the next few minutes I won't think of that or anything.

I go outside myself and look back from somewhere near the light bulb on the ceiling. I see a little man hunched over a table under the bright light.

I hate him.

I open my eyes. I'm back again. Now I feel fine, normal. It was a jolt. I don't like the feeling. I never wanted to be this way.

In the hospital I got morphine for the pain. The pain was bad and I would bribe the people to get a little more. When I finally came out I still had the pain, and after a day I knew I had the habit too. I scraped myself off the wall and went out looking. I bought my first bag in Bryant Park, like any other junkie with the shakes. Since then I try to shoot just enough to hold myself at normal. But you always want a little more. I've seen it happen to other people.

The dope still works to take the pain away. It doesn't do nothing for my dreams. I started to have the dreams when I got in the hospital. There was no way to get away from it. I couldn't even move. In all the years before, I never had these nightmares. I never even dreamed at all. There in the hospital it was all coming back at me. I didn't know why and I still don't. Nothing I could do would stop the dreams. I haven't found a way to stop them yet.

I stand up now and stretch my arms. My body feels all right to me now. I look down at the junk on the table. I should lock it back up and put it in the floor. Try to sleep some maybe. I have to be back in the park tomorrow. But I don't want to sleep. I turn away from the table and walk around the room.

There's more room to move around in here than there was in the cages. Past that it's not a lot different. I have an iron bed I sleep on when I sleep, my trunk, my table, and the chair. Over here on the wall is a picture of Mary that Johnny gave to me one time. He says it's a reproduction of what some famous painter painted. I couldn't care less, but maybe it's a good picture. I look at it now. Our Mother of Mercy. She doesn't look back. She's looking to the side, at Baby Jesus in her arms. A blonde, she doesn't look like any Madonna I ever saw, more like some kind of fast piece. On the picture frame is the name of the painter, Lippy Lippy or something like that. One of those crazy names they used to give people in Italy in the old days. Over here in the closet there's a toilet and a sink. Any landlord will give you that.

Now I walk into the front room. Over on the left there's a kitchen. I don't cook in it so it might as well not be there. If I want to eat I go out, but I'm not too interested in food these days, or booze or women or clothes or my house or a lot of other things. Dead ahead is the door that goes out, and from the door to the wall is nothing. There's another window on the wall, with another gate on it.

This is my house. I go back into the other room and sit down on the chair by the table. I look at the stuff on the table. I close my eyes. I open my eyes and look at my foot. I tip my head back and look at the light globe in the ceiling. It's a 500-watt light bulb and when I look away from it there's a big orange hole in my head. I never turn off the light. Not when I'm here. Johnny thinks it's crazy. He won't come in here without sunglasses on. But I don't like the dark. I don't even like shadows. My dreams come out of the dark.

The orange hole is turning red at the edges, and it reminds me a little of hell. I didn't take a good enough shot. If I had a good one I wouldn't have my thoughts for a while, but now they are crawling back at me already. Another jab would back them off, but I'm afraid of another jab. I won't have one yet. I'll sit still and try not to remember anything for a few more minutes.

I got sent down to Attica in the fall of '69. I had been on the way since the winter before. There was a lot of law-enforcement action that year, and it put a lot of pressure on a lot of people. We were under Joe Colombo then, and he didn't like us very much, because we had been with Joey Gallo before he got shipped away. I got picked up on a homicide, and the word came down that I was going to jail. There was no question of beating the case. A lot of people were in trouble at that time, and it was decided to give me up. I wasn't the only one to get thrown to the wolves that year. When the word comes down, you don't argue. If Johnny had been in court then the same thing would have happened to him. But he was involved in different things, and nobody went after him. He was lucky.

I was unlucky. The D.A.'s office decided to hit me with everything they had. I got indicted on about fifteen murder ones. Finally I was convicted on three of them. I took life on every count. I had my lawyers, and I knew I would be able to come out again in a few years. And I would be taken care of on the inside. The worst boss has got to give you that. He knows he might go up himself someday. But it was a bad day when I heard my sentences. Three lifetimes is long to anybody. I sat in the Tombs about five months waiting trial and after the sentence I was there another six weeks waiting to get sent away. Being in the Tombs was not so bad. Except you couldn't leave. I never bothered to try to get bail. I knew I was going away and I might as well start pulling my time. There were some people from the Honored Society in at the same time, made guys, and we owned the place. We wore our own clothes and got food sent in from the outside. I had been married then for about four years. Me and my wife had two baby daughters. I had bought her a house on Long Island, but when I went in jail she came with the kids to stay with her family in the city. She would come to see me every couple of days. Most times she would bring me something she cooked. The hacks got paid something for letting her pass it to me. These people don't make enough to say no, and who was getting hurt? They'll let you stay yourself in a city jail. When you get sent to the big walls you're going to have to change some.

A few weeks after my trial the court clerks did their paperwork, and a car came over to take me away. Two marshals came in my room in the Tombs. They didn't say nothing to me at all. They put a waist chain on me and locked my hands to it. Then they started to put some chains on my legs.

I asked them what they were doing this for. Did they think I was going to break on the way to the car? The marshals wouldn't answer me. They weren't like the hacks in the Tombs. Someone told them I was going up for fifteen homicides. What if I was? If the truth was known I was guilty of maybe thirty-five. Back then I didn't even try to keep a good count. Now sometimes I try to remember, but I can't be exactly sure. I only remember the special ones.

The marshals took my elbows and walked me down the corridor. All the guys along the way called out to me. I wanted to wave but I couldn't get my hands up, so I yelled as loud as I could. Nothing was getting me down.

They brought me out the back and I got my last smell of city air before they dumped me in the back seat of the car. Both of them got in the front. They didn't want to sit with me for the long drive, maybe they thought I might bite them to death. There was no way I was coming out of the back of that car anyway. They had a screen between the seats, and there weren't even handles on the inside of the doors. If the car caught fire, too bad for me.

I kept on cracking jokes to myself till the car got away from the city, but by then my sense of humor was beginning to fade. It was a long trip to nowhere. Attica is all the way up to the Great Lakes, and it takes something like six hours to get there. We left in the afternoon and got there sometime in the night. The marshals didn't say a word to me the whole time, and the trip seemed like forever. It started me thinking about the long years, and when the car finally stopped at the front gate, nothing seemed too funny.

You come into Attica through one of the guard towers in the west wall. There are fifteen of these towers with sharpshooters sitting in them, all around the outer wall, which is two feet thick and thirty feet high and cost one million dollars to build. They really don't want anybody to leave.

I went in and got put through a couple of hours' worth of garbage. They fingerprinted me again and took my clothes and gave me a strip search, which is not too pleasant. Then they cut off my hair and gave me a number and my gray prison gear. They took my picture for the files and showed it to me. Okay, I don't look like myself no more, I can handle that. Then they tossed me in a cell in A block, where I'm supposed to sit and wait for a permanent assignment.

I was keeplocked in my cell until my P.K. interview, which didn't happen for about ten days. Twenty-four hours a day I sat there in my cage. The hacks brought my food in to me. The cell was just like all the others in the four main blocks. It is six feet by nine feet on the floor, and in there you got a bed and a table and a stool and a toilet and a cold-water sink and a cabinet, which doesn't leave you a lot of room to play around in. There is nothing to do. There're no windows or facing cells. The cages run side by side down the gallery. They face a wall with windows in it looking over the yard. You can't see into the yard from the cells because the angle is wrong. You just see light at the windows. People in the cells can't look at each other unless they want to use mirrors. They can talk or scream if they feel like it. That's keeplock. It's supposed to be for discipline, the next thing before the box. Of course I hadn't even had a chance to do anything yet. I was being keeplocked for my safety.

All this is routine for new prisoners. After a few days of it you get taken to see the P.K., which is short for principal keeper. He asks you questions. He wants to know if you have any job skills or special problems, like if you are a queer already or if you know there is someone in the prison who wants your head. After the interview they put you in your permanent cell. You get your work time and your yard time, and you go to meals with the others.

I stonewalled through my interview. I didn't say nothing but "Hey, baby, here I am." This is what I was told to do. Everything was supposed to be arranged already. I thought the right people had been taken care of, and I was supposed to go into E block, where the rest of the wise guys were. E block is about the best place you can be inside the walls. It's supposed to be a vocational rehabilitation unit, and it is that for some people, but a lot of the space is used by the people with pull.

E block is even outside the main part of Attica, which is a big square with a cross in the middle. The four main cell blocks make the sides of the square. The corridors running across the yards make the cross. All the people in the joint call them the tunnels. Where the tunnels meet in the center of the yards is called Times Square. It has four gates and if they are locked then all four units of the prison are locked off from each other. They built it that way so they could seal up the blocks separately if there was a disturbance somewhere. You can't go anywhere in the whole prison without going through Times Square.

I was expecting to go into E block and be away from all that. But that wasn't what happened. After the P.K. interview they came and stuck me into D block. I was in there with the animals. I started to sweat some blood. In the interview I had lied my face off, of course. I had plenty of enemies in the prison. I didn't even know exactly who they were. But I knew they were going to be there. I had done too much on the outside. I was scared for about the first time in my life. I had no idea what I might be up against. When they turned us into the yard I wouldn't breathe before I got my back on the wall. They put me to work in the metal shop, and I stole a scrap to make a shiv. But how are you going to protect yourself when you don't know where you're going to get hit from?

This went on for like a month. From the second day, I started trying to make something change. But it was harder than I expected. I wanted to get a message to the outside, to Johnny at least, because at least he might be able to find out why this happened to me. But Johnny was a known criminal, and I wasn't supposed to communicate with him. You aren't supposed to write to anybody but your close family and your lawyer, and I didn't have the pull to break the rules. I tried to get some messages out through my lawyer but they read your mail and I didn't know what was getting through. The one thing I was afraid of was that Colombo or Joe Yack had decided to let me die. Neither me or Johnny was very well liked by them. Even though we had been with them for years they still put us with the Gallos in their minds. I couldn't stop thinking about the things I heard happened to Joey Gallo when he got sent away in '61.

It was never a matter of a contract. It was just the problem of not having protection. When Joey went down he didn't have a friend in the world except for his brothers, and practically everybody in the city was trying to kill them too. Joey gets into Attica with half the world gunning for him already, and what does he do? He picks a fight with the KKK. It wasn't because he was a great humanitarian. He was a psycho and he didn't like people to tell him what to do. The KKK told him not to deal with the niggers so right away he started dealing with them. The blacks didn't want him around either, and now all the whites had a knife out for him too. Even the hacks in the prison wanted to see him die. They weren't going to do it themselves, but they were letting the Klan get to him at night, that kind of thing. Joey was tough and they never quite killed him. After a few years somebody had mercy and he got transferred to Dannemora. When he got in trouble there they moved him to Greenhaven. At Greenhaven somebody poured gas on him and tried to set him on fire, but he lived through that too and got shipped out to Auburn. Then he dropped out of sight. Nobody heard anything for a while and when I came into Attica I thought Joey was probably dead.

I was afraid it was going to happen to me. I had never felt so alone before. The Klan wasn't so strong by this time but there was still plenty of race trouble and I had to keep in good with the white people. Most of the hacks were white, and sometimes you might get a little break from them. The blacks and Latins in Attica never got a break, and who'd be surprised if they didn't like it? But I had to take what I could get. I was just another prisoner with a number on my shirt. They turned us out of our cells for breakfast at 6:30 in the morning. In the day we had a work detail and a meal and a little time in the yard. At 5:50 they locked us down for the night. With all the animals carrying on all around me it was hard for me to sleep. The food was so bad that in that one month I lost around fifteen pounds.

I thought I might be doing my whole stretch like that, but one day it just ended. The hacks came in and took me out of my cell and transferred me over to E block. I didn't know where I was going before I got there. They could have been taking me to the box for all I knew. Instead I got a new cell, a room with a solid door like a real room, not like the cages in the other blocks. It felt good to be there. There were some people I knew before in the city, and some other Italians I hadn't met. They all hung together, like in a social club. Everybody was very nice with me, apologetic. I found out what the problem had been. It was nothing after all. Some guy in administration didn't get his cut, and he decided to be a bastard. It took some time to find him and get him fixed, and that was the time I put in at the zoo. After I had been in E block a couple of weeks, I began to think it wasn't so bad to spend a little time locked up with the animals. It gave you a feeling for the people that couldn't do any better. It gave you a feeling for what those people were going to think about and want.

E block was ours. There were just two things we couldn't get, women and out. Everything else was there for the money. I started decorating my cell. I put in a bar with the little airline liquor bottles. I got myself a stereo and a television. I even bought an aquarium and some tropical fish. I would go in my room and mix a drink, put on my music, and watch my fish swimming around. All the Italians on the block were friendly and we were in and out of each other's cell whenever we wanted. We all used to cook together and sit down to dinner. If we felt like it we might let the hacks come in and eat pasta and drink some wine with us.

The hacks belonged to us too. These are people that normally get paid about as much as your postman, and they know where the good money is coming from. They all played it our way. The Office has power that no one is going to ignore. All we were asking was to be let live like human beings. The hacks were our friends. They would bring us anything in we wanted. They would have even brought in dope, which they did do in other parts of the prison, but none of us wanted that. No junkies can work for the Office. If somebody is taking drugs, then that person is going die. Nobody wants to deal with him. Doping is strictly for the animals on the street. Some people don't even like to be in the trade, but the money is too good for most of them to pass up.

Even with these kinds of freedom it's boring to be in prison. The main thing you're going to be interested in is when you're getting out. All of us had lawyers that got paid to know what to do, but when you're just sitting inside the walls you start to want to know something about your case. A lot of good lawyers learned in prison that way. There were people in E block that knew as much as people with degrees.

So I started trying to learn some things. I got some law books to look at, and the people that knew more would explain to me. They had high school classes in the DVR program, and I finished high school there, which I never did on the outside. I always thought I was dumb around books and those kinds of things. Johnny was the smart kid who liked to read and he could have it as far as I was concerned. But in the walls you can look in a book and forget about where you are for a while. After about eight months, when I got my high school certificate, I sent off for college courses in the mail. Like some other people who were sent away, I became a smarter person in a number of ways. All the time I was studying my case, even though it was really a joke at that point. I knew I was going to sit where I was for at least five years or so.

After about six months inside I started to have some more legal problems, because my wife decided to divorce me. I was upset about this, but it was hard to blame her too much. My wife grew up in a nice quiet home, and she was only nineteen when we got married. She never knew exactly what I was involved in. She knew who I was working for, but she didn't know what I did for them, and if she thought about it she probably decided I was taking numbers or putting out loans or something like that. Then when it started to come out she felt like she didn't know who I was anymore.

That wasn't my fault either. Nobody who is deeply involved is going to say it to his wife. You can't do that. There's no way it can be good for her or you. If she knows things and there's trouble, then she might get into it. Or she might say something by mistake that would throw your life away. There were even a few cases where some woman got hot at her husband and decided to go talk to the FBI.

If I had been outside I never would have let it happen. But the way things were I couldn't really fight it. My lawyer told me I should handle it the nice way so that I could still see my kids when I got out. I could tell that he was right, so I let him settle the case my wife's way. I didn't even know what I was losing till a long time later. If you are inside the walls what happens outside just doesn't seem real.

After a couple of months in E block I got assigned a job as a runner. This was one of the better jobs it was possible for a person to get. I was supposed to carry messages, and it meant that I had a pass to go anywhere in the prison without a hack along. I knew more about what was going down in the place than most other people, because practically nobody ever got out of their own block.

Most of the people in Attica were in there for murder or assault-type crimes. They were not nice people. Nothing was happening to help them get any nicer. People were made to work and they would get paid maybe fifty cents a day for whatever they did. That would almost buy you a pack of cigarettes a day. If someone wanted more in his life than that, then that person was going to have to deal. So there was a lot of dealing, mainly drugs and queer sex and a few games. It got ugly at times, like it always does when people are hungry for something. It was no different from what I had seen in the street, except for one thing. These people didn't have any choice about what they were going to do. There was only one game in town and no way to leave. On the street you can at least try to believe that's not true.

There were more blacks than whites in the prison and when I came in both sides were mainly interested in holding their territory. There were only a few Latins and they had to hang with the blacks for the most part. Not much dealing went on between the races; if you tried it you were likely to get caught in the middle and squashed. Since I was a runner, I knew some people at both ends. I had to get along with everybody, which wasn't too hard since I could do little favors for people.

Most of the hacks in the joint were white and the blacks usually got it worse from them. This is one of the reasons that the Muslims got to be so strong in the prison, because they would take care of each other. No one really knew much about them at that time. They kept to themselves and the only thing you could tell about them was that they had some organization. They could get some respect from the rest of the people that were running around.

In July of 1970 the funniest thing happened. Somebody in the State Bureau had an idea and one day we all woke up and Attica wasn't a prison anymore. We had correction officers and no more guards. Everybody that had been a prisoner was now to be called an inmate. We were all being rehabilitated now. Everybody jumped for joy. Nothing changed but the names.

Then in November the news came into E block that Joey Gallo was alive and well. He was still in Auburn, but it looked like things had turned around for him, from the word that was coming out. Early in the month they had a thing in Auburn called Black Solidarity Day. All the niggers ran into the yard and started yelling into a bullhorn or something. It got out of hand and quite a few guards were taken hostage. Joey Gallo took a microphone and told all the whites to leave the yard and go back to their cells. The whites did what he said. One of the hacks had been hurt and after a couple of hours Joey went back in the yard and brought this guy out to get treatment.

All this was just swell for Joey. It was what got him paroled in the spring. And it made the wise guys in Attica sit back and think. A year ago everybody in the state prison system had been trying to kill this guy. Now people are hanging on to every word he says. He walks into a black riot and gets the podium handed to him like he was their guest of honor, which no one had ever heard of before. Then it turns out that the white people follow his orders too. Joey speaks and the people do. Everybody. It looked like he had done the impossible. He had figured out a way to play it from the middle.

This was an idea that made people worry and think. Joey was due to get out before long, and the word was that he had a new organization already set up, an interracial affair. It was a wild idea, and Joey was supposed to be completely out of his head, but then he was also supposed to be dead, which hadn't happened yet. Nobody was sure what was going to happen. Johnny was one of the people who worried about it the most, because he knew Joey would get in touch with him when he got out, and he wanted to be sure that he picked the winning team. I didn't hear much from Johnny then so I didn't know exactly how he was thinking. He had better things to do than come out to Attica and the most we talked was the odd phone call. Neither one of us was even going to say the name Gallo over the phone, but I knew Johnny would be keeping on top of it and I got the feeling he was starting to lean back toward Joey. Johnny is not a psycho but he does have a liking for wild ideas.

And the idea itself was hard to decide about. There was a possibility there. Black people have never had a big share in our thing, which is strictly a family affair. They might get paid to take numbers or deal dope, but they weren't going up any higher. A few years before, the Panthers had tried to take over some things in Harlem, but they hadn't been able to bring it off. The blacks had some manpower but they didn't know the business from the inside. Joey Gallo just might turn out to be their man. And you could never guess ahead what Joey might do. If he tried to turn the world upside down it just might work this time. With this thought in their minds the wise guys in Attica began to slide toward the middle. For a while everybody wanted to be pals with everybody.

By the summer of '71 things were beginning to change all over the prison. It occurred to a lot of people that if they all pulled together there might be some changes made. The race hating didn't stop. It isn't going to stop. But people began to talk together. There was discussion going on. That summer there were some wage strikes and things of that kind, which didn't change much. There was a feeling that it was time for a show of force.

Our people in E block didn't want to be very much involved in this kind of thing. We didn't have the same problems, we had too much to lose. But we were getting a feeling that these people were entitled to a little help. And with everything we were hearing, it seemed possible that sometime we might get some help back. It wasn't going to be our thing, but it seemed worthwhile to make a few contracts and give a little assistance. We were people who knew how to organize, so we did a little organizing. At least that way we had an idea of what was going down and when. When the riot did break we weren't going to get taken by surprise.

$\lor$

Porco

And now that I begin to think of these things I almost feel like my own face is slipping off. I'm sitting here on this bar stool and I feel like I have to cup my hands over my cheeks and brace my elbows on the counter just to keep my physiognomy from sliding off my skull into my drink. What a horrible sensation. It's like having no feet. If I had a horn nearby I would like to blow my whole insides into the mouthpiece and out of the bell. As it is, I think I'll go to the bathroom and look at the pipes in the ceiling.

So I peel my eyelids back once more and touch my face all over. Everything feels like it's still in place, but you never can tell for sure. I cut a glance at the mirror behind the bar, but there's too many gin bottles in the way and I can't see any sign of myself. Now I jerk on the counter and set the stool rotating, and centrifugal forces set me up on my feet. I flag the bartender and point at that last empty glass. Give the man something to do while I'm gone.

Now I'm on my way to the gentlemen's room, but here at the wall phone in the corner I see such an awful-looking object that I have to give it a second look. It has on spandex pants and a black leather jacket, with these adorable little chrome chains running through the straps at the shoulders. You can tell it's a male from the height and the bone structure, and it should never be wearing spandex pants, that's for sure. And this a nice neighborhood bar for dedicated gin heads. One of its feet is somewhat in my way so I give it an accidental stomp in passing. Then I go in the bathroom and hook the door behind me.

Well, here we are in the bathroom. There's slime-green paint dripping off the walls, obscuring all those little ballpoint cries of desperation, loneliness, nasty thoughts, and so on. The pipes up above are grinding and squealing and there's water beading all over them. I turn on the cold tap in the sink and let it run over my right wrist. Those first few drinks seem to have sent my blood pressure up a little high, though doubtless it's only an illusion that the cold water stream seems to be beating time with my pulse. I remove my right hand from the water and put my left hand in. With my right hand I chill down my temples and nose, and now I think that my equilibrium is sufficiently restored for me to chance a look at myself in the mirror.

But I can't see very much of anything in this mirror. Its reflective properties have dwindled over the years, probably because it's been forced to witness things you don't even want to think about. What little I can see of myself in this mirror is streaming in several different directions and looks like a ghost, or maybe two or three. Oh well, small loss. I already know I am no great beauty. I touch the surface of the mirror with my fingers and it is perfectly flat and clammy. Obviously there can't be any face in here, so it's no wonder I don't see one. All this is is a piece of glass with silver on the back. I'm drunk again. I shut off the water and take the Stone out of my pocket and look at it. It's very black. It doesn't reflect anything either. It even seems to be soaking up the light from the 60-watt bulb in the ceiling. I wonder if it has a soul and what it's thinking if it does. Probably it does have one. I put it back in my pocket. I bet my other drink is ready now.

Then when I open the door the first thing I see is a hand coasting through the air toward my shoulder. For one awful moment I think it's Yusuf Ali, but then I see that this hand is white and comparatively small, and in fact it belongs to the creature in the spandex and chains, et al. So I just move my shoulder out of the way and let him tumble into the bathroom. I don't know about these kids, they all take drugs or something. Bad for the coordination, also the ear. The bathroom door swings shut on its spring and I think I hear some bad language being used in there, but maybe it's only the graffiti finally discovering its tongue.

So I go back to my seat and sit on it. I have a new bourbon and a new beer waiting for me there. I put a little bourbon in my mouth, hold it for a second before I swallow. Then I take a pull on the beer and light a cigarette and blow some smoke up toward the light fixture here above the bar. In another minute the spandex thing is back at my elbow. I roll my left eye around so I can get a look at the front side of his head, and I see that he's got a bright blue streak in his hair, just as such a person should. Sometimes I think that someone has figured out a way to photoduplicate these guys.

"I think you're at the wrong address, my friend," I say. "Club 57 is still up there on St. Mark's Place right where it was last week." The only reply I get to this wit is a sort of spluttering noise, or maybe I'm not listening close enough to pick up any words. It's really more fun to blow smoke up past the tip of my nose and watch it rush into the lampshade. It's the heat that makes it do that. Convection.

"Better run along," I say. "Or you'll miss the party. Tonight they're going to lock you and all your friends inside, and then they're going to burn the place down." But even this doesn't draw a rejoinder. He just keeps gurgling and toying with the chains on his shoulders. I think he's hoping I'll turn around and be terrified by his clothes. But I just keep watching my smoke as it curls out of the lampshade, and finally he gives up and goes away. Can't perform without an audience. No dedication. My smoke turns a flip and rides away on the draft he makes when he goes out the door.

He's gone and I'm a little bored. People around here have no gift for repartee anymore. I'll miss that in Johnny B. A good talker, has read some books, knows some music, and can even think at times, if pressed. A jewel of a drinking companion, even if he can't keep up with the drinking. A shame that things turned out this way. But the best idea is not to brood. No, that's not my idea, that's his. Personally, I like to brood. One of my favorite pastimes. But for now I think I'll just go over and examine the jukebox, before somebody tries to get that Frank Sinatra song on again.

Yusuf Ali

Allahu akbar. La ilaha ill' Allah.
God knows everything.

I know little. I sit and watch the Spring Lounge. No one goes in. No one comes out. Here in the playground it is dark and very silent, so quiet I can still hear my own blood running. Time does not seem to pass. I stare at the diamonds of the storm fence before me. They run together and blur away from my sight. For another moment I have lost myself in the depth of this long night. Yet I know I am Yusuf Ali, a man of the manifest Book. I recite from the seventeenth Sura, the Night Journey, so:

> We have appointed the night and the day
> as two signs; then we have blotted out
> the sign of the night, and made the sign
> of the day to see, and that you may know
> the number of the years, and the reckoning;
> and everything we have distinguished
> very distinctly.
> And every man—We have fastened to him
> his bird of omen upon his neck; and We
> shall bring forth for him, on the Day

of Resurrection, a book he shall find
spread wide open.
"Read thy book! Thy soul suffices thee
this day as a reckoner against thee."

So it is written that I will know myself, and to remember is my obligation, as the heart finds comfort in the remembrance of Allah, in the recitation of the Most Beautiful Names. But I do not know the number of the years, even my own years. I never knew when I was born, or if I have a father. I was a child and I lived with my mother. They named her Sarah Lenox. She lived with a man who was called Sonny, but he was not my father. He would tell me so. Sometimes when he was drinking he would tell me that I was none of his blood and he would chase me out of the house, through the piles of garbage in the hallway, down into the street. At other times he would hold me and bless me in the name of Sarah Lenox, who was a good woman, Sonny said, like no other, and he would be a different man if she had lived. Probably it was a lie. But Sonny would still talk and shout and cry over my mother, sometimes, when he was very drunk, sick drunk. He would pass out and I would sit and listen to his breathing, and I would try to remember Sarah Lenox.

But I never could. I remember her dead, but I have never remembered her alive. It is my first memory, my dead mother, she is lying on the kitchen floor, on her left side, with a chair upset behind her, spun half under the table, and her head on an open newspaper. The name of the newspaper is *Big Red*. It tells about the numbers. My mother's eyes are open and liquid, and she seems to be still reading the paper, though I can tell at a glance she can't see it anymore. Blood comes from somewhere in her dress. I get up and walk over to where the blood stains the corner of *Big Red*. Sonny is lying on the floor, pressed into the wall. He is shaking.

"Get away from there," he hisses at me. "Get away from the door." There is a splintered hole in one panel of the door to the apartment. The wood of this door is not very thick. I heard a big noise and the chair fell over and now there is a big hole in the door.

"Get away," Sonny whispers. "Do you want to die too?"

The hole is above my eye level. I am just shorter than the kitchen table. Sarah Lenox was sitting at the table and died instantly so maybe she was hit in the heart. I bend over and look at the newspaper. It is drawing up the blood of my mother like a sponge. I can read the words in the newspaper. I never knew I could read before. I read the slogan at the top of the open page. The slogan says, "What Goes Around Comes Around, Y'all."

When nothing more happens for a few more minutes Sonny gets off the floor and crawls out the fire escape. I hear him drop the last few feet and hit the street. I sit and look at the numbers in the paper. The eyes of my mother glaze over and stiffen. The front door opens and Sonny comes in with two cops.

One cop goes down the hall and the other one comes into the apartment with Sonny. They look down at Sarah Lenox. The cop pushes a button on his portable radio.

"Calling from the shots fired," he says. The radio sputters.

"One black female, DOA," the cop says to the radio. Then he turns it off. The other cop comes in the doorway.

"Nothing. Nobody saw anybody." He fingers the hole in the door. "Nobody heard anything either."

"It was just like that," the first cop says to Sonny. "Just a shot through the door."

"Like that," Sonny says. He has straightened up and stopped shaking. "We sitting around the table. Bang, one shot."

The cop takes out a clipboard and writes on a yellow form.

"And you didn't see anything."

"No, man. How am I going to see through the door?"

"And you got no idea who or why."

"No." Sonny pushes his hands in the air. "No idea."

"A mistake," the cop in the doorway says. "Guy comes to make a hit, gets the wrong address. It happens. Sometimes."

"Yeah," says the first cop, writing. He pushes the clipboard at Sonny.

"Sign on the line where this X is," he says. Sonny holds the pen and the clipboard for a minute.

"Looks like he can't write," says the cop in the doorway. Sonny hands the clipboard back to the first cop.

"Okay," the first cop says. "What's your name?"

"Sonny."

"Sonny what."

"Just Sonny, they call me Sonny."

"Jesus."

"Write Sonny Smith," says the cop in the doorway. "We got to get back to the fort."

"Okay," says the first cop. He looks down at me. I see his face under the hat brim. He has sandy hair, green eyes.

"This your kid?" he says to Sonny.

"Hers."

"Got a name?"

"Leon Lenox."

"Got any family?"

"Not now."

"Come on," the cop in the doorway says. "Maybe you ought to have joined the Peace Corps or something. But if we hang around here anymore somebody's going to come shoot our badges off."

That was the first day that I knew any name for myself. From that hour I remembered that I was Leon Lenox. Sonny pulled the bloody newspaper away from me and burned it on the window ledge, but I remembered I could read. Then they came and took Sarah Lenox away from the apartment. Her body was not claimed for burial. I remembered that I was alone. But it is for those who are alone that Allah is named *Al-Qureeb*, the Nearest One, and *Al-Muhazmin*, He Who Watches Over and Protects All Things.

Then I lived a while longer with Sonny. We lived in the same apartment, in an eight-story building on Hoe Avenue, just off the Bruckner Expressway in the South Bronx. I did not know it was the Bronx then. It was the world, all that I could see. But the habitations of Allah are infinite in number.

Hoe Avenue was a part of the world's underside. The cars roared over the elevated expressway and the passengers looked down like men looking into the gate of Gehenna. Then the cars were gone and replaced by others. I was always there. I saw the gangs fighting for blocks of burned-out territory. I saw people shot for two or twenty dollars. I saw burning buildings and women in flames at the windows. Sonny was gone most of the time. If there was food in the house I would stay in and practice reading—the labels of cans and scraps of newspaper Sonny might bring in. If there was no food I would go in the street. Sometimes I would steal something from one of the bodegas along the avenue. Sometimes the numbers runner would give me a few dollars to hold his slips for an hour or take them somewhere. A few times I got paid something to hold drugs. I ate that way, or else Sonny fed me, if he had the money, or if he wasn't too drunk to remember.

The first winter after Sarah Lenox was dead, Sonny fixed the hole in the door with paper and tape to hold the heat. He put newspaper on the walls and in the cracks of the windows. But in the middle of the winter the heat went off. It was cold and people began to move out. Then the water went off too and more people were leaving. There were only a few people left in the building. Toward the end of the winter there was a fire. Too many people hit the fire escape at one time and it tore loose from the wall. Sonny said we were lucky to be near the bottom. He only got bruises and I only broke my arm. A man on the sixth story died when he hit the street. A man and a woman on the eighth floor breathed too much smoke and never woke up. Sonny put my arm in splints and it healed straight. They never proved it was arson. The landlord said someone lit a fire to heat his apartment. The insurance paid.

Sonny found a place on Seneca Avenue, on the east side of the expressway. We didn't have to worry about it being burned out. It had already been burned out. Sonny fixed the walls and the doors of a couple of rooms. He used metal sheathing from the ground floor. There was no water and no heat and no rent. We burned Sterno for cooking and a little heat.

I practiced reading by the light of the Sterno. Since it was too cold to stay in the building for long, I started to go to the school. I learned to read a little better there. I would read anything I could get. It didn't matter what it was. I did not know then, but Allah was preparing me for the day when I would receive the Holy Quran. For Allah is named *Ar-Rashid,* the Guide to the Right Path. *Allahu akbar, la ilaha ill' Allah.*

Not many people liked reading very much at the school. It was dangerous for me, since I was little. The bigger ones would tear my clothes and rip my books and beat my face. They would rob me, if I had anything to get. I found an ice pick down some basement stairs on Spofford Avenue and I sharpened it on a concrete trestle under the expressway, until the point shone. The next time somebody touched me, I put the ice pick through his hand. It took a few days. I never hit anyone to kill them. I only stabbed some hands and arms. I became very quick with the ice pick. People learned to leave me alone. I didn't make any friends. The ice pick was in my pants everywhere I would go. At home on Seneca Avenue, I practiced throwing it at a smudge on the wall.

Sonny was called a mechanic, but he didn't work on cars. He worked on cards and dice. He said that he was good at it before Sarah Lenox died and he began to drink too much, but that might have been a lie. It was true that he did drink too much. He would drink anything. If his luck was bad he would drink the juice he would get from squeezing Sterno through a rag. It made his hands shake. One night he dropped his second set of dice in the floating crap game on Fox Street and somebody blew him to pieces with a sawed-off shotgun. At least that is what I heard. But I never did find out exactly what happened to Sonny, because as soon as I knew he was not coming back I left the room on Seneca Avenue and hid somewhere else. I was afraid they might send me to the detention home and I knew that I would rather die in the street than go there. I put my ice pick in my pants. I went over to Fox Street and crawled down an empty basement. I don't know how old I was by that time. Maybe I was ten. Everyone I knew was dead. So it is written:

> In this house thousands and more are dead; there
> you are seated saying "Behold my household!"
> A handful of dust says, "I was once a tress";
> . another says, "I am a bone."

There were rats in my basement. There were rats all over Fox Street. They lived on garbage, cats, each other, sometimes small children. The bigger ones ate the tires off cars. The biggest ones were the size of little dogs. The first night I spent in my basement I sat up all night and stabbed rats with my ice pick. I threw the little rats to the big rats. By morning there was nothing left but their bones and their tails. The second night I made a big pile of scrap wood and old wallboard and climbed up on top of it to sleep. But the rats came up there too and chewed my feet. Over the next week I went to the Terminal Market up by the river and stole a few metal milk crates every night. I cut them up and built a cage to sleep in. I put the cage on top of the pile of scraps. The rats came every night to the wires of the cage and put their noses through. They breathed over my body while I slept. Their eyes were red and bright. If I lit a match in the dark the rows of red eyes glowed back at me. I could hear the rats rustling and gnawing all night long. When I got used to the sound it began to soothe me.

With the ice pick I taught the rats to respect me. I drilled a hole through the handle of the pick and threaded it with a fine cord. I could throw the ice pick from the door of my cage and nail a rat to the far wall of the basement. A jerk on the cord and the ice pick would be back in my hand. I decorated the corners of my cage with rat skulls. The rats honored my skill with the ice pick and stayed at their end of the basement. I stopped killing so many of them. We learned to tolerate each other. I stole a flashlight from the market, and at night I read scraps of newspaper aloud to the rats. I read them bits of the *Post* and the *News* and *Big Red*. Every few days I would take the ice pick out and kill a few rats so that the rest would have plenty to eat and so that they would remember my power.

In those first days I lived mostly off food I would steal from the Terminal Market. The old numbers runner was dead too then. They found his body under the expressway. Nobody ever found his head. I heard the Savage Skulls claimed the kill but I don't know what the grievance was. Maybe they didn't even do it. But the new runner was a Puerto Rican and he didn't like me. I had stuck one of his cousins in the school. He never threw me any work. So I went up to the Market and stole things. All the produce for the whole city was cleared through those yards and at night the place was jammed with prostitutes and junkies and thieves. Every few days I would go up there and snatch a case of noodles or a box of canned beans. On lucky trips I would be able to grab something to sell. I used the money to buy Sterno and salt and maybe a newspaper or a paperback book. It was hard to get any books then. I was afraid to go around the school, because of the detention home.

After I had been in the basement a couple of months, the people at the Market got to know me too well. I was beginning to grow, and people could see me coming a long way off. I couldn't get anything up there anymore. If I even showed my face in the yards somebody would chase me. I went back to stealing from small stores and bodegas, but I could never get enough to last very long from those places. People began to watch me in my own neighborhood, and I would have to walk fifteen blocks to steal one can of chili. I was losing weight and winter was coming again. At the same time I kept growing, and I was always hungry. I was hungry when I woke up and when I went to sleep.

One night I was reading to my rats by the light of my last can of Sterno. There were a lot of rats sitting close and listening to my voice, but I was too weak to concentrate very well. Then I got an idea. I slipped out the ice pick and stabbed five of the fattest rats I could reach. All the rest of the rats ran over to their end of the basement and sat there whispering to each other and looking at me over their shoulders. It had been a long time since I had killed so many all at once, and it was hard for them to understand. But I didn't have time to worry about that.

I ruined the first two rats completely, but the third one I skinned clean. I cut his stomach open and pulled out his guts and threw them to the others in the corner. Then I reached in deeper and found the liver and the lungs and heart. I took an empty tin can from the floor and put a little blood from the heart into it and fried the liver in the blood. It tasted a little sour but I could tell it had a lot of vitamins in it. As soon as I had finished it I felt stronger. It would have been better with salt. I cut the rat's hind legs off and toasted them over the Sterno and ate them like chicken drumsticks. They were not bad. The front legs were not bad either, even though there was not so much meat on them as on the hind legs. I finished eating and threw the rest of the third rat over to the others, since I didn't have anything big enough to cook it in. I was full anyway. I hadn't been so full in two weeks. I skinned the other two rats and hung them over a rod near the window. It was cold enough there to keep the meat from spoiling, and later I learned that hanging the meat for a while made it more tender.

After a few weeks the rat skins began to pile up in the basement. I learned how to make them into leather by scraping them and rubbing them with a little fat. The first thing I made was some moccasins. They came out sloppy looking, but they were warmer than my old shoes. Then I made a hat and some mittens. When I had saved up enough skins, I worked for a month and made myself a fur coat. It was a beautiful coat and very warm. It came down below my knees and had a fringe of rat tails all the way to my ankles. I put two small skulls on the shoulders, like a soldier's epaulets. The rat served as my omen, for that time.

People began to stare at me when I went in the street with my coat on. No one troubled me, but they gave me new names. They called me Rat Sticker or Rat Stabber or, because of the books, Professor Rat. I didn't care what they called me. I didn't deal with the people of Fox Street at all during this time. They were no different from the rats anyway. All they did was fight and eat each other and breed. I had already learned how to live with the rats and I was glad I could afford to stay away from the people. The Skulls and the Nomads both asked me to join, but I didn't. I wouldn't even talk to them. The Skulls were angry and about twenty of them tried to raid my basement one night, but my rats bit them on the feet and calves and drove them off. My rats were mean and suspicious around strangers. They liked routine and distrusted changes.

Then after a few more months somebody came to see me. I heard a voice calling down from the street.

"Hey, yo. Professor Rat. Put your head out the door." I stood on a box and looked up through the window. It was a man named Buzz. I knew who he was. Everybody did. He sold smack and had a big car.

"What you want from me?" I called through the window.

"Want to talk to you, come on the street." But I was not going. I did not trust Buzz, or anyone.

"Talk about what?" I called.

"About some money for you, my man," Buzz yelled back. I thought about money for me.

"You can come down here and talk," I said.

"Down there, no," Buzz said. "You come up here on the street." I went away from the window and went back to what I had been doing before, skinning rats. I could still hear Buzz walking back and forth on the sidewalk.

"Yo, my man," he called down. "Put your rats on a leash or something. I'm coming down." He started down the stairs into the basement. I loosened my ice pick and let it swing from the cord around my wrist. Buzz came in the basement and a few rats rushed him, but I shooed them back to the rear corner. I skinned another rat and strung it up on the rod by the window, where it would freeze for later. Buzz watched me. I took the fresh skin and hung it on my tanning rack by my cage. Buzz followed me over there. I started to scrape the new skin with a folded can lid. Buzz looked at my coat and the skulls on my cage.

"Yes, my man," he said. "You definitely got some style. Got a style all your own." I kept quiet.

"I got a lot of respect for you," Buzz said. "For what you done built up down here." He looked at me and then over at the rats in the corner. The rats stared back.

"You come down here just to tell me that?" I said.

"I come down here because I'm looking for a smart young man," Buzz said. "Might be someone like yourself, Professor Rat." He stopped. "What's your real name, my man?"

I told him. "Leon Lenox."

"Well, Leon, I'll call you Leon," Buzz said, with one eye on the rats, "it's like this. But first, how old did you say you were?"

"I'm not any old," I said. "A rat was my father. A rat was my mother. Rats don't have years." Sometimes I said things like that to people. If people thought you were that crazy they left you alone. Sometimes I even believed the things I said.

"Anyway," Buzz said. "Let's say you not more than fourteen, probably, let's just say that. And what that means, Leon, is that if you commit a crime, why," Buzz waved his hands in the air, "they just going to send you off to summer camp for a few weeks. But me, Leon, if I commit a crime, why, they going to lock me up and throw away the key. And that is the simple reason, Leon, that I need *you*, to work for *me*."

I took a day to think it over and I went to work for Buzz. He must have had too much heat on him then, so that he needed to put a few juveniles between him and the law. People do it all the time. Buzz had four other bagmen, all under fifteen. He paid pretty well, but the other four ran their pay right up their arms. I never touched the needle. I do not know why. But Allah is named *Al-Hayy*, the Living, and he who takes the needle belongs to the dead.

Most of the world belonged to the dead then, and Buzz had a good business. Everyone was buying. I sold to five-year-old children and eighty-year-old men and to everybody in between. I sold all over Hunts Point, from the East River to the Market. People wanted the needle, they could take it and forget that they were dead. They could even forget that they would have to steal a hundred dollars' worth of stuff or turn ten tricks to buy another bag tomorrow. I took a commission on every bag I could move. I was making money. I stopped eating rat and moved out of the basement. I grew some more, and my rat skins were too small and I bought some new clothes from a store.

But people still did remember my rat days. Buzz was the only one who knew me as Leon Lenox. I did business under one or another of my rat names. The santeros and the brujos all thought I had the evil eye. Most of them would turn away when they saw me coming. A few times they wanted to buy my secrets, but I would not talk to them. The reputation may have helped protect me, because no one ever tried to shake me down while I was dealing. But that could have been because of Buzz. He had organization contacts and they protected his operation. It was their operation too. If something went wrong with it someone would get a visit from downtown. One of those long black cars would roll up to a building on Fox Street, and everybody else on the block would suddenly go deaf, dumb, and blind.

So everything was easy for me until I finally got arrested. Then I got no help at all. I could not even find Buzz. He didn't even send me a legal aid lawyer. I pled to the mercy of the court and the court put me in the juvenile center on Spofford Avenue. It was like hell to me then, though now I know that the real Hell is to be veiled from Allah. Still, Spofford was bad enough. They took my ice pick away and I had to learn how to hand-fight so that I would not get raped. I was in there for about ten months.

I got out of Spofford in the summer and went walking in the streets for a few days. I didn't know what to do next. I did not want to go back to the rats, even though that did seem a little better than going among the people. I had got used to easier living while I was working for Buzz, but I didn't want to work for Buzz again. I wanted to stick him with something. He had lied to me. He told me I would not do time.

Then one day I was going along Fox Street, and a stranger with a white robe on came up to me.

"Salaam," he said.

"What is this crap?" I said. I never heard any such word before.

"Salaam, brother Leon," the man said. I looked at him. It was Buzz. I had not recognized him under the robe, and he had shaved his head.

"I don't need you telling me no more garbage," I said. "Take yourself on down the street. I listened to you once and what did it get me?"

"Now that wasn't me did that, Leon. That was my old slave self did those old things. I'm not the same old Buzz no more. Call me Ali abd Al-Ghaffir. It mean 'Servant of the Forgiver.' I got something for you here." Buzz put his hand under his robe. I grabbed a bottle neck off the street and swung it at his stomach. I still didn't have another ice pick yet. The bottle neck didn't do much to Buzz. It just tore a rag off his robe and scratched his hand.

"What you think you doing, little bastard?" Buzz backed off from me. I moved in for another try but then I saw that what he had in his hand was a book.

"I was going to give you this. That's all," Buzz said. "But now I ain't. You done lived with the rats too long. Won't do you no good now."

"I'll take the book," I said. I had not seen a book since before I was in Spofford. But Buzz shook his head. He started to put the book back under his clothes. I swung the bottle neck and the book fell on the sidewalk. I moved in and Buzz backed off. I put my foot on the book.

"Thanks," I said. "Now you can go on. Go somewhere and forget you ever knew me. Go somewhere and forget my name."

I watched his back until he was around the next corner. Then I threw the bottle neck away and took the book up in my hand. It had some kind of mark on the cover, like spilled oil or a streaked blood-stain. I looked at the inside. On the left-hand page there were just more of these marks. They looked like knots or entrails or some-thing that was broken and couldn't be fixed. I looked at the right-hand page. There were English words.

> This is the Book, in which there is no doubt
> a guidance for the righteous
> who believe in the unseen.

Something exploded behind me and I turned around. Four kids passed me going fast around the corner. At the end of the block a car was burning, and smoke rose up from it to the tops of the build-ings. No danger. I backed into a doorway and looked back at the book. I looked at the marks. I could not understand them. They were concealed from me. But I did know now that there was some-thing there to understand. For Allah is named *Az-Zamir*, the Mani-fest, as well as *Al-Batin*, the Hidden. I started reading the English.

I carried the Quran back to my basement. But I did not stay there very long. The basement would no longer hold me. I could even see through its walls. For Allah is named *An-Nur*, the Piercing Light.

Also, I continued to grow. By the time I had read my way to *El Hijr*, which is the fifteenth Sura of the Quran, I had grown so large that I could no longer even fit into the door of the basement. The weather was warm and I needed no shelter. I stayed on the roof-tops, and the light of the whole city was reflected on me from the sky, and I read on. By the time I had reached *Ta Ha*, which is the twentieth Sura of the Quran, I had grown so huge that no one I had ever known could even recognize me any longer. My head was seven feet above the street. I was changed. I did not even know myself. For it is also written:

> You become bewildered; then suddenly Love comes
> saying, "I will deliver you this instant from yourself."

And Allah is also named *Al-Waddud*, the Lover, who bestows com-passion. So I was delivered. I was not Leon Lenox any longer. I had become an aspect of the Nameless.

Porco

Not much of a selection on this box, but if you live in public places you have to take your chances. Maybe I should go for something long, to jam up the jukebox longer anyway. LP selections are down here in the corner, haven't been changed in so long you can barely read the labels, which might be a hopeful sign, after all. And here it is, "One-eyed Jack," Garland Jeffries's stab at the mainstream, which only managed to become another cut-out in the end. Not the best, but still better than some things that could happen to your ears.

So I drop my quarters. "Scream in the Night" isn't such a bad sequel to "Spirit in the Night," now I think of it. Cut has a nice lead-in but it drags in the middle, also at the end. But I make it back to my seat on that first upbeat line. And here by my bar stool is someone I know. Guy named Whelan. Sometimes hangs around here, not too much. I haven't seen him since before my last tour of the crazy house, a couple of months ago.

"Well, pal, when did you get back in circulation?" Whelan opens up. "And what are you doing keeping late hours in bars?"

"I'm marinating my liver," I say. "You should try it. Try it on me." And Whelan orders dark rum with no ice. His only drink.

"Why, did you inherit money or something?" Whelan says. "It seems like the last time I saw you you were walking up the Bowery with a bottle of Windex and a rag." This is not a nice thing for him to say, especially since it can't be true. What he is referring to is a scam which consists of cleaning the windshields of cars clogged up in the traffic around Houston Street, whether the drivers of the cars like it or not. Creates a false sense of obligation. This sort of panhandling is completely beneath me, though some of my best friends, etc. and so on.

"I got some sessions work," I say. "With an up-and-coming dance band of some sort. They wanted somebody to blow alto in three/ four time, blat blat. For money." This of course is not true either, but it wouldn't do to tell Whelan about the accident that happened to me in Terri's. Until quite recently Whelan was one of New York's Finest, though now he's off the force. Used to be a narcotics detective, but he got bad stomach trouble, too much pressure. Lately he works for a security guard shop, desk job, or that was the last I heard.

"Well, many thanks," Whelan tells me when the drink arrives. I fold a bill into a triangle and flick it at the bartender's shirt pocket. Whelan looks like the sort of guy that would slap you on the back, but luckily he doesn't. He's a big solid man going to fat and getting bald on top. Looks very much like a middle-aged cop or ex-cop, in fact, which is reasonable. Wears a blue polyester suit and a nice wide tie. Now he's staring into his rum glass, a little bit moodily, I'd say. He looks at the drink and then pulls a pint carton out of his coat pocket and fills his glass to the top with milk. Makes you blink, but this is the only way Whelan can drink the stuff, poor guy. He's had ulcers and complications ever since some hophead got upset during a raid and perforated his small intestine with .38 slugs. Whelan sips from his drink and sighs and swings his stool toward me.

"What news from your end of the world?" he says. And I put my hand in my pocket and close it over the Stone. Ah, I could tell you a story. But then I only get depressed. Who's going to listen to this one? I'll only end up in another padded cell. Try to find someone who'll believe in miracles these days. It's like asking the devil to go get you a glass of water.

"Nothing," I say. "Business as usual and not much of it." Whelan lets out a little groan of agreement and shifts his weight around on the stool. Then he starts to talk shop. Yes, he does still work for the security joint. In fact they're sending him on inspection tours, and that is the reason he is out and about so late. Just got back from driving around warehouses in Red Hook, pinching his guards to keep them lively.

"Like to get out of this racket," Whelan says. "Getting too old for this kind of a schedule. And the pay, why it's worse than being on the cops."

"Eat any bullets lately?" I say. After all I owe him for that crack about the Windex.

"You got a point," Whelan says. He stares into his rum milkshake. "But what I'd like to get into now is matrimonial surveillance."

"What? Oh, you mean keyhole peeping. You want to take that up at your time of life? What about the court dates? Drive anybody crazy. You'd blush yourself into a stroke."

"I don't want to go on the street, you loon. I want to open my own shop. There's money in it, believe you me. People that want that kind of work done, they don't care what they spend. And I have the contacts, but I need to make a nut to get it started." Whelan buys himself another rum and puts the milk in it and runs on for a few minutes about trouble death and taxes and the bills his wife runs up at A&S. Really he can be quite boring at times. But he often improves on his third drink, so I order it for him. He's my best bet for someone to talk to tonight, and at times he's not so bad at it at all.

"So where's your bad news friend tonight," Whelan says. "Whatever he calls himself now." Whelan never cared too much for Johnny B. It's only reasonable, considering who they used to work for, respectively.

"Who knows," I say. "We're not on speaking terms."

"Ah," says Whelan. "So much the better for you, I say." Whelan affects a great concern for my welfare and safety, at least where Johnny B. is involved. He started taking an interest sometime last year, when Johnny B. and I were spending a lot of time leaning over this very bar. One night in the dark of the moon Whelan invited me downtown and let me read a few files. That was really very touching, since Whelan was taking a chance on his job, though of course he dumped the job too, not very long after. And Johnny B. didn't have such a very hot file after all. Just a profile and a list of associates and a couple of arrests that never even made it to court, because Johnny B. has a talent for not having things hung on him. Holy Mother's folder, to which there was a cross-reference, was something else again. There were things in there that would make you think twice. But all the same, there's more to a man than meets his rap sheet. And that line even gives me an idea.

Santa Barbara

Hear the bata going down now. The drumbeats fading down and they stopping. The breaths of the others in my ears, and the voices calling to me by my name. A whispering from far, it saying to me, I. I coming back to me now.

I opening up my eyes, but it only the dark to see. Where I be now I don't know. Every place be the same in this darkness. The orisha come over me, and I closing up my senses. I rolling up in the dark like before getting born. So I don't be I no more but the god's body and god's mouth. *Subirse el santo a su caballo.* I closing up my eyes again but nothing coming anymore. It over now, come and gone.

Stretching out my hand through the dark but it not touching anything. Turn it over and it hitting something cold. My hand hot, too hot, and this I touch be cold. I hold the cold thing, let the heat go out by my hand. My head clearing up some little now. Can tell now they nobody in this place but me. So I not in the ileocha. Where then I be?

The heat run out my fingers onto this I touch. It feel like some metal. I more weak now than I ought to be. Long time since the orishas come to me. Since little while after I make the asiento. Been few months since then. I reaching up and touching my head. My hair grow out long again since the asiento. I remember like yesterday. Time dont mean nothing for the orishas. It dont change them.

Just the people change. The orishas not even living in time. If they coming to you, then they taking you out past the days and nights.

Just by the feeling of my hair do I tell how long pass since the asiento. Then they shave my head and now the hair grown out. For the asiento I come down to Loisaida to the ileocha one man name Martinez is keeping. He know Mr. Rivera for long time, so when Mr. Rivera die he become my yubbona for presenting me to the saints. I knowing him always as my yubbona while we both living. The day before he shave my head and clean it with butter and coconut pieces and some eggshells, how they call the revocacion de cabeza. It make the head clean for the orishas coming. It make clean the mind.

Next day he wash my head again and paint all over with dots. Dots of red and yellow and white and blue, going in a circle to the middle of my head. Making me not look like me no more. Making me look like something not a man. Then my yubbona he put on me a red robe. Red for the color of Chango. So Chango going to be sure to know me when he come. Because if the wrong orisha coming, this my first time, then it be bad for me. Other orisha going to be angry, and Chango be angry too. If they enough angry, then maybe I going to die between them. It known to happen to some few people.

These two days my yubbona keeping me in the secret eya, the room at back. Now it all ready to begin. He lead me out in the center of the ileocha. Many people there. All santeros who knowing Mr. Rivera when he alive. Most of them never see me but maybe one time before. I a little bit scared maybe. But I holding myself up straight while my yubbona saying a few words for me. Then the bata starting. I hear the three drums from behind me beating slow. They come up faster then and I hearing them from every side, all around me, the beats crossing over each other, and the songs and the voices calling, all the santeros calling for Chango and the bata playing now inside my head, all the voices one voice now in my head calling for Chango, and I calling him too, calling him so hard like maybe I will die, Chango, and

I too the one they calling for, who calls me, who calls Chango, I am Chango, big dark more strong than possible, I have a two-edge ax and a sword cutting every way and many lightnings, who calls, I jump down from my tower I tear hole in the roof of ileocha with my lightnings, I am here now, everyone bow to me, I, Chango, I will smoke strong tobacco and drink rum and more and more and more and

I not knowing any more till I coming back together on the floor on my knees. My yubbona blowing in my ears and asking Chango please to go now and now calling to me by my name. I hear and answer. I dont see nothing but light till my yubbona lift the white cloth from off my head and I seeing again the ileocha and all in it. My yubbona he pull my mouth open and make cross on my tongue with the flat side of razor blade, to show that this now a tongue the gods use to speak. He putting some pepper into my mouth and a little honey and some smoked possum meat. I take and swallow. I hungry and thirsty now, and weak. Someone bring to my yubbona a chicken and he tearing off it head and standing there with he thumb over the neck like he holding shut a bottle of wine. He make sign to me and I taking the chicken from him and hold it over my mouth. The chicken heart beat the blood into my throat and I drinking it. I drink it all. It food and water both. It make me strong enough to stand.

Then I get up. When the chicken blood finish I tear up the body and stick feathers on the blood where it spill around my mouth and on my chest. Why I doing this I dont even know, but my yubbona looking at me like it a good thing this I do. He take my hands and lead me to a chair over in one side the ileocha. This chair sitting up on a platform like it some kind of throne. I to sit down on this chair and watch over the sacrifices. This night they killing for Chango, many chickens, some pigeons, even one goat. Every time they killing one my yubbona bring me it head for me to drink some blood from it, like from a cup.

Then when all this be over I staying on in the ileocha for seven more days. I dont go out or look out of window. Keep in the dark. My yubbona staying with me all this time. He feeding me, little bits coconut and little bit smoke possum. This all I eat those days. My yubbona make the omiero from the twenty-one herbs of the orishas and some blood from the sacrificing. Each day he washing my head with this omiero and I drink few spoonfuls too.

Then the seven days over and I go out from the ileocha. I standing on the corner of Ludlow Street and it the first time in a week I see the daylight. Could be it any other day. I go home to my house in Hoboken. Next day I come to the city again and I working in the park for Yanni-B. Everything like before going on. Still something change in me. I belonging to the orishas now, and all these same things I keep doing, I know now they coming from the gods inside.

I still hearing the drumming, but it real slow now. The big heat run all the way down my arm and out my hand. I opening my eyes again, and I all the way back now. This drumming I hear, it only my own heartbeat. This breath in my ears, it just the wind of the late night. This cold under my hand, it the leg of an iron bench here in Roosevelt Park.

I sitting here on this park bench. Down between my feet the end of a cigar still burning. Myself I dont smoke no tobacco. But Eleggua and Chango, both them like the strong smoke. To Eleggua I offer some tobacco every day. The Eleggua Mr. Rivera making for me, I keep him in the closet next the door of my house. In the closet it just look like a piece concrete with shells for eyes and mouth, but this Eleggua. Not a picture—Eleggua. He too in the jar around my neck now, the Eleggua Yanni-B give me. Orishas can be many places, many times. That a part they power. So every day when I go out my house I leave one cigar in front the closet. All the time I carrying one in my pocket too. Maybe this Eleggua around my neck he some time want to smoke it. This one burning now by my feet I just let it burn itself up.

My eyes they see some through the dark now. This not Houston Street where I am. I see the streetlights of Houston Street now three blocks away. Not so much light down here. Eleggua he walk down here in the park. Wonder what he doing on the way.

Wind stop blowing and the smoke rise up from between my feet and go straight in front my face. It stinging my eyes. Now the smoke stop coming. Wind rise up and blow away the hot ash of the tobacco. The wind stop again and I feel something now near me. Not like something living but like something used to be. It feel like an iku here with me now.

Iku can be the body of the dead or else the spirit walking. We the santeros dont have to do with iku. We feed corn and water just one time each year, but no more. We dont use the iku. We dont want them so near.

It better to let the iku live alone and far from us. Still it is one other way, how Ti Jeanne and her people do. She know a way to make the spirit of the dead come back. In her house she keep some jars and in the jars the voices of her fathers and grandfathers. They speak to her when she ask questions. Then too she telling me a way for letting your own spirit out of the body, to keep in a govi. It the way to keep the spirit safe from enemies, so she say, and she want to do for me, but I dont want. I keep my spirit with my body, that enough for me. But maybe this the thing that Yanni-B doing, how he talk tonight, about the soul in the jar. Could be he would do this thing, because Yanni-B dont fear nothing. All I know is he got some kind of power. But to me it better not even to think about these things. But I still feel the iku near, and it dont let me forget.

This bench I sitting on stand here by a rail. Under the rail a wall go down. I lean over. The wall go down about six feet in the ground. It a big deep place cut out in the ground, almost as wide as the park. It for people to play games in, when the sun shining. Over there in the middle of the park I see some steps for going down inside.

It what I coming here for. To go down the steps in the ground. I come to find the babalawo that Porco talking of. I stand up now and my hair rising up on my neck and I getting a cold place on my back. But this not fear no more. Not since Eleggua coming to me. This cold like an arrow that point me which way to go. Now I walking around the rail and looking down into this hole. I dont see nothing down there. Just dark and a few old bottles shining back some light from the street.

I standing now behind the old park building. Used to be a place for the people going in from the rain or if the sun too hot. But too much go on in there. Maybe some people getting cut in there or maybe some women getting taken. Now the city come and seal all up with brick. Nobody going in there now. Nothing happening in there now. Nothing even inside except the same old air that cant get out no more. It make me think of Ti Jeanne jars, with the morts shut up inside. Those jars heavy. It take both arms to lift one, because so many morts inside. Heavy like Porco's rock heavy. Too many souls to lift up.

Now here in front of me, the stairs that going down. I taking a few steps down. A wind pass over my face like a door opening. I feel something passing over me, and a name rise up in my head. Anaguii, the name. It one of the faces for Eleggua, the face that watch the cemetery. I make a prayer to Anaguii and I go all the way down in this hole.

Still I cant see nothing. Nothing I looking for. On one wall here it say, Dont Break the Bottles. On the other side it say same thing in Spanish. But this still glass I walking on under my feet. I go straight across the middle to the stairs at the other side. Still I dont find this iku.

Now I feeling this cold place in my back telling me turn. I turning to my left, to where Forsyth Street is up there. I walking now along the wall. My fingers touching the wall. Here I see the spray painting of people's initials and the names of gangs. I coming to the corner now and I turn and keep going along the wall. I going now close toward the bench where I sitting up there before. Now I feel the iku close, the cold, and my hair rising. I push on the dark with my eyes. Here a shadow on the ground. Look like some wino sleeping. But this shadow too straight and still for sleeping. It lie with it feet touching the wall and it head stretching out across this hole toward Chrystie Street on the other side.

I make my legs walk me up closer. Now I coming up and standing over this shadow. I sure this must be the one. This the dead babalawo. The body here and the spirit still here too. I feel the spirit asking. It asking for someone to help it to let go. Help it let go the world so it can leave.

I feeling in my pocket for a piece of candle I keeping there. I light the candle but it only showing me my own hand. I kneeling down and holding it near. I let some wax spill behind the head and set the candle up there. So I can see him now.

The candle flame yellow and I looking in he face. Got flat nose, flat cheeks, brown skin. He look like an Indian, like Porco say. This the one. I stand up and step back and look again. Not a big man. Not any bigger man than me. He got on some old clothes like any wino wearing. Loose shirt with holes in front and some pants tied on with string. On his feet the shoes got the soles coming loose so I looking at the bottoms of his feet. From this he could be anybody. Someone been so close to dead so long and when they die for true nobody even going to notice. But this man got eyes open still. The eyes they staring back to where I looking at him. They black and hard and they don't shine. They drink up all the light from the candle. They got as much darkness as this whole night. Wind blow up now and the candle going almost out. It go down to just one spark at the end and then it come back slow till it burning high again. I looking at the body. This the one. The babalawo of the Stone.

But he not lying how he should. Not if what Porco say be true. Porco say he die from drinking the bottle, and if that true then he going to throw a fit. Then he dont be lying straight like this. He be all tied up in one big knot. I seeing this before one time. When they die they jump around and thrash. They dont lay out straight this way.

The wax spilling from the candle catch fire now. The whole pool burn on the concrete and it make more light. I see now behind the head of the babalawo. Some pieces from the bottle that Porco telling of. Quart tequila bottle like Porco say. The neck part it all broke up and lying on one side. But the bottom half it almost whole. It standing up there right behind the babalawo head. I see it got something inside.

I stepping around now to look at what in the bottle. I bending down and smelling it. It smell like some liquor, but it colored red. Too thick for liquor anyway. I putting my finger in and hold my finger near the candle. Some liquor in it I see now, but more is blood. Blood and tequila in this half bottle. What this man giving up to die.

But how it come here in this bottle, I dont know. Make more sense if it spread out all over the ground. Somebody have to fix it this way. Somebody coming here before me and laying this man out so straight and putting this blood back in this bottle. My hair rise again and I move out away from the light of the candle. Maybe this somebody still around, watching me now, I dont know. I lying back in the dark, by the wall. I looking all round, but I dont see nothing move. Only can see the streetlights shining over the far wall on the other side. I dont feel anybody near but me and this dead one. I looking up at the sky. Stars all gone out now. Clouds coming over the sky and it hot again. Feel like maybe it going to storm.

I looking back at the dead babalawo. I know Porco dont lay him out like that. He dont know enough to do it. He just walk off and leave him where he falling. And me, I dont do it. Then how it happen?

Then I know. It the god that do it. When just now he living in my body. Eleggua taking my body and coming down here to where the babalawo lying. It what I ask for, for help to find him, and Eleggua know what I dont know. He know right where the babalawo lying, down this hole. So Eleggua come down here and lay out the body and put the blood and liquor in the bottle. Then he walk back up to the street and sit on the bench and smoke he cigar and look down on all he been doing.

I looking up there now. Straight up from where the babalawo feet touch the wall is the bench I wake up sitting on. So it happen. Eleggua do this thing and then he put me down where I going to see it.

I walking back up the steps again and back around the rail to the bench. I walk soft under the line of little trees growing up beside the sidewalk. I come up in front the bench and touch the rail and look down again. Now I see the babalawo eyes looking back at me, like maybe I looking down a well to find my own face. Why Eleggua want me to see this, I dont know.

Some people saying Eleggua the oldest orisha. He born before anything. Before even Olofi coming and making the world. They say he born the son of Alabgwanna, that they call the Lonely One. When Eleggua still a child, he tie up Alabgwanna in a chain and go away by himself. For a long time Eleggua wandering. All this time he keep changing. He change and change until he having twenty-one different names and faces but he never grow any older. Always Eleggua staying a child, with the mind of a child for changing.

Then Olofi come and he make the world and live in it. The world go on and one day Olofi wake up and he so sick he cant get well. No one know how to make Olofi be well, but Eleggua coming and he make an ogbo with herbs only he know about, and this ogbo make a cure in Olofi.

So Olofi well again, and he give to Eleggua some more powers. He give Eleggua the keys to every door in the world and he make him the guard for every road and crossroad. So now when anyone move they go by Eleggua. When anyone start something they go by Eleggua. The santeros know Eleggua by many of the names, but they never know what face he going to show. Only he know that.

Eleggua living in all his names, in every place of this world I travel. He live in this world always and in my head sometimes. I know he living too in this shining ball that Yanni-B give me that I keep now around my neck with my elekes. Nothing show Eleggua better than this thing, how it break up into little ones and still it can be a whole thing. So Eleggua can change in all the ways, and still he be Eleggua.

Now in this night I think I know the right name to call him by. Eshu Oko Oru, the one that makes to live and to die. He come at the beginning of a life and he still there when that life over. And he bring me here tonight to let me see how sometime it going to be me lying dead somewhere. And somebody going to owe me, to clean my spirit and let it go free.

The last wax spilled on the ground burning up now behind the iku. Now I know what I going to do. I make the ceremony all myself for sending this man out of the world. Only thing I dont know now is where I going to put him and how I getting there. But now I know something going to show a way. The wax from the candle all burnt now and it dark down there. The dark warm and it covering me and nobody see what I doing.

Porco

Now I throw my head back a few notches. To get it into position for expounding that idea I just had. But the head motion turns out to be a mistake. It shoots blood into all the wrong parts of my brain, and since there is quite a lot of alcohol in my blood at this stage of the game I forget what the idea was in the first place. So I sit there with my head hanging off the back of my shoulders, looking at the room upside down, hoping the idea may decide to return. Then I realize that what I'm really doing is listening to Garland Jeffries, track 2, the Bob Marley cover "No Woman No Cry." With a nice little guitar line backing it, so that considering the beauty of the sentiments expressed, I think that this one deserves a toast. The past lives in the future, yes. I pull my head back forward again. After a couple of seconds my eyes come clear and who do I see but Whelan, good old ex-Detective Whelan.

"Why, hello there, hello," I say, taking hold of his shoulder. "Great to see you again, what you been up to?"

"I've been talking to you for the last ten minutes," Whelan says. "Do you feel okay?"

"Sure, I feel fine, I feel wonderful, very happy, "I say. And my head begins to reorganize itself, yes, I was talking to Whelan, not long ago. What was I thinking about? A toast, yes.

"A toast," I say, raising my shot glass. "Absent friends." Whelan is willing and we click glasses. "Dead friends." We drink. "Imaginary friends." I order another round.

"So what broke you up, you and the hood?" Whelan says. "Seems like the last time I saw you you were all sewed up tight with the guy." And he holds up two fingers touching. But the fingers have to change course and go to his mouth. Just too late to block the belch. Liquor's not sitting on Whelan too well tonight, the milk notwithstanding. His poor old tired stomach must have figured out that trick.

"A philosophical difference of opinion," I say. "Gentlemen's agreement to part ways."

"Give me a break," Whelan says, and his mouth takes on a slightly sour expression, though maybe it's only his insides bothering him. "I haven't heard such a pile of crap since Joey Gallo was reading Camus. These guys don't talk philosophy, they don't make gentlemen's agreements. What they do is steal and leech off of people and kill each other. That's the whole game, my friend, and you know it as well as I do."

"No, but which guys are you talking about, exactly?" I say. "Johnny B.'s not associated, hasn't been for a few years. You know that yourself, you showed me the sheet."

"Oh, the sheet," Whelan says. "Let me get a cigarette, I'm out."

I give Whelan a Delicado for spite and light it for him.

"But just because there's nothing current on the sheet doesn't mean he's out of business," Whelan says. "Probably means he's busier than ever, if there's no pressure on. That's the way it usually goes. These are pretty strange cigarettes you got here. Kind of loose, don't you think?"

"Look," I say. I hold my shot of bourbon over one eye and stare at Whelan through it. This makes Whelan look more like a person who might listen to reason. If I can conjure up any reason for him to listen to.

"I'm looking," Whelan says. "The only thing I can see is a glass of booze hanging in front of your face."

"I can fix that," I say. I drink the shot and put the glass back on the bar. "Now. Think of it this way. Think of Johnny B. and then the other one, the one that used to get called Crow. Now which one do you think is worse?"

Whelan considers this for a minute, drawing on the cigarette, burping again behind his fist.

"Well, the other one, I guess," he says. "That guy is really bad news, I mean, just think of all the stuff he's been into, been killing people since he was seventeen or eighteen, and that's as far as we know. And God knows how many it really is, half of them never get reported even. So he's worse then, if you want to know. Why do you want to know that?"

"Because it shows you got the wrong attitude," I say. "You're looking at it backwards, let me tell you."

"Attitude," Whelan says. "Sheesh, you sound like a bought politician or something. You on the payroll now, or what?"

"No, I'm not on the payroll," I say. "In fact I think I'm working my way up the hit list, not that it matters. The point is that there's worse things than killing people."

"Not many," Whelan says. "Not in the law."

"Well, the law," I say. "I think we both know that's not the last word. You notice that there's plenty of people. There's plenty of people right here in this room that you would never miss. And you know what?"

"What," Whelan says.

"All of them are going to die anyway. Fact of life."

"Jesus, you really are a nuthouse case," Whelan says. He spins his stool away from me. I've got him mad at me now and that won't do, it's killing the conversation.

"All right, I know that too. Not that it matters. But just listen." I reach out for Whelan's shoulder and rotate him back around where I can look at him. I feel like I've done this whole number a few times before. Hey there, I'm not really crackers, or if I am, I'm on to something anyway. I know I'm really on to something, I only wish I could remember what it is exactly.

"Look, I'm trying it the wrong way, sorry. Killing people is not a nice thing to do, okay, but some very nice people have done it. And there's a whole other class, you know, crimes against human nature. I can explain, just give me a minute."

"Okay, okay," Whelan says. "I'll give you a minute. I'll give you two minutes. Just try to make a little more sense, if you can."

And it feels so good to have a willing listener trapped that I could almost kiss Whelan. Only he would probably get very upset if I did that, and besides he has terrible breath from his stomach trouble and all.

"I'll make sense," I say. "I promise I'll make sense." Yes, nurse, if you will only turn off the electroshock machine, I promise I'll be perfectly rational. I'll talk just like a book, a psychology book if you like. "Get us another drink," I say. "I have to go somewhere for a second."

Holy Mother

I still remember. Yes I do.

The summer of 1971 was what you might call a long hot summer. There was things going down all over the place. Joey Gallo had come out that March, for one thing, and from what we could hear he was keeping himself busy, back in the city. Personally I didn't care too much what he was up to then. Enough was going on in my own backyard.

Even the hacks had the feeling that something was going to go down. They had no idea just what it was going to be but they could feel something in the air. You could tell by the way they acted. Even our hacks in E block began getting cagey, holding back, and we had always kept up very good relations with them. Now everybody was very worried. Half of the hacks wouldn't even risk carrying their stuff into the joint anymore. They'd leave their wallets and watches in their cars outside before they came on duty. They'd come in with just enough change in their pockets to buy a lunch.

You could see how the hacks might begin to get worried if they ever really thought about the shape they were in. There was only a hundred and fifty guards on the day shift, and these guys had to keep a grip on over two thousand prisoners. They have this saying that clubs are trumps, but when you are outnumbered better than ten to one, just see how much good you're going to do with a nightstick. There was just one thing that kept the joint from blowing apart from one day to the next, and that was that nobody could ever get many people together behind any one piece of action.

There was too many different groups in the joint for any good organization. In the blacks you got the Panthers, the Elijah Muhammads, the Sunni Muslims, the Five Percenters, and what they call the house niggers that just pull their time and hope nobody is going to bother them. With all that going on between all those people, you weren't going to get a decent organization off the ground. The Latins had barely enough people to keep their heads above water, and they hung with whoever they could for survival. All these groups held separate courts in the yards. Walk into some-body else's court and you got a good chance to get dead.

In a situation like this it's hard to get many people to back one idea. To take an example, Muslims can't eat pork, and you got a lot of pork in a prison mess hall. You also got a lot of stuff that you can't tell what it is. So the Muslims want to get the pork taken out of the kitchen: only the Latins, they like to eat pork. Then right away you got a problem between the Muslims and the Young Lords. A stupid problem, but still it's a problem. These little problems made it that not too many people ever got together. That way the hacks could keep control.

But in '71 all this was beginning to change some. The different groups began to see that if they all pulled together maybe they could apply some pressure. On the administration and on the State Commissioner, which was a fat cat named Oswald. Seeing a thing is not the same as doing that thing. Still, that summer enough peo-ple pulled together to send out a letter to Oswald. This letter was demanding things like better pay for the work details, better visit-ing conditions, less censoring of the mail, a lot of stuff like that. It didn't make a dime's worth of difference outside the walls. But it did give ideas to a few people inside. All of a sudden the courts began to open up and you would see some very strange conversa-tions going on. You had the Panthers, the Black Panthers that are supposed to hate everybody, probably even themselves, and they're going all over the joint trying to make some new friends. And the people they were trying to make friends with the hardest were the Muslims.

Nothing happened out of this right away. There was one guy, a Muslim minister he was supposed to be, that held it off for a long time. This was a guy that had three names. In the street he had been called Butler, and after that he had taken the name of Norman 3X, like the Elijah Muhammads all used to do in the sixties, and by the time he hit Attica he was calling himself Muhammad abd al-Aziz. Somehow he had more pull than any other Muslim in the whole joint. Why this was, I don't understand, because what he was supposed to be in for was whacking out Malcolm X in '65. That was okay by me I guess, but not by the Muslims, not by a lot of other blacks too, I would have thought. Anyway he had the pull and for a long time he used it to keep the Muslims from sitting down with the Panthers. Then the hacks got informed that the Panthers were thinking about putting him out of the way, so they got him transferred out to another prison. If I had been the hacks I would have left him there and let him take his chances, because after he got shipped out things really started to roll.

It wasn't long after Butler was transferred out that the Panthers and Muslims had a big sit-down in the yard, with the Young Lords acting as the go-betweens. Nothing happened out of this either right away. But it was unprecedented that a sit-down like that could even take place. What it said to the hacks was that they might lose their grip, and the grip they had wasn't too tight already. The next thing that happened was toward the end of August, when this guy called George Jackson got shot by the guards in San Quentin. Now this happened way on the other side of the country, but this Jackson guy was well known among the blacks, and the news caused a lot of people to get very upset. Because the story they put out on it was that Jackson had a piece passed to him while he was on a visit, and that he got back to his cell with this piece hid inside of his hair, and that later he tried to stick up the hacks with it, or some kind of garbage like that. But everybody that has ever taken a visit in prison knows that you can't get in and out of a visiting room with even an extra toothpick on you, much less a handgun. So what this story meant was murder. This was no big surprise to anyone. Not even to Jackson, who according to the wire had been expecting to get his for quite some time. But the way it was presented was taken as an insult, a slap in the face to people inside anywhere. The day after

the news hit Attica the morning shift marched all the cons to breakfast like normal. Only nobody ate anything. They all just sat there
and stared at the hacks standing along the walls, and they went on
back to the galleries when it was time. Nothing particular happened that day either. Only it was a little shock to the hacks.
Because the sight of a thousand or so people all doing one thing will
impress anybody. Especially if these thousand people hate you.

The Jackson thing happened toward the end of August, and
around the same time some people were beginning to wonder if
Oswald was going to do anything about the letter of demands that
had been sent up to him before. At the first of September Oswald
made a little visit to Attica. He started to sit down with the leaders
in the prison, only he got some bad news from home, or something
of that sort, and he decided to leave. The one thing that he did do
was to record a speech on tape before he left, and this speech was
played over the radio system that night. Everybody put their earphones on to see what Oswald had to say to them, but after about
two minutes people began to rip their earphones off and sling them
into the walls. Because the only thing that Oswald was saying was,
"Let's just wait and see for a while. Thank you for your patience."
But nobody had any patience left at that point. It was too late for
anybody to listen to that kind of garbage, and what Oswald had
done, though he didn't know it then and may not know it yet, was
to throw the game to the real serious militants who were attending
this party, and what these people had been wanting to do for
months was to throw down the whole prison and take hostages.

I knew. I was all over the prison during that time, since I was
officially a runner. I had plenty of chances to find out what was
going down. But I would have known anyway, because everybody
was involved by that time. Even all of us wise guys in E block that
didn't have anything to gain out of a riot, we were into it too.
Because when there is something that major about to go down
then it pays you to get in close enough to see what is going on. And
besides, even though we weren't that interested in lifer's law, even
though we were being taken care of outside the walls, there was
none of us that would have minded a little change in the scenery.
We came in on the thing and gave the help that we could. It mainly
involved writing up proposals to be used later and making sugges-

tions on the planning, even making a few contacts to people on the outside. In the end there were quite a few people, all the way up to the state legislature, that knew something was about to take place. We ourselves knew right down to the hour, which was supposed to be 9:30 a.m. on September 9. Myself, I was running around from one block to another, passing on messages and things like that, and I thought I knew all about it. I probably did know as much as anyone else did. But nobody, nobody knew just how bad it was going to be.

I open my eyes now because I don't want to see anything more of it. If I think this far I start to see it all again. I feel the pain and smell the blood all over again, and I don't want that. I open my eyes in this room and my head is bent over, so all that I see is the corner of the table with the rubber tube curling off of it, and my hypo. In a way it's funny. It's funny to think that these things wouldn't be on my table at all if Johnny didn't one day decide to send me a box of Amaretto cookies in the mail. These are a kind of cookies that come from Italy, and they sell them out of Ferrara's on Grand Street. They come wrapped up in little papers, and if you set these papers on fire then they fly away into the air, so this was one of Johnny's little jokes, having to do with me flying out of prison one day. And if they had even told me about the package on the eighth when it came in, then I probably wouldn't be a junkie now. But it's no use to think about that either, so I just close my eyes again.

I slept like a stone the night of the eighth. Back in those days nothing bothered my sleep. It was a habit from all the hits. But a little before eight in the morning somebody came in to tell me I had a call-out to go down to the package room. Since the guy woke me up coming in and telling me, I got out of bed. Nobody else was moving around much in E block that early, except for my fish in the fish tanks, so I decided I might as well go down and get the package, since it was still an hour and a half to show time. Besides it wasn't likely I'd get another chance to go to the package room in the near future. Besides I thought it might be fun to walk down through the joint, pick up on the excitement. It was overconfidence, and overconfidence kills people. I should know. It's killed a few people for me.

I wasn't the only one with the problem that day, and what I didn't know was that the day before, two guys had got cocky enough to punch one of the hacks in A-block yard. They were stupid to do that at a time like it was. They were even stupid enough to think they got away with it for a few hours. But that night after lockdown, these guys were removed out of their cells and taken off to the isolation unit, the box. Now it happens that one of these guys was locking into 5 company on A block. The guys in 5 company are all thought to be bad news, so much so that 5 company is the last stop a lot of people make before they end up in the box. So when the hacks came on the gallery to take this one guy out, all the other guys got upset to see that their buddy was going to miss all the fun next day. They began to raise hell and throw things, and they made a lot of noise and threats. This could have blown the whole show for the next day, if the hacks had thought to pay attention to it. But they didn't pay much attention. They just took their man off the gallery and left 5 company to cool down overnight. Only 5 company didn't cool down at all.

They went through the night on a slow boil and by the next morning they were ready to pop. They made it to breakfast all right, and they might have even made it back, but on the way back they ran across one of the hacks that had been on their gallery the night before, and that's when the lid blew off. Five company had just been locked through Times Square into A tunnel when they saw this guy. They jumped him and everything exploded. Me, at the time, I had no idea. I was just walking out of B tunnel into Times Square, with my package under my arm. The hack at the gate unlocked it for me, and I was just starting to talk to him, since this was a guy I knew pretty well, and A tunnel gate blew out behind him and the whole area was jammed full of people. The first thing I saw was some guy beating the hack I was talking to over the head with a stick. I could tell at a glance the guy was dead on his feet, and I was talking to him about the weather just two seconds before. I was already thinking, This is stupid, this is crazy, nobody is supposed to get killed in this thing or everybody in the joint ends up worse than they started. But there was nobody around that looked like they would listen to that argument and anyway this hack was killed already and I was being run down D tunnel like a cow or something before I could even open my mouth for a puff of air. About two minutes later I was standing out in the middle of D-block yard and I could hear the whole joint screaming to pieces all around me. I looked at my watch and I couldn't believe it—the thing was already dead out of control, and it was almost an hour before it even should have started.

I was shook up pretty bad. I'd lost my grip on things and I didn't know what was going to happen next. I'd never thought I'd get caught in the middle. I looked around. Not too much was going on in the yard. Just a few people were trickling in. But all hell was breaking loose in the tunnels, and I didn't see much of a chance to get out of the yard just then. I got over to the wall of one of the tunnels and sat down under a shadow, so I would be as much out of the way as possible if any shooting started. I wanted to keep a low profile anyway, because I had never planned on getting stuck in there, and if there was anybody running around that didn't like me or something, this would make a big beautiful chance for him to settle the score. I'd hung on to my package somehow, and I opened it up then, since I didn't have too much else to do. When I saw what was in it I didn't know whether to laugh or what. Holy Mother of God, I thought, I'm sitting in the middle of the biggest prison riot that ever happens in this state, and what am I holding but a ten-dollar box of macaroons.

Then I looked around some more and saw that D yard was starting to turn into a real zoo. There were guys pouring in now from all over the place, hundreds of people wandering around the yard. Nobody looked like they knew what they were doing. They acted like they thought they were at a big party or something. A couple of medicine chests had been taken out of the blocks already, and half the people in the yard were real busy eating pills. I thought the thing was supposed to be a business operation, but it looked like that idea had got lost somewhere, and the only thing that was left was about a thousand maniacs screaming all over the yard.

After a little bit of this the hostages started coming in, and things began to take on a little more shape. That is, a split developed between the people that wanted to whack out the hacks they had caught and the people that wanted to keep them alive. I was leaning into the wall of D tunnel when they started bringing the hostages through, and it was easy to tell those guys were going through hell inside. There were guys lined up on either side of the tunnel, swinging broomsticks and sections of pipe at the hacks as they ran through into the yard. Most of those guys had been stripped already, and a few of them I saw looked like they were hurt bad.

But when the hostages hit the yard the beating stopped for the most part. They all got taken over by the Muslims. When I first saw this happening, I didn't think it looked too good for the hostages. I thought they were going to get skinned alive. Because most of them were white, and what the Muslims preach is that the white man is the devil. Besides, nobody in a prison likes the hacks all that much. Not if the stick changes hands. So I was looking to see a massacre. But I got a surprise.

It turned out that the Muslims were the only people in the joint that never lost control. The political groups had lost it altogether, and they were all ready to drink blood. The Muslims kept cool through all of that and held their organization tight. Maybe it was because they hadn't been eating any pills. I don't know. They don't pass out any explanations to strangers. But as fast as the hostages came in the yard, the Muslims took them over and bunched them into a corner. There was one guy running it, and I watched him close for a few minutes, because I didn't remember seeing him around much. Then I knew who he was, he was the man they traded Butler for. And the funny thing was, he was supposed to be another one of the guys that got Malcolm X, according to the wire. That made him one of Elijah Muhammad's soldiers, and it was strange to see somebody like that taking such a big interest in the good health of a bunch of white people. But that was what he was doing.

The Muslims got the hostages into their corner. They made a line, shoulder to shoulder, in front of the corner, and they held it against everybody. And there were quite a few people howling to get through. There was all kinds of threats and yelling from a distance, but nobody really tried it. The Muslims just stood there like a bunch of goddamn statues and the message seemed to be, like, over

Holy Mother | 119

there you can say what you want to, but just come over here if you would like to be killed. And my guess would be it's several hacks that owe their necks to that. After a few hours went by the Muslims even managed to get the worst-hurt ones out of the yard to the hospital.

There were plenty of hostages to spare anyway. In the first couple of hours they must have rounded up about thirty, and all through that day they kept bringing in a few more. They'd find a couple of hacks holed up here and there on the galleries, locked into bathrooms, or barricaded into cells. I pitied those guys, waiting hours for the ax to fall. And all of them took a little trashing before they made it into the yard. They were bringing them in from all over the prison, and after a while I began to catch on to just how far it had gone. This wasn't just a couple of blocks. The guys had run over the whole entire prison. The only place they didn't take was the administration building. There were a thousand men in the yard, all of them yelling power to the people and acting like heroes. They had done some big stuff. They were sitting on top of the world.

Personally, I thought I was in a pretty tight spot. I hadn't ever planned on ending up in D yard. If it wasn't for the bad luck I'd have been over in E block, watching the action on my TV. But after I thought it over I decided I wasn't in that bad shape. Nobody in the yard really knew I had anything to do with the planning. Some people might have had some idea, but nobody really knew anything. And the way things looked it seemed like hardly anybody even knew that there had been any planning. I was more likely to have problems just because I was white, if I had any problems at all. But being a runner, I'd done some favors for quite a few people in there. I thought that would be enough to cover my head.

So I thought, well, I'll just sit back here and watch the party. And after a while I started to feel not so bad. It wasn't such a bad day outside, for September upstate. I opened up my cookie can and ate a couple of cookies. Then I rolled the paper wrapper into a tube and lit the top of it. It floated off on its own updraft, still burning. The ash almost cleared the top of D catwalk. I could begin to understand why everybody was acting like crazies. It was freedom of a kind. Even though they were still just sitting in the yard, inside the wall. At least nobody was going to come along and say, "Hey, boy, back to your cell."

By that afternoon a good deal of territory got lost back again. The State Police had begun to come in already and they took back A block and C block and all of the maintenance buildings before anybody really had a chance to notice. At that time in D yard people were trying to calm down and get some kind of organization back together. I was taking no part in any of this. It was getting too stupid anyway. These guys, the black guys mostly, they weren't even thinking about prison reform anymore. What they were asking for now was plane tickets out of the country.

But even after the two cell blocks were lost the position didn't seem too bad for bargaining. We still were holding B and D blocks, and the yard. Better than that, we had Times Square and all four tunnels, and without that it wasn't going to be easy for anybody to come in from outside. A little coalition got itself together for dealing purposes. The coalition talked to the Muslims and persuaded them to move the hostages into the middle of the yard. That way they could be seen easy from outside, and anybody thinking about an assault could see right away who was going to get hurt. There were forty or so hostages by that time. The Muslims put them in a circle of benches and tables, and they kept standing inside the circle, holding the ground. They ended up holding it all the way up to Monday morning.

By this time, everybody except the real lunatics had accepted that it was better not to hurt the hacks any more. Some order came back onto the scene, and some rules were laid down. There wasn't to be any more drug taking, and no sex was going to be allowed, and all the food and cigarettes there was around was to be divided even. The committee set up a security guard to enforce all this. The guard was armed with knives and sticks and they kept things together pretty well, at least at the start. By the time Oswald came into the prison that afternoon it at least looked like people knew what they were up to.

The first demands to go out of the yard that day asked for a lot of outsiders to come into Attica. Everybody had their favorite person they wanted to get in there. It ranged from politicians and lawyers to writers on *The New York Times* to the leaders of the Panthers and Muslims and Young Lords on the outside. Oswald decided to play along with this, and some of the people began to show up at the prison by that night. In one way it was dumb to get all those different guys in there, because it made everything that much more confused. But in another way it wasn't a bad idea at all. Because when the outside guys came they brought the news teams in with them, the reporters and the TV crews. And everybody in the yard was convinced at that point that as long as there were enough people watching, they weren't going to just get mowed down.

But the TV cameras had a bad effect on a lot of guys up front, the guys around the negotiating table. Some of those people forgot just how close their backs were to the wall, and they started carrying on like they were running for President or something. They would get up in front of the cameras and start talking about everything from here to the moon, when what they should have been thinking about was how they could get out of D yard with their heads and maybe a passable deal.

At the beginning Oswald was being a nice guy and putting up with all of this. He came in the yard himself to talk to the committee, and that is something I personally have to admire. No matter how much of a jerk he might be in other ways. It takes something to walk into a mess like that when you can figure pretty well that all half the people there want to do is to wrap your guts around a telephone pole. He did it, and the security guards had fun giving him a nice close frisk, but nobody did him any serious damage. Because that first day it seemed like Oswald was going to play ball.

The main thing that everyone was worried about already was amnesty. No reprisals, no extra time coming to anybody for anything that got done during the riot. It seemed possible to get that then, because nobody had got killed yet as far as anyone knew. It was all just property damage and minor assaults, and things like that you can maybe get waived. Oswald and some of the other negotiators said they would try for a court order. That word came through some time the first night.

So everybody went to bed happy on Thursday. It got cold after dark and people scavenged through B and D blocks to find some wood for campfires. Nobody wanted to try sleeping inside the cell blocks, because nobody wanted to get caught alone in there. It was safer out in the open with a lot of people around. Some people made tents out of blankets and slept under those. Me, I just stayed in the open, in my spot near the wall. I catnapped a little, but I thought it would be better to sleep in the daytime when it would be light and nobody could do anything without a lot of other people seeing it.

Then the next morning things started to get all fouled up. Oswald and some of the outside guys came back in the yard with a court injunction against reprisals and so on. But nobody was willing to trust it. They said it didn't have a seal on it or something like that. People were scared it was some kind of con job, and about then somebody happened to look out the back of B block and notice all the troopers that were lining up out there. Some more people went to check it out, and there were enough troopers for a nice little army. Everything started to fall apart right there.

Some jailhouse lawyer looked over the injunction and noticed that it didn't cover criminal amnesty. He saw that and started yelling, and he tore up the paper. Now I am a good enough jailhouse lawyer myself to know that probably there was no way to get criminal amnesty. But nobody was going to think about that, because everybody was beginning to run scared. I just hung back and watched and hoped I still had a chance to get out alive sometime. At the negotiating table everybody seemed to be just trying to do something that would look good on television.

It went on like that for a couple more days. There was a TV set built into one of the walls of the yard, and anybody who could get a word in at the dealing table could look forward to watching himself on the six o'clock news. Most of those guys were too stupid to realize they were turning themselves into prime targets. The ones with some brains put towels over their heads, which is why D yard ended up looking like some kind of Arab camp-out. But with everybody keeping one eye on the cameras, not much worthwhile dealing could go on. On one side you had a bunch of crazy cons that thought they were all of a sudden in Hollywood. On the other side you had Kunstler and a bunch of guys like that who had come down to get their names on a headline one more time.

So it went on like that up to Saturday, and Saturday there was almost a deal made. The dealers had worked out a lot of reform points that Oswald said he would accept, and for just a little while it seemed like it all might work out. The only problem was that amnesty still wasn't on the list. And also on Saturday the word came through that one of the hacks had just died in the hospital. I knew which one it was. It was the same one I had seen take it on the head in Times Square, and I knew he was dead even then. But when the news got out, it was all over. That tore it completely. Because to kill a guard is the death penalty. With that hanging over everybody, no deal that didn't have full amnesty in it was ever going to float.

Already on Saturday people were starting to get very scared, and the organization began to break down. People were afraid the troopers would be on top of them anytime. Some white guys were stupid enough to hang a white flag on top of their tent, hoping they'd get it easier when the strike came. The committee was going to kill those guys for that. But instead they decided to make them dig a trench along two walls of the yard, for defense, it was supposed to be. At the same time they built barricades along the catwalks on top of the tunnels, because everybody knew there would be big trouble before long.

Saturday night was like a bad dream. There was knifing and raping all night long. A lot of people tried to break through the Muslims and get at the hostages. Some people just freaked out all by themselves and started jumping around and screaming and trying to climb the cell-block walls. I still had my cookie box and I chewed up some of the wrappers till they were soft and stuffed them into my ears. I was afraid I might lose it myself, if I had to keep listening to all that.

Sunday morning my skin was crawling. I have an instinct, and by then I knew the end was coming and coming soon. The dealing was really all over by then and the air felt very bad. You could see troopers with rifles all over the roofs of A block and C block. But nothing happened that day either. There was a rumor that Rockefeller was going to come in and guarantee everybody a pardon. All through Sunday people were waiting for Rockefeller to show, but he wasn't coming. Probably he wasn't even thinking about it.

Sunday night it rained, hard. I hadn't ever made myself a tent, but it wouldn't have made much difference if I had. The tents were nothing but blankets and sheets and none of them would keep out a hard rain anyway. You just had to sit through it. At least it kept everybody quiet. By daylight Monday it had slowed down to a drizzle. The whole yard was just mud and dirty rags. Everybody was soaked to the skin and nobody even seemed to be able to think anymore. The troopers were still there on the roofs and they were beginning to group up at the end of catwalks at A block and C block. Around nine o'clock the last word from Oswald came into the yard. I don't know what time it was exactly because the rain had stopped my watch.

The last word now was, "Release the hostages now and then we can talk." It wasn't accepted. Probably more than half the guys in the yard would have taken any deal they could get by then, but it didn't happen. If they had known what was coming, all of them would have taken the deal.

What happened instead was that people tried to get ready to fight. The only weapons around were sticks and knives, but then the hostages were still there. A few of the hostages were taken up to the catwalks around Times Square and held there with knives on their necks. One of them kept screaming, "I don't want to die, I don't want to die." Over and over. It was driving me nuts.

About that time there was a lot of chopper noise and everybody turned around to look at a yellow helicopter that was flying over the corner of the yard. Some people were saying that it was Rockefeller coming in finally and everything was going to be okay. Big chance. I looked back in the other direction and there was another big helicopter hanging over Times Square. I never saw it come in and I have no idea how it got there. It was just there, and it was dropping gas. In a couple of seconds there was gas all over the place. I grabbed a wet rag off the ground and covered my face with it and rolled into the wall. But then I heard shots. Shotguns. I know a shotgun when I hear one. I couldn't believe they were using shotguns on a bunch of people with sticks and knives. The only firearm in the whole yard was one flare gun.

I got on my feet and started running for the trench. You can't aim a shotgun too well, and I thought the place for me was underground if I didn't want to get sprayed. I was running past the hostage circle in the middle of the yard. It looked like a slaughterhouse in there. The troopers had shot the hell out of it. Half the hostages were lying around full of bullet holes. The troopers had run over Times Square and they were jumping down off the catwalks and running across the yard. The whole place was crammed with them. It looked like a lot of ants coming.

I made it to the edge of the trench before I was hit. I felt it in my face and in my right side at the same time. It didn't feel like shotgun pellets. Whatever it was hit me hard enough to throw me over backwards. I slid down the pile of wet dirt behind the trench and rolled over onto my back. I couldn't really tell how bad I was hurt. My face was bleeding pretty good on the right side and I knew there was something in my body too. I felt tired. I was just lying there and looking up. There was another guy standing there right near me. I recognized him. He was a black guy that wasn't political or anything, a house nigger, and I knew him fairly well. He really liked those little hard candies they make with the honey inside, and I used to get them in the mail and sell them to him. Now he was just standing straight up there, looking like he didn't know where he was or what was happening. He had just choked and frozen, I guess. I was just going to yell to him to get the hell down, but he exploded. The center of his body just blew up while I was looking at him. I caught him falling and pulled him over me for cover. He was a big guy and he covered me up pretty well. The loose dirt by the trench was soft from the rain, and I was mashed down into it deep, and I didn't think I was going to get hit anymore.

I lay there quiet for maybe a few minutes. It seemed like it could have been years. The guy I was holding on top of me had a hole through him you could have put your foot through. I thought about it a little and I realized what had happened to him. He had been hit with a single rifled slug from a twelve gauge. This is a pretty big chunk of metal. They normally use those shells for stopping fast-moving cars or breaking down walls. Anyway, it had killed this guy very dead and he was bleeding all over me. I poked my nose out under his armpit and I could see combat boots walking around all over the yard.

The choppers still seemed to be up there somewhere, and I could hear a loudspeaker that kept saying, "Surrender, surrender." I decided I had surrendered already, but I stayed where I was, because the shooting was still going on. Then it stopped, and people seemed to be moving out of the yard. I got afraid that if I stayed any longer I might just get pushed in a hole and buried. So I rolled the body off of me and sat up. I could see a wedge of people crawling on their bellies toward D tunnel door. Somebody hit me over the head with something and I went down on my face and started crawling through the mud. I had to get up to walk across D tunnel but as soon as I got to the steps into A yard someone hit me across the knees and I went back down. There was an order for everybody to put their hands on their head. I put my hands on my head and started crawling on my elbows further into A-block yard.

The next order that came was for everybody to get up and strip. I heard it come over a bullhorn, but before I could get on my feet somebody else came along and put his foot on my head. "Get up," he said. "Why don't you get up, white nigger?" I lay quiet and he moved his foot and I got up and stripped. I was standing in a snake line that wound all over A yard. Everybody was buck naked and had their hands on their heads. Some people were getting clubbed pretty bad, but they were trying to stay on their feet. If they fell, they had disobeyed the order and it was all over.

There were troopers and hacks all over the yard. The troopers still had on the gas masks and they were waving their shotguns all over the place. The hacks were walking the snake line. Some of them had cattle markers. They were marking certain people, the guys that had been up front, with red X's. I wasn't at all worried when I saw this, because I had been very far in the background through the whole thing. But somehow somebody had fingered me. I never knew who or why or how. It might even have been something from my time in the city catching up to me just then. All I knew was I got an X put on my back and I was sure that meant I was marked to die.

Then they started to move the snake line into A tunnel. When I got halfway across the yard to the door I could already hear the clubbing. It sounded like drums. I might have thought it was drums except for the screaming. When I got in the tunnel they told me to run. Both sides of the tunnel were lined with troopers and hacks swinging clubs and yelling. I ran. I was praying I wouldn't trip. One guy ahead of me had fallen down, and he was getting stomped. I jumped over him and made it to A-block gate. They were running guys up the stairs into the cells and you could still hear the yelling and the troopers up there.

But I got pulled out of the line at the gate. There were three or four hacks waiting at the end of the tunnel, pulling out everybody with an X. Six guys with X's were there already, all handcuffed to one long chain. I got locked to the chain myself and they ran us all out the front of A block to a truck that was waiting there. It wasn't a prison truck. It was a laundry truck. I wondered about that while they were unlocking the first guys from the chain. Then I knew what was going down. We were getting slipped out of Attica off the record, and that meant that nobody was ever going to find out what happened to us. There was a hack standing inside the truck with a sap in his hand. Not a nightstick, just a nice little leather bag with something heavy inside. He was slugging the guys on the base of the skull as they climbed up into the truck. I could see he had a nice touch with the thing. Probably wouldn't even leave a bruise. Then it was my turn and I got on the truck and took my tap. I didn't have any choice about it. I was still handcuffed and I was too worn out to lift my arms. I just went to sleep for a while. When I woke up again I was in an isolation cell in Comstock, Great Meadows Correctional Facility.

When I did wake up enough to remember everything that had happened, I was surprised to still be alive. But since I was still alive I decided to play it confident again. I started banging on my cell door and yelling for a doctor. The fact was that I did need to see a doctor. The slug that hit my face had gone through and out, but the one that hit my body was still sitting in there somewhere, and I felt like I had a few broken ribs. After I had slammed around the cell for a while, a few hacks came and handcuffed me and took me down the gallery. The gallery I was on was about five floors up. They took me down to a little clinic on the third floor.

The doctor laid me out on the table and gave me a local and dug out the slug. He showed it to me after he got it out. It was a double zero buckshot, from one of the shotguns. Just nine of them will fit in a twelve-gauge cartridge, which makes them about the size of .32

slugs. I could see the thing sitting there in the doctor's tweezers, but it was still hard for me to believe. It was hard for me to believe that kind of firepower had been used on a bunch of guys with sticks. I never heard of such a turkey shoot.

So the doctor closed up the hole in my side and taped up my ribs and told me I was going to live. I wasn't so sure about that myself. I knew the other guys with the X's were probably dead already, and I didn't much expect that I was going to survive long enough to get invited to their funerals. The hacks ran me back to my cell, and I sat there thinking.

It was very quiet on the isolation block up there, and I didn't have a thing to do. There was no way for me to get a message out anywhere. I was alone in the cell for twenty-four-hour stretches, and I had no way of telling what was going on. I didn't even have a scrap of newspaper to look at, and the only thing I could do was keep thinking about what had happened.

I was in shock from all that, and it was no fun to think about it. I'd seen killing before. I'd even taken bullets before. But I'd never been in on anything like what happened in D yard. If I got hurt before, I knew why it was happening. And if I hit somebody else, they knew what they were getting hit for. But this thing made no sense at all to me. And because it made no sense, there was no way for me to figure out what might happen next. As it turned out, what happened next was even worse.

I think about it now and my back hurts and my legs get numb again. I want to stop it, now. I want to kill the memory. I heat the cup and load another syringe. Not much in this one. I won't take much. Just a little shot. I carry the hypo into the bathroom and open my mouth in the mirror. My tongue curls up to my top front teeth. I push the needle into the roots of my tongue and squeeze the bulb and pull it out. It only hurts for a second. Then my whole mouth goes numb. I couldn't talk now if I wanted to. I couldn't even say a word. I only wish there was some way to do the same thing to my brain.

I walk back out into the main room again. The pain in my legs and back is all gone now. Probably there never was any pain just now. Just the memory. I go between the table and the window and look out through the gate. Then I open the gate and the window and bend out over the street. When I look down my stomach clinches and I can feel myself falling all over again.

The whole time I was in Comstock the only time I got out of my cell was for hospital runs. A few hacks would run me down to the doctor and I'd get my bandages changed. Then they'd run me back up to the fifth floor. The whole time they kept after me. It was worst on the way back. They would call me nigger lover or white nigger. They would say to me, "This is your amnesty." They would prod me in the back where my ribs were broken. I had handcuffs on for the hospital runs, and there wasn't a lot I could do. I tried to ignore it. I tried to think about something else. But I didn't have much else to think about. After four days I cracked. I was on the fifth-floor gallery by the staircase, not far from my cell. The hack behind me gave me a gouge in the ribs and I spun around and hit him. I punched both my hands together and caught him on the mouth with the handcuff chain. I think I knocked most of his teeth out, but I didn't have long to enjoy it. There was two others, and one of them got me in the face with his stick. It was a twisting shot and it made a nice deep cut before it broke my nose. I was bleeding but I could still see. They got me under the arms and lifted me. I could see the ceiling floating up there like it was falling up away from me. But the ceiling wasn't falling up. I was falling down. I went out about eight feet and down about fifteen. It seemed like I was in the air for a long, long time. Then I landed. The small of my back hit the corner of a steel step and I passed out. I should have died. I was supposed to. Maybe it would have been better if I had. But instead, I just blacked out one more time.

That was a long dark sleep. It's what you call a coma. I've wished for sleep that deep again a lot of times since then. You don't dream in a coma. You don't think about anything at all. It's almost as good as being dead.

But I should stop this now. I better put the dope away. I could stop now and lie down. Maybe I could sleep for a few hours, some way or another.

Porco

Back in the bathroom again, and the only thing I really have to do here is transfer some more of the Terri's money out of my sock. So I pick up one leg and start feeling for the roll, but it seems I'm too drunk to make much of a stork. I tip over, and my shoulder makes a big racket hitting the door, and it appears that the best thing I can possibly do is sit down and rest for a minute here on the lid of the can.

Now I'm finding the bills folded down in my sock, yes, I peel one off the and leave the rest where they are, for future reference. Put the one bill in my pants pocket. Anything else? Yes, Whelan, Johnny B., I was going to explain it all. Where did that explanation go to? I can't seem to find it now. Did I leave it home on the piano? No. Did I write it in a matchbook? More likely, yes, probably one of the ones I lost. Yes, I think it was the one from the car lot in Paterson, I can see it now, a picture on the flap of a blimp, and hanging from the blimp is a little picture of a car, God knows why, and inside the flap is written everything I could possibly want to know or tell, it's in handwriting too small and crabbed to read, but I remember now anyway, yes, all about the man who went out looking for God with a very big bright flashlight, only all he could find out was that God seemed to be dead, killed by popular opinion, and that's it, yes, that's what's worse.

Up on my feet and out of the closet, I walk over looking for my stool, I seem to be having trouble seeing anything very clearly just now. I can hear Garland Jeffries howling away at "Oh My Soul" this time, with a paternoster chanted low on the back track, only I don't pay it much of my attention as I am too busy visualizing that mental matchbook. It's sprouting pages now, and on these pages I can read anything that I might wish to know, and now I have reached my seat and I see Whelan's face, floating up to me out of a cloud of smoke, don't see his body but just the face with the cigarette in the corner of its mouth and a curious expression, and I take a sip from my fresh drink, maybe it will clear my head, and hear my own voice now

how long has it been talking? what is it talking about? quiet, listen, and that is what the voice says itself, "Listen, listen, listen," even as a clock pendulum, and then declamatory, the voice rolling on with me listening to it from somewhere else, dislocated, shrunken to incredible density, hard and black and cold with knowledge and certainty, speaking of the immediate and perpetual assassination of God, and Whelan, "Keep it down, will you, but somebody got killed?" and the voice peremptory, cutting him off, and I full of delight hearing it, having for once lost conscience and with it fear and in this delirious freedom I hardly even care what the voice may be saying, and Whelan, "You killed somebody? or did he? killed who?" and the voice, "Nobody, nobody

"Nobody and that is it, either the worst thing or the best and I cannot tell you which because I don't even know but think of this then, if you can do away with your soul, if you can just stop talking to yourself then that is worse, or not worse but more daring and outrageous than strangling all the two-year-old girls in Brooklyn, or anything else you can possibly dream up," and Whelan, "What do you mean stop talking, the bastard talks almost as much as you," the voice, "Yes, yes, but

"Yes, he does talk, he talks to everybody, I know that, a perfect conversationalist, a great improviser, I know, breathing soul into accidents or at least it sounds like that sometimes, but the point is," and Whelan, "Yeah?" and "the point is that he can't hear himself at all anymore, he doesn't have an inner ear, he's found the switch and finally shut it off. And that's the power and the terror, that's the secret, and the most awful thing about the secret is that if you know it you don't have it anymore and if you have it you can't know it, because the will is deaf and blind all right, but it isn't dumb at all, you're right, he talks almost as much as I do, it's only that he doesn't have a monitor," and Whelan, "I thought you were going to tell what split you up," and the voice, "Oh, no, not at all, that doesn't explain it, because what better companion can you have for someone that can't hear than someone that can't shut up. . . ."

But it's only my own croaking voice again now, my voice is cracking, I'm losing it again. My tongue keeps beating on, but it's off the track now, too loud, too close to breaking, it sounds close to hysterics. So I clamp my mouth shut, I can't afford hysterics now, not here, not in front of Whelan. He'll turn me in and I'll have to do another stretch in the crazy house, white walls and white coats and white faces and worst of all nothing to drink, and months of it this time maybe, before I remember how to play dead well enough for them to let me back out. I'm getting too old for that, don't have the patience anymore. So I try to hold it back, but it's just too goddamn funny, I've got this agonizing laugh in the back of my throat that's screaming to get out, and if it does get out I'm in trouble. I'm only holding it in now by clenching my jaws, and the effort is making the veins pop out at my temples.

"Where are you getting all this anyway," Whelan says. "I can't tell what you're talking about."

"I read it in a book," I say, not paying much attention to my lies.

"Oh yeah, I know that book," Whelan says. "*Insanity Made Simple*. I got another one of those, on plumbing. Still can't do plumbing, though."

"Right you are," I say, pulling back together a bit. God bless Whelan for that line, I think it's maybe saved me. At that I can laugh like normal, and it sounds all right when I do, nothing exceptional, just a chuckle over a drink with a friend. That choking pressure is gone. A close call, but I made it, this time. Just let me catch my breath and I might even try it again.

Yusuf Ali

Allahu akbar. La ilaha ill' Allah.

Prayer is better than sleep.

So I make this takbir, for the sake that I have been guided out of my own dark and rage and defended from the ensnarements of Iblis, which are complex and subtle. . . .

For that I have been led out of my dark basement, out of the city of bones and ashes, into the light which is Allah, *An-Nur.* . . .

For that I have been preserved from the allurement of my own hatred and anger. . . .

For I was guided to the manifest Book, and in reciting it I grew in soul, as a believer, and it was permitted by Allah that my body grew also in proportion, to such a size that I no longer knew fear, even in this desolate city. So I have been defended. *Allahu akbar.*

I read and recited for a period, and the thought came to me, Where, then, are the believers? For much is written of the believers and of their community and of the obligations of all the servants of Allah. Then I might even have returned to Buzz to ask this question. But I had attacked Buzz, and I had wished to kill him, and I did not feel it probable that he would receive me again; moreover I thought that he might kill me this time. So I went out of the Bronx, searching for the believers.

And elsewhere in the city there were indeed many who professed to believe, yet more who did not, of course. I went among them, asking, "How is it that there are no believers, or only so few?" Then I was told that the truth had been hidden, veiled away from us by Iblis or Shaitan and their descendants and servants, and that this concealment was to endure for six thousand years, permitted by Allah's decree, but that the term of those years was almost done with now. Then I was told of Yacub and Yacub's history, which was represented as the true hidden history of the world and of our people in it.

So it was told me that long before our memory, all people in the world were black, and that these people were all the devout servants of Allah, and that they built a great kingdom in His Most Glorious Name. And in this kingdom Yacub was born, and Yacub had a big head which was filled with intelligence and knowledge, but Yacub's knowledge was all for destruction. He was known as the big-head scientist. When he grew to be a man he gathered a party of followers and led them to the island of Patmos, and there he bred his followers to one another in such a way that he weakened the black race to produce the brown, the brown to produce the red, the red to produce yellow, and the yellow to produce the white. The story tells how Yacub labored for twelve hundred years together to create this white race, because his knowledge had told him that the white race would be more susceptible to evil than any other. Then when Yacub had at last achieved the white race, he released it from the island of Patmos and sent the white devils out into the world. And every white man is not a man, but a jinn or a satan with the appearance of a human body. So the white devils raged all over the world, destroying Islam and enslaving the other races of men. And after a few generations the white devils destroyed the memory of the black man and caused him to forget his past glory, and taught him instead that he had lived in a tree like an ape. And all of this new, false history was the devising of the devil, I was told, but the history of Yacub was the very truth.

Such was the story that was told to me, and I believed it for a time, for in it there is much that is plausible, and many believed this story of Yacub and the white devils. For when this story meets the ear, it conforms with much that has already met the eye. And it explained to people much of what they could not understand without it. To some it explained prison. To some it explained drugs. To some it explained starvation. To me it explained the South Bronx. But still I questioned it.

And all during this time I traveled throughout the city, going among the groups of believers and asking them my questions, and I was possessed of a great feeling of freedom that I had never known before. Because I had not been out of the Bronx before, I had not known that there was any path that led out of it. Yet I already suspected that there are hazards in freedom, and I was cautious. The world was larger than I had known it to be, and I was wary of being confined to any one part of it too soon.

For when I went among any of the different groups of believers, then always there was some man that desired that I should join them and become one of them. This man would speak of the jihad that was soon to come, for the story went that the six thousand years of the white devils' dominion was passing through its final stage, and that there was to be a great holy war, in which the black man would purge the white devil from the earth and establish universal Islam. And I was often solicited to join this army of Allah, and often the man who was speaking to me would look almost with covetousness at my height and the width of my shoulders and the size of my arms, for I had grown to a great size by then, so that the man would have to bend backward to look up into my face.

"How do we call you?" he might say then. "By what name are you known?"

But I would always answer so, "I have no name, and am known by none." For I would not acknowledge any longer the names I had once been known by, and neither would I accept another name, from any one of these who said they believed, and who solicited me. So I kept passing from one such group to another, and always there was this talking of the jihad and the white devils and the great glory of Islam that was soon to come. But there was no unity among them.

Seeing this, I went again among the groups of believers, and I inquired of them how it could be that they were separate and lacked unity, if indeed they were all true believers. And in answering this question no man of any group could do more than pile up a mountain of words against the others, so that I grew weary of hearing it. And finally I said to such a one, "Cease talking, and show me where it is written, this of which you speak."

And at that I was given a number of books and tracts, and I was invited to read them and compare, but for the most part they had no authority, and I did not trust them, and the truth was not in them. Yet among these books there was one which did attract me, because the writer of this book was a man with no name, just such another as myself, and instead of any name he was called only X. So I began reading the book which was written by this X, and in the book there was some authority, though not so much as there is in the Quran, for X was not a prophet of the degree of Muhammad, blessed be the name of Allah's Messenger, but only a man like myself or another. So I was reading in this book, and though much of what was related by X had passed before I was born or was aware, there was yet a similitude, and a certain power which I could not deny.

And in the beginning of this book written by X, the history of Yacub was also related. But in the end of this same book, X spoke of how he went at last to Mecca, thus performing the hajj which is a sacred obligation laid upon the Muslim, and how while in Mecca he learned that this story of Yacub was not true. For there were people of all colors among those whom X observed circumambulating the Kaaba, and some of them were even white, and all of them were true believers. And this story told by X interested me greatly.

Now this account of the hajj made by X comes near the end of the book in which it is told, and the book did not proceed far enough to satisfy me, and so I returned to the man who gave me this book, to inquire where I might find X, because I desired to speak with him. Then I was told that X could not be found, or if he could be it was only in Gehenna, because he had been killed, and he was not considered to be a true believer. This I could not accept, and I was consumed with anger and disappointment when it was told to me, so that I demanded to know how this killing should have come to pass; and once again I was told such a multitude of stories that none of them appeared to be true. Then I was much embittered against all of the different sects of believers, for none of them were able to answer my questions. And at last I went to the Criminal Court in Lower Manhattan, and there I looked up the killing of

X in the book of the law. Now this book of the law has not the authority of the Quran or of any other holy scripture, yet all the same it is a book to which men have signed their witness. And there it was written how the killers of X were also among those who professed to be believers.

When I learned this I was greatly enraged against all the sects of believers I had visited, and I thought that perhaps I would turn against them and wreck their temples and their mosques. Because by this time my strength of body was even greater than before, and at first I desired greatly to work this destruction, for I thought that those who called themselves believers were indeed to be numbered among those who have gone astray, and that surely Allah must be wrathful against them. But I used time for consideration, and in time I overcame my anger.

For I remembered all that had been spoken of the jihad which was supposed to result from the end of the dominion of Yacub's people, the white devils, and I saw that it was no holy war at all, but only the same war which has endured among men since Allah sent Adam down from Paradise, with the decree upon him, as it is written. And I had already witnessed this war, and I had already fought in it, when I was in the Bronx, and I thought of how no one was winning this war and that I wanted no more of it. And if those who professed to believe were reduced to such a state that they killed one another, still I would find no merit for myself in working more destruction among them, but rather I should be quit of them altogether.

And I remembered too what is written in regard to the recitation of the Quran, for it is told that the recitation is rightly accompanied by weeping. For if a man should think upon what is written in the manifest Book and think also upon his own weakness, there is no doubt but that he shall grieve. And when all are reduced to weeping by that confrontation, then how shall any one of the believers have the arrogance to be angry against another? For the meaning of Islam is submission to Allah, not strife among the believers.

Then when I did return among the sects, it was with no show of anger, but with the peace greeting, salaam. And I called upon them to show where it is written in the manifest Book, any part of that which they had told me before. So they hastened to find in the scriptures some vague references to their belief, but all of this was false interpretation and a perversion of the incomparable message from Allah, and all of it was confusion. I knew the while that the Lord has distinguished the clear signs for those who are seeking, clear and impossible to confuse, and I answered the sects with words written of Abraham.

So we were showing Abraham the kingdom
of the heavens and the earth, that he might be
of those having sure faith.
When night outspread over him he saw a star
and said, "This is my Lord."
But when it set he said, "I love not the setters."
When he saw the moon rising he said,
"This is my Lord." But when
it set, he said, "If my Lord does not guide me
I shall surely be of the people gone astray."
When he saw the sun rising he said,
"This is my Lord, this is greater!"
But when it set he said, "Oh my people,
surely I am quit of that which you associate."

So saying, I departed from the sects of the false believers, and I did not go in their way anymore. I cut short my journeying and my inquiries and I returned again to what is written. For what is written has its own pure tongue and does not require an interpreter.

So I went then to the public library on Forty-second Street, and in that library there is a room in which all the writings of Islam are gathered together. And in that room there is everything that one must know in order to comprehend the message of Allah. I returned to that room day after day. I began to learn the original language of the message, which is Arabic. The learning was slow and difficult and painful, yet it increased me in understanding, and it increased me in peace also, for peace is a meaning of Islam. And though there may be an appearance of confusion in the Book, in fact there is no doubt anywhere within it. And in all other respects I lived as best I could.

In coming and going from the Forty-second Street library, I was beset with many temptations. Because the library stands at the edge of a park, which is named Bryant Park, and this park is full of vice and corruption and is held by the purveyors of the same, and this park is not even very different from the Hunts Point Terminal Market, except perhaps for the trees. And after nightfall, Bryant Park is dark and hazardous, but the lights of Forty-second Street run west to the Hudson, enticing to lust and depravity and addictions of one kind or another. But for a time I was made blind to all this.

I was changed, but the world was not changed. The seasons moved, and there was another winter. In this winter I suffered much from the cold. I needed more food and better shelter, and to obtain those things I needed money. And to get money, there was only one way that I had ever known, and it was going on out there still, even all around the library where I sat reading. I knew I could break back into it if I decided to.

For some little time I debated this matter with myself, but in the end I yielded. For it is written, among other things, that a duty of the Muslim is to make the pilgrimage to Mecca, and much may be forgiven to one who has made the hajj, and for this also, money is required. And it was also true that those who were involved in the traffic were unbelievers, all of them, so that whatever might come to them could well be taken for the punishment of Allah, who is swift at the reckoning. So I went back into business.

Once again, I took no name, and answered to none. I needed no name for my business, for I was so big by then that no one could confuse me with anyone else. I worked Bryant Park a few hours each day, and spent the remainder in study and prayer and meditation. For it is written:

> If the sea were ink
> for the Words of my Lord,
> The sea would be spent before the words of my Lord
> are spent.

I worked Bryant Park for a little more than a year, and I prospered, and I laid aside a fund for making the hajj, and I moved to Independence Plaza. My mind was easy, and my life was comfortable. But after a year my size began to work against me. I was becoming too well known. So I left Bryant Park and moved downtown to Washington Square. There I was anonymous again. And for what did I need any name? For I was only one calling upon Allah, and it is written:

> Say: "Call upon God, or call upon
> the Merciful; whichsoever you call
> upon, to Him belong the Names Most
> Beautiful."

Yet after all, I was not without a name for much longer. For it soon came to pass, as it has been written, that my own signs too were distinguished most clearly.

> It is God who splits the grain and the date stone,
> brings forth the living from the dead, He
> brings forth the dead too from the living.
> So that then is God; then how are you perverted?
> He splits the sky into dawn
> and has made the night for a repose,
> and the sun and the moon for a reckoning.

Porco

Well, that was a very close call indeed. I'd better watch it now. No more wild and ill-considered ravings. I'm catching the bartender's eye, and when he gets over here, I'm ordering nothing other than a big glass of ice water. The biggest glass you got in the house, baby, if you don't mind. In which I plan to drink a toast to discretion.

"What's with you?" Whelan says. "I thought water makes you sick."

"Oh, I don't mean to dampen the occasion," I say. "I just want to give you a fair chance to catch up. You'll find I make better sense once you catch up. Go ahead, have another drink." And since I see his glass is empty I yell for the dark rum bottle.

Whelan gives me a wink and a grin, and I see he's got new silver caps on his canines. He tosses the milk carton to the bartender to throw away, and ducks out the front door. Going around to the bodega for another carton of milk and maybe a roll of Rolaids. Well, I have no objections.

The ice water arrives and I hold it till it chills my hand. Then I drink it all up and call for some more. Halfway down the next glass some clarity begins to penetrate my brain. Also my teeth hurt from the cold. Okay.

I get up and consult the cigarette machine. I'm tired of Delicados now. Besides, they're all gone. Get a pack of Camels and light one, stroll by the jukebox. Walking much easier now, except I'm gurgling from the water. I'm looking for something to follow the Garland Jeffries, and what do I find but Bob Marley, the man himself. It would be nice to find something with a horn in it, but if you go for a horn section in this joint you get stuck with the vocalizations of Barry Manilow or someone like that. I'll settle for this. Drop the coins, it's coming in now. It's got the beat, and it's got a sneaky little guitar line that sounds like the footsteps of alligators in the swamp.

Okay, I think I've earned another drink. A finger hooked at the bartender and I've got a little bourbon on the rocks. The schedule now is one sip liquor, two sips water. This method keeps you on your feet for extra hours. Try it sometime.

"Funny weather," Whelan says. He's back and mixing his drink. "Looks like a thunderstorm maybe." I raise my glass to him, the whiskey one.

"Here's to alligators," I say. "Here's to the alligators down in the sewers under our feet."

"Alligators," Whelan says. He drinks. I drink. I take two sips of water.

"I don't much think that's true," Whelan says. "I never believed that story."

"Well, maybe it's not true," I say. "But it would be funny if it was. Think how they hate us all, those alligators down there. They're down there getting bigger all the time and storing up resentment. I hate little Johnny, he flushed me down the toilet. Then one day, boom, enormous alligators. Eating up subway trains under Times Square."

"Sure," Whelan says. "What was it we were talking about before?"

"Okay," I say. "What's your name?"

"What do you mean, what's my name? You know my name."

"What's your name?"

"Tommy Whelan," Whelan says, exasperated. "Okay? You happy?"

"How do you know?"

"How do I know? How do I know? I got a birth certificate."

"Seen it lately?"

"All right. I know because people call me that. Everybody calls me Tommy Whelan, then I'm Tommy Whelan. Right answer?"

"Check. How about when you're getting shot at. You think, hey, I'm Tommy Whelan, getting shot at?"

"Hell no, I don't think that."

"Think any words at all?"

"No. Not if I'm getting shot at. I don't think nothing. I just do."

"Aha," I say. "This leads us to an important point."

"This leads us straight to the nut house as far as I can see," Whelan says.

"Not at all," I say. "Well, maybe. But no matter."

"If you say so," Whelan says. "Here's to no matter."

"Right you are," I say, with another hit on the bourbon. But in my private mind I make this one a toast to the Socratic method. It helps you keep your cool.

Santa Barbara

So I going now through the full dark. This dark feeling heavy and wet and hot on me now. Now boom goes, and it thunder one time. Boom and thunder again. Not too much I hear it thunder in this city. Most times it too much other noise going on all around. Boom, I hear the thunder sounding. It feel like it giving me strength. Thunder coming from Chango. I going fast down Forsyth Street, alongside this park. Not seeing nobody move nowhere.

I going by Delancey and Broome and coming onto Grand. Past the corner there I seeing one man moving. It stop me a minute there. I not thinking to see anyone. I stand back in the shadow and I watching him. But it only one small man. Hair cut close by he head, and one small gold ring in the ear. I seeing him stand in the light from the door. Now he make with the key and he going inside. The door banging closed behind him when he go. I stop where I standing and think for one minute. It time for thinking what I going to do.

I could go maybe to the ileocha of Martinez my yubbona. But if I wake him now, four in the morning, he dont like this I know. Then the questions he must ask. Who is this dead one you talk of? For what you calling him babalawo when no one know him ever? And all I got to say to him, I know it true. Maybe he dont believe. Then he dont help me. So I dont go. I dont go to Martinez. This thing is for my doing it alone.

If there be only someone for talking and giving advice. But I dont got so much time for using up. Daylight coming on soon. When the light come, then the babalawo end up in a garbage truck maybe. I got to move him quick out of the park some way. How? How? No way can I walk around with him on my back. If I doing anything like this then the law coming to say something to me sure. No way any taxi going to pick up him. I laugh thinking this. It the voice of Yanni-B speaking in me, to say such a thing. But no time now for laughing. Time now for the good idea.

I touching my elekes, think now. The thunder stopping. The air get some lighter. Not too much. I feeling under the beads of my elekes and I finding this small small wire. Around my neck too this wire. At ends of wire be heads of two little steel alligators kissing mouth on mouth. So I know what I going to do. It some stupid I dont think it before. Maybe it only because my head tired out from holding Eleggua inside.

Dont matter this, now I know what to do. Some few cars standing right here on Forsyth, but better I go more far away. Somebody see me from building windows, and they calling cops maybe. Then they finding me in two three blocks. East the better way to go. I closing my hand over my alligator clips and I going off east on Grand now.

One two my feet beating fast on the street. Dont see no cars parking on Grand Street. Not all the way to Allen Street, no cars. Allen a wide street and got trees down the middle. I going in the middle and walking under the trees. It feel good to me now to walk on dirt and be under these trees. It seem good to do after too much time walking concrete. I following the trees till Allen meet Delancey. There I turning east again.

Delancey Street empty all the way down. No one walks. It a wide street too and many stores and places along. But no one walking here so late. Only thing moving is some big truck coming out of Brooklyn. Big trucks coming down off the bridge. They making sound like thunder again coming over. I look up to the sound and seeing the lights of the bridge going off in the sky. Trucks going on past me to the Bowery behind. Then nothing, nobody.

Now I stopping by a car standing in front of fabric store. Car fine car to me. Dont much matter how it is. American car. Big Buick maybe. I looking in at the window of store. Much lights still turned on in there. So no one breaking in at night. I going up to the gate and looking in. See all the cloths hanging from the ceiling. Big pieces all different cloths, hanging in the light. No one there inside I can see.

I looking back to the big car. I holding my alligators. I break off they mouth where they kissing, hold them loose in my hand. Thinking. I know they no be any place open the whole way down Delancey. Except the coffee store up at Clinton where the bridge touching down. And way back down off the Bowery the hotel where the whore standing outside. But the hotel too far to even see. Still I dont feel so good for taking this car. It too much light all over the street. All the storefronts throwing out light, and the lamps in the street. It make Delancey bright like the daytime. Maybe some man not sleeping still, in the rooms above the stores. I dont risk it. I wrapping alligators few times over my wrist and snapping they mouth back together again. Going back down the side streets for trying down there.

Going down Essex Street now. It good and dark down here. Up high even the sky black and heavy. No light shine anywhere in this sky. No lamp on the street or by the doors of the buildings. But nobody leaving any car on a street so dark either. Two blocks fast walking and nothing comes. I worry some little. But now I seeing a car up another street. Little bit over on Grand. Other side from project house tower.

I going up to this car quick. It looking good to me. Little Japanese car. Body on it some beat up, and the tires way low. But I dont care nothing for that. Not if it roll. I feeling now up under the hood for the latch. My fingers touching and pulling and the latch click open. I lift on the hood and pushing it back. No engine inside this car. Somebody getting here before me.

It make me feel bad. It making me feel like the luck go against me now. But what I think that for now? I know better. No such thing as luck to me. What happening belong to the orishas. It for them to say and make happen. And I know too well this thing given to me by the orishas for me doing it.

I going now to the corner of Ludlow. Not too far now from ileocha of Martinez. But still I dont go there. Standing by the corner. I taking the alligators from off my wrist. I loose they mouth and fit back together so it make a V. Touching my elekes now. Holding the jar of Eleggua, asking him. Show me how I must go. I throw alligators straight up in air and listen for where they going to fall. They falling, and I step quick to where I hear the noise. It so dark I got to light up a match to see what the alligators going to tell me. I light the match and I seeing where the alligators pointing me to on Ludlow Street uptown.

Now going just as far as the next corner and stopping there. I asking Eleggua again, and throwing the alligators high. When I lighting the match this time the alligators show me to go west on Broome Street. Now I going that way. I coming up to the corner of Orchard. Looking every way. Down Orchard a little bit I see a car.

Now I going over to this car. I know this got to be the one. American car. May be a Ford. I dont know. I dont care. Clicking the hood open. Nobody stripping this car yet. Good. Good. I letting the alligators bite on here and here. Going back around to the driver side door. It locked. All the doors locked. I going back up quick to the corner. Where I pass by a trash pile before. Digging in this trash till I find one piece stiff wire. I taking this up in my hand and putting a hook on one end. Go back by the car and fish down under the window. Sliding the hook around till it catch something. Now something catching and I pulling up and the lock lifting up inside.

Getting inside now and reaching around. I finding the gear stick up under the wheel. Putting it in neutral. Put my foot down outside and push. But I cant move it this way. Car too big, too heavy. I getting out and pushing on the frame and turning the wheel out. Car rolling out on the street now. I bend down and give one good push and jump back inside. Car still rolling, but slow. Put it in gear and pop clutch out. It dont start. Not moving fast enough. It stopped dead now.

Back out and pushing it again. It hot still and much water in the air. I sweating while I pushing. Car going over a little hump on the street and going faster now. I jump back inside this car. Putting my foot on clutch. Now I seeing lights come up behind. Another car turning down Orchard and coming. I worrying too much now. If car dont start this time then maybe I have to run. If I running I lose my alligators. Then I dont know what I going to do.

But here the street going a little bit down. It feel to me like the car moving some faster now. Only thing to do is try. The lights behind close now. I pop clutch out and push my foot on gas. The car choke and turn over. I pushing gas and it jumping ahead. Good. Good. Running. I put in next gear and switch on lights.

I make the right on Grand. Other car behind it following me on the turn. I worrying maybe I going wrong way on this street. Dont drive much in the city. I not sure which way it supposed to go. This car behind me, I hoping he not a cop. I make the right on Allen Street but he still following me. Cant see him good enough to know if it a cop or not. Dont want to keep looking back. Driving now slow up to Delancey. Sweating too much now. I come to Delancey when light changing. I make the left. Car still coming behind me. But under the lights of Delancey I seeing well he not a cop. Anyway got no lights on the car and no marks.

I breathing easier now. Wipe off the sweat from my head. Rolling down the window to let in the little breeze. It so hot now and the air so heavy. This little wind feel good to me. Car behind me coming up and passing by in other lane. Dont have to worry about him no more. It feel good now to drive this car. I making much money with Yanni-B, maybe one day soon I buy a car for my own.

But I forgetting something I must do. Now holding wheel in my left hand and taking the jar of Eleggua up into my right hand. I making a prayer, a thank you for Eleggua. For him leading me by the crossroads. And now I taking the eleke of Oshun into my hand, the yellow bead necklace. It hang by the eleke of Chango. Oshun the sister of Chango and the lover too. Now I make a thank you to Oshun for the help coming to me through the alligators. To Oshun belong all the rivers where the alligators living.

Now I finished with that I need to do. It better always to thank. The orishas, they always listening. They knowing what you think about. They knowing if you give respect or if you dont. So now it done well and I watch where the car going again. But already I go too far. I going past Second Avenue already and coming up on the Bowery. Passing through the park now and it too late to turn. Couple black whore walking out from the hotel and coming toward the car. They faces grinning at my window. I pass them on by. I turn down on the Bowery and looking back to see where they shaking the hip at me.

But this not any time for the whores. Time now to go for the babalawo. Get him in this car before somebody else finding him down there. I making a turn on Grand Street and driving back to Roosevelt Park. Pass through the park where the street go through it. There by the subway stop. I turning now uptown on Forsyth Street. Driving slow on the left side. Looking close at the benches and trees there. Look for where I sitting before. Now here I coming up on it. Here the same bench standing, and the rail that go around the pit.

So I stopping the car. Best way I leave it running. Look at the gas marker now. It gas enough for running some little time. I take out of gear and find the brake and push down. Getting out of the car and going over by the rail.

Cant see nothing down there. Too dark and the candle all burned up long time ago. But I feel him. I feel him down there still. Still waiting for me to come. Now I go down and carry him. I going over to where the stairs are now and going down. Walking straight over to where I know he lie. I wait for my eye widening so I see. Now I see the edges of the bottle piece shining. Now I see the babalawo head lying in between the pieces. I bending down and reaching my hands out for taking him up.

But something stop me now. I stop before I touching him. I standing back up on my feet. Maybe it better if I find something for wrapping him in. Before I move him anywhere. Sure that way it better if anybody see me. Also too I think it better respect to the babalawo. To let him have a covering for this journey.

I go now back to the stairs and up. Come back by the car and open up back doors. Feeling on the floor and finding something feel like wool. I pull it out of the car. It a blanket I holding. Good. I put on the lights of the car and see this blanket be red. That seem good to me too. It some worn, but it clean enough. I using it to cover the babalawo. Close up the doors of car now, and put out lights. I going back down the stairs now, with this red blanket in my hands.

Porco

Ah. Rebel music. Let us now collect our thoughts. Maybe we want to give them to the poor. And take two sips of water, for safety's sake.

"Now," I say. And I signal for more water, light another Camel, pass the pack over to Whelan, who forgot to get any while he was out. "Let's review. You are Tommy Whelan. You know because people call you that. You call yourself Tommy Whelan. Except when you're getting shot at. Let's just call this a condition of severe stress. In this condition, I'm quoting you now, you don't think nothing. You just do."

"Fair enough," Whelan says. "What's it all supposed to mean?"

Why, absolute freedom and power, I think, with the voice kicking at my heart and lungs, it wants to get out and start shouting again, no no no, stop it. Take two sips of water, listen to the nice music. Cool out.

"Just this," I say. "Now suppose you could feel the way you do in this condition of stress like all the time. Then what would you be like?"

"I'd be scared out my pants all the time," Whelan says, chewing at the end of his cigarette. "Doesn't sound like much fun. In fact, I'm here to tell you that it isn't any fun at all. That's why I went off the cops."

"No," I say. "Not the being scared, not that part of it. The not knowing your name. The not thinking in words."

"You mean like being retarded or something?"

"No, I don't mean like being retarded." Patience, oh my soul. "Listen, now. You're in this condition of severe stress. Bang bang, the junkies are shooting at you. And what do you do? You don't start any arguments with them."

"You bet not," Whelan says.

"And you don't even start any arguments with yourself. You don't have to bother with that. In fact, you better not bother with that. You duck. Or you shoot back. You just do something. You don't even have to think about it."

"Okay, okay. But believe you me, it's still no fun to get shot at."

"Fine. I know. But if you could just act that way all the time. Not that you want to feel like you got bullets going by your ears. Just that you don't have any debates with yourself before you go do something."

"Oho," Whelan says. "I think maybe I'm beginning to get you. Keep talking."

"Right," I say. "Wrong. Talking is no good. Talking is just what we want to dispose of."

"No, I don't get you now."

"All right. Now just let me tell you the history of the world."

"Jeez, now?"

"I'll keep it short. In the good old days, before all this talking got started, everybody was very free and easy. Nobody knew what they were up to at all. Everybody just ran around doing what they felt like and didn't worry about it."

"Caveman days, huh?"

"If you say so. Fine. Now let's say, one day one caveman wants to make a deal with another caveman. And to do this, he has to talk, you see? He has to make up some symbols for what he wants to do. He has to make them so the other caveman will know what he's cooking up."

"So?"

"So first of all this is hard to do. Because the signs, the words, they turn out to be a travesty of what the first guy had in mind. As soon as he makes it so the second guy can understand it, it loses something."

"Okay. Maybe so. Then what?"

"Then this goes on for years and pretty soon everybody is talking and making deals. After a lot of deals are made, you have language and writing and stuff like that. Civilization. And cities. Here we are in a nice big city. This city we're sitting in comes about from a lot of talking and dealing. How do you like it?"

"There's not much I can do about it now, if I like it or if I don't."

"True enough. Now. During the same few thousand years, all this talking and dealing gets internalized. People start talking and dealing with themselves. Whatever they do, they see in the mirror. They worry what other people are going to say about them. They worry what they're going to say about themselves. This is called consciousness."

"This is history, you say? Where did you pick this all up from?"

"Around. Don't worry about it."

"I don't know, my friend, but seems like every time I see you have this many drinks you start talking like some kind of a college teacher."

"So listen and you might learn something."

"Okay, then, what's the point?"

"That consciousness isn't natural. Who needs it? It only messes things all up. It interferes with everything. It makes you a slave to the other people. It keeps you from doing what you want."

"Sure, baby, but that's just the way things are."

"For most people. Not for everybody. What if you could turn it off? What if you just didn't care? Then what?"

"You'd be a psycho. You'd be a criminal."

"You'd be happy. That's what's up with our mutual friend. That's why he's a happier man than you and me."

Holy Mother

But sleeping is just no good anymore. I sleep, I dream. I stay awake, then I got to think. No good at all.

I woke up. I was in a bed, in a row of beds. A lot of people were lying on the beds. With IVs and other kinds of doctor machines hooked into them. There was a tube in my arm too. I couldn't feel it. I wasn't hurting anywhere. There was a window at the end of the ward and sunlight coming in.

A doctor came over to my bed. He pulled back the cover. I had on a white nightgown. It came to my knees. It looked silly. My feet were white. I tried to pull up my knees. Nothing happened.

The doctor put his hand on my foot.

"You feel that?" he said.

"I don't feel anything," I said.

The doctor pushed on my legs here and there. I couldn't feel anything. I couldn't move my legs. The doctor rolled me over and touched my back above the waist.

"I feel that," I said.

"Good," the doctor said. He wrote some stuff on a clipboard.

"Where is this place?" I said.

"Hospital," the doctor said.

"I'm out of jail?" I said.

"For now you are," the doctor said. "It doesn't look like you're going anywhere real soon, though." The doctor went to the next bed. I went to sleep. I had a dream.

Somebody comes over from Jersey to talk to Larry. The guy from Jersey has a problem collecting for some drugs he sold to a guy up in Harlem. He has a car and a driver and another guy. He wants an escort up there. Larry gives him me. We drive up to 116th Street. The crib is on the sixth floor. We all go up to the door and look at it. I tell the driver and the other guy to give me ten minutes. I get up to the next floor and find a window on the hall. I go out the window and walk the ledge to the fire escape. I go down to the sixth floor and look in the window. I have a .357 Magnum in my hand, under my coat.

The dealer doesn't have a lot of company. There's a woman there. Maybe it's his wife. She's sitting on the bed by the window where I'm peeping in. I can see into another room and the dealer is sitting in there in a chair. The doorbell rings. The dealer gets up and moves out of my line of sight. I kick in the window. I point the gun at the woman and move her into the next room. The guys from Jersey are already in. They have their pieces out too.

We all sit down in the living room. There's a little argument. The dealer says he doesn't have any money. He says if he did have any he would keep it. He says some bad things about Italians. This goes on for a while, and I get bored and annoyed.

We don't want to mess around anymore, I say. We don't want to waste a lot of time.

The dealer calls me a motherjumping guinea.

Bad things can happen to you, I say. I reach out and break the woman's nose with the barrel of the Magnum. She bleeds down the front of her shirt. The dealer just sits there, keeps calling me names. I hear a baby crying. I go in the bedroom. There's a little nigger baby lying there on the bed, fenced in between two pillows. I pick it up. It shuts up the crying when I do. I take it back in the other room and stand there by the window.

You want to be polite and helpful, I say. Or this kid is going out of this window.

Holy Mother | 155

The dealer says some more bad stuff about me and my family. I put the baby through the window. The window is shut.

I woke up. I was still in the big ward. Johnny was standing at the end of my bed.

"How you feel?" he said.

"I don't feel much of anything," I said. "How is things down in the city?"

"There's some things going on," Johnny said. "I'll tell you about it sometime. You're going to move to a private room, they'll be moving you in a couple of days. Right now I just came up to tell you hello."

"Hello," I said. "I'm tired." I closed my eyes. I thought, What I dreamed should have been a nightmare. It wasn't. It happened. The Jersey people said I was crazy. We tried to beat it out of there. But people in the street had got to the cops. They don't usually do that up there, but seeing the kid drop six flights was too much for a few people—about three people, as it turned out. The cops picked us up in two blocks. I made bail that night. By the next night Larry knew where those three people lived. Go up there and clean up the mess you made, he said. I went up there with the .357. I shot it six times. There wasn't any indictment. In the hospital I went back to sleep. I dreamed about the baby, falling very slowly, the same speed as the broken glass.

I woke up. Johnny was sitting by the bed in an armchair. I was out of the ward, in a little room. There was only the one bed in there.

"You sleep a lot," Johnny said. "I came in here three times already."

"I'm all worn out," I said. "A lot of things happened."

"I know," Johnny said. "I hear that thing didn't work out the way it was supposed to."

"Not at all," I said. "It was one big mess."

I went back to sleep. I dreamed about falling down a deep stairwell. I fall very slowly, like I'm floating. At the bottom of the well is a lion on a chain. When I land I'm so close to him I can see meat scraps on his teeth and smell his breath. The lion pulls at the chain. It breaks.

I woke up. Johnny was still sitting there in the chair. Maybe it was another day.

"You sleep a lot," Johnny said. "You want to hear some things? I checked the room out, it's clean."

"Okay," I said. "What's going on?"

"Not too much is really going on now," Johnny said. "But people are still feeling kind of nervous over Joe Colombo."

I didn't say anything.

"You remember Joe Colombo?"

"Sure I do, he's the big boss man."

"Not anymore he's not. Not since June. For Christ's sake, did you fall on your head or what?"

"Sorry. I got a lot of things on my mind."

"Okay then, listen. Colombo started the League, a little while back, you know? To stop all the bad press on Italians, let people know there's really no such thing as the Mafia, all that, right?"

"Yeah, I remember that."

"And it was getting to be a very big thing. A lot of rallies, big rallies in the park, lot of members, and every member pays some dues so the money is rolling in. And they're taking *The Untouchables* off the air. Even taking Alka-Seltzer commercials off the air. Big stuff. Civil rights for Italians."

"So what makes people nervous?"

"I don't know. It seems like Colombo is skimming a lot of money off the top of this thing, so maybe he makes a few people mad at him. Also Joey comes back to town. You remember Joey, right? Un Paz, the Crazy One, our old friend, you know?"

"Yeah."

"So back in June the League has a big rally up in Central Park. Colombo is up there, of course."

"And then what happens."

"Somebody shoots him in the head a few times. In front of about a million people and his family and all. So he's not the boss anymore. In fact, he's not much of anything anymore. He's lying up in a hospital somewhere, and he doesn't wake up at all is what I hear."

"Yeah, I remember about this now. It's coming back, but it's fuzzy. Who got to him?"

"A black kid, kid named Johnson. He pulled the trigger."

"A black kid. Joey have something to do with this?"

"No one says for sure. There's a story it was someone closer in. You remember Jerry Ciprio?"

"Ciprio, yeah, he was Colombo's bodyguard."

"Right. Well, when Colombo takes it, Jerry Ciprio is somehow not around. Then about five seconds later, he is around. In fact, he's right there blowing Johnson's head apart, so Johnson never gets to talk to anybody."

"Ciprio stepped aside, you think. He let Colombo take the fall."

"It's what some people say."

"Ciprio was in pretty tight with Joey, I recall."

"So they say. But nobody is talking about it too much. Besides, Joey was away a long time."

"He busy now?"

"He's doing all right now. He's got most of the South Brooklyn stuff back."

"Oh yeah? I thought Colombo took all that over, while Joey was at college."

"He did. But Joey seems to have it back now."

"That's nice for Joey. So who's the man now?"

"No one seems to know. But Joey seems to think it's him."

"That's nice. We always get along with Joey."

"Yeah. Only it seems there might be a few people that disagree."

I went to sleep. I had a dream. I'm in a big tenement up in the South Bronx. I'm in an empty elevator shaft in the middle of the building. I have some gas and some blocks of paraffin and some fuse that I'm stringing up the shaft. After I go away from there, the fire goes up the building like a rocket. Next day I read in the paper, a few people got killed in a fire. The newspaper starts burning in my hands. I try to drop it. It won't fall. My hands are burning.

I woke up. It was nighttime. No one was there. I buzzed the nurse and got a pitcher of water. I lay there and thought about things. I tried to stay awake for a while. I tried to remember how I got there.

_____

I remember: I'm a nice little kid. I got a very nice lady for my mother. My father I don't remember. My mother tells me he passed away from a severe illness about the time I get born. When I get older, I find out that this illness is a kind of lead poisoning that comes on real sudden. But for a long time I don't know anything about this, and my mother takes me out to the cemetery, and we lay flowers on a grave, and I say a rosary like she shows me how to do, for the peace of the soul of my father. And she cries, and she tells me she knows I'm going to be a good boy and keep out of trouble, and I say yes, that's what I'm going to do. She tells me to pray to the Holy Virgin for the soul of my father and for my soul and her soul too, because the Holy Virgin has all the mercy and she whispers it into the ear of God, and it takes mercy to protect you from Sin, no matter how good you are. So I pray to the Virgin, like she says, and I'm in the Catholic school, and every week I go to confession. Also I get pretty strong, for a little kid, so if anybody gives me a hard time about how I am, then maybe I give them a fat lip. But if I do I confess it on Saturday.

I have a little cousin. His name is Gianni Dellacroce, and he is a wild kid, even when he's only about ten. He has a little gang of kids, and they raise a lot of hell here and there, and one year they all start calling me Holy Mother, which makes me mad. I figure it's Gianni that thinks of this name, so I give him a fat lip one day, and then they all leave me alone for a while. Then the next year it comes up again, only Gianni gets bigger over the summer, and when I go to give him a fat lip, instead he knocks me down. I'm sitting on the asphalt in the playground feeling kind of surprised, and Gianni looks kind of surprised himself, and he squats down beside me and says, "Hey. Hey, what are we fighting for, anyway, why don't we be friends?" "Okay," I say, "only quit calling me that name all the time." "Okay," he says, "just don't be so holy all the time, and we can stop calling you that." "Okay," I say, and Gianni says, "Hey, let's go around to the candy store and boost some magazines." Which we do.

Then about five more years go by, and Johnny and I stay good friends, and I don't go to confession no more, and my mother, she has to do all the praying now. It's summertime, I think maybe 1960, and it's very hot down Mulberry Street, so Johnny and I are walking around in the early evening, trying to get cool by drinking a lot of beer. We walk up till we get to Spring Street, and there's a brand-new Porsche sitting outside the little café up there. The motor is running, but no one is inside and no one seems to be watching, so Johnny says, "Let's go for a ride," and the next thing I know we're in Coney Island. We pick up a couple of girls there maybe, and we go to Jones Beach and play in the sand, and sometime the next morning we dump the car on the Bowery and go home to sleep for a couple of days.

Then about a week later, we take a walk across Spring Street again, which is probably not a good idea, but we do it. We go in the Spring Lounge and get a couple of beers and take them out to drink in that little playground across the street, which is on the other corner from that same café. We sit there drinking our beers and trying to think of something to do, and a long black car pulls up by the playground. Then we think we might like to leave, only we can't, because there's a fence around the playground and the car is stopped across the gate. A man gets out and comes over there to us, and he says, "Go get in the car." Johnny and I look at each other, and we don't say anything, but we both figure we have to do what the man says, because we know who he is, all right.

His real name is Albert Gallo, but most people are calling him Kid Blast, and he's fairly well known in the neighborhood even though he lives over in Brooklyn with his big brothers Joey and Larry. Them and one other guy are famous as the Barbershop Quartet, ever since they got to see Albert Anastasia while he's getting a haircut and play him a concert with pistols. Before this happens to him, Anastasia is famous himself, because he runs a business called Murder Inc., and when people don't show up anymore, you figure Anastasia has something to do with it. But now when people don't come around anymore, it's maybe the Gallos that know where they are, and they are mobbed up with Joe Profaci, who let out the contract on Anastasia, and everybody knows all about that. So we don't argue. We get in the car.

The car is done up very nice inside, and there's a couple of other guys in there that we don't recognize, and they don't say hello. The car starts rolling, and Johnny asks what it's all about, but he doesn't get any answer. The car rolls along for an hour or so, and when it stops we're in Brooklyn on President Street. "Get out," the guys say. We get out and they take us in a building, they put us in the stairway that goes to the cellar and bolt the door behind us. It's dark and we can't find any light switch at the head of the stairs, and we got no idea what's going on.

"What the hell," Johnny says, "let's go down and see what's there." We go down in the cellar and it smells real funny. "Let's find a light," Johnny says. "There's something down here besides us." I feel on the wall and I find a switch. I flip it and we both freeze. The thing that's down there with us is a lion. A real lion like TV or the zoo. It's coming our way and the only reason it can't get to us is it's chained to a little bracket in the wall. I'm scared but good. "Let's get out of here," I say. "How we going to do that?" Johnny says. "I think we better tough it out." So we stand real still, as far away from the lion as we can get. Some time passes, and a door opens up at the other end of the cellar.

We know who this guy is too. It's Joey Gallo, and no mistake. He's all dressed up in pinstripes and got on shoes that look like spats, like he's going to be in a movie or something. But this is real, and Joey is grinning at us all over his ugly face.

"Hello, boys," he says. "I wanted you to come out here and meet my pet."

Then it's quiet for a while, and Joey looks at us, and the lion looks at us.

"Thanks a lot," Johnny says. "We didn't do nothing to bother you, did we?"

"You might have," Joey says. "You boosted a car belongs to a friend of mine."

"Jesus," Johnny says, "we didn't know. If we knew, we wouldn't have done it."

"You don't get any points for being stupid," Joey says. "You get a few for having nerve though."

We don't say nothing. I'm not even breathing.

"There's three things I can do with people got nerve," Joey says. "I can put them in the river. I think you saw the river on your way in. I can feed them to my lion here. Or I can give them a job. You boys need a job?"

"We're dying for a job," Johnny says. Joey laughs.

"Okay then," Joey says, "come on upstairs and we'll talk."

I went to sleep. I woke up. The doctor came in.

"You're getting an operation," he said. "Roll over, I got to give you a shot." I tried to turn myself over with my arms. Too weak. An orderly came in and flipped me. I couldn't feel the needle. The orderly put me on a cart and I rolled into another room. A mask was on my face. It was sweet. It made me sick.

I woke up. I puked in a basin. Johnny put the basin away on the floor somewhere. He cleaned my mouth with a wet cloth.

"I'm sorry," Johnny said. "I'm really sorry." He put his hand on my knee. I couldn't feel it. I closed my eyes.

"The doctor says they can try again," Johnny said. "You still got a chance." I went to sleep. I had nightmares. I woke up.

1960 turns out not to be the best possible time for making friends with Joey Gallo. What he's mostly making about this time is enemies. But to me and Johnny it don't seem too bad at first. What Joey ends up having us do is to go out and take numbers around Bed-Stuy. The game out there is supposed to belong to old man Profaci, but we don't know about that. Since the Anastasia hit, Joey feels like he should have his own private piece of it. Since several other up-and-coming types feel sort of the same, things aren't too tough for me and Johnny. We'd go out there and collect from the spics and the niggers. Every couple of months we introduce ourselves on a couple of new blocks. If there's already somebody else there, maybe there's an argument, but we both carry little pieces of pipe we know what to do with, and we watch each other's back. If things get too hot, we know there's somebody behind us. And the money is good. When we go back in Manhattan we got bucks in our pockets and we got some respect because of who we're with.

So about a year goes by like this, and one night Joey calls us into the fort over on President Street. Kid Blast and Larry are up there sitting around a big table, and so are a couple of other people, and there's two new-looking pieces lying there in the middle of the table.

"You boys been doing real good," Joey says. "I been thinking I like to give you a new project." He looks at the guns on the table.

"There's more for you in this one," he says. He names a price.

"It's got to be a hit," Johnny says.

"It's a hit," Joey says.

"Who is it?" Johnny says.

"No way," Joey says. "I ain't telling you before you say if you want it or not."

"Okay," Johnny says, "do we get to think it over?"

"Yeah," Joey says, "why don't you take a walk around the block and come back in a few minutes."

So we take a walk around the block.

"I don't like this at all," I say, "and I don't want in."

"I don't know," Johnny says. "We better think about it."

"Yeah, I'm thinking," I say, "and what I'm thinking is, we could do some big time for this."

"Maybe not," Johnny says. "We're juveniles, remember. Besides, who says we get caught?"

"If we don't get caught, maybe we get unpopular with somebody," I say. "I want to live to grow up, you know?"

"Look," Johnny says, "I think we better do it. There's two reasons."

"What are they?"

"One is if we do it, we're made around here. We'll pull more weight than we do now, a lot more."

"Maybe the other reason's better?"

"It is. The other reason is if we don't do this now, I think somebody's going to do it to us later."

We went back to the fort.

"Well?" Joey says.

"We're taking it," Johnny says.

"Good," Joey says. He gives us a name. It's a Brooklyn guy, we don't even know him. Joey don't say why he's getting whacked, and we don't ask. He tells us where we can find him, several places.

"You got two weeks for this," Joey says. "My advice is you follow this guy for a while and watch him. He knows something is up already. In a few days he'll break his pattern and you can take him on the street."

So that's what we do. We follow this guy around for a while. Sometimes we even eat in the same restaurant with him or drink in the same bar. He's just an ordinary old guy to look at, in his forties or so. But it's funny how nobody seems to want to talk to him, any of these places he goes. It's like he's a ghost and nobody can see him but us.

In a few days we think we're ready. The guy has quit hanging in his usual spots and he spends a lot of time just walking around by himself. The night before we go out and steal a car. Already I'm so nervous I'm shaking and sweating.

"You don't have to sweat it," Johnny tells me. "I know I got us into this, and I'm doing the shooting. All you got to do is drive. The only way you pull the trigger is if I slip up, and I don't think that's going to happen."

The next morning we're up real early, because the guy always is up early too, he walks a couple of blocks to a bakery when not very many people are around. So we get about halfway down along the path he takes, and we're sitting in the car. We can see the guy coming a good block away because of this old-style hat he wears around. Johnny pulls his piece and checks the load.

"Start the car now," he says. "You don't want a problem starting, not today."

I start the car. "I'm going now," Johnny says. "I'm taking him on the other corner. When you see him drop, you pull out and pick me up." Johnny gets out of the car. I watch him cross the street and stand by the lamppost. The guy is coming, getting closer. Johnny takes his gun out and aims it at his head. The guy looks at him. He don't slow down or speed up. Johnny don't shoot. The guy walks right past him. Johnny turns around. He still has the gun up but he still isn't shooting. I watch the guy crossing the street toward me. I take the other piece off my belt and get out of the car. I hold it out at the guy and start pulling the trigger. The first couple of bullets knock him over. I keep squeezing, all body shots. I keep jerking the trigger. I feel cold. Then Johnny is pulling my arm.

"Come on, come on," he says. "This guy is as dead as he's going to get; we got to get out of here." I look at my hand. I'm still dry-snapping the gun, how long I've been doing it I don't know. The guy is on the ground and not moving. I keep jerking the trigger, it's like I can't stop. Johnny drags me to the car and pushes me in the back seat.

"Snap out of it, snap out of it," he says. He's sweating all over his face.

"I feel okay," I say. "Gimme the other gun." I take the other gun and brace my arms on the window of the car. I put a couple of shots in the guy's head so he won't turn up alive sometime later. Johnny punches the gas and takes off out of there.

"I'm sorry, I'm sorry," he says. "I don't know what went wrong with me."

"It's okay," I say, "it don't matter." I pick up the empty gun and start dry-snapping it again, out the window. I'm still doing this when we get to the river, and Johnny takes it away from me and throws it and the other one into the water.

I went to sleep, I woke up. Johnny was sitting in the armchair.

"I got some good news," he said.

"About what?" I said.

"We've been working on a few people in the courts," he said. "I've got a new lawyer on your case."

"What's going on?" I said.

"Reduction to time served. I hope."

"That's nice."

"Nice, hell, you're going to get sprung, can you hear me?"

"It's nice," I said. "When you get through with that, see if you can spring me out of this bed." I closed my eyes. I went to sleep.

We go back to report to Joey that the hit was good. He gives us the money, a lot of money. Next couple of months we do a couple more hits. Johnny drives now, and I pull the trigger. Johnny don't like it much, but it don't bother me. And the money is good for both of us. I buy a nice new car, some other stuff. But people are starting to turn up dead all over. And the next thing you know, it's a gang war.

The trouble is, nobody likes old man Profaci anymore. Practically none of the younger guys in the family. This takes in the Gallos and the Persicos and Joe Yack, and they swing about half of the Profaci guns with them. So it's a real mess. It starts because Profaci don't like to give people enough for what they do for him, and he interferes when they do things for themselves, and the guys are tired of this. They want to put a little pressure on Profaci, persuade him to treat them nicer. So there's a lot of shooting going on, and President Street starts to look like an army post or something, and no one can really tell exactly what's going on. Joey Gallo wants all the guns he can get, but Larry Gallo don't want me and Johnny around so much anymore, maybe because we're still juveniles. So he tells us to get the hell back to Manhattan and stay out of sight and call up if we hear anything interesting, and that's what we do.

And it's lucky for us that we do it, because right after we get out of there everything screws up for the Gallos. Because now Joey wants to whack everybody on the other team, everybody, and the Persicos and Joe Yack think that's going too far. So it ends up that they break up with the Gallos, and what they do then is go have a sit-down with the old man, Carlo Gambino, and they tell him that Joey is off the wall altogether. Carlo says, "Okay, you settle it among yourselves, and I'll keep Profaci out of it for you, so you won't have any trouble at that end."

Then Snake Persico calls Larry Gallo to go have a peace meet at a closed-down bar on Utica Avenue. Larry is dumb enough to go, and when he gets there the Snake starts to choke him with a rope, and the only reason he doesn't die then is that a cop wonders why the side door is open and comes in to see.

So Larry gets away that time, and now everybody knows what's up. But the Gallos don't have many friends any longer. They only have about twenty people left, in fact, and they're barricaded on President Street, and they don't go out much at all. And probably it ends with a lot more people getting killed, only about this same time Joey gets nailed on an extortion thing, and he goes up to Ossining. Once he's gone everybody decides to try talking again.

Now Larry is running the Gallo show, and old man Profaci dies of natural causes. This makes some more confusion, because the first guy to succeed him gets in the soup with Joe Bananas, and he loses his head. Then the next guy to come in is Joe Colombo, and he makes a deal with Larry, who is always easier to deal with than Joey. Larry goes back in the family, which is now the Colombo family, and me and Johnny go back out to Brooklyn and work for Larry.

Larry has a piece of the Bed-Stuy numbers officially now, and he puts Johnny out there as a button man, which is a good deal for Johnny. I get kept around as an enforcer and sometimes a hit man, and it's okay for me too. I have a knack for the work, and the money is even better than it used to be. If Larry don't need me himself, he lends me to somebody, so I get around a lot and I keep busy. Johnny don't go out on hits anymore. It's my private party, and I'm doing well enough to get married and buy a house to put my wife in. When I have a job, which is often, I go alone. I go do whatever it is, and I dump the gun and the car afterward, and then I go home and watch TV or crawl in the bed with my wife if it's late, or whatever. I sleep like a log and I don't worry about nothing.

Everything rolls along pretty smooth for a few years. Nothing much goes wrong at all, until Larry gets cancer and he dies. Joey is still on vacation, so Kid Blast is supposed to be running things, only he can't do it because he's too much of an idiot. He can't even hold on to what he has, and Colombo is getting it all away from him, and Kid Blast can't figure out what to do. People start to get nervous again, because it looks like there could be some more shooting. Only all of a sudden everybody is in bad trouble with the law, and personally, I take the fall. Then I go on vacation myself and it's not my problem anymore for a while.

I woke up. The doctor was standing at the end of the bed.

"We're going to try it again," he said.

"What are the chances?" I said.

"Fair," the doctor said. "We won't kill you, anyway, and we might get you on your feet again."

"Okay," I said. We went through the same number with the shots and the orderly and the little meat wagon. I had the mask on my face.

"Breathe deep," they said.

———

I woke up. The doctor was back at the end of the bed.

"You feel anything in your legs now?" he said.

"I feel the worst goddamn pain I ever had," I said. "And my back, the bottom of my back, it's killing me."

"That's good," the doctor said. "That's very good."

"No it's not," I said. "It's terrible. Can't you give me a shot or something?"

"We gave you a shot," the doctor said.

"Well, give me another one," I said. "This one's not working."

I woke up. Johnny was sitting in the armchair.

"Congratulations," Johnny said. "You're going to walk one of these days."

"I hurt bad," I said. "Get the nurse in here." I hit the buzzer. The nurse came in with the needle. Then she went back out. I felt better.

"You want to watch that," Johnny said. "Don't get any bad habits."

"Well, they're the doctors," I said.

"I don't think they're going to say no to you," Johnny said. "You're going to have to watch yourself."

"What do you say we talk about something else for a while," I said. "What's going on in the city?"

"No action much, yet. But I'm getting some funny feelings."

"Who about?"

"Joe Yack, mostly."

"That bastard."

"Joe Yack is definitely a bastard. I don't like him, and he doesn't like me, or you either, for that matter, all because of Joey too. Yack doesn't like Joey, never did. And on top of that he's a creeping crawling nut case, I think."

"Well, who's got the button?"

"I don't know, and I don't think anyone else does either. I think maybe Joe Yack would like to whack Joey over the Colombo thing still. But it's been a few months now and nothing seems to happen."

"Who is Joe Yack to let a contract anyway? He running the Colombos now?"

"No, not officially. Officially it's Vinnie Aloi. But you know Vinnie, he's practically a stockbroker. I think Yack is running a big end of it."

"That's not so good, maybe."

"Maybe it's not. You can't trust Yack to even be reasonable. He's the most paranoid guy I ever even hear about. Anytime he goes somewhere he changes cars three times. Lives out in Jersey in a house with his mother, and he's got an eighteen-foot fence and dogs and I don't know what else, a machine-gun nest on top of the house, maybe, or a mine field in the front yard. And anybody that runs scared like that is going to be dangerous, and the one he's scared of right now is Joey, I think."

"So why don't he move?"

"The story seems to be that old man Carlo put the word out that Joey gets left alone. That the old man doesn't miss Colombo too much, because of some problems they had over the League and all that."

"That's good then. Everybody listens to Don Carlo. I guess they still do. Joey happy?"

"Who knows what he thinks about? He gets around plenty though, that's for sure. He's playing around with a lot of celebs uptown and they tell me he's writing a book. He just got married again. And he's moving in on the Persicos."

"Is that a good idea?"

"I really can't tell you. The Snake is away, you know, so that's a help. But personally, I think Joey is moving a little too fast. I think maybe he should slow down some."

"You tell him that?"

"Who am I to tell him that? He won't listen to me, he won't listen to anybody. He's still Un Paz, he hasn't changed. I don't see him so much anymore."

A woman started coming to give me therapy. She would bend my legs back till my knees were in my mouth, that kind of thing. She had muscles on her like a hockey player. It hurt like a bitch.

I kept on having the dreams, the bad ones. I'd wake up shaking, sometimes twice in a night. I had some money around by then and I made a deal with the night nurse for shots off the record. It was the wintertime. Snow piled up on the ledge outside my window. The pain was very bad.

The pain was always there. I remember it so well now, better than anything else, really. I think I'll have another shot. I think I'll open up my pants and put one on the inside of my thigh. If you're going to shoot, you might as well get high. That's better now.

I woke up. Johnny was in the armchair. I lifted myself by the rail of the bed and took a step and a half to my wheelchair. It hurt so bad I thought I was going to die. I shut my eyes and ground my teeth. Then I opened my eyes and rolled the chair around the end of the bed to Johnny's side.

"That's good," Johnny said. "Very good."

"Yeah."

"I have the good news. You're out. You got the reduction. You're as free as I am now."

"That's good. That's great. It cost you?"

"Don't worry about it."

"I appreciate it. I do."

I rolled the chair back and forth on the floor.

"What's going on in town?" I said.

"I think something's going to happen maybe. I think maybe Joey stuck his neck out too far."

"Where did he stick it this time?"

"He put too much heat on the Persico people and they got together with Yack. Yack thought it all over, and what I hear is he asked for a sit-down with Carlo."

"And what did you hear Carlo said?"

"No one seems to know for sure. But the argument seems to be that if Joey takes over the Persicos, he's going to go for the Colombos next. If he takes the Colombos, he's going to be a very strong little guy, Joey is. Then maybe Carlo has to worry for himself."

"Yack thought that up? What did Carlo think, you know? It's a good argument."

"It's a very good argument, yes. I think Carlo probably listened to it real careful. The thing is, he doesn't need any problems at all right now, because he's got an extradition problem, you know? So he doesn't want any trouble at all."

"Then maybe Joey's still all right."

"Yeah, and maybe he's not. Because if something happens to him, then maybe it's all over quick. But if nothing happens to him, he's going to keep running around and rocking the boat."

"Is that what you think? You think Carlo dumped him?"

"I don't think about it. I don't think about it at all."

"What does Joey think about it?"

"I don't know that either. All I know is he's running up and down Mulberry Street like nothing's the matter at all. But I don't see him so much anymore. I see him as little as possible."

"Well, who the hell you work for now, anyway?"

"Tell you the truth, I don't even know that. I work for the next guy up, and which way he's going to jump I don't know and I bet you neither does he. But I'm not that busy anyway. I kind of try to just stay out of the way, you know. I've been taking night classes to fill in the time. Because nobody knows what's going on down there, it's too crazy."

Think I'll have another small one. Since my pants are still open. I put it in the left thigh this time. And buckle up my pants, they look silly open like that.

Dreams, nightmares. Free shots. The snow melted off my window ledge. The therapist woman started making me walk. I had a walker to lean on. Up and down the hallways. It hurt me plenty. The weather was warm and my window stayed open even at night by then. If I was lying awake in the early morning, I could hear all the birds carrying on outside. It got warm enough for me to go out of the building. I'd take my wheelchair down on the elevator. The hospital sat in the middle of a park. It was a nice place, upstate somewhere. I would walk around as much as I could stand and then roll around in the chair. The therapist would be there or else Johnny would be.

"Big news," Johnny said. "Big bad news. Somebody cracked the safe at Ferrara's."

"So what do they got in the safe at Ferrara's? What they make in a week selling Cinzano and cookies?"

"That and Vinnie Aloi's whole loan fund. Oh, and Vinne Aloi's books too."

"Jesus. You know who's in it?"

"I hear Jerry Ciprio."

"Yeah, him and who else?"

"Him and some safecrackers, I would guess. But there's another thing I hear."

"What's that?"

"Ciprio's been having a lot to do with Joey lately."

"Oh no. Something's going to happen. Something's going to happen, right?"

"I think so. I think soon."

I started going out without the chair. With just the walker I could move good enough to get from one bench to another in the park. The pain was still bad and the nights were as bad as ever. I had to give the night nurse some more money. She got tired of coming in all the time, so she got me a needle and showed me what to do with it.

So now I know what to do with it. I think I'll have one more cocktail. I roll down my sock and put a little in my ankle. That's the way.

I was sitting on a bench in the park, holding the walker up in front of me. It was a warm day, hot even. Johnny came up the path. He had a bundle of newspapers with him. He was coming fast.

"They hit him," Johnny said. "They got him last night. In Umberto's, and his wife and his sister were there."

"That's bad. That's the worst way."

"Yeah, it's bad all right. But he never should have been there. He had any sense and he wouldn't have even come in the area. But no, he has to go have himself a little birthday party."

"Who made the score?"

"They say it's Sonny Pinto. Pete the Greek was in there with Gallo. He got shot up some himself, but he's not in too bad shape, at least so far. I hear he made Sonny, and there were a couple of guys he didn't make."

"You talk to Pete the Greek?"

"Hell no, I didn't talk to Pete the Greek. I don't even want to know him, not right now."

"Who's Sonny Pinto with now anyway?"

"Sonny Pinto is with Joe Yack," Johnny said, "and they tell me Yack has got a hit list as long as your arm, only nobody knows who's on it for sure."

"Oh, that's great, that's just great. You don't think they're coming up here, do you?"

"No. Not for you. You've been out of it long enough, they'll leave you alone. Me, I'm not sure about that."

"Maybe you should go on a vacation."

"I'm going on one now."

"Where you going to go?"

"I got a motel room over there in Millbrook, nice little town, Millbrook. Lot of fresh air."

"That's good then. Let me know what you hear."

"Oh, I will, I will. I'll stay in touch."

By the fall I could walk okay on crutches. I didn't need the walker anymore. The pain wasn't so bad anymore either, but I still seemed to need a lot of shots. As many as ever, maybe a few more. I didn't know what to make of it at the time. I put it down to the bad nights and the dreaming.

Now I know what to make of it. I'm going in my other ankle. There we go.

Johnny went back to the city, after things settled down some. The next time he was up to see me, I was walking with just a cane. It was hard going, but I could do it. It was cold in the park. I sat on a bench with a big woolly scarf around my neck like I was an old man.

"I got news," Johnny said. "We're off the hook."

"Off what hook?"

"We're out. We're out of the Thing."

"What do you mean, out. Nobody goes out. Except in a box."

"No. Things are changing, a little anyway. I went to see Carlo myself this time. I told him how it was with us. How we hadn't known what to do in ten years under the gun and we were getting tired of it. And you all busted up and everything. And we get loose, is the deal, and nobody is going to bother us. We don't come around and we keep quiet, and we're going to be okay."

"For what did you go and make this deal for me? I never asked you to do it. What are we going to do now? What am I going to do?"

"Look," Johnny said. "You're going to stay alive, first of all. And believe me, this is the only way."

"What are you saying here now? What is this that you're telling me?"

"I'm saying that first of all, nobody loves us anymore down there. Everybody we used to know is in the river or in the ground, I mean everybody."

"Okay. But we could still go in with somebody else, it's the usual way."

"We can't. There's something else, and I don't know if you want to hear it."

"Talk to me."

"All right, you asked. The story down there is that you're junking a lot, you know. I'm not asking you about it, okay, so you don't have to say anything. But that is what the wise guys think, and you know how they feel about things like that, you know it as well as I do. They don't trust you anymore, and you're going to get hit. So I make the deal that we go out together and I'm going to take care of you. Otherwise we both go down, you know?"

"You're out of your mind. If that's the way it is, they're going to hit us anyway."

"They're not. They can't."

"Sure they can, why not?"

"Remember Luparelli?"

"Joe Fish, I remember."

"Well, it turns out that he's driving one of the cars, that night down at the Clam House. And after that he broke up with Joe Yack, and he gave himself up to the FBI. He's turned around, and he's got a lot to talk about, and he's got everybody all tied up in knots. So they don't want to whack anybody else just now, except Joe Fish of course, and I think they're going to hold the murders to a minimum, for a while anyway. Especially Joe Yack can't do anything, and he's the only one that would bother coming after us anyway, just because he's paranoid. But he's all tied up, he can't do anything. I tell you, we're okay."

"All right. I guess it's not a bad deal, maybe. And anyway it's done."

"It's done. We can't go back on it. I'm sorry I couldn't let you know before, but this was the only way."

"It's okay. I can see it now. But what are we going to do?"

"Oh, I don't know." Johnny laughed. "I'll try to think of something."

So Johnny thought of something, and here we all are. It works out pretty neat, all things considered. I got a nice steady source of supply, and that's just so nice for me. But I'm not kicking. I got what I'm due. I might even say I've been lucky. But I don't like it. Not at all. I don't want it anymore.

What do I want?

Mercy, maybe. The forgiveness of sins. The forgiveness of memory. I'd like to get rid of it all.

I get up and move around the room. I'm very tired somehow, feel like I'm swimming through the air. I look at the empty walls. I stop by the picture of the woman and the child and look at that.

Hail Mary, full of grace. . . .

It isn't that easy, not now. No one is listening out there. I haven't got a penance. There's no one that can give me one.

It's a nice picture. A nice picture, I guess it is. I turn back to the table and the chair, the needle and the bag.

I want it stopped. I want out. No dreams, no more thinking. Finish.

I sit down in the chair and load the hypo. How much, I don't really look to see. Just shake some in the cup. I'll take a little chance here.

I look out the window. The loose gate moves in the wind; I think it must be near morning. There's flashes of heat lightning, down east. The gate moans on its hinges.

I feel the side of my neck and press and squeeze until that good big vein comes up. I only did this once or twice before, and then I used a mirror. But I don't want to bother with that now. Besides, I got to sit down. I'm tired already, and if I'm standing up when this hits me, I think I just might fall.

So I set the needle in there by touch. I'm still holding on to the bulb. If I don't let it go, the stuff won't release. I can still take the needle out of my neck. Maybe I will.

I look at the window. Lord, show me a sign. But I can't even see the window, not really. There's too much in the way.

I let go of the bulb.

I can feel it working. It's finally doing what it's supposed to. I don't feel anything now. My thoughts are gone. I see the end of the table and the windowsill. I see the window, the swinging gate, a few raindrops on it now. And now I see nothing. I see nothing. Nothing.

Porco

"So what you're saying is, he's a guy with no conscience, right?" Whelan says. "And that makes him happy, well I think that's great. Me, I'd rather be unhappy, I think, that's what it takes."

"So would I, if it comes to that," I say. And saying it, in fact, I do feel very unhappy. I don't have a good snappy answer, I'm losing my chain of thought. I'm tired and I'm drunk and I wish there was some place I could go to and sleep for a while, just some place, not a hotel, not some jerk that owes me a favor, well, no use thinking about that. I'm not the only one, for sure, I can feel the Stone, dragging my coat pocket down, the weight of all that unvoiced misery. Happy people have nothing to say for themselves, after all. Wake up, here we go again.

"It's the wave of the future though," I say. "There's more and more people like that running around, they'll put us all out of business in another hundred years or so."

"I don't get you," Whelan says. "Guys like that, don't give a damn, they've always been around. I used to deal with them in a business way, you know, down at the precinct. And I could walk down this street and round up a couple of dozen right now."

"Not like him," I say. "There's a difference, try to understand." But it hardly seems worth trying to explain it, maybe I don't understand it myself. Maybe I'm wrong.

"I'm trying," Whelan says. "But I can't do it, is all. You got a guy, small-time wise guy, or ex-wise guy if you say so, not that I believe that—what's different about him? What's he got the rest of them don't?"

"Nothing is what," I say. "A whole lot of nothing. He's got nothing on his mind, you know, and that gives him a good imagination. There's not so much already sitting there, so he can put whatever else in he wants to. Very good at forgetting things too, he is."

"I'll back you on that one," Whelan says. "Got some things to forget, I think."

"Oh, that," I say, and I try to wave the remark away with my hand. But my hand just flops down on the bar like a dead bird. "I don't care about that, beside the point. Those things he used to be into were just around for him to be into, an accident. If something else had been around he would have been in that instead. And I didn't even know him then. I don't think about that, I doubt he does either."

"Sure he doesn't," Whelan says. "There's some people that do though. There's some people that remember him, I think."

"Maybe there are," I say. "Though from what you tell me and what I pick up, a lot of them are dead. Gone and forgotten about as far as he's concerned."

"Sure, that's always been the way. Somebody making difficulties, something happens to him, he's not around anymore. They forget those guys, all right. But everybody can't be that way, turn the whole world upside down."

No, I think, everybody can't be that way. I can't be that way, though right now I wish I could. Then I wouldn't remember, for instance, how bad I feel right now; I just wouldn't have to know that. But maybe it's just the wrong amount of liquor. I should sober up a bit and start over.

"Hey there, friend," I call to the bartender. "A coffee over here."

"Coffee, is it?" Whelan says. "Did I catch up yet?"

I sit quiet with my chin in my hands. The coffee comes and I have a swallow. It's bitter, chase it with water. The old runaround, thought and memory, and good old Johnny B. doesn't have to bother. It's like he's got somebody else to stand in for him there, be his memory and all. Tonight I'm elected maybe, or maybe it's somebody else.

"Hey, babe," Whelan says. "You running out of gas?" He yawns and stretches his shoulders back away from his belly.

"The weight," I say. "This place, it's got so much history, it can't even begin to assimilate it. You're better off to turn your back. Shut off the signal. Live in the permanent present, or otherwise go nuts."

"What, this bar?"

"This town, you cluck. Two hundred years and two hundred million maniacs trying to figure out where they are and how all the other ones got here too, is it such a surprise if they don't get along so well most of the time?"

"A historian you are now," Whelan says. "And me thinking that you were just a bum or a musician or something. But what's the tie-in?"

"To what?"

"To your wise-guy pal."

Oh yes, there he goes again, making me think, when all I really want to do is go to sleep here on my folded arms. But after all, I might as well think. It's in my nature.

"That's just one of the things he knows that most people don't," I say. "You could even call him an example, on a small scale. The things he's doing now, for instance."

"And what might they be?"

"That you don't need to know," I say, remembering I should watch my mouth, Whelan being who he is. I don't want to get caught in the middle of something.

"You brought it up."

"Forget that. All I'm saying is he's got some new friends now, and not the kind you'd expect. Got a Muslim and a Puerto Rican witch doctor and gets along with both of them like coffee and cream. Couple of other guys too that you wouldn't expect to see at the same party, and all of them rolling along together like they were raised in the same cradle. And if he wants them to do something, why, there's never a question."

"Put the arm on them, I imagine."

"Not that."

"So what's the gag," Whelan says, yawning once more.

"Just what I said. No consciousness, no memory, it makes you very charismatic."

"How's that?"

"People can come along and run into you, and they can't tell you're you. They think you're them, you get it?"

"Oh, sure they do. And what happens when they find out they're wrong?"

"But they're not wrong. That's the whole thing, it's what he's got going for him. He wants to get along with people, he never even has to think about it. He soaks it up direct, knows where they came from and what's on their minds and what they want. He just turns into them for a little while."

"And what does he want them to do, after all this?"

"Oh no," I say. I finish off the coffee, and shake my head to start it moving. Mistake. Makes my head feel like a steel spike got drove into it. I hold still till the pain goes away, and after that I do feel a little more lucid.

"He wants them to peddle fruit and nuts in Times Square, all right?" I say. "Or maybe he wants them to sell Girl Scout cookies or something like that, but it makes no difference to what I'm talking about. And what you're asking about, I don't want to tell you anything. So you can stop asking, okay?"

Yusuf Ali

Allahu akbar.

A blessing for the Namer of All Things.

I hear thunder. A mist of rain settles on my face. A few light drops and then there is no more. It stops with the second roll of thunder. But the rain rouses me. It must be near dawn. I had almost forgotten my purpose. To find Porco. Porco hit me. That is why I am here. Porco. The Spring Lounge, there on the other corner, the red and blue lights over there. Now I should rise and go there.

Porco. I have never had anything for or against him. He was just around sometimes, and then he was not around any longer. Santa and Holy Mother hate him, but that is only because he beat them in a fight. That was their pride, for he was only one small man, and they were two. And Johnny B. was a friend to him for a time. Until he interfered with us. The shouting and the screaming, I could hear it at the other end of the park. Porco has a strong voice. I could make out no words. Then Johnny B. was calling, and I was going toward that voice. But when I arrived, there was a crowd already gathered, and Santa and Holy Mother were slipping away through it, and the cops coming in from another side. It was only Porco in the center of a thick ring of faces, the pleasant faces of our customers, and Porco screaming, no words at all now. And if anyone came near him, Porco knocked them down. Very quick and very strong, Porco. Then Johnny B. gathered us and we departed from that place. When we were far enough I asked Johnny B. what happened. We were walking fast down La Guardia, the five of us, and I next to Johnny B., and he was angry.

"He's raving over things he can't help," Johnny B. said through his teeth. "A mistake I hope you'll never make. Because you won't get anything out of it, nothing at all."

And this I well understood. For it is Allah that knows that which we do not know, and there is no further use in pondering, though it may be difficult to refrain from pondering, as I now do not refrain. And I said so to Johnny B., and he smiled at me, for these are the things he also understands. But still he was worried and angry.

"He's making himself into a menace," Johnny B. said, looking down at his fast-moving feet. "A fool and a menace." He spat on the sidewalk and stepped on it. *"Porco miserio."*

But Johnny B. does not hate him, I would testify to that.

He named him.

I remember watching Johnny B. in the park. Long ago, it seems. Watching him watch me. He had Santa then, and that was all. Santa doing all the footwork and the hawking, and Johnny B. just around, watching the people, and it took a practiced eye to see that the two were together. For a week or more his eyes were always on me. It began to worry me and disturb my mind. When they watch you so, then perhaps they are thinking of you more than is safe. It is time to look for something to happen, and what it is likely to be is the gun or the club or the knife. For they want something from you, when they look at you that way. And I did not believe that anyone would want anything from me except my stock or my business, but it was not so, not with Johnny B. He watched me and I watched him do it, until there was a line between his eyes and mine, a tension waiting for something to break it. I stood above the fountain, and Johnny B. leaned on the arch, and the line was so taut it amazed me that the strollers could walk through and across it as though it were not there. Then Johnny B. broke it. He walked down to where I was waiting.

"I know you," Johnny B. said, looking hard. "I know you for a long time, Yusuf Ali."

I returned the look harder. But already I believed his words. For I was reading, translating still, even in my mind wherever I might be standing, the parallel columns of English and Arabic, arranged there by the first man of that name. I too a translator, and could think myself into that name as well or better as into any other. It fit me well.

Then Johnny B. spoke again, and now it was he who recited:

"God is not ashamed to strike a similitude
even of a gnat, or aught above it.
As for the believers, they know it is the truth
from their Lord, but as for the unbelievers
they say, 'What did God desire by this
for a similitude?' "

And he smiled, and when I still spoke nothing, he said, "But perhaps I am mistaken. . . ." He began to turn away, but I caught hold of his arm.

"I am he whom you have recognized," I said. "You are not mistaken."

Hence I, Yusuf Ali.

I was given a name, though perhaps I am still growing to fill it.

I took it as an act of love.

And Johnny B. named Porco too. Not when they were together, but when they were apart. When Johnny B. was angry against him. But Johnny B. does not get truly angry. He only cuts his losses when it is necessary to do so. He does what he sees he must do. I think he would have let Porco come back if it had been possible.

Assuredly he does not hate Porco. You do not give a name to something you despise. The naming itself is a gesture of respect and honor.

I wonder how Porco received his name. If he understood the gesture, the recognition. My surmise is that he did understand. I feel now that he understands a number of things. And I think that Johnny B. meant to do an honor to his pain, whatever the source of it, even while putting him aside. He recognized Porco, a thing in him, and he told him so.

I want to talk to Porco.

I did talk to Porco. Tonight. I remember, I have got it now. The wind blows, drying the last drops on my face, and I hear them again, Porco and Johnny arguing across the chess table. Porco holding up a burden in his hand and talking of it. "The storytelling stone," he said, and we were laughing at him, I was laughing behind my hand. It seemed nonsense to me then. I mocked Porco, and he hit me with his stone. So I am looking for him now, to kill him perhaps.

But now I think that it was I who was at fault. I should not have mocked him and his talking. Yes, I think that after a night of talking to myself I can say that I should not have mocked him for it. I wonder what it was, that stone he had.

I had one quick look at it. Johnny B. was shining his light on it and I saw over his shoulder for one second. It was not much in appearance. Just a rock, small and black, not even shining in the light, and then it was all covered in Porco's hand. A black stone.

And now I recall the Black Rukn of the Kaaba, which is far from this place, in Mecca, and I have never seen it, though I hope some day I will. For it is a sacred place, and the Black Stone within it is sacred, and it is an honor and a duty to go there and lay a hand upon the stone. For that is what the Prophet of Allah, peace be unto him, did when he was circumambulating the Lord's House, and when he laid his hand upon the stone he pronounced a takbir. *Allahu akbar. La ilaha ill' Allah.* And the stone was set there in its place by Abraham.

It is written how Abraham was building the House of Allah, which is called the Kaaba, he was building it up with stones, and Ishmael was bringing the stones to him on his shoulders. And when Abraham had completed the first level of the walls, he stood at the place of the Black Rukn. He spoke then to Ishmael, and requested him to go and discover a stone of another aspect, to distinguish that corner, so that the people should know where to commence their circumambulation. Then Ishmael departed, and he searched for a stone that would be distinctive. But when Ishmael returned he saw that already another stone was there and had been set into the place which Abraham had shown.

Then Ishmael inquired of Abraham where the stone had come from, and Abraham spoke to him and said, "It was brought to me by one who would permit the use of no other." For the stone had been delivered to Abraham by Gabriel. And it was from Allah. And at that time it glowed exceeding bright, so that Abraham and Ishmael could scarcely look upon it, and yet it was also exceeding in beauty, and it pierced all the corners of the House of the Lord with its light.

And it was the same stone that was sent down upon Adam in the first and earliest days, and when Adam saw it he was enchanted with its light, so that he embraced the stone, and he would not be parted from it. Yet when Adam was led astray and out of the garden by Iblis, then Allah chose to part Adam from the stone. And at the time of the Flood, Allah concealed the stone in the mountain, Abu Qubais, against the day when Abraham should be born to build the House of the Lord. For the Kaaba is built on the foundations of the first house which was raised by Adam, and this is confirmed by the presence of the stone, though the stone itself has changed.

For in these latter days, the stone is no longer white and gleaming, and it emits no light to our eyes, though yet it may be a light unto the spirit. It is a black stone, to the eye. It was made so, I believe, by the touching of hands, the infinite generations of pilgrims touching and kissing the stone, to lay their burdens upon it, to confide unto it all that they cannot speak aloud to tell. So it is a stone that is full of the secrets and woes of the ages of man, and if it is darkened, to me it is no wonder. For the face of God even may seem veiled and dark, and the mouth of God be muted, but he is no less God for that. *Allahu akbar*, God knows everything, in silence as in any other manifestation.

So it is I who was at fault, I confess it, I obstinate and blind. Though I am not such a fool as to believe that Porco is walking around with the very Black Stone of the Kaaba in his pocket, yet I can perceive a resemblance. And neither will I be such a fool as to ignore what I perceive, for God is not ashamed to strike a similitude, and God knows the things that you do, and God knows everything that you do. *Allahu akbar*. And why should God refrain from striking a similitude in the world as well as in the Book?

And that Porco is an unbeliever, for that I care nothing. I have come too far to make that an issue, and I have seen too much. If there are professing believers who are in fact astray, then perhaps there may be among those who do not profess someone who has a

knowledge of the right way. For the world is nothing if not confus-
ing, and its paths are dark and occluded, even as are the paths of my
own mind.

So I am getting up now, stretching my legs. I will go and speak
with Porco, if in fact he is there. And if he is not there, I will seek
him out on another day. For I have conquered my anger now, and I
will not permit it to blind me to a new knowledge, if any awaits. And
I will not be the first to pass out of rage into comprehension.

Sword in hand, Umar comes intending to slay the Prophet, he
falls into God's snare, and discovers a kindly regard from
fortune,
Or like Adham's son he drives toward a deer to make the deer his
prey, and instead discovers another prey,
Or like a thirsty oyster shell he comes with a gaping mouth to
take a drop of water into himself, and discovers a pearl within
himself.

As they were, so shall I be, and I hope I may find Porco tonight,
while this mood is fully upon me. I have crossed the street, and I am
nearing the glass double doors of the bar. And now I see that he is
there, hunched over the bar with his head in his hands, talking to a
fat white man with a balding head. *Allahu akbar.* I will forgive and I
will ask forgiveness. I strike the doors with my palms and they swing
open.

Porco

"So sorry," Whelan says. "Just go ahead and talk about what you want to then."

"Right," I say. "Where was I?"

"Your pal turns into other people, you were saying. Which I don't get what you mean by, at all. Why don't he just turn into a bird and fly away?"

"Sometimes I don't know why I bother," I say. And I don't, at that. What I should do is get a shave and a new suit and a pair of patent-leather shoes, go out to St. Paul, Minnesota, and start a nice swing band. The big bands are coming back, so they say. But will I do that? No, I won't. I'll sit around here till my teeth fall out, wondering about the people I know and what goes on in their heads, if anything. The price I pay for staying awake. I'm yawning now myself.

"Ahhh," I say. "Just consider one more thing. The world is constantly changing, you know, and so are the people you see around. There's a new breed coming along, and they're not going to be the same as you and me."

"They're going to be taller and stuff," Whelan says. "I read about it in *Popular Science*."

"It's going to be worse than that," I say. "They're going to have different stuff in their heads."

"Like mud or something?" Whelan says. He gives me a friendly poke on the shoulder, which makes me rock on my stool. "Like too much booze?"

"Like a whole howling lot of nothing," I say. "Like something that can make itself into whatever it wants for as long as it wants and no longer."

"Yeah, yeah, back to that," Whelan says. "Back to your little friend."

"Yes, that's it," I say, getting a little bit interested again. "He's one of them, I'll give you a line on it, he's one of the new breed of cats."

"I don't think I'm going to like these people," Whelan says, "if that's how they're going to be."

"No, you won't," I say. "I probably won't either. I might envy them, but I won't like them. They won't listen to me and they won't talk back, and I'm not going to like that at all. But there's not going to be anything to do about it, you know. The monkeys didn't like it when we came along, and where are they now?"

"Africa," Whelan says. "The Bronx Zoo."

"Okay, forget the monkeys," I say. "One more time, let me give you the rundown on Johnny B."

"It's late, jeez," Whelan says, looking at his watch. "I got to get out of here."

"It won't take long," I say, holding up my hand. "For one, he's done a lot of things which aren't considered to be nice, that we agree on, and these things don't bother him at all. He forgets them as soon as they happen. And for two, never mind he doesn't remember and doesn't really think—if he needs to know something then he knows it, and right at the right time. He needs a new man, he looks him over, he can find out everything that goes on in his soul, and he doesn't have to be bothered with believing in any of it himself."

"So?"

"So, these two things together, he's got a different kind of mind. He's a walking brief habit, that guy. He's the Superman."

"You're making me tired," Whelan says. "All this talking over a second-rate con, he's still nothing but a second-rate con."

"Look," I say, losing patience once and for all. "He is something else than that, and this is the reason, get it—nobody would bother to know the things he knows and not believe them, nobody but the Übermensch would go out and learn the Nine Million Names of God just to facilitate pushing smack in Washington Square."

"So that's what it is," Whelan says, waking up quite abruptly. "That's what he's up to, is it?"

"Just a minute," I say. I've blown it now, but good. Why do I do these things? Now I'm so jumpy my tongue is knotting itself over every word I can think of. "Jesus Christ, you can't do this to me, it's a private conversation. You use it and you'll get me killed besides."

"I can keep you out of it," Whelan says. "Who's going to know?"

"I'm going to know," I say. "And that's plenty. And not only that but—"And looking over Whelan's shoulder I see both bar doors fly open fast and hard, slapping into the walls on either side. It's a wonder the glass doesn't break, but I don't wonder about that for long, because coming through the door is none other than Yusuf Ali, with his hands stretched out like the grabs on a power crane and his eyes burning a hole right through my head. Oh no, oh no, I didn't think I had to worry about him yet, why couldn't he take the night to sleep it off, why? I guessed he'd catch up with me sometime, but not this quick, but it's no time for vain wishes and regrets, it's time to do something and do it now. I swing my arm hard to the right along the bar, sweeping glasses and ashtrays and loose change to the floor back there. The bartender's head snaps around and I see where I missed one beer bottle, so I pick it up and throw it at the range of bottles in front of the mirror, breaking quite a few of them, I think. "Hey, what the hell—" the bartender is shouting, and he moves to the right to investigate the damage, while Whelan has taken me by the shoulders, the last thing I need at this point. I point over Whelan's shoulder at Yusuf and when his attention is a little distracted I raise my hands and knock his away, and while diving over the bar I notice out of the back of my head how Whelan has put a hand on Yusuf's chest to slow him down and Yusuf has picked him up bodily and set him down gently behind him near the door. Now I'm on my hands and knees scrambling toward the trapdoor I think I remember being there on the left side, "Excuse me," I say to the bartender, kicking at his shins to discourage interference, and I hope I'm right about that trap, because this joint has no back door. And bless my soul, there it is, my luck still holds, if barely, I crack it open and pour myself through the crack like a glass of water and let the trap fall shut over me. Here I am on the flimsy little stairway, feeling around for some way to lock the trap, no light on down here so I can't see, but here is a nice heavy hasp under my fingers, and beside it hanging from a chain is a nice thick bar to put through the hasp, which I do. Done. It will take even Yusuf a little time to rip this thing out of the floor, so I've got a moment to catch my breath, and when I do I feel much better, pretty well in fact. Nothing like a little abject panic to clear your head of any trifles that may be bothering you and make you appreciate life again. I even feel sober now. I press on my chest to shut my heart up some, so I can listen to what's going on up there. I hear a lot of scuffling and thumping, but it's nowhere near the trap, it seems that someone is giving Yusuf some resistance, and I wish them the best of luck, I'm in no hurry to see him myself. But I won't have to, not if there's a service entrance to the cellar, which I'm hoping there is, and preferably on the back street. Then I will be out of this place and gone before Yusuf can get down here, and after that I'll move to another country maybe, that would probably be the best idea. But enough deliberating, I'm going down now, looking for a light.

Yusuf Ali

Allahu akbar.

It is no doubt the will of Allah, whose will is manifest in all things, that now when at last there is in my mind clarity, confusion should arise from the world all around me. And for that, I will have patience, though I enter this place full of a desire for peace and understanding, and yet I am received as though I were the person of Azrael himself.

I have entered the room and the room has exploded. One moment ago I looked through the glass and all was quiet and calm, but now that I have passed the barrier it has all dissolved into madness, as if the touch of the air from the street were sufficient to madden all these people—Porco is struggling with the man he was speaking peaceably with only a moment before, and now he is throwing bottles, and the room is full with breaking glass and shouting, and I can no longer think so clearly as before.

It all must stop, this is not the way it was meant to be, I must arrest everything for a moment and have the room still again. I move farther inside and raise my hand to command quiet, but everything only grows louder, and there is still more commotion— now Porco is jumping over the bar, his fat friend coming forward to shove me in the chest, causing me to become angry, when anger is just what I ought not to feel now.

Patience, I command myself, thinking in this instant of the whole length of time, and I take this fat old white man by his upper arms, grasping him just below the shoulders, and I lift him up so that we are eye to eye. I think that with his feet removed from the ground he may perhaps become more calm, and I stare into his pale eyes, seeking to share with him my patience. But there is no comprehension in his face, only fear and outrage and injured pride, and after all he is only an old fool of a white devil. I did not come in here to look at him, it is Porco that I wish to speak with, so I put the old white devil down behind me, out of the way, and I move on toward the bar where Porco must still be.

But the noise continues, everyone seems to be yelling and howling, and glass is still shimmering from the shelves behind the bar onto the floor. I am becoming confused and I must move slowly, carefully, for I do not want to make a mistake or injure someone. And there are so many people running around the room, some of them turning over tables, some of them diving toward the door, several blocking my path or pulling at my arms. All of these people seem to be shouting but I cannot hear any words they may be saying or even separate their voices, it is only one sheet of sound fanning the air without meaning.

Then I hear one voice.

"Freeze, you," is what this voice says. And the tone is familiar, I have heard this voice at least a dozen times, and from as many different mouths. It is the sound that a man makes when he is pointing a gun at your back. This voice is coming from behind me where I just set the old white devil down.

And I do freeze. But not for long. I stop moving for a second in which I know the shooter will relax, and in the third quarter of that second I am already pivoting on my outside leg, out of the line of fire, and sweeping my arm toward where I know the hand with the gun must be. It is there, and I grasp it and push it downward, so that the shot, when it comes, goes into the floor. One shot, and abruptly it is quiet again, and everyone has stopped moving. Ah, at last silence and peace. I hear nothing now but the blood thumping in the bruise beside my temple.

Now I reach out with my free hand and take the barrel of the gun and pull it out of the fingers of the old white devil, for it is he who has the gun, just as I thought. I hold the gun by the barrel, and I look at him. He looks back at me, and he does not move, does not break for the door though it is just behind him. The old white devil is rubbing his right wrist with his left hand, but certainly his wrist is only bruised, and he is not badly hurt at all for someone who just tried to shoot me in the back.

Another time I would be angry. Another day and this white devil might possibly be dead. But now, tonight, I look at him and I only feel sorrow, and a great disappointment. It has all gone wrong. But I will not make it any worse. I will maintain my patience. I hold the gun up by the barrel and take hold of the butt and pull the two together till they touch, till the barrel is bent in a U and I am quite certain that no one can shoot this gun anymore. I look hard at the old white devil and I drop the gun at his feet.

Just as though this were a signal, all Gehenna breaks forth in the bar again. Truly, all of these unbelievers must be madmen, crazed by wine or equally by misguided thinking. Now they are all scurrying around again like small insane animals, most of them headed for the door, darting between me and the old white devil, who is still standing there staring at me as though he were trying to memorize my face. And surely, that is just what he is trying to do, for the gun that I have just bent up was a standard-issue police weapon, which means that this old white devil is very likely a cop. Still, I am not too concerned with that, not now. Most of the crowd has got out by now, leaving their drink spilled on the floor with its fumes offending my nostrils, but I have not seen Porco go, so I must look for him.

I go over behind the counter where I saw Porco jumping not long ago, but there is no one there, no Porco, only the bartender just now picking himself up off the floor. When he sees me he jumps back, and that makes a bitterness in my heart, for I had no intention to bring fear and confusion into the house, though surely this too, as well as everything that passes, is the will of Allah.

"Brother," I say, raising my hand again, "I wish you only peace and comfort."

The bartender does not answer me, though I see his mouth working at the edges. He speaks nothing from where he stands in a puddle of splintered glass and reeking alcohol, but he waves his hand around the room as though he wishes to indicate that it is not peace and comfort I have brought, and this is true enough.

"Brother," I say again, "believe me, I am very sorry for your trouble. Believe me, it was never my wish that any of these things should have happened."

Now I think of the money, my payment from Johnny B. for my night's work, which is still in the fat envelope here in my back pocket. It is written that in such a case as this it is right to make restitution, and I open the envelope and begin to count out a given sum. Then I also recall that it is written how it is best to be unstinting. So I take all the money out of the envelope and hold it toward the bartender.

"Brother," I say again, "I hope you will accept from me this token."

But he will not stretch out his hand for it, though his eyes widen looking at the money, he only backs farther away. So be it, for me this is a night of error alone. I put the stack of small bills down on the bar at the length of my outstretched arm.

"And now, brother," I say once more, "I must ask one small kindness. The small white man, he who jumped over the bar. Where is he now, this little man, do you know?"

The bartender's mouth works again, and this time he makes a sound, but it is not a word, only a kind of croaking. Then he points to the floor under my feet. I do not understand this, unless he means that Porco has gone to Gehenna, but he still points, shaking his finger, and I look down and see a handle, and I see that I am standing on a trapdoor. I raise my head again to say my thanks. But the bartender has vaulted over the bar and is already moving toward the door, not forgetting, I notice, to snatch the pile of money from the counter. Now he and the old white devil, the last to remain here, are backing out of the double doors together, both staring at me yet, as if they were looking upon some marvel, impossible to believe. Surely, the unbelievers are all madmen. I bend down and tug at the handle of the trap.

The trapdoor lifts an inch and stops. I see that it is locked from the other side. Indeed, there is no good fortune with me this night. I am weary of these obstacles. But I do notice that there is just room for my fingertips under the edge of the trap. I set my hands and squat on the floor, pulling hard, but the door will not give. I am tired from all that has passed this night. Perhaps I have not the strength. I stop and rest a moment, breathing hard. Perhaps I will give it up, for now, and seek out Porco on another day. But that prospect does not content me. I shift my feet and grasp the door and strain, closing my eyes and feeling the knots in my legs and along my back and shoulders. I try to forget that I am forcing the door and think only that I am simply trying to stand up. Then there is a tearing sound and a crack and I am standing up, staggering backward, and my shoulders are stopped by a wall. My head clears and I see two halves of a broken board in either of my hands. There is a dull yellow light coming from a hole in the trapdoor. *Allahu akbar.*

The trap is still shut, but now it is easy to reach through the hole and unfasten its lock. I pull the door open and let myself down directly to the basement floor. The ceiling is very low, my shoulders scrape it, and I must thrust my head out like a turtle. I crouch down, to see what I can see. There is a single yellow light bulb in the ceiling, with a string hanging from it, and a piece of flypaper. I see no one in the basement. No Porco, no Black Stone. Only rows of crates and cartons and boxes and bottles of the devilish alcohol, some open, others closed.

Then I have come this far and caused this much trouble to myself and others only to crouch on my hands and knees in a basement full of liquor. I stand up, as much as I can, and walk stooping between the packing cases, up one aisle and down the next. I do not see Porco anywhere, nor do I see any place he might have hidden. As I move toward the rear of the basement, the light grows dimmer, but I feel a different air, not fresh exactly, but it has the smell of the street. And here in the rear wall is another stairway going up, and the door at the top stands open. Then that is where Porco has gone. I have lost him back to the street.

I climb to the sidewalk myself now, and I look in both directions, but there is no one. It is too late, and I was delayed too long. Porco might be anywhere, and surely by now he is far away. I am grieved beyond reason by this little failure. Certainly I will meet Porco on another day, but that does not seem sufficient.

It is good to be out of the basement, and to stand straight again. Yet the air outside is heavy and choking, and the sky lightless, bearing down on me like a lid. Perhaps it is only waiting to rain, but I am oppressed by it. I am lonely and desolate under this last hour of the night, and I cannot even think of any place where I might now wish to go.

Darkness. It strikes me now that even God has withdrawn His light from me. I am exhausted and alone, and now I feel that I have even been deserted by my belief. And most of all I am weary of the sound of my own voice whispering within me without cease. For once, I would speak and be answered.

Yet there is no one here to speak to. I must move now, for these thoughts are evil. And as I begin walking I repeat the takbir, though it is dry in my mouth when I start the repetition, *Allahu akbar, Allahu akbar.* I walk with the phrases falling aloud from my lips, in rhythm with my footsteps. And I notice that I am not walking west toward my home, but eastward, and this thought comes to me, that possibly Santa is still in Roosevelt Park, and the park is only a few blocks ahead.

I would not choose Santa for a companion, for he is not only maddened in the ways of all unbelievers but possessed by a whole host of demons besides. Still, he has witnessed all that I have witnessed tonight, and it is not impossible that he has understanding. And indeed, I now feel that it is Allah who provides me with this thought. My steps gain strength as I walk toward the park, and my spirit is lightened, and the takbir becomes as a rich fruit in my mouth. And I do repent of my moment's lapse of belief, for it is written:

> They say, "When shall this promise
> come to pass, if you speak the truth?"
> Say: "It may be that riding behind you
> already is some part of that you seek
> to hasten on."

Porco

A very bad moment that, yes, a nasty few seconds I've just lived through. But it appears I'm none the worse for it so far, maybe even a little better, the head cleared out a bit, so to speak. I'm slipping down these few steps here, with one ear tuned to the thumping and bumping up above. In case there should be any sign of approaching danger. And at the same time I've got one hand sliding along the wall, and hoping to discover a light switch. But I slip and sit down at the bottom of the steps without finding any such thing.

Stand up now, and reach around for a possible pull cord. Nothing. Can touch the ceiling though. I begin to pat myself down for broken bones. Or matches. Take a step ahead and here's something scary and sticky all gummed up into my face. Gives me a start. Nerves on edge already. I flail at it, and now my hand has blundered across a piece of string. I give this a pull. Light.

So, I have a look around. The sticky thing, I can see, isn't a tentacle from the great beyond. Nothing but a tatter of flypaper with a few ripening flies attached. Nothing to worry about at all. But before I have time to savor this relief there's a bang and a ricochet and glass breaking too close for comfort. Not off upstairs, but right down here with me. And I roll up in a ball at the foot of the steps and wrap my hands around my head like all three of the no-evil monkeys. That was a bullet, or I'm losing my fine sense of hearing.

They're shooting at me through the floor. I lie quiet with my knees tucked in, trying to guess what happens next. But what happens next is nothing at all, and as I lie here waiting for it, my nose fills up with a certain smell, with which I am very familiar. Half horse urine, half gasoline.

Mescal.

I unroll myself and sit up for a minute. Open my eyes to the yellow light of the fly-specked bulb in the ceiling. I don't see the stuff yet but now I can hear it. It's dripping in a fast little beat— plop-splat, plop, splat-splat. Makes me feel like whistling, and I do, getting up onto my feet and looking at all this whiskey lying around with nobody watching it. Anything and everything you could possibly wish for or imagine, wall to wall and ceiling to floor. A few undisturbed hours down here and I could explode my liver faster than a *pâté de foie gras*–destined goose.

Mescal. I can't tell you why I feel such an urge to go and find the stuff and dabble my fingers in it and even possibly drink it. It makes me ill, it can bring on hallucinations even more grisly than the ones they design in the crazy house, and it tastes even worse than it smells. Also, it's the worst thing possible to put on top of anything else. But right now it's drawing me like a magnet. I get up and go after it, following my nose. And here it is. A packing case with the lid off, on top of a stack. I peep in and see a double row of quart bottles padded with Mexican straw and gila monster dung. Five whole bottles and one smashed, with the liquor bleeding away from the pieces through the boards. And here in the top slat is a small black-rimmed hole that a bullet has drilled.

For now we'll just put aside the question of why the people upstairs are picking off stray bottles with gunfire through the floor. For now, let's just pick up a whole quart and hold it to the light. Yes, this is just what it smells like, mescal. The wicked yellow ichor I see through the whorled glass, and three quarters down in the bottle is suspended the bloated white carcass of the worm. I tilt the bottle and the worm gives a wiggle and wave of his tail, swims to the edge and kisses the glass.

Of course this swimming and kissing bit is an illusion. This worm is as dead as the cold concrete I can feel through the nickel-sized hole in my left shoe. He's totally saturated, locked in an irreversible alcoholic stupor, a bender from which he won't ever return. But you wouldn't think it to look at him. Not now, with the way his calm red eye meets mine. And now the worm gives me a wink and a dare, and here is what he is saying: If this stuff can do so much to me, my friend, what do you think it will do to you? I open the bottle.

It's you and me, old worm. Or is that you or me? No matter. Cheers.

Aurrgh. Mescal every bit as bad as I remember. Burning tears in the eye. Razors in the throat. And almost dropped the bottle. Not something I usually do. Ah. I hold the bottle up again and look at it. The worm rocks quietly in a yellow wave.

But what am I doing standing around talking to worms at a time like this? When the binding of my body and soul is in danger. Yusuf Ali is up there and will be down here soon if no one stops him and probably no one will. And instead of going somewhere far away fast, I'm hanging around drinking tequila and daydreaming. No time for this. It's out, out, out of here. Now.

I slap the bottle back in the case and take a bound for the far end of the basement. But then I think better and go back and get it. Might as well take it along, since I opened it. No use leaving it to sit here and evaporate. It's kind of a tight fit here in my inside coat pocket, being a quart and round and all. But I can wedge it in good enough. And if the neck of the bottle sticks into my chin, why, that just helps me hold up my head. I fold my arms across my pockets and burrow for the rear of the cellar. A sure thing there's a loading door here somewhere. Nobody would hump all those boxes down those stairs. Here's hoping it just isn't padlocked.

Ah, the stairs in back, and oh, the door. And a blessing on which-ever gods or demons rule my destiny, it is shut with nothing but a bolt. Which I slide open. Then I stop a minute. I'm all turned around. Can't think if this is the front of the joint or the back. But the best I can do is hope it's the back. I push up on the metal lid and it falls over and down and smashes against concrete. Here I am with my head sticking out in the middle of the sidewalk on Kenmare Street.

Fresh air and freedom. Not a light burning on the block. A good dark night to get lost in, and that's what I'm doing. As fast as I can. A zig here and a zag there. Don't even know where I'm going.

Don't care. Just get a few blocks between me and old Yusuf. Who might be already out looking around. Running out of breath here. But. Here's a place. Deep enough to slip into. Out of the way for a sec. Big set of stone posts with a stretch of iron fence in between.

Feeling too drunk now. The exercise. Sends it to your head. I bend over. Hold the rails. Can't hold a thought. Or remember what I've been up to. A touch of a stitch in my side. Not all I used to be. But it's passing. Though I'm not clear. Where am I? Straighten up now, see where we've got to.

Oh yes. I look above the lance heads on the gate and see the dome back there. Been a long time. A very grand building it is, for down here. Built for a church. Then a precinct house. It's nothing now, so far as I know.

No one keeping up the back yard anyhow. Underbrush all over down there. Choking the ramp that goes down—wonder what that's for? Roll coffins into the crypt maybe. But all grown over now and the brush running out through the rails of the gate. I pull at a branch of something, and it pricks my hand. A thornbush. No, a rosebush, an actual rosebush. With red roses on it, back there inside. Hard to believe, sometimes, what you'll find. The roses look in good health, all things considered. Stretch my arm but I can't quite reach the nearest. Can smell it though.

A cat watching there under the thorns. Down low where the bush is thickest. Come out for a look at the stranger at the gate. A wild street cat, ragged and hungry. One eye shut or missing, the other shining yellow and doesn't blink. Lives here, no doubt. Old gray mangy street cat, but got a nice place.

Could slip in myself, I suppose. Have a little nap among the roses. Easy to hide there where the bushes cover the ramp. Could climb the gate easy enough. And curl up at the door of the crypt. Or somewhere.

Don't think I like that cat though. He'll sit on my face and breathe my breath. Cats do, they say. You never know. Don't know just how hungry he is either. What he might get up to.

Oh well then. Sit down here on the pavement. Where I feel at home. Okay, cat. To you yours. Me mine. With my blessing, cat. And he sits down and curls under that rose, just out of reach. The one yellow eye shuts up and I can't see this cat anymore in the gray night.

Time to inventory. Some funds here, still in the sock. No point counting it. Little lump there still feels solid. Enough for . . . I lost some though. A few bills left standing by my glass on the bar. Couldn't say how much. Had my scare, forgot to pick them up. Must be slipping. But no helping it.

And the bottle, here in the inside coat pocket. Right over my heart. And my trachea. Have a look, a good bit left. Almost all, in fact. I put my head around the post and look both ways in the street. We're all alone here. Sky thick and dark as a blanket. Have another drink.

Ggrrhh. Like eating a raw cactus. Spines and . . . But it does open things up. Great desert spaces. Oh, my vision is limitless. New horizons multiplying. Excelsior.

Mistake. Scraped my chin falling. But the bottle didn't break. Can see it lying whole by the railings. Quite near my hand. With the cap on too. What luck. A scrape on the chin will heal itself but a broken bottle is lost forever. A proverb. Cheek on the cool concrete, eye-to-eye with a sleeping tiger through the bars. No, an alley cat. Can sit up now and reach the bottle.

Ah. Goes down smooth this time. I've beaten it. Who is master, me or the mescal? Me. But then why am I crying? Great bloated tears dropping straight from my eyes and bursting on the pavement. Why, how funny. Why, I'm laughing. And I can't stop. Can't stop. To breathe. Got to stop and I do for a minute. But the whole center of my body riots and it's started again. And here come the tears again. How really funny. I can hear myself laughing. Shaking too hard to hold the bottle. Head jangling off the rails behind. Oh it's funny, got a stitch in my side laughing. But I have to stop this. Before I drown.

And I'm making too much noise. Someone could come by and take it the wrong way. Well now. Sit up straight and breathe through the nose. As much as can be. Stops the sobbing. That's better. Just dribbling a bit at the corner of the eye, tears of pure alcohol. Now wipe the nose on coatsleeve.

But where's the reason? You have to find a reason for this kind of thing. Or else you're off your head. Or alcoholic. Maudlin fits a sure sign of that. Can't have it. But here's the bottle. Have a drink and look for the reason. Lean back with the eyes shut and still leaking under the lids. Let me know I can cry all night if I let go of myself. And maybe I will. It makes a change. But now I'm floating off in a mescal haze. . . .

Half dreaming. Here we are in the vacant lot off Stanton. All three of us. The lot all grown over and the bushes taller than we are. Almost like a garden. And water beading on the leaves. An hour ago, it rained. Summer showers. A leaf shakes drops into my face and wakes me up from the wine I've been drinking. With the little brown man. And his little hard stone. He's holding it my way. . . .

Now here we are in the dugout playground. Roosevelt Park. Propped into the bike racks near the wall. All done talking. And up above it looks like the sky might clear. Me and the brown man and a bottle of . . .

Mescal. How could I forget all that? Me and the little brown dead man. Me and my Comanche. He gave me the Stone. Wouldn't answer my questions. Just drank himself dead. Wasn't looking for that. Not too pleasant either. Sent me out of the park double time. When I knew he was gone. There was nothing to do. No time. Except watch it. It was what he wanted. The look of him, he knew what he was doing, more than most. Maybe more than me.

Was it what he wanted? What he said. What It wanted. It. Gods and demons, have I still got It? Yes. In the side pocket. Check up and down the street again and take It out to look at It. But it's too dark here, or my eyes are running, or anyway all I can see is a blur. But I feel the weight on my hand, against my ribs. And there's the sad thing. That Indian lying out there over east, not saying anything anymore. Could be any of us. And me, running off and leaving him like that. Not that it matters at all.

But it's coming back to me. Mescal notwithstanding. I remember everything I've done tonight and it's beginning to look like a miserable mess. I squeeze the Stone in my hand, but It doesn't give. Bastard, you started this. So long ago I can't even see the beginning. And what do you do to help out? You are supposed to *make things count.* I carry you around all night, you mother, and you still haven't said a goddamn word.

So maybe things are just exactly how they are. How they look to Johnny B. For instance . . . The hell with it. I lift the rock to sling it into the intersection, but after all, I think, maybe I shouldn't do that. After all we've been through. Really, I should try to hang on to it. It has Its uses. Can hit somebody solid with it, this much we already know. And if I stand up and put the mescal in one pocket and the Stone in the other, it will help me keep my balance. Like so. Off we go. Though not so steady after all. In fact I'm so far off center that I'd fall if I didn't hold to the rails.

Can't really blame it on the Stone, though. No doubt these things are really all my own fault, not Its. A safe assumption. Hold the rails. While that sick-drunk cloud passes on over. And even if I don't believe I might as well go through the motions. Just in case. Now. Got to get a grip. Now I can stand.

Now I even know where I'm going. Back to Roosevelt Park. Not that there's any point. Practical it's not. Won't help anything. But I'm going. I can see if he's still there. Have another good cry, maybe, and clear out my sinuses. And be the witness when Sanitation comes in the morning, to take him to his everlasting home.

How to get there. Forget where I am exactly. But east is that way. Simple to walk east, if not for the stumbling. Toward Mecca and everything. With the park somewhere on the way. Too bad I can't manage to stay on the sidewalk. Keep turning my ankles when I drift over the curb into the street. It's my eyes that's the trouble. Keep shutting on and off like a camera shutter running off speed. Got to get a grip. I stand still. And concentrate till there's only one street, not six. Clutch the bottle and the Stone, like imaginary canes. And off again.

What's this. Wide-open spaces. Stop and focus. Benches and trees. And Delancey Street. Looks like I've arrived.

That was quick.

Where were we sitting? Further down, I think. On the east side. In the dugout, yes. Should be right down here. But here's a running car standing on the next block. Funny, late for that. Makes you wonder. I stop short of the streetlight. If there's anybody in the car they can't see through the light to me. Best be careful. All the good guys around here are asleep.

Cross to dark side of the street. Slip along the doorways. Stop and focus eyes. There's no one in the car. Double funny. And this should be just the place, I think. The dugout is right down under that rail. And just over the top of the car I can see the sign, that place across the park where they serve the 80-cent noodle soup.

Flat in the doorway, somebody coming. Maybe the car goes away now, and I can go look in the dugout. Wait, now. I press the corners of my eyes to see.

It's Santa Barbara. I see him passing under a streetlight. Carrying something all wrapped in red. And loading it into the back seat of the car. Very strange. So strange I think I'm sober. The door bangs, and Santa is looking toward me over the top of the car. I freeze. But I know he can't see me in the dark. Not unless I move. But I don't even think he's looking. His eyes all glassy. Like he's on something. Johnny doesn't let his people dope. But maybe he doesn't know. Santa moves off now, back around the dugout rail and into the dark.

What's he up to? These hairs standing up on the back of my neck know, but I don't know, not yet. Think I'll chance a look though. Hope Santa's down in the dugout.

Bang. I'm across the street and down behind the car. Couldn't have done it better sober. This drunk has been coming in waves though. I peep in the window, but I can't tell what's there. Just a smudge of something red on the seat. Now I'm trying the door and it pulls open. Still can't see much. Get inside a minute. Check through the windows first. No Santa. I slide onto the floorboards and let the door fall shut behind. I run my hands over the seat. Something lumpy wrapped in something woolly. Then something else I'm touching. Which my fingers slip inside.

A hand.

Stiff and hard as concrete. Rigor mortis. I've found him all right. But I wouldn't have expected any of this. What's going on here, I don't know.

But at least something is. And that feels like a big comfort just now. Can't say why, but I feel like the tide's turning, luck running my way. This started out looking like my night, and maybe it is after all. Not that it's most people's idea of luck to get to hold hands with a corpse. But did I feel that hand squeeze mine?

Steps. I peep, it's Santa. Slip my fingers up to the wrist, dead for sure, and won't ever know if I run for it. But I feel like hanging on for the ride. Not to make a big fuss about it, but I'll stay. So down to the floor, and quiet and still as I can manage. Solid as a rock.

Yusuf Ali

Allahu akbar.

They say, "Why has a sign not been
sent down upon him by his Lord?"
"The Unseen belongs only to God.
Then watch and wait; I shall be with you
Watching and waiting."

I stand in a deep doorway on Forsyth Street, in its shadow, where none may observe me. I have found Santa already, even as I intended, but I have not spoken, and he cannot see me, here in the darkness where I stand. Santa has a car now, and because I know him and because it seems that he cannot turn it off, I think that it is a stolen car. I would speak to Santa, I would have spoken before now. But when I look at him closely I can see that one of his demons has touched him. That is apparent in his walk and in the posture of his head. And I think it will be better for me not to offend Santa and his familiar jinn, not now. I will watch and wait my moment. I watch Santa removing a red cloth from the car and taking it with him down into the park.

Santa's car stands still at the edge of a pool of yellow streetlamp light. I hear no sound but the motor, that and the low muttering of the small-hour breeze. The air of the city moves only in secret. I hear steps of someone walking down the sidewalk. They stumble and stop and I strain to hear. Now the steps start again, and they are coming nearer. I press back in the doorway for the walker to pass. But he does not pass. He swings into the doorway to my right, and something he must be carrying meets the wall with a clink. I hear his feet shifting in the next doorway. Perhaps, if I reached around the corner, I could touch him. It seems most strange to me that there should be another here, watching and waiting. Yet already it has been a night of many strange things, and it is only Allah, the Most High, who observes them all.

There is motion across the street, and I see Santa returning from the park. He is carrying something wrapped in the red cloth, something long and stiff and oblong, though what it is I cannot tell. But it would appear that he or his demons or all of them together are practicing their mystery. The moment to speak is not yet. Santa goes back in the park.

Now the unseen watcher next to me bursts across the street in a ragged blur and stops, crouching, at the near side of the car. I see his profile against the fender, the features acute and brittle, a face that sucks in on itself, around the eyes and the busy mouth. The head shrinks into the collar of the coat that is too big. Of all people, it is Porco.

No sooner do I recognize Porco than he opens the back door of the car and wriggles inside like a lizard. The door shuts behind him and I cannot see him anymore. Perhaps he was never there. But I did see him, for a second. Now Santa is coming back out of the park again, carrying a small cylinder, dark and glistening, held in both of his hands before him. Possibly there is an agreement between him and Porco, though I do not think it very likely. And Santa does not even glance toward the back seat. He slips into the front, behind the wheel.

Then there will be no moment, unless I make it, and there is surely no time to puzzle the matter. I leave the shadow of the doorway and move in two long steps across the street. But demons or no demons, Santa is alert. He is lunging for the far door before he probably even really knows outright that anyone is coming. But he is not quite fast enough to get it locked. I open the door and move in beside him on the seat.

Santa looks at me, and he does not seem to know me. He is still half-leaning toward the door where I came in. Then his eyes change and he straightens. He knows me now, I see, but he is not pleased.

"You," Santa says. "Yusuf."

I make no answer. It now seems that I cannot think of a word to say. I can only think that there has never been any love between us, and perhaps I would not be pleased either if Santa came upon me so and took me unaware.

"What you do here, mon?" Santa says. "In my car."

I have no answer ready for this either, or not a good one.

"It is not your car," I say. "It is no one's car now, I think."

Santa takes his eyes off me and looks off at the street up ahead. He raises his hands to the wheel. I see that he will not argue, not about the car.

"I drop you somewhere maybe," Santa says. "You need a ride someplace."

But I shake my head, no, I do not need a ride.

"Then out," Santa says. He brushes at me with his right hand. "Out now, Yusuf. I have things to do. No time for talking to you. And nothing to talk of, mon."

Now I might tell him about Porco, hiding in the back. For it must be that Santa does not know that he is there. But time passes and I do not mention Porco. Indeed, I do not even open my mouth. I sit and look through the windshield, while Santa looks from me to the street and back at me again, shifting back and forth behind the wheel. I know that he is trying to think of some way that I can be out on the street and he driving away and leaving me there. But there is no way that Santa can bring this about, and he knows it, and I can sense the knowledge galling him. Finally Santa spits out the window and looks at me once more with disgust in his face. Then he puts the car in gear and it begins to move.

Santa drives the car slowly, turns it east on Delancey. There are no other cars and no people on the wide street. I watch the streetlights beating by and wait to discover my tongue. But there seems no room for a voice in this car, because it is too full of Santa's anger.

He turns the car into Ludlow Street and slows it to a crawl. Every window of every building is solidly dark at this hour of the night, but there is still a heavy smell of pork and fried fat in the street, where the air is not moving enough for the odor to disperse. The buildings lean close toward each other from either side. Santa points the car to the curb and lets it roll to a stop.

"Why?" Santa says. "Why you come to bother me tonight? How you even find me I don't know. What you want with me? It better if you go. Go where you live and rest your head for tomorrow."

"I have no rest tonight," I tell him, and wait to see what may come out of my mouth next. "There are voices talking in my head. They say things which I cannot explain," I tell him, "not by myself. I have even addressed Allah," I tell him, "and searched an answer in the Book."

Santa shapes his mouth to spit again, but he does not. That is well for him, that he does not spit. Though if he thinks little of my belief, no more do I think of his.

"Then go to the mosque," Santa says. "Go to your temple." It is spoken in the tone of insult. But this I will ignore.

"I have been thinking about everything which has happened this night," I say, and Santa turns toward me, looks at me with a certain interest. "About Porco coming back again," I say. "And the stone."

"Ah," says Santa, leaning his head toward me. "And what you think about it?"

"That maybe there was more in what he said than what we thought."

"It could be so," Santa says, and I see that he is smiling. "Anyway, it was more than what you thought, my friend. What was it you were thinking of, when Porco caught you in the head?" I am angry at this mockery—Santa should know better than to push me so far—but it surprises me to discover that I am starting to laugh. Now Santa is joining in, and I am laughing very hard at the thought of myself being caught flat-footed and hit in the head with a rock, and the two of us together are making a great deal of noise and even rocking the car. It is strange that I should be laughing over this, and that thought makes me stop.

"More than that too," I say. Santa looks at me, not smiling anymore, and taps his fingers on the dashboard.

"Yes, mon," he says. "There is more." Now he is looking at me in such a way that I almost feel I should be ready for the blow or the knife. But neither comes.

"Wait here," Santa says to me. "Watch the car." He gets out, closes the door softly, and slips across the street. There are no lights on Ludlow Street. I sit quietly in the dark humming of the car. I should be thinking about whether or not Santa is going to set me up, but somehow I am not. He has left me with the feeling that we are together, as though we were in the park and working. There we are together to a degree, though also and always separate, and knowing we can depend on each other, and how far. Here there is no boundary, but there is the feeling which suffices. I listen for any sound that Porco might be making in the back behind me, but I can hear nothing. I am tempted to look over the seat and make sure he is still there, but I will not do this. Everything waits its own time to be known. *Allahu akbar.*

Santa stands outside the gate of a storefront across the street. Somewhere in the store a night-light is burning, so that I can see in the display window the shadows of the figures of the saints. I see Santa in silhouette against the barred window—the hook of his nose, the pointed beard, the lips drawn back in a smile of sorts. Santa's hand moves to the wall and somewhere within there is the distant rasp of a buzzer. That sound repeats and repeats until a light comes on in an upper-story window. Then the light is blocked by the shadow of a man, who comes forward and shouts down in the street, speaking Spanish, so that I cannot understand him well. My Spanish is not good and the man speaks too quickly. But to my ear it seems that most of his speech is cursing.

Santa answers softly, and the shadow gabbles and curses more. Another soft answer, and the shadow stands quiet for a moment looking down. Another short phrase I cannot quite catch, and the man moves away from the window. Santa moves away from the gate and I lose him in the dark; then he returns with a cardboard box in his hand. A light bulb flashes on above the door behind the gate where Santa waits, the door opens and a man appears in the frame, an old man, humped and stooping. His head is thrust out in a curve from his bent shoulders and I can see it clearly under the light—the face mashed flat and toothless, a few white hairs still bristling from the head. He peers both ways, then fixes on the car. More talk which I cannot understand, and then the gate is opened and Santa passes inside.

The car cramps me, there are pins and needles in my legs. I move around to ease them and jostle something on the seat beside me. I find it with my hand; it is some glass vessel, with a broken rim. Whatever is inside it smells of pure evil. I take my hand away. Across the street the gate is locked again, but the door has been left ajar and I can see shadows moving in the room inside, though they do not cross the window. Now I notice lettering above the window, and my eyes have dilated enough to read it—Botánica Martinez. The door is opened wider, and the old man appears in it again. I see he has the features of a black man, though his skin is very light. The old man lets Santa through the gate and locks it, shuffles back into the store. Santa holds his cardboard box in both hands, and he also has a long loose cloth bag, bulging at the bottom, the mouth of it run through his belt at the hip. He walks around to my side of the car and puts the box through the window onto my lap.

"Put you hand on top," Santa says. "Hold it shut."

I cover the box with my hand and at once something hits the top, under my palm. I look up; this is some trickery designed on me out of Santa's devil worship.

"Do not fear, mon," Santa says. "It is only a little chicken."

Then I open the box, and there is only the small stupid eye of a black rooster looking up at me from inside. I cover him again. Santa has put the car in gear, and already we are rolling around the corner. Santa leans over the wheel, his eyes slanting secretly like the eyes of a cat that sees food.

"Yes, there is more," Santa says. "You miss it all, Yusuf my friend. Right to the big boom in you head.

"It true everything that Porco say to you," Santa tells me. "Some things in the world and you don't know them. Because you be too busy, mon, looking in the book. One day your god come up and poke you in the belly and you be looking in the book and don't know. You got a god that talk to you off a piece of paper. My gods, they right here with me now."

"It is not gods you have with you, Santa," I say. "It is seventeen devils."

"What you think, then," Santa says, "maybe it be so. But here you are coming to ask me question." He taps the brake and the car stops again. "Long time ago maybe the father of your father's father be sitting in a treetop talking to mine. Now it different between us, but the gods, they don't change. Still they talk to me, and now they give me a thing which I must do. The gods the same as ever, Yusuf, only you don't ever see this, I don't think. So you can get out now and go on your way."

"Not yet," I say. I sit where I am. Santa cannot throw me out of the car, he could not even pick up a box that weighed as much as me.

"I don't hear your insults," I tell him. "Even though you have said enough already to not be alive anymore."

"I fear, Yusuf, I fear too much," Santa says. "Maybe you going to do me how you did Porco." And this time he really does spit out of the window. I reach, and before he can move I have got him by the forearm. I squeeze it just a little to get myself some respect. But Santa reaches over to my folded thumb and presses the joint and the pain is so swift and surprising that I have let him go before I know it. An old trick which I had forgotten. When my voice comes again I am surprised to hear that it is pleading.

"Keep telling me," I say.

"How I going to tell you anything?" Santa says. "When you don't know how to hear. Porco tell you everything already and all you can do is make fun."

I think he is going to drive me out my mind with his teasing, this making me a fool. I reach again, but not for Santa this time. I only want something dead to squeeze and tear. My hand closes over the plastic rim of the wheel and I pull it toward me. I grip the door frame with my other hand, lock my teeth, and strain to bring my two hands together. Perhaps the strain through my body will ease my anger and frustration.

"Then I make a mistake, tonight," I hiss through my locked teeth. "But don't play with me. Don't play with me now." Under one of my hands there is some kind of crack.

"All right," Santa says. "But if you tear up the car then we can't go nowhere."

I relax, fold my hands back over the box that holds the chicken.

"Now. I try to tell you. It is this way. There is a kind of a man." Santa stops talking, though his mouth still is making words that do not quite come out.

"You call him a man of power," Santa finally says. "The gods are closer to this man than to the others. So he has power and the gods are with him and they help him to make things happen. And this man don't sit around looking into a book. He go down the street with the gods speaking right in his ear.

"But it comes a time this man must die," Santa says. "Then he must pass his power. To some other one. He must pass it." There is now a change in Santa, in his posture and the tone of his voice. I feel that the jinn are coming near him again, perhaps they are already in the car. Surely, it is a host of demons that whispers in his ear, and also in mine now as I listen to him speak, interpreting the wiles of Shaitan, for only in Allah is there real and true power. But still I listen.

"And who he pass it to. The man know for certain. When the gods tell to him, 'There, there. There is the one.'

"And this time it is Porco," Santa says. "Why, I can't tell you. When he just a little crazy man and a drinker. Somebody Yanni-B let come around so he can make us laugh."

"He can fight though, " I say with a grin in the dark. I know that Santa and Holy Mother both have been eaten up all summer by the idea that they couldn't handle one little man like Porco.

"Yes, mon," Santa says. "He is very quick sometimes, Porco. You think, Yusuf?" And Santa gets in a quick jab near the swelling on my head, in and out before I know that he is only playing. It seems that everybody gets to make a fool of me tonight.

"Also Yanni-B don't fool around," Santa says. "And tonight, it is two times now for Porco. Two times he walks away. Maybe we all miss something there. Maybe there is more in Porco than it show.

"Maybe Porco, he will become himself a man of power," Santa says. "But some things, he don't know them yet.

"Like tonight," Santa says. "Porco don't know the right way. The man of power die and Porco walk off and leave him lie there. Walk off with the power in his pocket and leave the man lie there. This you never can do."

"Why not?" I say. I remember Porco's story now, but I still do not think much of it. "All Porco did was watch a wino die, and that is something which happens all the time," I tell Santa. "And if this was a man of power who could make things happen as you say, then I do not think he would be dying in the street a block off the Bowery."

Santa shrugs his shoulders.

"Yusuf, mon," he says. "Why you want to talk to me, I don't know. But to be close to the gods is not to go riding around the city in a big black car. Because they are there where you are and it don't matter where. Especially when the time come to stop living it don't matter.

"But the body of the man," Santa says, "the people must take care of it. Someone must do this. Because if not his spirit will stay near. It will be near and hungry and use for its eating the people who don't know the right way."

"It is not true what you say," I tell Santa. "You are in the way of the devils and it is the devils' speech you are saying."

But Santa is not listening. He jerks forward, stiff as a board, and then droops all over the wheel. It is as if there is no Santa, but only his clothes hanging there. Then he sits up, very straight and rigid, and he looks somehow larger than before. He turns and places his hands on my shoulders and it seems that the pressure of his hands draws my glance to his face and holds it there. Santa's eyes are yellow and they are even shining from some light inside his head. I do not like to see this, but my head is fixed and will not turn away.

Listen, a voice says out of Santa's mouth, but it is not Santa's voice, it is deeper and stronger and full of authority. *Listen, Listen, Listen.* Though there is nothing to hear, not even a noise from the street or the car's motor nor yet the sound of my own heartbeat, it has all stopped and it is silent and my eyes are fixed on those two burning yellow eyes, and I feel that even my thoughts are not my own. And I feel a presence behind me in the back of the car, not Porco but something altogether else, something that touches that cold button at the base of the spine where you know that someone is watching you, not the presence of a man but something other, hungry and expectant, and the voice rises again but I cannot tell if it is someone actually speaking or only the words surfacing in my own mind. *So many, Yusuf Ali, there are so many dead. So many dead who cannot depart that the living have followed their example and walk the city like galvanized corpses in a night which no sunrise ever lightens. So many, but only this one which is so near to you.*

I know this is some devil's trick, or else Santa is trying to hypnotize me, though Santa does not seem to be trying anything really. His own eyes are now so dilated that they have turned all black. I shake my head and the sharp pain of the bruise dispels the witchcraft. The pressure that I thought I felt is gone. I take Santa's hands away from me and set them on his own knees. Santa twitches, then a long shudder runs through his body, all the way to the feet. I watch his eyes shrink down to normal. He turns away from me toward the wheel. When he speaks again it is in his own voice.

"So you see, Yusuf. I have a thing to do. And do it now. Because it is night for maybe one more hour. And everybody else in the city is as stupid as you are, and if they see what I be doing at sunrise, then they going to lock me up, mon. So I tell you everything I can. Now get out and go your way."

I look outside of the car. The night does not seem to be lifting yet, but that is because of the clouds waiting to rain. When the morning comes it will be sudden.

"You need help," I say to Santa, "to get it finished by sunrise."

"I help myself," Santa says. "You I don't need. For nothing."

"I want to go with you," I say. Santa looks at me. The problem has not gone away. Santa still cannot put me out of the car if I do not choose to go. And I can see that he is tired from being again touched by the demons, and he knows that he is losing time.

"You want to go," Santa says. "But one thing. This is what I have to do. You don't mess with it. Whatever, you don't mess with it."

"I don't mess with it," I say.

"Then you promise me," Santa says. "Promise on your book."

"In the name of Allah."

"In the name of Allah what?"

"In the name of Allah, you will do what you do and I will not interfere." And Santa surprises me with a smile as he moves the car back into the street.

I do not know where we are going. But the car is moving east, through the maze of the Lower East Side, the narrow breathless streets, which are almost never quiet but are quiet now, an hour before daybreak on a Sunday morning. Loisaida, as the people say, or Alphabet Town, in the mouth of Johnny B. when he comes in to buy the stuff for us to sell. In the name of Allah, I just said. In the name of Allah, I associate myself with the jinn and increase myself in vileness. These are my words. My words, I am not bewitched, not hypnotized. In the name of Allah, it is written, everything which is to be. The streets begin to open up and now I smell the river.

Porco

"You," Santa says. "Yusuf."

Oh Jesus, Mary and the little saints, I have screwed myself right to the wall this time. I have stuck myself in a car with Yusuf Ali, and I am dead meat this time, I know it. Come, dead body, hold my hand. Here's even money you and I will be stretched out in the same place shortly. And let it come soon, please, because this waiting for the fatal moment is hard on a person. Think I'll just close my eyes and listen for the sound of my neck snapping.

Why-oh-why does it not come? Why do Yusuf and Santa sit there talking about not much instead of getting on with the job? There is absolutely no chance Yusuf does not know I am here. He moved in right behind me, not a second to spare. Could be he was tailing me all the way from the bar. But then why didn't he hit me outside the church? Or anywhere?

Well, who knows? Maybe all they want is to scare me sober, the bastards. Or no, I don't think Santa is in on this. Not from the talk I can hear, which sounds more like Santa does not want Yusuf along on this trip at all. Then what is he cooking? Possibly I will live long enough to find out. The car rolling out now. Wish I could tell where it's going. Right turn says east. Up through the side windows I see streetlights strobing over the covered corpse. Turn down the blanket from the head, maybe he is only faking. No. The lights flash on and off over a face as dead as a brick wall, eyes unmoving as pebbles on the sidewalk. Another right turn tells me south and the street-lights are gone. Cover of darkness.

I let go the dead hand and work my own down toward the pocket where the mescal is. Quietly now. I will anyway have my one last drink. I'm drawing the bottle carefully toward my head, using my own body for a sound muffle. Clash as it crosses my belt buckle. I freeze. But not a move from the front. Can't even see them up there. They've stopped talking. Well. The bottle brought level with my chin, and I raise my head as much as I can. Still a bad angle. But could formerly drink a glass of water, standing on my head. No coughing allowed.

There. Not so bad after all, and whatever gods or demons are in charge of my luck anyway get credit for some sort of sense of humor. Jerking me around this way. Ah, but we're stopping. This could be it.

No, but it is only more arguments between Yusuf and Santa. And would you believe it? They are talking about me behind my back. Plotting my doom, no doubt. It's coming. I reach for the cold dead hand. But no, if I can believe my drunk ears, they actually want to hear what I'm talking about. I finally got them interested; these guys are for once ready to stop running around and start thinking. This is my big chance. I pull myself together to sit up and tell them everything.

But now I can't remember what I was going to say.

More's the pity. I can hear them laughing now, can't blame them. I'm always just a hair out of sync, it's my destiny. And drunk tonight, very drunk, as I can tell from that short effort to lift my shoulders off the floor. Probably nothing would come out of my mouth anyway now but goobly-goobly-goo.

Santa's going off somewhere. Here's my chance to make a break, maybe. But I'm too cramped up down here to get a very good start. Besides, I'm beginning to feel like I would really rather die. Depressed as I am, I think I'll just lie here. Come on, Yusuf, finish it off.

Come on, Yusuf.

Why does he just sit there like a bull asleep in Times Square?

Well, you have missed a good chance, Yusuf. Santa is back and there is more arguing. These two are talking past each other, I think, might as well save their breath. Santa explaining all about his voodoo gods. They're putting me to sleep with all this talk, I can feel my eyes rolling back into my head. Santa's voice rolling along like black water lapping over the old verities, the gods, the devils, power, even my own name floating up here and there to let me know I am only asleep and dreaming. . . .

. . . *Listen* . . . *Listen* . . . *Listen* . . .

My eyes snap open like firecrackers popping—there's something very strange in this car. I twist my head toward the front but I still can't see anything but the back of the seat. But there is a something here besides the three of us, or a someone, old and cold and quite foreign to me. It is running a current from the dead man's hand across my body to the pocket where the Stone sits cold as an iceberg.

Perhaps the Stone is speaking at last.

Snap and it's over. It did not speak to me. Yusuf and Santa begin again, in quite ordinary voices. Whatever it was is gone for now, but everything is not quite the same. Point—I seem to be quite sober now. Point—I am not afraid anymore. Feel a little numb, maybe, but that's all. Point—I was wrong to worry back then when I lost my words. Whatever is going forward here has its own voice and does not need mine.

The car is rolling again. I try to guess where we are going, but I've lost count of the turns. Only as the minutes go by it seems that the feel of the air is changing. Either the weather is breaking at last or we are getting somewhere near the edge of the island.

And here we stop. Santa and Yusuf Ali get out and the car rises on its springs, relieved of their weight. The doors bang shut. And the back door opens. Now for sure they have got me. But they don't seem to notice or care. The body is drawn along the seat and out of the car and the door slams behind it. I'm alone. Where are we anyway? Finally, I sit up and slide to the open window.

East River Park.

Quite some time since I've been here. What with funds not permitting taxis and things, and it being a long lonely walk through hell on foot. But this is it, the park, trees, the river, even though we're still on the wrong side of FDR Drive.

I see Yusuf and Santa standing like tombstones on either side of the body stretched out on the sidewalk. They pick it up, head and feet, and carry it up the stairs to the footbridge over the highway, Santa leading.

A strange business. Neither one of them has bothered to give me so much as a bash in the face. And here is a beautiful chance for me to split out of here.

But curiosity killed the cat. I get out, stretch, touch the Stone and the mescal. I feel very clearheaded, even up to a moderate drink. There. One meditative sip on the mescal leaves me no worse off than I was before. Santa and Yusuf have already come down on the other side of the highway. What can I do but follow them. I'm going up the stairs to the footbridge.

It's not so high, this catwalk, but I can see clear to the river, with Brooklyn squatting on the other side of it, the dull line of buildings brooding into the night sky. Behind me a wall of brown project towers. Overhead, a mesh to prevent me from lobbing bottles onto any cars that might be passing below, and a heavy starless sky. I roll my head around a couple of times, and all in all I feel rather happy it's still on my neck. And the cold sweat which this trip has raised on me is dried by the breeze blowing back off the river.

From the stairs on the park side I see Yusuf and Santa, with the body between them, passing through the first tree line, crossing the field. I go down the stairs and follow them, walking into the wind. It's a real weather wind, coming in fits, and in between the gusts it's just as choking as it's been all night. But this wind is blowing something our way. Possibly, who knows, good fortune. I see Santa and Yusuf pass through a second row of trees, the last screen between us and the river. It seems as though I am floating across this field. One solitary raindrop touches my face, and there's a flash of heat lightning out over Brooklyn.

Now I have reached those trees myself, and here I stop. Santa and Yusuf are standing on the promenade above the water, right up against the fence. They are possibly three steps away from me, but they still don't seem to notice I'm here. A few blocks down south the Williamsburg Bridge is flinging its chain of lamps out over the river.

Santa and Yusuf stand at opposite ends of the body. Santa is holding a long loose sack, reaching into it with one hand. He crouches over the body, turns back the blanket, works over the head with something from the sack. I move along the trees to a better angle of view. Santa is cutting the hair off the head with a long straight razor, roughly but close to the skull. A cluster of hair grows in his free hand.

"Yusuf, the box," Santa says. Yusuf bends with the fluid ease of a sleepwalker, picks up a cardboard carton, and carries it to Santa. He lifts something alive and flapping out of it and holds it to his chest. Santa reaches into the box and takes out a large, clumsy-looking clay bowl. Hair falls into the bowl now as Santa goes over the skull again, shaving it close this time.

There is a loud roll of thunder somewhere behind Brooklyn. Santa stands up abruptly, almost at attention. Then he relaxes and turns to Yusuf.

"Hold him rooster close," Santa says, "but not so close you kill him." Yusuf loosens his hold on the chicken, which cackles a little now. Santa bends back over his sack, taking out a candle and four or five small pots. A match flares, and Santa sets fire to the hair in the bowl. It burns bright enough for me to see Santa's face and his mouth moving soundlessly. Then it burns down to a network of sparks. Santa lights the candle and begins to paint the head with colors from the few small pots. I can't quite see what the colors are. Santa works quickly with one forefinger, making columns of dots which run from the back of the shaved neck to the forehead. When it is finished he pours what is left in the pots into the bowl, over the smoking hair ashes, and puts the pots back in the sack.

It thunders again, this time I think lightning struck somewhere on the river. Santa stands up suddenly again. It is peculiar how he does it, almost like he is being pulled up by a string attached to the top of his head. The thunder stops and Santa goes back to his knees. He takes the bottom of a broken bottle and pours from it into the bowl.

I smell a smell I know. And I have seen that bottle. I think that what Santa has got is a piece of that man's death, scraped up from the stones of the park. Gives me shivers to think of that. I have a shot from my own bottle.

"Porco," Santa says.

I jump. Hands trembling. Santa isn't even looking my way, he's still looking down at the dead face. He knew I was here all along. I glance over at Yusuf. He is looking south toward the bridge.

"What is it you drinking?" Santa says.

"Mescal," I say. The word comes out clearly.

"Give me," Santa says. Still looking down at the body, he stretches his hand toward me.

I step away from the trees and hand him the bottle at arm's length. Santa takes it, pours from it into the bowl. Doesn't use it all, I notice. The air is getting heavier and heavier, and the wind has stopped. Santa dips a finger into the bowl and paints symbols on the dead forehead with the mixture. Then he raises his head.

"The otan," he says.

The what?

"The stone, Porco," Santa says. "I must have the stone."

"No," I say. I put my hands in my coat pockets. Santa stands up jerkily and moves toward me. We are the same height and eye-to-eye.

"The stone," Santa says. He opens his right hand and the razor unfolds with his fingers.

"No way," I say. I close my hands, one over the Stone and the other over something softer I don't recognize. What's that? I trace it with a finger. Box of cigarettes. The razor tilts in Santa's hand, catching what little light there is. Somehow I am full of confidence. Though somewhere I hear a voice screaming that I've got to be out of my mind.

"Leave it," Yusuf says. My knees should be knocking, but they're not.

"Leave Porco the stone," Yusuf says. Santa turns back toward him.

"May your Allah step on your head and squash it," Santa says. "You promised not to mess with me."

"It is only what you said yourself," Yusuf says. He is still standing unnaturally straight and looking down toward the bridge. The rooster squirms in his crossed arms, craning its neck.

"The man gave him the stone," Yusuf says. "Then it is his to keep and watch over. So it seems. Even from what you said before."

Santa hesitates. It thunders nearer and Santa shudders. The

razor folds in his hand and disappears inside his clothes.

"No more time," Santa says. He turns the blanket down further, to the body's waist. He opens the shirt and places a tuft of hair on the bare chest. The candle flickers and the eyes wink and glitter, staring up into the cloud cover.

"Yusuf, the chicken," Santa says, reaching. "And both you, turn the back."

Yusuf shifts his feet and faces the river. I turn back to the city. The rooster begins to crow, and the sound is chopped off in the middle.

"Turn back around," Santa says. We turn. The rooster is now lying on the top of the big bowl. All except for his head which I don't see anywhere.

"Finished," Santa says to the corpse. "We owe each other nothing now." He lifts the bowl and sails it high over the river into the darkness.

The next lightning flash fills the whole sky and catches the bowl at the top of its arc, where it looks no bigger than a subway token. After the flash there is blind darkness, the dark falling down like a hammer. And the darkness is filled with a voice deeper and louder even than the thunder, coming more or less from where Santa is standing, but no way is this Santa—

CHANGO MANI COTE CHANGO MANI COTE OLLE MASA CHANGO MANI COTE OLLE MASA CHANGO ARA BARI COTE

—another bright flash of lightning shows me Santa's mouth grown large and working hard. I look for Yusuf but the dark comes back before I find him—

CHANGO ARABARICOTE ODE MATA ICOTE ALAMA SOICOTE YE ADA MANICOTE ADA MANICOTE ARAN BANSONI CHANGO MANI COTE CHANGO MANICOTE

—flash and I'm looking at Yusuf gone limp against the rail, mouth parted and eyes shocked wide. He looks smaller. How was I ever afraid of him? . . . then the dark and the booming voice—

ELLE MASA CHANGO ARAM BSONI CHANGO ARA BARICOTE ODEMATA ICOTE SONI SORI CHANGO ARA-BARICOTE ARASORI HE HE GUE GUE HA

—flash and I see on Santa's bared tongue a cross etched in red, leaving a bright afterimage on my eye as the dark falls again—

MAYO AMAYO GUERA OKOKOTE ARO EGUE ARO AMAYO GUERA MANICOTE CHANGO MANICOTE OYE MATE MANICOTE OYE MATE ALABAO CHANGO

—flash and Santa has picked up the body and raised it above his head, the body, stiff as a plank, seems to be rotating on his hand and then the dark—

ARABARICOTE CHANGO ARABARICOTE ALAGUO BARICOTE OYE MATA ARABARA COTI SORI ACHE CHANGO MANI COTE

—flash and I see Santa spinning on his heels and chanting, the body spinning too but at a different rate. No way is Santa strong or agile enough for this, it is another power in him. The dark returns, the wind rising suddenly, and it begins to rain. Only scattered drops but under the wind they pelt me like bullets—

SOICOTE ARA ADOMEMATA ODE ODE MATA ODE ODE OYE

—flash and Santa throws the body out on the river, the body still turning on its own axis thrown as easily as a bolus caught in a series of short bolts in different positions against the sky—

MATA ARA BARICOTE SORI SORI SORI ODEMATA ODE-MATA

—flash and I see the body on the point of meeting the water, falling, the blanket fanned out around it like wings—

SORI ACHE BARICOTE

Lightning strikes the river directly in front of us. I see every electric vein reflected from the black water.

ARA BARICOTE SORI ACHE CHANGO.

The next flash is only heat lightning somewhere over Manhattan, behind us now, and in that light I see Santa dropping hard to his knees on the pavement. It begins to rain seriously now, and very hard, the rain falling on my shoulders like blows. Santa kneels under the rain, his feet tucked up behind him, his head shielded in his hands. Whatever it was has left him. He is only a small man kneeling in the rain, in the very dim light of a grim city predawn. This is the morning. The rain has straightened out the kinks in Santa's hair, water pours out of his beard.

Yusuf Ali stands at the fence with his hands behind him, palms down on the rail. Looks like he was struck by lightning himself. His eyes still fixed on Santa, water running from the slack corners of his mouth. I move over beside him on the rail, but he doesn't notice me. I jog his arm with my elbow.

"What the hell?" I say.

Yusuf, startled, turns my way.

"It is only his devils," he says vaguely, "or his gods. . . ." He nods, chin to his collarbone.

"What do we do for him?" I say. "Is there anything that we do?"

"I don't know," says Yusuf, coming to again. "How would I know?" But while he is speaking he is stripping off his shirt. He steps out from the rail and drops the shirt over Santa's head. Much good that will do, the shirt is as wet as anything else around. But the rain is beginning to slacken. It is only a summer storm.

Santa's shoulders are heaving. Now he sits up on his heels, his head still completely covered with the shirt.

"Santa," I say. I don't know why.

"Santa Barbara," says Yusuf.

"Santa," I say.

Santa pulls the shirt off his head and looks up. He gets up and hangs the shirt over the rail and leans on it, looking down into the water.

It has stopped raining.

I flex my fingers, still in my coat pockets. And feel the cigarettes again. I pull them out, wrapped in my hand, they're still dry. What a nice break. And there's even a pack of matches stuck into the cellophane.

I start two cigarettes and pass one to Yusuf. I hang the other in Santa's mouth, where it droops. Santa's eyes are glazed. I light a cigarette for myself and draw on it. It's still very dark. Santa's cigarette glows red and rises to the horizontal. He turns around, coughs, takes the cigarette out of his mouth and looks at it with some surprise.

Well now. I look down on the asphalt in front of me and there is the bottle of mescal standing beside the drenched cotton sack. I pick it up and have a shot and pass the bottle to Santa. Santa has a shot. He raises the bottle and nods to me. His eyes are his own again.

Santa passes the bottle toward Yusuf Ali and it hangs in the air. Yusuf turns, opens his mouth.

"The Prophet—"

"—is not looking this minute," I say.

Yusuf Ali tilts the bottle up and keeps it there for some time. When it finally comes down, he is grinning.

"Allah is always watching everything," he says. "But He is also called the Merciful." He passes the bottle back to me. I take a shot, Santa declines, I put the bottle back in my pocket.

"I am sorry for the night," Yusuf says. "I spoke to you in haste and without thinking."

"The fault is all mine," I say. "I only hope that your head is not hurt too badly."

"On the outside only," Yusuf says. His teeth flash white in his head for a moment. "Inside I think it is much better than before."

I hold out my hand and Yusuf grips it.

"Between us let it be as if it never happened," Yusuf says. "When we meet again it will be in friendship. And there are several things I would like to ask you of."

"At your convenience," I say, with a little bob of the head. Even at five in the morning Yusuf can always talk like he just wandered in from some other century. Hard to match him at times. His thinking is sometimes a little peculiar, but what can you do? If you don't like tautology, you can take paradoxes.

"But what Johnny B. laid down, that will have to stand," Yusuf says. He looks at Santa and Santa nods.

"All right," I say. "I know."

"My man," says Yusuf Ali. He snaps his butt into the river. "Thanks for the smoke. We'll see you later—till then stay off our turf." He pushes himself off the rail, crosses the asphalt, turns around at the trees.

"Let's hit it, Santa," Yusuf says. "The day is waiting."

Santa touches three fingers to my coatsleeve.

"Later," he says. He shrugs. I nod. Santa swings away, stoops for his bag, and follows Yusuf off through the trees.

They're gone. I'm standing here, wet as a rag, and beginning to shiver more than a bit since the wind has picked up again. I have another pull on the bottle to ward off pneumonia, and then I start walking again.

Best get back to the streets, I suppose. I cross the park back toward the city, taking the odd shot from the bottle as I go. Now I'm crossing the catwalk over FDR Drive, and now I'm back in town. The car is gone, I notice, and no one is out and about but me. I'm drying off somewhat now anyway, as I drift along through the streets. Still quite dark, and I don't really know where I'm going. Got no urgent appointments in any case. More than a few things I might want to think over, but no thoughts seem to come. There's nothing but random actions and pictures floating around in my head, along with odd broken bits of music. I'm very tired, I think, too tired to make sense out of all these things. Too tired to even figure out where I am, my eyes won't focus on a street sign.

Oh, but this is Delancey Street again, and that is the lone police car parked there at the foot of the bridge. I walk down by the stark white lights of the all-night coffee shop there on Clinton, and stop here on the corner. That great stone stairway is leaning out over me, and it seems I might as well go on up. So I cross the street, passing the two dozing cops in their car, and begin slowly climbing the stairs.

I come up and out of the stairwell and for a moment it seems that I am about to put my head directly into the sky. Of course, this does not really happen, and as I move forward I can plainly see that I am still here in the city, walking between the project towers that stand ceremonially on either side of the bridge—unlit at this hour, they have become obelisks. The first concrete stage of the walkway opens out ahead of me like any city sidewalk, except for the steady incline upward, and except for the absolute silence; I hear no sound other than the mescal thumping against my hipbone with each step I take. That, and the voice of one solitary car moaning over the grating at the top of the bridge, a smooth and desperately lonely aural curve building toward a peak it never reaches, a phrase spliced away into nothingness when the car hits the asphalt, its lights dropping away behind me now, the car falling into Manhattan. This is the last night music, for the night is finally breaking, the glare of the bridge lights fading into the even illumination of the dawn.

My own feet are beginning to trip me up, but I move to the rail and keep going. I am walking eastward, climbing into the growing blue light. Already my eye level is raised above the tops of the black towers. The steel webwork of the bridge's main arch gathers me in and there is enough light from the sky to throw shadows, all over my face, my hands, the spot just ahead of me where my foot will fall next. I am walking along the arc of a shadow, but this is metal under my feet, and each of my steps is answered, the bridge ringing like a great gloomy bell. And through the rust-edged holes in the walkway, I can see the river flickering, returning fragments of the gathering light.

I stop, turn around, and look back. This is it, the precise center of the bridge. I have no way to calibrate it, but when you are there you know. I look back, standing straight and unsupported for once—I see the sunrise bringing the city up whole, out of the nightmare river. Every nerve in me is exhausted beyond any capacity for knowing even one more thing, and in this weariness and freedom from the business of thought, what I see is falling into absolute order. The sky brightens to the west and there is a breeze running through the girders and across the back of my neck, and for this moment even the air has forgotten to be polluted, it is fresh.

This morning there is no fog, no mist. My vision extends over the whole island, the range of buildings structuring the sky, one object seen through this long distance of clear air, with the sun reaching further toward it now and touching its outlines with color. There are no more isolated notes and broken phrases, I have it coherent and complete, the fulfilled city found in this red dawn. It is impossible, unreal, not true, but I am seeing it. Thank you, gods and demons, I have seen it all.

Well. Nothing so nice could last forever. I might as well finish the bottle. I lift it from my pocket and it's empty already. But the worm is waiting in the bottom. I turn up my mouth like a hungry baby birdie and shake the worm loose from the bottle neck. Then I chew it thoroughly and wait for results.

The results are terrible. I should have quit while I was ahead. Now I think I'm going to . . . yes, I am. I lean far out over the rail, and the river begins to twist and spiral down below, but I'm too miserable to care if I fall in or not. I hang there until there's nothing left but the dry heaves and then I make myself stop. And sit down with my back resting on the balustrade. A foul taste in my mouth.

No more than I deserve for drinking mescal on top of everything else.

I stand up and test out the operating systems. It appears that I am still able to walk. Slowly, daintily, I start down the walkway, one hand on the rail.

It's been quite a night, all in all. Would make a good story to tell to someone, but who have I got to listen?

Bingo, I know the very man.

I walk down the stairs and cross to the phone booth on the corner of Clinton. There's a couple of dimes in my watch pocket and I tilt one into the slot and start punching a number. It's not listed, this number, but I remember it well from the days of our happy friend-ship.

Good morning, Johnny B.

Johnny B.

It's Sunday morning, 4:25 a.m. as I check out my watch, and I'm standing here on Twenty-second Street watching Holy Mother's back receding into the dreary distance, watching the display on my watch dial turn over to 4:26 now, making a long and weary night this night, for a hardworking man of few and simple wants like me. And this lateness of the hour may also explain, now I think of it, why Holy Mother has been so cross and edgy these last few minutes, because he needed to fix quite some time ago, I believe, and the guess is confirmed by that unmistakable urgent hunch in his shoulders as he swings down the street, a man in a big big hurry to nowhere. At least that's one problem I do not have. I can stand here in the mouth of this garage and talk to the car parker for the rest of the night if I feel like it, and no monkeys on my back, but all in all that's not such an interesting prospect, and what I'm going to do instead is go home. Holy Mother is almost out of sight and it won't pay me a nickel to think about his troubles. I need to go get my beautiful sleep, for tomorrow is another day, and it's already here.

And slipping away eastward on Twenty-second Street I begin to feel better already, as though what ties me to Holy Mother and his dead weight of gloom were only a long strand of pink bubble gum attenuating as I get farther away from him, snapping altogether now as I make the block up to Twenty-third Street and start across town. Maybe I'll pick up a cab here or maybe I'll walk on across to where there'll be some going up the right side of town. Just here on my right I see the Allerton Annex, Transients Welcome (if they got the money), and several of them are hanging their heads and their wine bottles out of the windows at this moment, hoping no doubt to obtain some relief from the heat and humidity, for it is becoming very sticky and clammy tonight. Very strange place the Allerton, I remember I went in there one fine day to see if you could really rent a room in the joint, I needed a brief change of address at the time. I went in the door and there was no lobby whatever, just a big molding ornamental staircase, and when I got up the first flight I met the clerk, sitting there behind a chunk of glass that must have been a foot thick, I kid you not, and he was milk-white all over his body, this clerk, and not a hair on him anywhere, not even eyebrows, and no color even in his eyes. I rapped on the glass but he didn't look up, and when I noticed the gills moving up and down on his neck I realized the Allerton was really an aquarium and this guy was a prehistoric fish, I swear before god and the devil. So I beat it back down to the street and I went somewhere else, thank you so much, and the next time I need to drop out of sight I'm going somewhere else again, not the Allerton.

Not the Chelsea here either, just because they charge you too much for that notorious atmosphere, while sleaze is not really all that hard to come by, artyfax in the lobby notwithstanding. Passing by the doorway now I see what looks like a new sculpture there in the center, *Whistler's Mother* in the round, but then it moves and I see it's a client, not part of the decor, just an old man in a wheelchair with a long black blanket drawn up over him and some sort of cowl over his head. He doesn't seem to be able to move his neck very well, but he pivots his chair around to stare at me or the street, which I can't tell as his eyes are too glassy, only because he's just had a stroke I suppose, but that look chills my bones for a moment just the same. Verily, this is a night of dreams, also signs and portents which I most definitely would rather ignore, provided I can afford to ignore them, that is, but now in any case I am well past the Chelsea and I can forget about the old man in the chair and let something else, or preferably nothing, gnaw at my memory now.

So in view of my present precarious state of mind I think the best thing to do is to just keep walking, seeing that exercise is always of benefit to the troubled intellect, and at this moment I have no wish to sit still in a taxi, for there I might have to review and consider an activity I find for the most part is futile. Better by far to keep rolling along the street taking things as they come, which things will never fail to do. That is one thing you can count on in this world for certain, and here to prove it, before my eyes, is the Last Beat Poet of Twenty-third Street, standing between two sandwich boards which announce his willingness to write you a poem this minute on any subject of your choice, LOVE, however, being his specialty. Not that I'd expect he'll be getting much trade at 4:31 on a Sunday morning, but then I'm no expert on the poetry market, and no doubt he knows his business better than I. So I hand him a dollar for luck and for giving me a nice leaving-alone, as I do not wish to hear any poetry at this time, yet neither do I wish to be considered hostile to the Arts, for life is short and Art is long, though not so long as eternity.

I leave the Last Beat Poet here on the corner and cross over to the donut shop there behind the IND stop, to purchase one coffee-to-go through the take-out window facing the street. It's not that I need or desire any more coffee, but I do want to smoke some more Kools as I go walking along, and my mouth seems to be rather dry at this point. It's Greeks they have running this place, and the lady who takes my order must have been a knockout twenty years ago or maybe only ten, tall and lean and energetic, with the hot eyes and the hungry mouth. A Melina Mercouri if she'd had better luck, and still not bad, though the blue polyester waitress rig-out does not set her off to great advantage. She moves out toward the coffeepot, and noticing the steam on the window, I realize that this place must be air-conditioned inside, so in I go to stand by the register and pay for my cup while the sweat goes cold and clammy on my brow.

I put a big splash of milk in my coffee as a hedge against acid indigestion, won't somebody stop that bubble machine, bite a semicircle out of the lid so I can drink without spilling, and it's bye-bye Melina-Might-Have-Been, back to the street. *Questo è la strada*, and I love it for staying just what it is, ask it no questions it'll tell you no lies, and if you do ask it questions it still won't say anything. You don't have to worry about it, just keep rolling along, finish a Kool and snap the butt into a culvert. There goes Sixth Avenue, here comes Broadway, I cross under the trees of the park here and head up Fifth, into a trace of a cooling breeze.

A few more blocks and I'm on top of the Golden Corner before I know it, the Golden Corner which serves up an irreproachable businessman's lunch by day and a significant percentage of the midtown streetwalkers by night. Here comes one now, a sort of mod-rocker hooker, bruise-purple makeup and a little gold star at the corner of her eye, like what maybe Teacher once gave her for being a good girl and it's,

"Going out?" and

"I'm out now and staying that way, thanks the same," and as I pass on by,

"Right, bastard, and I hope it falls off."

Which surprises me. Mine was just an idle pleasantry, or so I thought, nothing to call forth insults and angry words. People make me tired sometimes, and yes, I'm tired now all over, so I toss the empty coffee cup and throw up my hand at that cab coming across Thirty-third Street my way.

The cabby swings the car into the curb, and I get in the back and bang the door shut, start reading the little signs they have posted back there, driver cannot open meter so do not bother to shoot him, etc., as the cab moves out, panning over the side windows of the Golden Corner and rolling across Madison Avenue. The cabby opens the sliding glass and turns his head to me.

"Where's it going to be?"

"Uptown," I say. "Park and Seventy, that would be fine." So he presses the gas and the cab picks up speed. I look at the back of his head up there and can't see much more than a knot of black curly hair falling out from under his cap onto the limp denim collar of his jacket, but then he turns back again and gives me his profile, a nice young white kid he is, around twenty years old.

"Not much doing tonight," he says. "Not making no money tonight, no way." And he gives his meter a sad sort of look.

"You been having fun?" he says. "I hope somebody's having some fun tonight, you know."

"Somebody must be," I say, "but not me, not tonight. I've been working, that's all I'm doing." It slips out before I think and the cabby turns farther around to look at me, a sharp-looking kid he is.

"Yeah?" he says. "Whaddaya do? Whaddaya do keeps you up this time in the night?"

"I'm a manager," I say, thinking on my feet, as it were. "I got a few little acts I handle, music stuff, folk singers and that."

"Folk singers," he says.

"Yeah," I say, getting into the swing of it, "and tonight, see, I got this guy, he's worthless is what he is, and he's never getting any action in this town, no way."

"Umph," says the driver.

"So what I did for this kid is, I got him some dates up in Canada. You know, up there it's all right, I slap some stickers on his guitar cases that say Carnegie Hall on them, and nobody knows the difference. So I get him a chance to make a little money up there, and if he never comes back even, that's okay with me."

"Know what you mean," the cabby says. "Long as you get your cut and all."

"Oh, I get my cut," I say. "When they sign the contracts I take mine, so that's okay. No problem. Should be no problem at all, but what happens is, the kid takes off for Canada in his home-design hippie van with the mandalas all over the outside and the carpet all over the inside and that, and they don't let him over the border."

"Dope?" the cabby says.

"No way," I say. "He's not quite that dumb, or anyway I told him not to be."

"So for what did they hold him, then?"

"Because he's stupid, this kid, he forgot to take his contracts along. And in Canada, it seems they have this law, why they have it I don't know, but it says if you come over the border with more than so many instruments to a man, then you become an importer, and you got to pay taxes and duties and tariffs and this and that, till hell freezes over, in fact."

"So where do you come into this, this time?"

"Because the cluck forgot his contracts, and he has to have them to show he's giving a performance and make it all right, but he doesn't have them to show. So, two in the morning he's calling me up, whining at me over the phone, and what he wants me to do is fly up there, like physically bring him his contracts, that's where he's starting, if you can believe it. My bad luck he's not quite so stupid he doesn't remember I got copies of them all. So anyway, I tell him a thing or two, and I put down the phone and go back to sleep, and if they keep him up there till his hair falls out I don't much care. But then he starts calling me back, you know, and I can see I got to do something or I don't get any sleep at all, so I get up and go down and copy the contracts, it's three in the morning, I got to find a place to make copies, and then I got to go over to the post office there, and get them off express. And why I bother I don't know."

"It's tough," the cabby says, shaking his head. "It's tough all over, but you must be doing all right, you live up here."

"I don't live up here," I say. "I got a girl friend, she lives up here."

"You visiting your girl friend, five in the morning?"

"Why not?" say I. "I got to suffer, let her lose a little sleep too, is what I think."

"Hey, who else you manage anyway? Anybody I might know?"

"Not a chance," I say. "Just little groups you never heard of, bread-and-butter stuff. I got most of them working out of town, you know. No big names. What's up, think you want a manager?"

"I'm not a musician," the cabby says. "I'd like it if somebody could manage me some better luck though. The corner okay, or you want me to drop you at the door?"

"The corner is good," I say. I take a bill out of one of my wallets and hand it up to the guy when he stops.

"Keep the change," I tell him. "Maybe the luck will come."

"Oh, something usually happens," he says, folding the money.

"It always does," I say as I step onto the curb. "Drive careful." He turns the radio on and up as he pulls out and I catch a snatch of the song as he goes.

> Hey busdriver, keep the change
> Bless your children, give them names
> Don't trust men who walk with canes
> Drink this and you'll grow wings on your feet. . . .

And now he's gone. These short-term friendships are just what I like. No mess, no fuss, no consequences. Seventieth Street toward the park, it's time for a big dose of the sleep here. I cross Madison once again, and I can see the canopy over my door.

Alonzo the late late night doorman is asleep on the job, and I can just barely see him slumped on a chair in his little room to the side over there, under the sickly blue light of his tiny television. Got a finely tuned ear though, Alonzo does, and he wakes up when my key clicks in the first lock, and here he comes, rubbing at his eyes and buttoning up his uniform coat over his greasy gray undershirt. Alonzo the doorman holds the second set of double glass doors open for my ease and pleasure and gives me a little bob of his head as I go through.

"Good evening, Mr. Jenkins," Alonzo says to me very politely, Harold Fellowes Jenkins being the name I am known by up here. "Or good morning perhaps I should say, sir," he says, with an uneasy little smile, pleading with his eyes I won't tell the manager he's been napping, not that it would ever occur to me to do that anyway.

"Good evening or good morning, whatever it is, Alonzo, it is definitely superfine, and a nice time for a man to get himself some sleep, that's what I think." And I give him a nod and a wink as he hands me into the elevator, for I do not want Alonzo to suffer any anxiety on my account, there being trouble enough in the world already without that. And now I am standing in the little box of the elevator, and a very plush little box it is, with fleur-de-lis patterning on the walls of it, and gilded moldings too, not that this interests me a great deal as I have seen it already about a million times, so I just push the button for the eleventh floor and wait for the elevator to take me there.

And now number 11 is lighting itself up, up there on the grid, and the doors slide open smoothly and silently just the way they are supposed to do, and I step out and go down the hall to the door at the end, where I let myself in with my key just like I am supposed to. And now I am standing inside my house and locking the door behind me, and I do not bother to turn on a light, as I know my way around this room without one and there is not much to bump into in any case. I stand here for a moment and listen to the comforting drone of the central air conditioning, the coolness most welcome to me after my hot night on the street. Now I walk to the far end of the room and draw the double curtains away from my big picture window which overlooks Seventieth Street, and standing here at the window, I can look down and see the fountain splashing in the courtyard of the Frick across the way, though I cannot hear this fountain, as the window is quite thick and does not open. And when I have drawn the curtains, enough light enters the room from the street outside for me to be able to see the room and the things which are in it.

And what there is in this room is not much, or anyway a good deal less than there was when I acquired it, several years ago that was. The then tenants, an elegant couple of means, kept this room full of many nice things, such as a white grand piano here by the window where I am now standing, various and assorted antique furniture along with a few chairs you could actually sit on, and most notably a trompe l'oeil painting all over the walls and ceiling, complete with fauns and cherubs and other things of that kind. And every item in the place sang harmony with this painting, doing its bit for the unique and special ambience which characterized this apartment at the time when it was lived in by the elegant couple, who when I met them, however, were most anxious to move all the items to some other location. So I bought the place from them and I own it outright, this building being a co-op, and no one can get me out now even if I prove to be undesirable, which I will not do anyway, since Harold Fellowes Jenkins is a very respectable fellow indeed, albeit a little eccentric perhaps and keeping rather odd hours, but then again he is believed to live off investments of a most substantial nature, and certainly causes no trouble to anyone, does not even make any noise that can penetrate these sound-muffled walls.

So the elegant couple moved out, taking their ambience with them, but leaving the painting of course, and I moved in. And as I have no wish to keep company with cherubs and fauns, the painting had to go. I considered having another one done, of Forty-second Street perhaps, but in the end I settled for off-white, and I brought nothing else to this particular chamber aside from a big tatami mat for the floor and some small padded rice bags for the walls, and also a couple of sizable mirrors. For I do not do a great deal of entertaining, and if I did do any I would do it somewhere else, so I have no great use for interior decoration. So this room I employ as a little home exercise studio on the theory that the sound body supports the peaceful and untroubled mind.

And as I stand here and survey my domain it occurs to me that a spot of exercise right now might do something toward easing me of the troubles and frustrations of this very night. So without further thought I take off my shirt and slip off my boots, and I step out onto the mat, meeting my reflection head on in the long mirror on the right wall and seeing its back in the long mirror on the left wall, and so on and so on in infinite recession, and owing to the half-light none of these images seems to have any face, so that they could be anybody, not just me.

So now I begin to work a little, and what I am doing is certain things that were taught to me by a little old man down in Chinatown, Li is the only name he goes by, but he knows his stuff, and now I know some of it too. Because when the time came that I had to do something to keep my figure and all, I decided it might as well be something with practical applications. Now I begin with stretches and neck rolls for flexibility's sake, since I am stiff from a day walking the street. And when I am loose enough I start my form, slowly the first time through, stopping on each technique to inspect myself in the mirror and make sure that all is as it should be, and there is nothing at all in my mind now except perhaps the voice of my Chinatown master, calling the numbers sharply in my ear, and that imaginary count carries me through the steps until I am done with this first round.

And now I move back to my original position and run through the whole thing once for maximum speed and power, there is nothing on my mind at all now, not even that voice, and my feet fall silently on the mat, so that the only sound I can hear is my own breath punctuating the hum of the air conditioning. I do not even watch the mirror this time, though I catch glimpses of those shadows in my peripheral vision, precisely repeating everything that I do, and now I am finished, brought up hard and sharp against the wall. I hold my stance and glance down at my glowing watch dial and see that it's taken me about a minute to get through the form, not much at all off the ideal forty-five seconds for executing these fifty-odd maneuvers.

Not bad at all for a man my age, not that I'm old but I'm no kid anymore, and if I want to stay in shape I have to work at it now. Besides, as I said, it's good for the head. The form has carried me just opposite one of my rice bags on the wall, so that I can reach it without shifting my feet, so I close my hands and drive them into the bag and through it, feeling the grains separate under my knuckles, focusing on the wall behind. The shocks are solid and pleasant, they travel up my arms and across my shoulders, and finally go out my heels into the floor. This makes noise, but not that much, just a dull, even thumping, and if the people next door hear it they will put it down to the ventilation. Fifteen each and that's enough, I'm not looking to wear myself out just now, all I want is a warm-up.

I step back from the bag and relax, breathe deep for a minute or more. My skin is still cool, owing to the climate control in here, but I can feel the heat deep in my muscles. So I'm leaving this room, going down the hall to the bathroom at the end, where I turn the shower on nice and hot. I take off my watch and put it in my pants pocket, take off the pants and hang them on the doorknob, no need for formality here, I'm at home after all, and then I get in the shower and stay there a while. The hot water matches my body temperature at first, and after a few minutes I begin turning it down slowly until it is cool and I am cool and my heartbeat and breathing are back down to normal. I feel very fine and healthy and sane as I get out of the shower and dry myself off, and when I am dry I go in the bedroom and turn on the light.

My cat wakes up when the light goes on, and she slides off the pillow at the head of the bed, where she's not supposed to be sleeping in the first place, owing to the fact that she sheds. But really she's not such a bad roommate to have, in spite of these petty disobediences, anyway she's got the right conception of the litter box, and that is the main thing. She doesn't have a name, doesn't need one, since she's my only cat. I just call her the cat, or Cat.

"Hey, Cat," I say now, but she slinks out of the room with her tail in the air, feeling guilty no doubt for being caught napping in the wrong place, but trying to carry it off with style. So I go over to my closet and slip on my robe, it's smooth Chinese silk and one of my luxuries, and then I look at my bed, but I don't feel like sleeping just now, though really I probably should. But I feel a bit tense for some reason or other, though I can't think exactly why, and after all I really don't want to. It's just a little prickling at the back of my neck, no more. I take a Kool out of the cedar box on my bedside table and light it with the lighter I also keep there, it tastes fresh and good after the workout and the shower. So now I'm going down the hall and into the library, and there I'm making myself a drink.

Right here in the cabinet at the end of my bookcase, I have my whiskey and I have my soda and I have my little highball glasses, and now I am pouring some Bushmills over some ice, reaching for the soda siphon and thinking better of it after all. On the rocks, I can taste that peat moss, and it tastes very good to me right now. Now I am looking over my bookcase to see if there is anything relaxing to read, but really I don't see anything that would soothe me in my present mood, for most of these books I use in a business way, and I am very weary of thinking about that. There are several volumes up here that would be of some interest to Yusuf Ali, such as about eight different translations of the Koran and a nice little shelf of Sufi poetry and a few fat books of Muslim theology, al-Ghazali being my really strong suit there for when I need to make an impression.

And there are also a few things here on my shelf that might interest my little friend Santa Barbara, if Santa knows how to read, which I doubt. But that makes next to no difference to Santa, since brujeria is and ever shall be an oral tradition in the main, without much of a literature at all, and for that very reason my shelf on the subject is not so respectable, consisting of a couple of very dull theses more or less in the anthropology line, fleshed out a bit with various pamphlets I pick up in the botánicas here and there around town. Or sometimes I order one straight out of the *National Enquirer*—"You Too Can Beat Your Fate and Make God Himself Bow Down to You with This Amazing Creole Mojo Stick," Satisfaction or Your Money Back, et cetera, and so on. Santeria isn't really so hard to handle once you've got the basics down, I buy these pamphlets to freshen my ideas from time to time, but if I really need something particular I just make it up, and why shouldn't I? It's what the santeros do themselves, I suspect, and what have they got I don't?

But I can answer that one too, the secret they have is that they believe it, and that is a trick that I can't master, not that I even want to try. But it is amazing how they do it, the info travels no farther than from one end of their brain to the other, but somewhere along the way it gets incarnated as The Truth. And sometimes I do think it might be nice to have one of those neat little sets of absolutes to call my very own, that would relieve me of the burden of ever having to make another decision all by my lonely little self. Yes, sometimes I think it would be very nice indeed to dispose of myself in one loud self-annihilating shout, *Allah allah allah akbar* or something of the sort and it doesn't even matter what, and be done with it once and for all. Even Holy Mother has got the hell beat out of me in that department, with his guilt and his pain and his dope and all that, he's still measuring himself against those same old changeless laws. But why I am even thinking these kinds of thoughts at this time I cannot understand, I do not want to think them at all and the fact that I am doing so is a sure sign that something is wrong inside my head. Now I am wondering what that thing might be, but then again I probably don't want to know that either, so I am going to cease all this troublesome thinking once and for all, put on a record, and sit down and drink my drink.

So now I am scanning my long shelf of records, perhaps my principal pride and joy, and I am looking under C, for Coleman not Coltrane this time, for I believe that it is only Ornette that can lift me up out of this gathering gloom. And my eager fingers are now alighting on my record of choice, which is entitled *New York Is Now*, and I am removing the disc from the sleeve and placing it on my Philips turntable, which responds to the heat of my fingertips and is so accomplished that it will do almost anything except make dinner.

But all I am asking it to do at this moment is to set its diamond tip down on the vinyl, and now this has been achieved and I am sitting at ease in my armchair, with my drink balanced on my navel, hearing from the mouths of my tiny Jap speakers the opening strains of side one, track one, which is called "The Garden of Souls." And Ornette lays open the gate to the garden with several horns and even some strings, a set of long dirgelike phrases, with a little interrogatory uplift at the end of each. And after this opening has teased at my ears for a moment or so, all the horns drop out but one, the bass and drums setting up a nice easy hint of a swing in the background, while that last horn drops into a nice coherent sax solo, and I close my eyes and take a sip of my golden alcohol.

And it seems that my cat is allured to my side at this point, whether by this lovely music or the smell of the drink or something entirely else I do not know, but she comes in the room and jumps into my lap, curls up there and begins to purr against the beat, as I sit and listen and stroke her warm fuzzy sides, Baby-Loves-You-Back, maybe that's what I'll name my cat, for she and Ornette are making me very content just now.

Yet as I continue to sit and listen to the plastic horn, it seems to be losing the line, or losing its mind, or I don't know what, but the solo is making less and less sense to my ears. That comfortable swing is gone altogether and the line that the horn is traveling is now choppy and broken, it sounds less like music now and more like voices in an argument, the voices nagging at my worried ears, and now the argument seems about to get hysterical, and yet here for a second it does fly away into an intelligible run, and the swing is back now too, only now I do not feel so certain that I can trust it.

And I am right to be suspicious, as it turns out, for now the bass is constructing a ladder, and the one horn is climbing down this ladder, and every now and then a rung snaps and the horn falls free and out of control and barely recovers itself. And everything is very uncertain in the garden of souls, so that you cannot be sure what is going to happen. But here at the foot of the ladder the first horn falls away and another one comes in, very low and very pained, moaning like a big foghorn over a large body of water. Three long moans and the third is held interminably, chewed back and forth in the horn player's mouth, and as he chews it, it begins to scream. And what I am now reminded of is Porco Miserio, for this is even very like his style of playing, which is why he can't get any more sessions, and so far from being relaxed and contented as planned, I am gritting my teeth at this moment and practically choking my unfortunate cat, listening to this manic shrieking horn and thinking of Porco and his sneaking Porco tricks, creeping back into my mind in this disgraceful nasty way when I have contrived so carefully to keep him out. It's the bad-luck curse that made me play this cut in the first place, for now I remember that what I really wanted was "Toy Dance," the next one, which is wholly free of these emotional acoustical complications.

But now I am entirely out of the mood for listening to any music whatever it might be, so I am slinging my cat out of the room by the scruff of her neck and getting up to shut off the record. I will not freaking sit here and think about freaking Porco against my will, I will listen only to the silence and the air conditioner and have one other drink, not more, for no matter how distressed I may presently feel I will not become a drooling slobbering sniveling drunk, like Porco Miserio. And now I am tossing off my last short drink and turning out the library light, and I'm stalking down the hall to the bedroom, as angry perhaps as even my cat. Now I'm throwing myself at my bed as if it were a punching bag, and when I hit it I am bouncing up maybe a foot, and landing on my back this time, to stay there, and what I am not going to do is think about insoluble problems, and what I am going to do is sleep.

And indeed as I lie here on my queen-sized mattress, I can feel those ugly nagging tensions seeping away through the double-ply padding and foam. Let Porco tie himself in a knot with his freaking talking rock in the middle, if that is what pleases him, but I am not going to worry and listen. I have my little system of self-regulation and it will suffice me, as it always has up to now. There are certain types of things that I do not let bother me, and tonight must definitely go on the list. For the rule of thumb in case of worry and doubt is that if you expect the worst you can count on getting it, so it is a far, far better thing to roll onto your stomach, crawl under the sheets, and let the rest of the world take care of itself. I'm yawning, I'm dozing, I'm immune to anxiety or even discontent, if you prick me I won't bleed, I'll just change colors and move farther down the branch. That is the last thought that I think as I go sailing away into sleepland, I am dreaming myself as a small observant lizard in a minor, but nonetheless classy, tree here in the garden of souls, and those souls may moan and groan to one another across the garden and dress in black cerements if they so choose, but not I, I will sit in my tree and watch and listen and learn and adapt, tossed on my branch in a cool springy breeze, and though I am almost a-sleep already I can still recognize this for the beautiful dream that it is.

Johnny B. | 243

Part Two

THE GARDEN OF SOULS

—We too back to the world shall never pass
Through the shattered door, a dumb
  shade-harried crowd
Being all infinite, function depth and mass
Without figure, a mathematical shroud

Hurled at the air—blessed without sin!
O God of our flesh, return us to Your wrath,
Let us be evil could we enter in
Your Grace, and falter on the stony path!
      —Allen Tate

Tommy/Sal

"Hello?"

"Hello, this the Brasi house?"

"Yes?"

"Lemme speak to Sal, he up?"

"You want Sally now? I think he's sleeping."

"Well, this is Tommy Whelan—"

"Oh, Tommy, sure, he'll talk to you. Just a minute while I get him."

"Yeah?"

"This Sally?"

"Yeah. Who is it?"

"It's Tommy. Tommy Whelan."

"No kidding? Tommy. So what you doing, calling people up this time Sunday morning? Thought you was working nights or something. Don't you ever sleep?"

"Working nights, yeah. No, I just thought I'd try to catch you before you went out to early Mass."

"Very funny, Tommy. You was lucky to catch the wife here though. She's just going out the door right now."

"She taking the kids with her?"

"Kids? Yeah, she's taking the kids. Nobody here but me. Come on, Whelan, what's up with you, you want me alone in the house or what? What's on your mind?"

"Oh, nothing special, Sally. Just thought I'd call you up and see how everything was out to Queens. Long time since I was in Queens."

"Yeah? Well, things are very nice out here, Tommy, since you ask. The wife got up, and she went to Mass, and I was just lying here having this nice dream about how the phone wasn't going to ring and I wasn't going to have to get up till noon. Then I talked to you, which was really great, and now I'm going back to sleep, okay?"

"Wait a second, Sally, don't hang up. I got something for you, I think."

"Oh really now, Tommy, I thought that might be what it was. Come on across with it, there's nobody here, phone's not tapped, nothing."

"Okay, now, but it'll take a minute or two. Sit down there, get comfortable. Now, you remember Johnny Dellacroce? Name mean anything to you?"

"Johnny Dellacroce? Johnny Dellacroce. Gimme a minute now, I just got up . . . seems like I remember the name. Yeah, I do. It was back in my kid days I knew a kid named that, younger than me. Yeah, right when I was about to move out of the old neighborhood, there, he was a bad little kid coming on around the block, stealing stuff from the candy store. You can't be calling about that, it must be twenty years ago."

"No, I'm not calling you about that, Sally. Statute of limitations is run out on this guy stealing stuff from the candy store. I wasn't thinking you'd remember him from the neighborhood anyway, I was thinking more like you might remember him from the rap sheets."

"That's it, is it? Well, it makes more sense. Don't know what I'm thinking about this morning anyway. Dellacroce. Tommy, you gonna have to tell me. I can't come up with a thing. We get this guy on something sometime, or what?"

"No . . . not exactly. Nothing particular. Be back around '68, and on up to around '73, he's just kind of around all the time. Suspicion of one thing and another. Lots of bad company and that."

"Ah, come on, Tommy, I could paper a room with guys like that.

Ten years ago and it doesn't mean a thing. You know it as well as me."

"I'm serious, Sally—"

"Okay, okay. So tell me who this guy's hanging around with ten years ago."

"Joey Gallo. All the Gallos. Then something to do with the Colombos. Also very thick with that hit man they used to call The Crow. You remember him—I think you had something to do with him going to the walls in '69."

"Yeah, I did at that, but Chrissake, Tommy, all those guys are long gone. Let the dead bury the dead, you know?"

"The Crow's not dead. Matter of fact he's back in town."

"He's what? Whelan, you're putting me on, he went up for freaking ever."

"But no, Sal, he's back out now. Walking papers and everything."

"Where'd you get this?"

"Called downtown."

"They're not supposed to talk to you."

"But they do."

"Jesus . . . trust Pardons and Paroles. They get you every time. But I don't see how I come into it. You gonna give me something on The Crow or what?"

"Just that every time The Crow does something it seems like this Dellacroce guy is just around the corner."

"Hey, come on, Tommy, it's early in the morning, Sunday morning here, I can't keep up with all this stuff. Besides, it's not my angle anymore, I'm off the mob squad, totally. Strictly narcotics, these days. Somebody else has the conspiracy end now and tell you the truth I'm glad they do."

"But this *is* narcotics, Sally baby, that's what I'm trying to tell you."

"You what? Okay, now, just tell me slowly about the narcotics part. And make sure you don't tell me nothing about guys we couldn't get indictments on ten years ago."

"But it all goes together, Sal, just listen to this. I got a tip this Dellacroce guy is now in the drug biz."

"Yeah? Okay. Where. What. And how much of it."

"Washington Square."

"Jesus, Tommy, this must be a bad dream. You're calling me up Sunday morning, tell me about guys selling joints in Washington Square? Go get some sleep, Whelan, sounds like you're not getting enough rest."

"Not joints, Sally. Hard stuff. Smack."

"Oh, no, Whelan, I'm not buying this. Everybody's always trying to tell me the Italians are heavy in heroin, and you know what? They're not and they never have been. You know who's really heavy in that, for real, it's the Jews. Even the word, *smack*, it comes from a Jewish word, means taste. A guy was telling me just the other day."

"Very interesting, Sally. But no kidding, I think we got one Italian down there that's in it enough to turn over some serious money. Come on, don't I usually give you good stuff?"

"You do, Tommy, you do at that. I'm still listening. Who tipped you into this?"

"A guy I know."

"A guy you know."

"Look, I can't give him to you, okay? And you don't want him anyway, he's not in it. But the information is good. You can take it to the bank."

"Tommy, on the level now, I don't see anything in this. Sorry, but I don't. I look up the files on this Dellacroce, I'm going to find stuff from '68. I send my guys into Washington Square, they're going to bring me sugar and oregano and stuff. Better I should leave them down the precinct where at least they can answer the phone."

"Okay, all right. You still play chess, Sal?"

"What . . . yeah, sure I still play chess. We played, when was it, coupla months back, right? I beat you, I remember that."

"Well, look, it's a nice day. Let's meet over to Washington Square, play a little chess in the park there."

"Oh no. Look, you want to play chess, come on over here and we'll play. The wife be glad to see you, Tommy, it's been a long time."

"Too long, Sal. Sure, I'll come over there, but today, let's play in the park, and maybe we might see something interesting."

"Ah, Tommy, do I have to do this? When did you get such a case of the hots for dope dealers anyway?"

"Well, let's see. First, you might remember, it was a junkie shot my guts out and left me where I can't have a drink or eat nothing I like—"

"Sorry, Tommy, stupid of me—"

"—and then you remember my kid Stevie? About the same age as your Tony, I think."

"Sure I remember Stevie. I don't see him in a long time now, how's he doing?"

"I don't see him in a long time myself. Not for over a year. But about three weeks ago I get this letter, and you know what? He's in with the Moonies or something like that, and he won't even say where he is. And he says he's very happy and he hopes me and Mom are happy and he forgives us for everything and a whole lot of crap like that—"

"Jeez, Tommy, I didn't know—"

"—but the point is, it seems that Stevie was out and around, and he got on the junk and we didn't know. Then these Moonies or whatever took him off it, and now he thinks they own him. The kid is ruined for life, and besides that there's one thing and another—"

"Okay, Tommy, okay. When you want me to be there?"

"Say twelve noon? And Sal—"

"Yeah?"

"Have some guys around. In case there's a collar."

"What . . . okay, okay. I'll make a call. Anything else?"

"Yeah. I'll bring the chessmen. You bring the clock."

Johnny B.

Brrnng. . . .

It's not the alarm already. Why, that's not possible, it's hardly light out. I lash with my sleep-laden hand at the dresser, hoping to smash the alarm clock.

Brrnng. . . .

No, but it's not the alarm after all. It's the phone. Now who the hell. . . ? I roll to the other side of the bed where the phone ought to be, but instead I only come up with the cat. And what are you doing in the bed, I'd like to know. I pitch the cat into the far wall and she hisses out of the room, and the same to you, bitch.

Brrnng. . . .

And here is the phone, at last, on the floor.

"Hello, what the hell?"

"Johnny B.?"

Chilly fear weakens my bones. Nobody, but nobody, should connect that name with this number. Except for Holy Mother, and this isn't him.

"You have the wrong number," I say.

"Wake up, Johnny B., it's a lovely morning."

I roll back to the dresser and grope for my watch.

"Morning it is, whoever you are. It's six o'clock yet, now state your business and get off my phone."

Then there is silence. Not even the sound of a breath on the line, but suddenly I know who it is, I can even picture his miserable face.

"Porco, you horrible bastard," I say. "I let you live. All right? All right? Why can't you let me sleep?" Then I hang up the phone and unplug it. Hats off to the boys down at Bell Labs, these modular jacks are so very convenient, and now it's back to my poor broken sleep.

But now my sleep refuses to return. I'm lying here with my face tucked into my elbow, listening to my watch tick, and that is absurd, because my watch is electric and ticks not at all. Now I turn over onto my back and lie looking up through the morning murk in my eyes at the immaculate paint on the ceiling. I keep telling myself everything is okay, but I feel like the ceiling is about to fall in.

There's a horrible odor of rat in the room, and it's getting ranker every minute. Something is wrong. I sit up and swing my feet to the floor and find that I feel not so hot, which isn't really surprising on not so much sleep. If I ever see Porco again I think I may pull his head off personally. He has no conception of when to lay off. My cat comes back in and pours herself over my bare feet, she's begging forgiveness, and I pick her up and give her a pat. It's Sunday morning, pushing six-thirty now, but why does the room feel so full of devils and ghosts? Let us assume it is only a fractured dream, but since I can't sleep I will go and make coffee.

There are no ghosts or demons in my clean bright kitchen, where I stand spooning coffee into the pot, and there is nothing particularly troubling to me while I'm setting the pot on the fire. I go cheerfully down the hall to the bathroom and wash up my face, and it is not until I meet myself in the mirror that the shades and tremors return. That's a very jumpy-looking guy in there, you can see that the rodents of worry are gnawing inside his head. Those red-rimmed eyes are a big part of the problem, and I tug out the mirror and reach for the Visine behind it, which adds some sparkle to my view of the world and does in fact seem to improve my expression. And my pants are right here on the knob where I left them, so now I am putting them on.

Now I'm going back down the hall to the kitchen, where the coffee is calling me with smug little gurgles, and pausing in the library to snap on the radio for a touch of morning classical music.

While I am there it occurs to me that just a quarter inch of Irish in the bottom of my cup might aid in dispelling the remains of whatever nightmare Porco woke me up out of, so I take the bottle with me to the kitchen when I go. And I'm measuring out a small drop of the Irish and covering it over with hot black coffee and topping it off with whipped cream, why not? And halfway down this lovely confection the morning feels very much better indeed. So I break a healthy pair of granola bars out of the box and enrich myself with energy to meet the challenges which the day will doubtless be bringing. Then in comes the cat to clean off the crumbs from the top of my shining round table, and out go I to replace that bottle back in the bar.

But what's this they're playing for get-up-time music? Some dismal depressing string thing in D minor, which hits exactly the wrong note with me. I off the stereo, but it's too late already, and I plop down into my comfortable chair, overwhelmed once again by that odor of rat, that deadly sensation that somewhere, somehow, trouble is waiting. It's really too bad, but I know this feeling too terribly well, and when it won't shake off there's always a reason. Now what can that reason be? I catch my hands finding and lighting a Kool without any conscious instruction from me, and as the slow column of smoke mushrooms off of the ceiling, I scan the board for symptoms of danger. I tap on the walls and wait for the rat inside to respond.

First, the usual series of dread possibilities: Holy Mother may have finally crossed over the line, it's possible but no more likely this day than the last. Or something may have gone wrong with the car, or somebody may have tipped me into the cops, or some unsavory colleague from the long-distant past may have decided to take action against any or all of us. But these are all standard occupational hazards, covered by contingency plans that will work or not if the occasion arises. Forget them. I stub out my Kool, it's not good to be smoking already at six in the morning, and I get up and go feed the cat.

Items of special interest for the day are first of all . . . Yusuf Ali. That crack on the head may have skewed Yusuf permanently, or he may indeed have died in the night, carried off by concussion, complications, and so on. But I do not think that this threat is a serious one, and in any case I will find out in due time. There's the fact that Carlo is missing, but Carlo has always been more or less missing, as far as being useful goes. Then there is Porco, always an imponderable. But even Porco has some common sense and surely he won't be around today, not after last night, not after the call. And if he does show up that is it, no more breaks for Porco, and surely he can feel that in the wind for himself. Forget him. That covers the board as far as I can see it, and it looks more or less like a normal day, the odd problem lurking here and there up ahead, but nothing so very exceptional. Then why no abatement in that crawling sensation that keeps traveling up and down my poor spine?

The rat has not left my mansion of thought. He is only lying quiet for the moment, he's waiting for my attention to wander. But I will fake him out of the wall, I will think about other things for a while, and when the rat does put his head through the baseboard, I will still be waiting there with the brick.

So I wash up the cup and the pot, and I toss them into the drainer. I stand waiting for the cat to finish her breakfast, and when that bowl has been washed there is little to do except listen for sounds of renewed rat movement, so I decide to move on to the street. I go back to the bathroom and get a nice shave, find a clean shirt and socks to put on. I pat myself down for my keys and my cash, and now I am ready to go.

There is not much at all doing on Fifth Avenue, not at an unreasonably early hour like this, but it looks like being a very nice day. No doubt about it, it's cool and clear and the air is reasonably fresh for this town anyway, and the leaves of the trees in the park are still carrying the drops of a recent rain. And it is pleasant to walk by the wall on the cobbled sidewalk, alone and unhurried on this Sunday-morning stroll, with the little warm sunbeams slipping down through the branches of the trees that spread over my head. It seems that those rodents of worry and doubt have remained behind in my tidy apartment, so that I am just walking along with nothing much at all on my mind, and in fact I am feeling so light-hearted that I even attempt to swing through the zoo, but this is not much fun, because all the animals are asleep and won't come out to say hello. So I go back up to the sidewalk, and I keep on walking downtown, and I am so cheerful and carefree and thoughtless that before I know it I'm standing in front of the Plaza Hotel.

I stand here watching the sparkling fountain, and it occurs to me that since I have come so far I might as well go on and perform my daily duty at the Port Authority. So I make three quick blocks across the foot of the park and turn down Eighth Avenue, becoming just a little leg-weary by the time I arrive. This early on Sunday, the station is quiet, and there is no one to see me as I step up to locker 581. I transfer the contents into locker 582, and for only a quarter I have bought myself another day's worth of security. Good deal.

I move off from the lockers and a plan begins to take shape in my mind: since I have already journeyed this far from home, it makes perfect sense to go on and begin the business day. I am not going to summon personnel at this hour, but there is no reason not to go down to the park myself, I can smell the flowers just as well down there as up here, and I can also eliminate certain sources of groundless concern, such as the car. Let that then be the first order of business, to pick up the car and move it down to the Square.

So I crawl down to the nethermost regions of the bus station where the IND subway is, find a token for the machine, and start walking the platform and reading the signs. I have the station very much to myself and it is a bit gloomy and boring down here, I having forgotten to pick up a paper, but then the train is not long in coming, and the first to arrive is the double A, which suits me perfectly fine. For the double A carries me straight down to Twenty-third Street and spits me out right back at the Greek donut shop, where the morning shift is coming in now, Melina having packed it in for the present, and just a short walk from the donut shop is the garage where the car has been left for the night.

That is where I am going this minute, and it is not until I am standing in front of the place that it strikes me that after all this, I don't have the ticket. And what a shame it seems, after so many years, that I should start to behave like a screaming incompetent fool. Not only that, but those unwelcome feelings of doubt and anxiety have returned to me now in a great formless flood, the rat catching up with me at last, and really I'm too nervous and jumpy to go back uptown. Then there is nothing to do but go get Holy Mother, who will think I am out of my mind, that's for sure. But having come so far, I must follow through, so I swing back up to Twenty-third Street and walk west, trying to conjure up a nice opening line. I can always claim I got up for Mass, which should get a laugh out of the man if anything will, which, thinking it over, it won't. Poor Holy Mother, but we've all got to suffer, and he can always roll over and go back to sleep. All he's got to do is give me the ticket, and he won't really have to wake up to do that.

So my plan for the morning should work out after all, and my sense of contentment returns with new strength as I pass by the wall of the closed A & P and walk down by the row of shells near Tenth Avenue. And I see signs of renovation going on here, boding a nice little co-op opening up here soon, which will tone up the neighborhood and raise everyone's rent. And give Holy Mother a better class of neighbors, not that he'll mingle with them much, I suppose. Here is his building coming into sight, and now I am standing on the opposite corner, all ready to cross over and lean on the bell, but suddenly that rat has come out of the wall, and he's sinking his teeth in my throat.

It's the gate. The gate across Holy Mother's third-floor window is unlocked and swung open out over the sidewalk. This is it, the place where my intuition for evil was leading, the door where the rat got into my mind. I've lit another Kool without planning to, and I'm standing here trying to tell myself that maybe, just maybe, nothing is wrong, maybe Holy Mother is up early too. But up early or not, I know he never opens that gate. Not since he came back from the walls, since then, all the windows and doors and boxes stay locked.

I cross over the corner and stand under the fire escape, looking up at the gate with the sun winking off it. What to do? I could ring the bell now, but I don't want to wait a long time for no answer, that would jangle my nerves worse than they already are. Call the cops? Very funny, I'm not doing that yet. I look up and down and see no one at all on the street except for one kid in white coveralls sweeping in front of the Empire, and in a minute or two he's gone back inside. I back down the sidewalk and take a short run, jump up and just catch the first rung of the ladder. And I find I can just pull myself up to the next one, and when I have done that a time or two more, I've got a foothold and I'm on the first platform. I climb up the second ladder quite quickly, before the second-floor tenants can wonder what's up, and here I stop to catch my breath.

But really I'm not breathing so terribly hard, which is not bad for a man of my age, and a smoker. If all else fails I may yet have a career as a second-story man. Once again I feel healthy and wealthy and wise, and reluctant to remember I'm not doing this only for the exercise. In truth and fact, this fire escape has always been my favorite part of Holy Mother's residence, and when I am hanging around here, not so often in recent days, alas, it is where I will usually end up. Holy Mother himself doesn't like it so much, having a distaste for heights and ladders which is really quite reasonable, all things considered, but then I don't much care for that shrieking bright light bulb he won't ever turn off. So I come out here, regardless of weather, and perhaps Holy Mother will sit near the window ledge, and maybe we make conversation. Nice little visits, they used to be, but as the years go by there is less and less to say, and maybe Holy Mother is pacing the floor inside, while I stand here looking down at the street. Because the more time goes by the less time it takes him to get edgy and jumpy and wish me to leave, because the pressures of the habit are growing, and shooting up has always been a very private affair for Holy Mother. And that has cut into his social life.

Still, it is pleasant to stand here with my hands on the rail, looking across at the black and silver front of the Empire Diner, where the hired help is cleaning up for the morning's trade. And here on my right is the abandoned old El track, and I believe there are weeds sprouting up through the rails, all very nice and pastoral. I can even hear birdsong, from some hiding place, and far away down at the end of the street I can see the prow of a big white ship nosing up the river. Since the angle is such that I can't see the water, it looks like one of the buildings down there has just thrown up its hands and started walking away. Then the ship has passed by, and I still don't see the water, and I'm not getting any younger standing up here, and if I don't make a move fairly soon someone will come by and wonder what I am doing.

And so to the business at hand. I turn around and find that the gate giving onto the platform is properly shut with two padlocks, one in each hasp. All shipshape and correct, and it would take me a painful hour to get the thing down, if I had a screwdriver, which I don't, not to mention how foolish I'd look up here when the citizens come out and start walking their dogs. And behind the gate the blind is pulled down, so I can't even see what is waiting inside. But the blind is shot through with a hot white glare, which means Holy Mother is still burning his light.

That is no news, he sleeps with the light on, how I don't know. The last year or so, he's been scared of the dark. So maybe everything is still all right, Holy Mother is stretched out in there on the bed, sleeping whatever sleep he can manage. I can almost persuade myself that it's a good omen, that gate hanging open, a signal that Holy Mother is loosening up around the edges, gaining some ground on his torments and fears. Thinking this happy thought, I reach out my hand to tap on the window, but then if I'm right it's a pity to wake him. If I am right the thing to do is forget it for now and meet him later down at the park. But I look back at the open gate and the rat gnaws the molding. It seems there is only one way to get in.

It is some little distance from the platform to the gate, just about a foot more than I can possibly reach. If the gate were swung this way, it would stretch to the railing, but it's hanging straight out, right-angled to the wall. I stretch and strain, but I can't get it, I call it and it doesn't come. Well, it isn't really so much of a jump, and these little risks add spice to my life. I climb up on the rail and crouch on the balls of my feet, my fingertips pressing the wall for balance. I'm only hoping the hinges will hold.

Swish, and I make it, I'm glued to the grid like Spiderman, and guys, this is really fun. The gate is swinging around from the force of the jump, cruising back into the window frame. Now I am hanging in front of the window, and there is Holy Mother sitting cross-legged behind his table, looking back out. I am so very relieved, and after all, life is so very wonderful.

"Surprise," I say, grinning already, all over my face. But then I see that the joke is on me.

There is a crack and a groan and the hinges are giving, the gate is sagging under my weight. But now I can steady myself with a toe on the windowsill—it's not me that buys it this morning. It's him. I can now see the needle stuck in his neck, like someone has hit him with a poisoned dart. The cords in his neck are tightened and stiff, and the whites of his eyes are turned out. All this and the bluish tinge of his skin informs me that it is only the corporeal husk of Holy Mother which I see, the soul, such as it is or was, having fled. And around this vacated shell of my man, all the nebulous and ominous harbingers of the night and the morning are clustering into one grim little aura. The hinges give more and I almost fall out. I work my way around the gate and sit braced on the ledge, looking down at the shape of my bad dream come true. After all, this is exactly what I was expecting.

Porco

"I let you live. Why can't you let me sleep?"

And that's it, dial tone. Hangs up on me and leaves me standing here with the receiver beeping in my hand. He's still got no idea what's been going on. A guy that could sleep through a night like this, what the hell is the matter with him? He should have listened. I slam the receiver back in the cradle and feel in the slot for a lucky dime. But there isn't one. I turn away from the booth and almost pass out on my feet. Great floods of darkness coming up from behind my eyes. I hold on to the frame of the booth to keep from falling, if I go down in front of those cops on the median, I'll wake up in the tank. When my vision comes back I feel a little more charitable about Johnny B. A nap wouldn't hurt me either, I think, it's something you do need to do now and then. Right now I've got to sit down a minute.

Well, the coffee shop is waiting there across the sidewalk. Can I make it? Yes. I go in and totter to a stool at the counter. Nobody in here but the counterman, no sound but the fan grinding away in the wall at the back. Low-class establishment, about the size of two elevators or half a tenement hallway.

"Number one breakfast," I say. "Coffee light." My appetite is theoretical only. But if I eat something it might give me the juice to walk out of this neighborhood before I fall down. Which would be a good idea. I scratch my left ankle and come up with what's left of the money out of my sock. Two twenties there, and the singles. I put the bills into my inside coat pocket. Checking through other pockets, I find some more singles and most of a pack of cigarettes and enough change to probably pay for the breakfast. Not so bad at all. I thought I'd been more profligate in the Spring Lounge, but of course it's cheap there. I stash all the bills away in one pocket and load the change onto the counter. Number one breakfast appears as two fried with potatoes and toast. Surprises me how hungry I am when it comes. In seconds I'm down to the last vein of egg yolk on the last scrap of toast. Doing me all kinds of good too.

Feel a bit more lifelike now. Refill on the coffee, and have myself a smoke and a quiet think. Time now to try to sort some information out of my swimming head. Seems certain that Johnny B. won't give me any more play just now. Sad, but true. With what Yusuf said, I should probably give them all a big miss for a while. No visits, no more calls. Show I can follow directions. I've done as much pushing as I can for now, don't want to push myself into a coffin.

Which leaves another whole weary day to get through. And only just beginning, by the clock on the wall. I count out a buck twenty-five for the counterman and pocket the rest of my coins. I swing off the stool and out to the street. My breakfast keeps moving around when I walk, but I feel a lot better than I did before.

I push on across Delancey Street, back toward the middle of town. Getting painfully bright out here now. I rummage around in my pockets and come up with a pair of green glasses. Nothing much wrong with them except one missing earpiece. They balance okay on my nose. Not much doing on Delancey so early. Only a few storekeepers puttering around behind their locked gates. It's shaping up to be a hot day.

Well, what am I going to do with it? Still feel just a little lonely and outraged. Rude of the man to hang up like that. Not giving me any kind of shake at all. But that's gone on by now. A little music would be nice now, I think, and in order too. Must keep my chops up somehow, and it's been several days. Let's see now. The cash on hand is not quite enough to unhock the alto. This reduces me to the kindness of friends. Which is often not to be counted on at these early hours of the morning.

There is always my friend Cynthia, who's holding my sopranino. But then I'm not in the mood for Cynthia now, nor she for me, probably. Besides, it's way the hell up the West Side, never make it up there, the shape I'm in. Then there is the tenor left in Bradley Todd's loft over on Crosby Street. That seems like a better prospect. Though I am not much in the mood for Bradley Todd either; in fact I'm almost never in the mood for him. But then I don't so much mind waking him up at six in the morning. Better he should suffer than Cynthia, also Crosby Street is much closer than West End Avenue. Then if I save Cynthia for later in the day, I might even swing some practice time up in her place. Haven't asked her many favors lately that I can recall. Then again there seems to be enough money for a couple of days in a flop, once I pick up the horn. And by the time they throw me out I'll be ready to leave in any case. Well, we'll see. But at least the great desert spaces of the day ahead seem to be filling up with something or other.

I'm picking up the pace here at Allen Street and crossing over now to Maxie's for a coffee-to-go, keep up my strength. Maxie's all full of dark yawning hookers from the hotel next door. All worn out from Saturday night, and catnapping away the first hours of Sunday. I pay for the coffee with the last of my change and go swinging across Kenmare Street, then up Lafayette and over on Spring. And the cup falls empty at the corner of Crosby Street.

Now I'm wavering in front of the buzzer and trying to guess the time. Can't say for sure, but it's early to come calling on Bradley Todd. He's not going to be very pleased with the visit, and what if he won't keep the horn anymore? Put me in a bad spot is what. I pull at the street door, thinking not much. And strangely enough it opens. Must have been left ajar by someone. So now I just go in and walk up the stairs.

But the door to the official Soho artist's loft belonging to Bradley Todd is absolutely locked. Keep pulling on it and nothing happens, you can't expect too much from dumb luck. There's nothing to do but start knocking—or is there? Always a chance I still have that pouch of masters on me. Takes a full-scale pocket inventory to find out, but I have nothing if not time. I sit down and begin dealing things out of my coat onto the corrugated steel steps around me. The usual jumble of god-knows-what, and no keys. Now I take off the coat itself, and here is something which feels promising in the lining. I push it around the bottom of the coat until I can fish it out through the original hole in the left pocket. Yes, my nice flat manila envelope full of twenty-five spare keys.

So now I put everything back in my pockets and put on the coat. I stand up and address myself to the lock. Keys one through nine do not even go into it. The tenth key fits but will not turn, likewise the eleventh. The twelfth key, much to my surprise, both fits and turns. The atelier of Bradley Todd is now open to my depredations. I kiss my envelope of keys and stick it back into the coat lining.

Now I'm pushing the door open, softly as I can. Now worming my way around the edge and shoving the door quietly back. If anyone is here they must be sleeping. Can't say if anyone is or not. This loft runs through to the street on both sides. Windows at either end, curtained with some sort of straw matting which shuts out most of the light. The style is Soho Art-Loft Package #4, which includes cleaning and whitewashing of the window frames and columns, if any, plus sanding and waxing of the floor, plus the installment of the obligatory International Style rabbit hutch, also called a living module. The rabbit hutch in this instance conceals bedroom, bath, and kitchen, also perhaps a sleeping Bradley Todd with or without friends.

The rest of the space in this loft is mainly filled up with air. At one end there's a long table for eating. And under the Crosby Street windows there's another long table for cocktails and hors d'oeuvres. Bradley Todd being a prominent hostess, or no, that's not quite the term. Then there's a few dangerous-looking chairs scattered about here and there.

Plus also the artwork of Bradley Todd. Without that he couldn't even pass by the zoning. Todd has a rep as a conceptual sculptor, or some equally resounding title—these things sometimes slip my mind. The rep is based on a couple of sculptures now present in the room. I tiptoe over to one of them and observe that it hasn't changed a bit since the last time I was here. Which does not surprise me too much at all. The sculptures consist of dried mud in large boxes. This mud has been molded and shaped by the conceptualizing fingers of Bradley Todd so that it resembles the Badlands of South Dakota, on a small scale and unfortunately without the nice colors. And that's all.

A person might jump to the conclusion that the talents of Bradley Todd are really quite negligible. But that would be a mistake, because Bradley Todd is really a consummate genius in his own way. His genius finds its true expression not in the mud boxes at all, but in the magnificent, elegant scams he has been running on the National Endowment for the Arts and the New York State Council on the Arts for the last six years or so. The *locus classicus* of Bradley Todd's artistry is grant-writing, and the cash flows his way in thick fragrant streams. Meanwhile I run around all over downtown cheating bartenders on the change and sticking my fingers up pay telephones. However, all the money Bradley Todd makes is not worth having to be Bradley Todd. Or so I believe, at least most of the time.

Bradley Todd's main problem at present is that he's fallen into the habit of believing his own PR. Used to have a charming cynicism about his whole operation, but now, alas, no more. He now talks very ponderously about his early work, that being the mud boxes. Which is really quite funny, because the mud boxes themselves have not changed at all. In fact, the only fresh mud that has entered the loft lately has come in inadvertently on Bradley Todd's feet. And if he's done any sculpture in the last several years it must have been in the realm of concept alone. Meanwhile this horrible habit of taking himself seriously keeps getting worse and worse. So that now he's almost intolerable. Though up to the minute his perception of what is of true value in this world has remained lucid enough for him to play host to me now and again, and more often to my tenor sax. With which thought I abandon the mud boxes and return to the real issue of the day. Where in all of this predictably bare-and-spare elegance has Bradley Todd hidden my horn?

It is not anywhere in plain sight, that's for sure. Which means it must be either in the rabbit hutch or else in the dandy pine cabinets built all along this one wall. I try the cabinets first and find no horn. I do find lots of clothes and a hidden stereo set and some unusually clean-looking sculpture equipment.

Well now. Exploring the rabbit hutch is likely to be a matter of great delicacy. My preference this morning is to come and go unobserved. If I can swing it. Of course it would be truly wonderful if Bradley Todd was vacationing in Madrid. Then I could make all the noise I please. I could probably even stay here through August, now I've got a working key. A pleasant thought, but more likely Bradley Todd is in residence and snugly tucked up in his bed. Well. I take off my shoes and move into the rabbit hutch on soft moving socks.

Not much to my surprise, I don't find the horn in the kitchen. Nor yet in the bathroom. Then there is a loft within a loft, a storage space on top of the hutch. I creep up there with fairly high hopes, but the horn isn't up there either.

Bradley Todd wouldn't have hocked my horn, would he? Certainly not. One of my few remaining prerogatives is doing that stupid thing myself when I feel like it. Probably the horn is in Bradley Todd's bedroom. Under Bradley Todd's bed. Under Bradley Todd himself, in all probability. That's where he always keeps it, after all. I was just hoping I might not have to go in there. But now it appears that I do.

The bedroom is the last room in the hutch, which runs up on the last wall of the loft itself. I give the door a push of a fingertip and let it float gently open. There he is, my darling coney. Bradley Todd is a trim little guy. Every hair stays in place even while he's asleep. His mouth parted slightly, his breath fanning his nice little mustache. And the sheet drawn up flush with the red lower lip.

What a picture. I inch to the end of the bed and crouch down. Then to my horror I see that there are not two feet hanging off the end of the mattress but four. Either Bradley Todd has grown another pair of legs or else he's got company. And things could get awkward if the company wakes up.

Eyes still on the feet, I reach under the bed as far as I can. And a blessing, the first thing I touch is clearly the marbled case of my horn. I pull it very cautiously toward me, and something on top of it seems to fall off, making a terribly uncouth loud sound. All four feet (nicely formed they were too) flash abruptly out of my field of vision. Then I hear the commencement of feminine screams. Bradley Todd and his friend have gone straight up the wall. The friend continues to shriek with great verve. Of all things, it's a girl, and a girl with no clothes on. And I always assumed Bradley Todd was gay.

Well, maybe it's his sister. I get hold of the case by the handle and pull it completely out from under the bed. Time to put the best face on the matter I can.

"Good morning, Bradley, good morning to you," I say. "How's the mud pie business coming along?"

"What? What? What?" says Bradley Todd. He gives his head a vicious shake and his hair fans out in all directions. Then it miraculously drops back into the contours of the fifty-dollar clip. Now Bradley tries to cover himself with the sheet. In the process he further denudes his lady companion, whose screams rise a notch in pitch and intensity.

"Oh my God," Bradley says. "Oh, it's you." This last in the tone you might use for addressing a slug. While Bradley and friend still fight for the sheet, I notice he's now got a perfect full-body tan. All over his neat little physique. These conceptual sculptors, they know how to live.

"Oh my God," says Bradley, repeating himself. "How did you ever get *in* here." And he gives an uneasy glance at his friend, who's still screaming determinedly, eyes squeezed shut and chest heaving admirably. I see what's bugging Bradley now. He'd like to play outraged householder all the way, but he's deathly afraid of being unhip. Though the lady, after all, is responding in a perfectly conventional way.

"Oh, I just stopped in to pick up my horn," I say, picking up my horn to prove it. "Believe me, nothing could be further from my intention than to disturb you in any way at all." Hearing my voice, the lady friend scales another octave. I'm impressed—this girl can really sustain.

"What I said was, '*How* did you get in?' " says Bradley. "Not *why.*"

"Oh, ah, well now, Bradley," I say. It would only upset him to hear about my magic keys. This I know. "Do you think maybe you could ask your friend to sort of like be quiet now? Hate to make trouble, but I've got just a bit of a hangover this morning."

"Celeste, Celeste, it's okay," Bradley says, in a voice of deep understanding. "It's cool, it's a friend, well, it's someone I know." Gives me a bitter look on that one. I spot a blanket folded at the foot of the bed and toss it over to Celeste. She pulls it up to her shoulders, then opens her eyes and closes her mouth. This simple reversal reveals her to be a very pretty girl indeed. Model, I shouldn't wonder. Got the bones for it.

"What is it, Brad?" she says. "What's happening?" And she looks at me with her eyes very wide and appealing. The latter effect being accidental, I imagine. After last night I doubt I look much worth appealing to.

"Dear lady, allow me to present myself more properly," I say, placing one hand over my heart.

"Oh God not the Barnum and Bailey routine," says Bradley, all of a rush.

"My humble cognomen is Porco Miserio," I say, with a bow. Celeste is now so astonished that she takes her hands off her blanket and tucks all ten of her fingers into her mouth.

"Will you please take your horn and go *away*," Bradley says. But I really can't stop myself now.

"My intimates call me quite simply Porco," I go on. "And I would be absolutely enchanted to number you among them."

Now I step forward, intending to take one of her hands out of her mouth and kiss it, that being the action which seems best suited to the diction. But instead I fall largo over the saxophone case, which I seem to have put down directly in front of my feet. I pitch very gracelessly onto the bed itself and into Celeste, who's now lost her blanket. With my head fortuitously pillowed on her bosom for the moment, I'm thinking that now is the time for my nap. But then it occurs to me that from the objective point of view, the situation is really going from bad to worse. So I bounce back onto my feet. Like Bozo the Boxing Clown.

"It certainly has been an extraordinary pleasure," I say to the girl, who's still floundering. "Bradley, I'll stop back in sometime when it's more convenient." But from the burning brick color of his sputtering face, I think he doesn't really appreciate my solicitude. So I pick up my sax and walk out, shutting the bedroom door. Making the best of a bad job. But at the worst it only means eviction for my horn. I walk out of the rabbit hutch and stop cold.

There're still voices going on in the room behind me. Bradley's soft and repetitive, the girl laughing now, she's either in hysterics or honestly amused, I couldn't say which. It doesn't matter anyway, because the voices suddenly stop in my ears. They must be still there, but I don't hear them now. Snap, it's like turning off a radio. I blink my eyes and look down the long plane of the loft. I watch the dust dancing in the bars of light that shoot through the matting over the Crosby Street windows, and I listen to the deep silence that has risen inside my head.

Now I walk down to the table by those windows, not even hearing my own feet striking the floor. I open the case and take out the saxophone and put it quickly together. There's about ten times as many moving parts on this thing as there are bones in both of my feet, so I run over the keys to make sure they're all working. Then I find the hook on the lanyard that always hangs inside my clothes and slip it into the ring on the horn. I stand up, cradling the horn, and now something tells me to take the Stone out of my pocket and put it in the center of the table. I stand back, sucking my reed, regarding the Stone. This will be a serenade.

The bars of sunlight play into the Stone, not reducing its blackness. It seems that the objects in the room and even the walls and the floor are beginning to tilt toward it. I find myself expecting this world to pass into and through the Stone, emerging inverted on some other side beyond my imagining. Yes, precisely beyond my imagining. The Stone rests in the center of my vision, small, infinitely heavy, of a darkness that is simply a negation of color. It is the limit for the asymptotic approach of my understanding. Thus it knows, beyond my imagining. Nothing in fact comes out of it other than a sonorous emptiness, a resonant silence parallel to the vacuum in my own head, that silence now filling with the opening lines of the correct idea: Coltrane's "Spiritual."

I arch my fingers and draw in my breath. The first notes of the tune curve up into the air like an enormous question mark. However, this aural formation also expresses great certainty. It makes an answer of the question itself. So I permit myself to forget the question for now, knowing that what will be required of me in the next few minutes will be perfectly simple.

Johnny B.

So now I know. I'm hanging here in the window, looking into the room, not exactly at Holy Mother, but over him, at the wall. And after some amount of time I begin to hear voices and cars rolling by on the street below, business going on as usual down there. So I push the window open far enough for me to duck inside, and I land heavily on the floor, worrying about the noise I made, which is foolish, since there is no one to hear it. And now that I am inside, the first thing I do is cross the room and turn off that glaring hot light bulb, for which there is now not any further use or need.

And in the new dimness of the room I walk back and forth, paying no attention at all to the man in the chair, because I do not want to look at him, and in fact I would rather look at almost anything else. The first thing which I choose to inspect is the picture on the wall, which is indeed the only thing on any of the walls, and which I put there myself. I look at the face of this girl with her baby, the face being so very full of life, also full of vanity in the frivolous hat, and with pleasure, one assumes, in the fat healthy child. I think how little she is like the Madonnas of the churches we both knew, and also I think that the placement of this picture here is a joke which perhaps did not pay off. And now I resume exploring the room, but there is little else in it of any aesthetic interest, because it has been a long time since Holy Mother has taken any interest in the things of the senses, or in any other things, for that matter.

What I find in the room is a hole in the floor, with an old army trunk pushed aside from it, and the loose floorboard propped on the trunk, and this is Holy Mother's hiding place, empty now except for a folded blanket in the bottom of it. What was once in the hiding place is now in plain view on the table by the window: a bag, a Bunsen burner, a length of rubber tubing, all the little odds and ends of addiction. And other than these items there is nothing in the room of any especial fascination.

So I find myself standing near the man in the chair, and after a moment has passed I grasp the syringe and pluck it out of his neck. I'm standing here holding it, not knowing where it goes, and it occurs to me to be a good housekeeper and put it and everything back in the box, back in the hole, and under the floor, but of course that would be the wrong thing to do. So I pull out my shirttail and wipe the needle for prints, and then I let it fall on the floor by the chair. And when I have done this I find a chair for myself, and I pull it up to the table and sit down.

It is amazing how very like himself he looks, how little less alive than yesterday. I find the pack of Kools in my top pocket and I hold it across the table to him.

"Smoke?" I say. But he doesn't answer.

"You won't mind if I have one," I say, lighting it. "I know you claim you don't like menthol, but that's just because you're an ignorant fool. There's really nothing like it on a hot summer day."

I sit and I smoke, tapping ash in my hand, and I look at him. He is sitting quite still. I notice a piece of blue paper peeping out of his shirt pocket, probably that is the parking ticket. I pull it out and it is.

"Excuse me," I say, "but I'll be needing this for later today when I leave."

Now my Kool has burned down to the filter, and I lean to the window and blow it and the ashes outside.

"Remember," I say, "the pool on Vandam Street. The summer we used to climb in there late at night? Ah, that was nice, it was so hot that summer. We must have gone in there almost every night until the night the cops came and we had to blow. Left our shoes there too, and next day Timmy the cop was all over the neighborhood—'Hey, who knows these shoes?' And of course, we had to tell everybody, and the guys dared us to do it again, and a few of them came along. The cops were watching it that night, naturally, but we all got away that time too, all except for Artie, because he was already too fat to get over the fence. Then Artie wouldn't say who was with him, and they were that mad, Artie would have ended up in Spofford if it hadn't been for his father. Good old Artie, the stand-up guy, twelve years old. It was a gas, you remember?"

No.

"Remember ten years later, when Artie turned up shot?"

No comment.

"Sorry, that could have been one of yours, couldn't it? Silly of me, I really wasn't thinking that."

Nothing.

"You remember the time I stole the church wine? Got it right out of the sacristy, it wasn't locked up or anything, and argued with you an hour that it wasn't consecrated yet before I could get you to drink any. Then we finally did crack into it, and it was so loaded with water we knew it was blessed. You thought we were going to hell for sure, you've got to remember that one."

No.

"Remember the girl from Carmine Street?"

No.

"I know you remember the girl from Carmine Street. But we won't talk about her if that's the way you feel."

I light another Kool and smoke it and unload the butt out the window.

"I understand your position completely," I say at last. "All things considered, you're probably right. We did what we did and it's all in the past. There's no use dragging up all those old stories now."

No comment, once again.

"Well, it's been nice to talk to you," I say, standing up, "but I have a lot of things to do now. I hope you don't mind, but I'm going to have to kind of look around the place, check if there's anything that might lead back to me. You understand, I have to keep on living."

And I get halfway across the room before it hits me between the eyes like a hammer. What it is is a picture of Porco sitting last night in the park with his rock in his paw and that superior smile which is trying to tell me, "You too will come to this." And I have just spent the past half hour reminiscing with a corpse.

An uncomfortable thought, but I will have to consider it later, if ever at all, because right now I have other things to do. I have got to run through the whole place and be absolutely certain that there is nothing around which would especially connect me with him. What I have in mind are things along the lines of letters, date books, diaries, photographs, none of them the sorts of things that Holy Mother would ever have around anyway, but you can't be too careful, you know.

I begin the search in the kitchen, where there is nothing in the drawers except some unused-looking cooking tools. Nothing in the cabinets but very dusty dishes, and nothing on top of the cabinets at all. I open the oven and all there is in it is mouse dung. And in the refrigerator I do not find anything of any interest to me. And there is no place else in this room where anything could be hidden.

In the next room, I look first behind the picture, and then between the picture and the frame—clean. I open the trunk and go through the clothes in it—zip. I reach in the hole through the floorboards and shake out the folded blanket, but nothing at all falls out of it. After thinking it over, I drop the blanket in the hole and put the boards back over it and the trunk over that, no reason not to.

Between the trunk and the bed there is a bureau. On top of the bureau there is only a brush and a comb. In the top drawer of the bureau I find socks and underwear, and turning them over, I begin to find various old pens and pencils, and these may be some cause for concern. And at the bottom of this drawer I find a date book and an address book, and these could be very hot items indeed, just what I am looking for. But when I open them up it turns out that there is nothing whatsoever written in either, nothing at all besides what was printed there by the National Notebook Company of Metuchen, New Jersey. So I tumble them back in the drawer under the socks and the underwear.

There are three other drawers in the dresser, and nothing in any of them other than clothes. I even go through the pockets of all of these clothes, and I don't find anything other than the odd matchbook or cigarette pack. So I close the drawers back up and move on to the bed, which is made up so professionally tight and square that a flea could not creep into it under the sheet, and there is nothing between the bed and the frame and nothing under the bed either except big clots of dust.

I get up sneezing and go into the bathroom. In the medicine cabinet I find toothbrush and paste, a safety razor and a lot of old blades. On top of the cabinet, nothing, and nothing in the soap dish or the shower. I lift the lid off the toilet tank and behold, there is something in there, at the bottom. I reach down in the water and lift the thing out. It's tidily packaged in two Ziploc bags all wound up with tape, and what the thing is is a gun. That is of no concern to me now, though Holy Mother has it against my advice and counsel. He was keeping it for sentimental reasons perhaps. Let it remain to amuse or perplex the next tenants. I let it sink back in the tank.

That's it. The monastic simplicity of Holy Mother's domestic arrangements has made this task very simple and easy. I'm grateful for that, but all the same it's a bit disappointing not to have found any mementos at all, though in theory I approve of this straight down the line. Still I have this feeling that there should have been something, an item or two for me to get rid of. But there's not, I've looked everywhere, I'm done and now I can leave. For simplicity's sake I will leave by the door.

I stop for a moment on my way out and take one more look at the man on the chair. Holy Mother, or by proper christening Aniello Di Angelo, which translates, believe it or not, as little lamb of the angels, though half of it is a fix perpetrated on the man by his mother. And perhaps he is now in the fold of Jesus' arms, though in truth that seems very doubtful. He is dead and gone somewhere anyway. And looking at him now I feel a sudden and pointless movement of pity, which on close examination turns out to be mostly for myself, since Aniello is out of it now in any case. He is dead and there is now no one who can remember any of the things that I know. In fact, there is no longer anyone who knows who I am with any degree of certainty, and that is a very desirable thing from the practical point of view. And probably there never was anyone to remember, not when I have made such a careful practice of forgetting it all myself. It is now time to go.

I turn away and then realize I forgot to check the pockets of the clothes he has on. A disagreeable thing to do, but I had better do it. Hopefully, most of it can be done just by touch. In the shirt pocket, only a pack of Luckies and matches. In the left boot I know there's the double-edged tempered-steel stabbing knife, but I'm not going to put my prints all over that. His wallet is peeping out of his left hip pocket, and I can just draw it out with a thumb and forefinger. In the wallet there is money, a driver's license, a little this and that. Also a cellophane folder with pictures, but these prove to be only the wife and the kids, and are ten years old besides. I push the wallet back down in the pocket. I feel nothing at all in the right hip pocket. In the left front pocket I can feel change, but there is no need to examine that. In the right front pocket there's something I can't identify by feel. With some difficulty I hook my fingers into the pocket and draw the thing over the unyielding hipbone. It is, of all things, a rosary.

Well, how do you like that. But after all, I almost like thinking that Aniello may have brought off some last-minute deal with the Lord. Maybe, and in any case it isn't my problem. I shove the beads back into the pocket, get up, and walk to the door. It takes a hard twist to open these four lock bars. I turn back to the man in the chair. What do you say on an occasion like this? None of the usual lines seems to fit. Also I keep thinking I've overlooked something.

Oh yes. There is just one thing that my man would want, and that is a nice Catholic funeral. Well, what do you want from me, old bones, I really can't make the arrangements myself. So sorry, but no can do. I'm leaving, but then I'm not. In this situation there seems to be a particular necessity. In the words of the Prophet, it is written. There must be a way, and now I have got it.

I walk back to the dresser and open the drawer, find the pens and the books and take them to the table. I open the address book and begin to write, changing pens now and then in the interest of plausibility, and how well I do remember them all, a mother, father, grandparents, aunts, uncles, cousins, and friends. I remember the addresses and the phone numbers, also the voices and faces and tastes in clothes and movies and everything else, and each new name I write in the book calls up another memory, another persona appears in the room at my back, and soon the room is filled with solemn faces and voices soft with regret. *Holy Mary, mother of God, pray for us now and at the hour of our death* . . . I can even smell the candles and hear the murmuring, as though it were all really happening, as though it really were a wake.

Now I have filled out the address book from Abbadano to Zambone, and now I turn to the date book. And I find it easy to write that on Monday, my man went downtown to play cards, Tuesday, dinner with the family, Wednesday, the phone number of an interesting girl, and so on and so on until the date book also is full of information, until it has constituted a life. An interesting life in which many things happened and which has been concluded now, today, in the year of our Lord 1980. I put down the pen. They will not give him the big funeral procession, the long cars and the wreaths and the men in dark glasses, because they do not do that anymore, not for anyone. But there will be the church and the Mass and the priest at the grave. Though I will not see it, I know it will happen, this much can be depended on. I take both books and crack their spines to give them a look of use. I sponge the pages around on the floor, and I put them on top of the dresser. It is finished.

Almost. The nice thing about all this is I get to finish it off with a gag, as a matter of fact I have to finish it off that way. I check all round to make sure I haven't forgotten anything, and there are the pens on the table. I put them back in the drawer with the socks, and now I am walking to the phone on the wall.

I pick up the receiver and dial 911. A voice answers on the second ring.

"Police."

"Get somebody over here quick," I say, panting. "There's a murder going on here."

"What? Where are you?"

"I don't know, I don't know," I say. "But there's a lot of shooting going on. Twenty-third and Tenth, the northwest corner, the third floor."

"Who are you, anyway? Who's making this report?"

"It can wait till the car gets here, can't it?" I say. Then I hang up the phone. Now there is really not much time. I walk out the door, leaving it standing open, and jog down the two flights of stairs.

There's a Sunday *Times* on the floor in the entry, and I wedge the door open with that as I go out. Now I cross to the south side of the street, walk over to the row of shells on the other side of Tenth, and sit down on some steps out in front. I look at my watch, it's 11:08. How time flies when you're having fun. There's a little green tree planted in the sidewalk in front of me, craning toward an empty window on the second floor up above. I light another Kool and lean back on my elbows, blowing smoke up through the leaves.

Two-thirds down the cigarette I hear a siren, and the car comes flashing down the street. It screams to a stop at the corner, and two uniformed cops plunge out of it and into the building, hands on their holsters. My watch now says it's 11:15. Seven minutes on an emergency call, not so bad. Seven minutes is a long time to get shot in, of course, but I realize our boys do the best that they can.

I stand up, stretch, and step on my Kool. Back on the corner, I give a glance of the most casual interest at the car, which is still flashing its dome lights. I turn my back, and now I'm walking in front of the Empire, and now I'm around the corner and gone.

I walk up Twenty-second Street toward the garage, feeling a queer sense of emptiness after all that just happened. But I know that the *I* who is now going slowly along the sidewalk, dressed in a crisp white shirt for Sunday, has nothing to do with the *I* who spent those hours in the apartment with the dead man. That *I* is already lost in the past and indeed cannot be proven to have ever existed at all. There is now only the *I* who stands in front of the garage and presents the claim ticket to the cheery attendant, the *I* who waits patiently for the car to come down in the elevator, unsuspected and undisturbed. And now there is only the *I* who gets into the car and puts it in gear, the *I* pressing his foot on the gas, and the car jerking forward, into my future.

Tommy/Sal

"Your clock's running down, Sally."

"Shut up, will you? Shut up and let me think."

"You'll never think your way out of this one, Sally. Admit it, you're screwed."

"There."

"Hit the clock. Now I do this, now what?"

"This."

"Ah-ah-ah. Nothing for you, Sally. Your flag just dropped. Time's up."

"Okay, Tommy. One down. You only beat me on time though."

"Only on time, he says. Wait, don't pick up the pieces. Notice how you're up against the wall here. Right now you're a piece down and you're about to lose the exchange."

"The hell you say. How?"

"Like this, okay? Look at the board, you got no way out of it. And with that much material, you know I'm going to beat you. So don't be talking to me about time. Feel like trying it again?"

"Sure. Set it up. Hey, Tommy?"

"Yeah?"

"It's after twelve already. When's this Dellacroce guy come around?"

"He'll be here. Relax. Just go ahead and set the clocks."

"Okay, I'm hanging around for just one more game though. Some things I got to do this afternoon besides sit around in the park."

"Why, you must be planning to lose again, Sally."

"Make a move. Why's that?"

"Best two out of three, right? And you shouldn't play the English against me, Sal. It's a lousy opening, I'll ram it down your throat. Your move."

"We'll see about that, Tommy. Don't get overconfident. Hey, but you can tell me something."

"What's that?"

"Tell me something about where this tip you got came from. Who is this guy that I don't want?"

"You don't want him, like I said. He's just this guy that's around. I see him in bars now and then."

"So what's he do besides go in bars?"

"Not much, Sally, that I know about. Says he's a musician though, plays the horn. Matter of fact he threw me a ticket one time, go hear him play somewhere."

"You go?"

"I went."

"How was it?"

"Terrible. Some kind of modern jazz kind of jive, didn't even have a tune. Best I could do to sit through it. Got so bad I had to tear up napkins to stick in my ears. Never again."

"So what else about your guy?"

"Not much. Down and out now, I think. More or less of a bum these days."

"Oh, no, don't tell me. You meet this guy in a bar, right, Tommy, and you buy him a couple of drinks while he's telling you some kind of a story, and for that you drag me out of my house Sunday morning."

"It's not like that, Sal, the guy is all right. He's an egghead kind of guy. I think he's pretty smart even. Just a little off sometimes, you know? Got these wild kind of ideas he likes to talk about, don't make any sense. But he knows if the sun's shining, he's okay on facts. And he bought the drinks himself, if you got to know that. But forget him. That reminds me, there's something I wanted to ask you about too."

"How do you like the English now, pal, you just lost a pawn."

"But you're all overextended, Sal, I'll get you later. But tell me what you know about this Chinatown scam."

"Nothing. Don't even know what you're talking about."

"Saw it in the paper, couple of weeks back—hey, now, wait a minute."

"Something bite you?"

"No, but that's him. Over there, that's our guy."

"Where?"

"Up the corner. See him? Black hair, sunglasses. White shirt."

"What, way up there in the north corner? I can't make anybody that far off. Well, maybe I see a white shirt."

"I think you better get glasses, Sal. That's him, for sure. Stop the clock a minute."

"Stop the clock the hell. I thought you wanted to play some chess."

"Sure, but I want to see what he's gonna do."

"You going up there to take a close look?"

"No. Not yet anyway. Might make him jumpy."

"So your clock's running, play the game."

"All right, all right. There. Your move. Ah, now he's going down in the middle, see him?"

"Yeah, yeah."

"Probably he'll come back this way."

"So what were you saying about some Chinatown thing?"

"Oh, just what I saw in the paper. Some of your people running a front restaurant down East Broadway, and last week they broke it open and collared two guys. Six months they were running it, the paper said, and they get two guys. Sick is what I call it."

"Yeah, now I know what you're talking about. But what are you calling them my people for? That wasn't drugs, that was gangs. I had nothing to do with any of it."

"No connection between drugs and gangs, is there?"

"Look, Tommy, I didn't even know about this gag until it broke, and all they were going after was protection. And anyway, China-town's not my beat."

"The hell it's not. Half the time, I try to call you over the Village house, they tell me call down Chinatown."

"So I go down there sometimes. Maybe today, if you get me any-thing. They got me moving around some these days."

"If, he says. I'll get you something. But all I want to know is, what were those guys doing down there for six months? Cooping? Eating egg foo yung all day? Waste of my tax dollars is what I call it."

"Lay off with the taxpayer bit, Tommy, you know how it goes. And it never was my setup anyway, like I told you."

"Okay, okay, I was just giving you a little bit of the stick. Can't you take it?"

"Sure, I can take it. Maybe you'd like me to ask you some stuff about the guards business, eh, Tommy?"

"No, I wouldn't like that. Wait, here comes our guy again. Right down the path. Cool it, don't turn around. Just get a make on him when he goes by."

"Yeah, okay now. He's familiar. I think I know him. Used to have his hair shorter than that, didn't he? And lost some weight too, if it's the same guy."

"Yeah, he's changed some. Not enough to matter though. What's he doing, just walking around? Yeah, casing the place. Don't stare, Sally, not polite."

"Whatever you say, boss. Well, there he goes. Didn't see him sell anybody any smack either."

"Patience, my son. We just got to watch who he talks to. Just watch him awhile is all. Stop the clock."

"What are you going to do, follow him in there?"

"No, no, Sal. I'm just going to walk over and get us a couple of hot dogs or something. You're hungry, right? Lunch time here."

"Want company?"

"No. You just stay here and hold the table."

"Fine. Make mine with mustard and onion, and get me a Pepsi too, you don't mind."

"You got it. So stop the clock."

"No need to stop the clock, Tommy. The game is over already."

"What are you talking about here?"

"Just this. It's my move now, so check. Then you go here, then I get mate in one."

"But I go here instead."

"If you say so. But then I get mate in two. Now aren't you sorry you said bad things about the English?"

"The hell with you. Okay, one and one. I'll see you in a couple of minutes."

"Remember not to talk to strangers."

Porco

Indeed, completely simple. I just blow through the second line, the same, but with a little more lift. I get to breathe, and now I go bridging way up high, stretching out toward the last line of the intro, that descent. I take it down and hold it, sustain it, feeling the sound swell into the room, and then I sneak out at the bottom. Nice and easy for the next few bars. These spots drifting in front of my eyes tell me I almost blew a blood vessel back up there. But now I'm entitled to just noodle around for a while. I've tipped forward onto my toes, leaning into my own air pressure, to push through the intro. Now I step back and relax, let the next few bars slide out by themselves, more or less, nothing fancy or difficult. When I've cooled out some and my eyesight's stopped swimming, I begin to punch it up a little bit. Punch and probe, like feeling the way along a wall in the dark, the odd twist here and there, but never straying too far from the main line. Yes, and now it's the main line again, full and clear, and I begin to walk up and down, swinging back and forth on a semicircular track around the corners of the table, feeling more confident now.

Would be nice to have a rhythm section to lean back on, but it's okay not. I'm hearing ghost voices, I think, but then it's only Bradley Todd and his Celeste muttering behind me, back by the rabbit hutch, maintaining a steady chorus of aggravation and despair. I have better things to listen to, but every now and then a whole phrase seeps through.

". . . my God, you just can't get away from it, it fills up the whole place . . ."

That's the girl. And what a pretty compliment, because that's just exactly what it's supposed to do, exactly what I had in mind. A song of the inevitable, and I'm so pleased that I make a wild run up the scale, *aawonk aawonk* with wails of joy, building volume and biting the reed lightly at the very top, at the point where tl.e whole thing can go screaming away into madness if I choose. But I don't. I let my wild line fall back down to the parameters of reason, where the main line still waits reliable as the safety net which shimmers under the flying trapeze. The drop is retarded by the net, soft and easy. Now I start to build back up.

". . . Bradley, can't you do something?"

"All right, all right, I'll try . . ."

And swinging on my heels at the corner of the table, I notice Bradley Todd sneaking into the corner of my eye. One hand raised in warning and a mouthful of remonstrances. This will never do. I aim the bell of the horn at him and set my line into oscillation, as fast as I can manage and approaching the point where its own energy must shatter it. It beats in my mouth like a live electric eel. One eye still open, I see Bradley hesitate, and this is my moment to get him. I shove my bottom teeth into the reed and the sound splinters like a large pane of glass. Through squinted eyes I see Bradley Todd struck and flung back by this first wave of acoustic shrapnel. I shake my head, worrying the mouthpiece like an angry dog, then bring the line back full and wide, covering Bradley Todd with a stream of sound like water from a hose, and pushing him slowly backward, across the floor, to the wall of the rabbit hutch.

". . . You see how it is, he's not very responsive when he gets like this."

"Well, whose place is this anyway?"

"The only thing to do is wait it out . . ."

I rotate around on the balls of my heels, turn my back on them, and face the Stone. I'm ringing the changes, sounding my questions in a series of short, sharp attacks. I let the short phrases move more and more into discord—clear notes, but querulous. Sounds quite mad with no rhythm behind it, only the silence coming up hard against the ends of the phrases. So now I let them lengthen again, run together and glide.

It's not easy, blowing so hard after these long days not keeping up my chops. My knees tremble and my eyes won't see for me, the Stone swirls off the table into the air to become a series of hurtling asteroids, then just one unitary and absorbing blackness. The dark full of panic, holding all the fears and alarms of the night past, and not only for me but for all of us. But the music still carries itself somehow and draws me along after it like a fish on a line, rising steadily, sustained and still climbing, though how I'm still breathing I don't even know. Now the music and I break the surface together, bursting into clear air, and jangle away into joyful brassy laughter. I open my eyes, not blacked out after all, and the room comes back in one piece, the table solid in front of me, the light dancing in through the window and breaking on the surface of the Stone, which has not changed one iota. I did that run, didn't I? not bad for this out of practice, not bad for an old fool, oh no. But slow it down now before the coronary.

So I slide back down to the comfort and security of the main line, but almost immediately it starts to run away with me again, headed I know not where, but it seems to know what it's doing. I shift my feet and shrug my shoulders, I'm off the ropes now, and my head clearing. I have only to keep anchored here in the present and keep back from the edge of the void. But not too far from the edge, after all, it's a game of attraction and revulsion. Conceive these notes as strands of light flung out over the pit, an aural webwork I attempt to stitch, though not only a bridge over the howling darkness but also an engagement with it. I inquire into the dark, thrusting my whole interior up and out through the bell of the horn, at last reaching and rebounding from the Stone. The Stone and the worlds it holds in abeyance, that glossy silence of unarticulated thought, ah, talk to me, come on, talk to me, I laugh and scream through the horn. And the music is spinning away from me, in spite of all I can do, whirling on into suspect and hazardous territory where I have to navigate blind. I give up, close my eyes and resign, giving in to the heart of the night, with afterimages of my own acts and everyone else's still burnt deeply across it, an unlikely chiaroscuro built up from the surface of time. The sound of the horn comes back to me again, more and increasingly frantic. I pull myself together and look at the Stone, still unaltered and outrageously silent. With an effort, I break the tempo in half and plead as eloquently as the horn will allow, talk to me, talk to me, just tell me the things I already know. But in that case, why am I raving? For no good reason, it occurs to me, and I pull the piece into a gentle decline. A soft serenade to the Stone. It won't reduce, won't decode itself. Very likely that is just as it should be. Let it be its own sufficiency. At my end I will do whatever I can, which now amounts to winding up the piece, the last slow inflated notes rising up unprompted from the bell of the horn, garnished with all sorts of frills and adornments I didn't even know I was planning to put in. On the last bar I bow over the Stone, I salute its intransigence. Quite a pair we make, I think, pulling up from the last tremolo.

Well, I'll never know exactly what I did back there, but it was a nice little workout, at the very least. I let the horn swing loose from the lanyard, while I lean with both hands on the table, hearing the echoes recede inside my head. Then there is also some sort of dull thumping noise, actually present in the room, I believe, yet not my heart. I turn around, and there's my forgotten audience. If I can trust my eyes, Bradley Todd is clapping, slowly and steadily, thud thud thud. While Celeste is slumped against the wall of the rabbit hutch and plainly in the grip of a serious sulk. Well, fifty percent. Not so bad, and a good deal better than average for me.

Tired myself out once again. I pocket the Stone and start crossing the loft, steadying the horn with one hand. But the distance between me and the door has suddenly got as big as the Sahara. Bradley is still clapping along, albeit in a rather affected way. By the time I get close enough to see the whites of his eyes, he stops.

"Great show," he says. "Really something. You're it, you're it." He comes grinning toward me, hands extended as if to present me the key to the city. Though his hands are empty, in fact.

"Yes, indeed. You'll go far." And then the very campy stage-whispered confidence—"And could you . . . do you think you

could go far right now? You see, I think I've got a problem here"—
with a gesture behind him—"I mean, Celeste is not really musical. . . ."

"Absolutely," I say, remembering even in my dazed exhaustion
that the ilk of Bradley Todd tends to be impressed by absolute
words such as *absolutely.* "I absolutely dig what you mean, all the
way to China, baby." I squeeze one of Bradley Todd's hands in
great good fellowship, and without breaking my gait I veer toward
the door.

"I mean, come back later and everything, the more usual hours,
you know, but glad to see you anytime. . . ." Etc., etc. My only
wish now is to get out and off by myself without any further exchange of pleasantries, but that wouldn't be politic, would it? With
one hand on the door latch, I turn back with my best sociable smile.

"Right, Bradley, I hate to break in on you like this and all, but I
needed the tenor for a studio date today, good stuff for me, you
know, and I had to have it right away. . . ."

"Oh, I see. . . ." says Bradley Todd, not sure if he should swallow
this or not. I give him a wink that could mean anything. But "break
in" was not the phrase to choose, was it, I'd better keep talking.

"So my apologies all around, look, I've really got to run right now,
late already, I'll stop by later for the case, okay?"

"Right, right, see you soon," says Bradley Todd, ushering me
onto the staircase with a big smile and a lordly wave. Then bang
goes the door, and I'm standing at the head of the stairs, looking
down into two blinding panes of light far away in the door at the
bottom. It's out of the palace of musical dreams, back to the street
and the bitter bright daylight. I fumble out that half pair of sunglasses again as I go tottering down the stairs.

Soldiering on up Crosby Street, I take stock of the situation.
Looks like I didn't totally tear it with Bradley Todd after all. He
didn't absolutely kick me down the stairs, for one thing. Also, I can
get my foot in the door one more time when I go back for the case,
and maybe then I can renegotiate the stashing of the horn. Though
on the debit side I don't have a case for it now so I have to walk
around cradling it like a baby.

But at least I can still play the damn thing. Always wonder if you
can or not after a while not trying. But that wasn't so bad, not for an

old dissolute drunk with a horrible hangover. Or I think it wasn't so bad, but how do I know, maybe it was terrible. Hardly listening to myself anyway, just dreaming into the Stone.

Zap—here comes the blackout again. Falling over a corner curb, I have the blind luck to hook my elbow around a lamppost, embracing it like a long-lost brother, or somebody good for a loan. Pull it together now, but now I hear my own music shrieking back at me, though my horn is hanging down over my sternum, making no more actual noise than a dead and decaying albatross. Only my ears ringing, but this isn't the regular morning-after tremors and shakes. This is the authentic whirlpool. I've been pulled into the vortex of the Stone, myself entire. With the terrible weight of an infinite star-studded vacuum pressing in on me from every side. And I'm completely convinced that if I open my eyes at this moment the world will not be there anymore. I've fallen off the edge at last, or between the stools, ha-ha, and now comes the dreadful suspicion that when I do open my eyes I'll be in that little white cell with the little wire window, reeling out of an electroshock daze, having peed all over myself and everything else besides. Because it's often turned out that way before. Or perhaps this time, no return at all. I will peel back my eyelids and find no relief of the darkness, wake up to face the coffin lid and the shades of everlasting night.

No use waiting, let's see what we can see. I open my eyes and find that I'm still in a world which, if not the one I just momentarily left, is indistinguishable and therefore just as good. With this difference, I'm now on the inside looking out. Enveloped in the Stone, part and portion of its weight and obstinacy. Myself, the Stone, me. I the inexplicable. We're through quarreling, me and the Stone, we both know what we know. I look up at the sign on the lamppost, it's the corner of Prince and Crosby. I turn the corner, feeling fine now, and walk down to West Broadway looking for someone new to perplex.

And here she comes now, supple and tall, with bright blue trousers tapered tight to the ankle, and a black T-shirt, the Clash. Plus the Soho crew cut and fat cylindrical purse pendent from a loop of gold braid. She's in perfect disguise, but she can't be for real. She has to be a tourist from Slovenia, or else there is no way she wouldn't know that there is nothing for her to spend money on at this time Sunday on West Broadway. Except me.

So I take a bow as she approaches, catching her surprised eye. And raising the horn to my mouth, I begin to finger "Greensleeves" with my right hand, while extending my hat with my left. Support the arts, madam, make a small contribution. The only catch is that my hat is purely imaginary. She doesn't get it, or doesn't like it. It isn't done in Slovenia. A leap and a bound and she's on the other side of the street, leaving me only a look of dismay. There she goes, my heart of gold. And she knocked down my day's rating to thirty-three and a third.

But here comes another prospect, a solvent-looking old gent decked out in silver hair and a seersucker suit. I segue rather clumsily into "Night in Tunisia," hoping to evoke a memory of better or different days. And as he comes nearer I flourish the hat, kind sir, would you . . . I've got him, he's stopping to listen, actually propping himself on the wall and settling in. I give it the best belt I can, though the bop is not really my strong suit, especially tired as I am. But my prospect seems to be sliding down the wall. If my eyes don't deceive me. Yes, and when his tail hits the pavement, he keels over sideways.

I stop in mid-phrase. Can't see worth a damn through these scratched-up green glasses. I push them up to the top of my head and move in for a better look. But this guy is nothing but another bum. That's right, the suit is a rag out of a barrel, and there's a column of wine-soaked breath whistling out between his last two brown teeth. I really know how to pick them, don't I?

I case the street in both directions and there's nobody. But really I shouldn't, not to a brother in misfortune. Probably nothing to get anyway. Ashamed of the very thought, I find a cozy-looking piece of a carton and push it under his head. My ethics are slipping, as well as my eyes. What I need is to lie down myself, I think, only some place not so much out in the open.

Time to get off West Broadway. I go across one street and up another. Greene Street this is, I think, and here's the perfect place. A good two feet of space behind a Dempster Dumpster up there on that loading dock. Up the steps, and down we go. I curl myself around my horn, flattening my cheek on cool sheet metal. Down for the count. One, two, three . . .

Johnny B.

And I feel like a completely new man as I step into the northwest corner of Washington Square, ready to seek the day's fortune among the flora and fauna surrounding me, the fauna most especially. The horizon of possible futures expands all around me, and I pause in the pincers of this circular array of concrete benches, in the dense shade of tall overarching trees. It is cool and dusky and damp under these trees, in the grasp of the benches, and the air is impacted with chlorophyll. This is a genteel end of the park, on the benches I see only two old men in loose cardigans, looking down at the liver spots on the backs of their hands, and three old ladies in tired Sunday best, talking together in vanishing voices, and one polite and listless poodle dog. They look like they're dying by inches, all five of them, but they're causing no one any inconvenience about it, least of all me.

So I don't look at them. Framed in an arch of the trees and out in the open sunlight there's a kid juggling some multicolored ninepins—three, now four, and now five, throwing them absurdly high but keeping them quite nicely under control. Outsized and garish under the sun, the ninepins loop end over end in the air, returning surely to the hands of the juggler, who never even looks at them. For that is the secret of juggling, not to think where the thrown object was or will be, but only to know where it is, a knowing that doesn't even know it knows. It's a secret which fascinates me, as you may well imagine, and I stand stock-still, spying on the trance of the juggler until something breaks it and the ninepins bounce and scatter over the lawn with the juggler scrambling after them, a magician no longer but only a redheaded freckled college kid, running and frightening pigeons.

Now I rotate my head around like an owl, but there is still no action on any of the benches, only the old people still sitting there lifeless as waxworks. Now a fat black fly comes droning into the park, bloated and sluggish from a visit to the Häagen-Dazs stand up on Eighth Street, and as he makes his first pass along the benches, the old man holding the ivory-handled cane raises one eyelash, then becomes even stiller than before. The fly loops a turn and comes back again, teasing the hair of one weary old lady, piquing the dog for a second or less, and settling finally and foolishly on the mottled knuckles that hold the white cane.

Whop—dead fly. The old man blinks, smiles to himself, and scrapes with a long brown fingernail at a spot of dirt and blood on the back of his hand. And that is the only thing that is likely to happen around here for the next hour or so, so I am going to snap out of my daze and go down into the park to find whatever is awaiting me there on this particular day.

So I go along down the diagonal path, and the trees get thinner and the shade fades out behind me. No more senior citizens on the benches along the way, but a different clientele, mixed up some but mostly black guys in sneakers and sweats, maybe basketball players from the courts on Sixth Avenue, come over for a breather and a couple of joints. And then there're the radios, big box radios, thundering at me from either side.

I walk through the noise, half-catching a couple of lyrics, and fade into the usual scrimmage at the end of the path and the edge of the trees, crossing toward the open center of the park, free ground. There's four or five guys drifting around the border, and a couple of them seem to be new enough to the area that they're trying to catch my eye.

". . . smoke, smoke, joints and bags . . ."

". . . smoke, my man, you never too old for Gold, just got to be bold . . ."

Johnny B. | 291

I keep walking and the two freelancers warp away around the edges of my very useful dark glasses. Eye contact is where it all begins for these guys, then they're in your pocket and smoking your cigarettes and giving you all kinds of good advice and ripping you off just as fast as they can. So you don't want to look at them, but then it's also nice to know more or less where they are. Not that I care too much, they're all a bunch of lightweights and most of what they deal is garbage. They don't interest me, except that it's nice to have them around to create confusion so the cops can't find the right people when they come visiting. And then they're also a useful pool for recruiting purposes, which it now occurs to me is something I'd better start thinking about, and soon. I'm going to have to get at least one other man, and a good man too, not another Carlo. Yusuf and Santa are great as far as they go, but I really can't stretch them all over this territory. I need someone reliable, and unfortunately I don't know of anyone like that.

I come up to the edge of the fountain, turn around, and sit on the rim to watch the action. Two girls come down the diagonal, walking with difficulty because they're each twined around a boy friend. Both pairs get the runaround from the hawkers and shrug it right off, passing on by. They go, and now an old black guy I seem to see around a lot calls two freelancers over to his bench. It's the same two that tried it on me, and when the old cat says whatever he says to them, they both turn and look my way and nod their heads like puppets. He's warning them off of me, the old guy, telling them not to waste their breath. I can't quite put a name on this old guy, though I've seen him around quite a bit, and he's easy to spot by the light patches in his beard. He's operating something though, that's easy to see, and maybe those guys aren't exactly freelancers after all. It gives me a cold spot in the small of my back to have the finger laid on me like that, even though I know I'm as clean as a newborn infant, cleaner in fact. With the time I put in down here I can't avoid a little recognition, but it doesn't suit my modest and retiring disposition at all, and I especially don't enjoy being pointed out to newcomers and people passing through. Who is this guy, anyway? I could have Yusuf say something to him, but what can you do, you can't stop word-of-mouth. And I'm covered for that, I'm clean, so forget it.

The old man finishes his rap and the two kids catch themselves looking at me and stop. That's very subtle, children. I watch the old man, nodding and mumbling on his bench, and I decide that here's someone that knows what's what. And maybe he's the man to take on, but no, it's too complicated, and he's probably happier with his own show, the loose joints and that. Better I should find somebody new and working alone, but I can't think of anyone that would do, not offhand. I have to admit it, Holy Mother is going to be hard to replace, hard if not impossible. Holy Mother, Aniello, where is he now, I wonder, in the meat wagon, or already in the morgue? But I can't let my mind go wandering off in these perverse directions, because I have to get on with the day.

The day, and so far everything is as usual. This side of the fountain everything is very pluralistic, it's open territory. The long sweep of benches is full of people, all kinds of people, you can take your pick, artists and intellectuals up from downtown, teenage runaways, semiamateur musicians, lunatics, Frisbee throwers, apostles of strange beliefs, anything you want, and all melting together in the hot midday sun, a bit like human peanut brittle. Here's the balloon man, and there's the hot-dog man and also the knish man, and in and out through the crowds go a couple of amateurs with tin buckets full of cold beer, only slightly illegal, ladies and gentlemen. I stand here with my back to the falling water, picking over the crowd from behind my dark glasses and looking for anything or anyone that might give me some cause for unease, but I don't see it, nothing at all to worry about at the minute. It's now twenty to one by my watch, twenty minutes to clocking-in time, and all systems are go, assuming my staff turns up when it should. I've got the car stashed a few blocks off the park, and so far I don't see anything here that shouldn't be, though I haven't yet covered all of the ground.

I walk around the other side of the fountain and spot Alex the fuzzbox guitar player sitting off in the shade, not building any audience as yet, just jerking around with a few of his friends, the volume turned down low. But here's hoping Alex will do his whole number a bit later in the day to pull in the tourists and stimulate commerce. Right now the arch spot is taken by the Trinidadian steel drummer, rolling his sticks with a great sound of bells. He's not bad, this guy, but he's not drawing anybody, I'm afraid he'll go home hungry tonight. And now I see Charlie the Joker coming down Fifth, spiffed out in red pants and a white fishnet shirt, and flanked by two bodyguards about twice his size. He's a very small guy with a very big mouth, and I'm always glad to see him around. Not only because his routine is quite funny, but also because he brings his own crowd down from the Upper West Side, all guys with money they're ready to spend. Charlie's just here to secure his spot, his show won't kick off till the late afternoon, but it will pull in the people when it does.

Hey, it's all right, it's okay, I'm going to make some money today. A yellow butterfly materializes in front of my nose and I follow him into the east end of the park, losing him finally among the trees and the stained tattered grass. It's quiet over here and not much going on. Here's a pale reedy girl sitting cross-legged, playing the flute in the general direction of a boy with a backpack who's reading Camus. Over there on a bench there's another old lady, tapping a black orthopedic shoe. A mongrel dog comes along and propositions her and she gives him a taste of the old steel toe, so he runs on ahead to check out a wino stroked out on the next bench down the line next to two black guys in knit caps, passing a joint. I follow the dog as he keeps going, now scaring an overweight pigeon into flight, now homing in on a loaf of wheat bread and a bottle of carrot juice, which sit in a circle of gray-haired hippies. So the dog blunders in and makes friends and gets some organic peanut butter for his trouble, as aging hippies believe in niceness to dogs. And there's nothing else going down in the east end, so I swing back and climb the steps to the platform patio on the south side.

I hear a buzz of wheels over brick, and a sweaty girl skater whips by my left shoulder, missing me by a hair, and when she comes out in front where I can see her she makes a snap turn and glides backward, momentum unbroken, along the curve of the street-side benches and trees. And now she pulls another two-footed turn and careens backward straight toward the small fountain there in the center, and I think she's going to break her neck for sure, but now I see she planned it. She swoops down into the basin and catches herself on the fountain's top pipe, bent over backward like a ballerina with water pouring all over her face and her red one-piece suit.

A very classy way to cool off, I would say, and I am even tempted to start applauding or something like that, but then I feel eyeballs drilling into my back.

I hold still and listen, but all I can hear is a squirrel climbing around in the trees behind me, the same trees that screen this patio from the rest of the park, so that no one will see what is about to happen, if anything is. I turn around, there's four of them, Latins over from Alphabet Town, and I don't know them, but I think I know what their problem is. Their attention is bound on me by a line of need and urgency substantial enough to pull their heads after me in unison when I start moving off to the left, enough to pull them out to the edge of the bench they're sitting on. Junkies all four, and not in good shape, I'll bet they've been sitting there waiting all day. Junkies have extra senses all their own, and either that or the word-of-mouth has told them who I am and what I've got. A minute more with my back to them and they would have jumped me. Another minute and they might yet. I pull off my sunglasses and give back the stare.

It's a long strained moment, while I try to communicate by mental telepathy—patience, my friends, you'll get yours when the time comes. Meanwhile don't do anything you might regret later, and whatever you do, don't kill the goose that lays the golden eggs. Now the one nearest to me relaxes, sits back on his bench, sags until the back of his head catches on the top rail. One by one the others lean back also. It's over. They don't look at me. They look up into the trees over their heads. That's right, my children, never be hasty. First thing you learn is that you've always got to wait.

I walk down the steps on the other side, putting my glasses back on as I go, and move back toward the center of the park. I've got no symptoms of nervousness other than a couple of ligaments twitching at the backs of my knees, but I don't like little encounters like that, not at all. We're getting a lower class of customers these days, sent to us by, of all people, the cops, who in their wisdom decided to make a big push and shut down all the shooting parlors in Alphabet Town, which had the happy effect of putting all the action back into the street. It's wonderful how the cops work it out. So now we've got guys coming over to the Square who would happily cut your throat for your watch, and although I don't mind getting whatever money they may happen to have, I really don't think it's worth the bother of having them around. Maybe there's some kind of pressure play we could pull to send them all somewhere else for a while, I should talk to Holy Mother and see what we can come up with.

But there I go again, it's funny how my mind keeps running in these habitual channels, no matter what I try to do about it. I walk up to the edge of the fountain and look down into the water, not really seeing it. Repeat until learned—there is no Holy Mother, there is no Aniello Di Angelo, not anymore. I see my own face reflected from the dark water, tight-lipped and drawn and shielded behind the sunglasses. Where is he now? . . . *in the morgue, the coroner's assistant dialing the phone, holding the address book open with a scrupulously clean thumb, the receiver clamped between his shoulder and jaw, dialing for the next of kin. Next of kin, I'm sorry, I have some bad news for you, hello* . . . but enough of this. Let the thought be as dead as the man. I raise my head and look at the top of the fountain and think only of how many times I will breathe in and out before all other thoughts purl out of my mind and drown in the muttering water.

Now I snap back into the soothing singularity of my present moment, and now, void of memory, I begin constructing the world all over again and naming it to myself: this flowing substance in front of me is water, and this hard substance containing it is concrete, and the pavement I'm standing on is also concrete, and it is my feet that I'm using when I now turn around. I see the old black guy that pointed me out to the young ones, still lounging on his bench. I think I'll call him Lemon Peel, for the lemon-yellow stains in his beard around his mouth. I will, and when I've called him that enough times to enough people that will be his name, because that is the way the world works, and what you call a thing is what it is. I call this a good summer day, with plenty of sun and green grass and idling people who have certain needs that I can satisfy and others that I can't. A good day to do some good business and lay hands on some incorruptible money, and I am socking away all my spare change into AT&T stock and the money market for a nice blend of high gain and security, and probably by the time I turn forty I will be able to buy a condo in Florida and start boring myself to death in a big way. Maybe I'll do that and maybe I won't, but either way I have no problems or worries, not now, not today. I take a step forward, walk down the diagonal to the southwest corner and the chess tables.

This time the hawkers don't give me a tumble. I walk by them and Lemon Peel without getting so much as a glance. Two college kids in long cardboard streamers are chasing each other all over the playground to my left, commandos of the insane, yelling orders at each other through six-foot cardboard tubes. This place is getting really crazy, sometimes I wonder if I'm seeing what I'm seeing. But down in the chessboard circle everything is very normal. At this time of day it's so sedate that it's barely even worth checking out, but we always have to stick to the drill. So I look all around and it's the usual crowd: Chinese whiz kids from Taiwan, and computer programmers with inch-thick glasses, and random aging gents ruined by chess more surely than by liquor or women, the usual run of chess nuts, in a word.

I'm about to turn around and go back when I feel eyeballs on me again, and why should that happen down here? I turn around and scan a row, the same one where Porco was sitting last night, so maybe it is only an afterimage of Porco come back to bother me some more, not satisfied after last night and this morning. The hell he's raised with his talking rock, I'm really beginning to think I should have had him taken out. But now I spot the two guys that just don't look quite right, and looking them over for why, I see that the reason is their coats. Both of them have on thick polyester suit jackets, on a day like this when I am sweating all over my light summer shirt. I watch them at an angle, hiding behind my glasses, and as the near one reaches out to move a picce I see the fabric stretch tight over a lump in the armpit, probably not a goiter, probably a gun. Cops. These guys are absolutely cops, and about as inconspicuous as a pair of orangutans at the Metropolitan Opera. I even almost recognize their faces, but not quite. I've never been personally acquainted with these particular cops I don't think, though of course we may have mutual friends. Anyway, it's no use to stand here and stare at them, so I head back into the center of the park.

My little heart is going pit-a-pat and no mistake, even though I'm telling myself in all reason they're probably not after anybody here. Oh no, I'm sure they just came down here to play a little chess, with their nice plaid coats and their guns on. However, probably whoever they're after isn't me, and anyway I'm clean, so the best thing to do is wait and see if anything develops. I get back to center and drop onto a bench across the path from my man Lemon Peel, and I pat my forehead down with my handkerchief, because my sweat is beginning to chill.

And now right behind me comes one of my cops, and he gives me a half-look in passing and checks it, walking on by. I follow him from the corner of my hooded eye, watch him stop at the Sabrett wagon and talk to the vendor, then check me out to see if I've moved.

The hell with it all, my day is shot, completely and totally out the window. I start smoking a Kool for consolation, but the wind carries the spark all down one side, hotboxing it so bad I have to throw it away. Nothing, but nothing, goes right anymore. My cop lingers by the hot-dog stand for five minutes or so, marking time and still watching me. Finally he gets a box lid full of hot dogs and soda and goes away to report to his friend, leaving me sitting here chewing my lip.

My cop fades out among the chess tables and I get up and wander around the fountain, trailing my fingers along the raised rim. Two white kids arrive on the wall opposite me and plop down under a miserable stunted tree, catching my attention with the two huge Panasonic radios they're carrying, both tuned to PLJ. Blocky couple of kids they are, and don't look like they're from town. Bet you a nickel they're fagbashers in from Jersey City, sitting there with matching mean looks on their faces, waiting for dark. Not that I care, bet you a dime I'm not working this park again for a couple of days, maybe even a couple of weeks. I don't like it, but I know how to follow directions when they're written all over the wall, and when the rest of my people show up I'm just going to tell them they're all getting a vacation. Another vacation, on top of the first one Porco let us in for when he bugged out on me back in June, and both in summer prime time. This is going to get into my end of the profits, not to mention the aggravation.

The aggravation and the worry. I turn back toward the south

side, but I can't see my cops at this distance. I just don't see what they're after me for, when I've been an exemplary citizen for the last ten years or so, as far as anyone can be presumed to know. And I don't understand how anybody knows any different, not unless somebody tipped me in. I'll have to look into that, and the first thing to do is send Holy Mother down there to see if he can make them—ah, no, not this again. I push back out of the memory through my trusted five senses, concentrating on two skaters on the volleyball court, half dancing together, half ignoring each other, and notice PLJ is playing the Pretenders . . . *while somewhere the coroner's assistant has connected his call: "Hello, sorry, I have some bad news for you"—the thumb pinning down the address book like a specimen on corkboard, and the coroner has completed the pointless autopsy, pointless because the cause of death is obvious from a cursory glance at the remains, but now he can write on a yellow form that the ratio of opiates to blood in the body of the deceased was found to be this over that* . . . and how tiresome it is that I can't shake this morbid chain of thought.

New distractions. In between me and the skaters there're some Rastas grouping up, six or eight of them, not quite enough for a good soccer game, though enough to make even Yusuf Ali think twice if anything were to occur. They're making Rastas pretty big these days. They circle together and chillum, spliff between little and ring finger, mouth over thumb. This way you get a nice air mix and can hold the smoke down longer and if you are lucky have a vision of Jah. And Jah lives, and two o'clock we play soccah, mon. I get a whiff of what they're smoking, brought to my nostrils on this cool little breeze, and it smells good and rich, like cedar. I almost wonder where they're getting it from, but then I really am not interested, the turnover you need to make money off that is much too big and too dangerous.

The paired Panasonics sound good to me, putting out a nice solid bass line, still the Pretenders. The Rastas split up and start toeing a soccer ball, and look, here comes Eva the Swede, up La Guardia Place past the Loeb Center, taking the curb neatly on her skates, and she's in the park a good three hours earlier than usual. Maybe she had a bad night herself. But she looks fresh as an ice-cream cone, and wearing blue satin, which becomes her greatly. Nice idea, Eva, and swish, she goes by, right under my nose. Sometimes I think I must be invisible, but then I suppose that I'm trying to be. Eva is communicating in body language to one of the Rastas, while the Pretenders play on. Eva pirouettes and Chrissie Hynde sings and I am drawn into this twirl—she's got my attention.

Nice spin, Eva, but I'll take Chrissie Hynde if I can get her, her voice has that fine edge of desperation which is so attractive, and her little leatherboy backup band is not at all bad. And cute too, I've seen her picture in the window down at J&R. I wonder what she takes. Eva, skating backward, raises her arms and gives her shiniest smile to a long bony Zulu with a wide-brimmed hat and a feather. Anybody but Eva would know with her back turned that this guy is nothing but trouble, and low-grade trouble at that. It depresses me to watch her dig her own grave. Time to take a walk and think about something else for a while.

So I move off down toward the south end again, shaking out my legs, which have stiffened from standing in one place for too long. Down on the corner of Fourth and MacDougal I spot that blond girl singer that's starting to come around on weekends, dancing behind her black guitar and singing so strong and proud I can hear her from where I'm standing, over the crowd noise and the passing cars. She won't be playing the parks long with the voice she's got, and writes her own stuff too, they tell me. For some reason it lightens my heart to see her down there, and I'm about to go down and throw her a bill, but then I remember my cops, and I don't want to give them another free look. Let them come up here if they want to see what I'm doing.

I stop in my tracks, feeling more than a little piqued and annoyed, because I haven't lived this long to get into a state where I can't walk across the park without having to stop for second, third, and fourth thoughts. I didn't live this long for that, no . . . *while somewhere the coroner slides the corpse into a long numbered drawer, a tag tied to its toe for double security, and the coroner's assistant returns the address book to the manila envelope with the other personal effects and waits for a claimant to arrive* . . . and the feeling now sweeping over me is not irritation this time, it's panic. I'm in a box but good this time, all my efforts at keeping the horizons empty and open wasted. I'm caught in a corner between all these unlikely circumstances on the one hand and the conspiracy my treacherous mind has mounted against me on the other. I look at my watch and it's one already, my staff should appear at any moment, though I won't take an attitude if they're a little late, last night was so tough on all concerned. But I want to get out of here as soon as may be, turn over the car to Yusuf, I suppose he's the best I've got left for that job, and blow out of here before something snaps permanently. I've got to get off by myself somewhere and not think about anything for a while, because I'm so shaky right now I might do something really ridiculous, like take a shot of my own dope. And maybe a little vacation won't be so bad after all, the way things seem to be going.

I'm back at the fountain again and none of my people have come along yet, but I'm cooling out anyway, at least enough to go back to admiring the scenery. Those two Panasonics are still beating it out, and I roll around on my toes in time to it, one more device to stop myself from thinking. I see Eva has shaken the guy with the feather, and now she's holding conversation with some of the Rastas. She says something I don't catch, twirls away on the toes of her skates, wrists crossed over her head, then rolls back into the group. And what's this? One of our Rastas is hitting Eva a good solid clout across the side of her pale face, a backfist without too much weight behind it, so it's easy to see that my man has finesse when it comes to beating up women. Good woman no show armpits to other man, that would seem to be the message. Eva, sitting down on her blue satin behind with her legs stretched out before her like a child of ten, doesn't seem to get it. What could she have done to offend this gorilla with the foot-long dreadlocks, who's walking toward her now? Probably she doesn't even remember his name.

Eva has a bad-looking bruise on her left cheek, red with blue filling into it, and with her fair skin it could be a month before she can take her face out in public again, and summer will be over. And Eva is also in a bad situation at this very moment. If she was only on her feet she could be skating away at ninety miles an hour, but unfortunately she's not on her feet. Now this is Washington Square, not Union Square where you can take two hours and torture somebody to death. Here you've got ten minutes at the outside to waste someone, then comes the man. However, time flies when you're getting badly hurt.

I'm thinking all of these thoughts on the wing, because it seems that my legs have just walked out from under my brain. Am I dancing? No. I am walking toward this big Rasta in a businesslike way, and with my mouth I am shouting, *"Hey, whaddaya think you're doing?"* Just exactly like a Boy Scout. My man is simply attired, wearing only Adidas, gym shorts, and muscles. He's staring at me in sheer amazement, because nobody gets into other people's problems down here. Then he appears to wake up, and I get the backfist square in the middle of my chest, which is more or less what I deserve for behaving like a freaking fool, and it's such a good solid backfist that it's flipping me head over heels.

Now I land on the pavement and start rolling across my shoulder blades, tucking in my arms and legs and head so as not to get them all broken, and while rolling out I'm making this little list on my little mental scratch pad:

1. I still hear the Pretenders. "Mystery Achievement" now. What a lot of one group on one station.

2. Yusuf Ali is not here right at this moment.

3. Neither is anybody else I know and love.

4. Even if they were all here I couldn't ask them to bail me out of this one. Because I have to follow my own rules or life will become meaningless, and it's perfectly clear that I got into this entirely through my own stupid fault. I got myself into it and I will just have to get myself out.

5. In order to do this I will have to resort to the secret weapon I reserve for real emergencies. Not the tear-gas pen, which would be of very little use against six or eight people on a breezy day like this. Secret weapon number two.

I come out of my roll with my thoughts all in order and squat on the balls of my feet. I've managed to put about eight feet between me and the first Rasta, and he's only about eight feet tall. And he's in no hurry to cover the distance. A good sport, he doesn't kick another player when he's down, or more likely he's just overconfident. Whichever it is, he'll regret it for the rest of his life, or about forty seconds, if I have my way. Now I am reaching into the loose top of my not-so-fashionable left Dingo boot and taking hold of the thing I keep there for times of real trouble. A gift from the Orient, useful for shelling rice, as well as other things. I stand up and send it lashing behind my neck and under both my arms and through my groin once for show, all too quickly for these hashheads to really see. Then I drop into a shallow crouch and hold the thing extended in front of me for them to look at for one second, holding it lightly by my fingertips like a flute.

It's not much of a thing to look at really, just two tapered sticks joined by a little piece of chain.

But check it out, my friends, I'm ready.

Ras Tafari.

Tommy/Sal

"A Pepsi, I said. A Pepsi I ask you for, and you bring me a god-damn root beer."

"Shut up and drink it already, Sally, it wasn't the first thing on my mind."

"Oh, excuse me please, I forgot you went up there to take a peep at your guy. Personally, I think you'd done better keep the order straight."

"Just drink it, Sally, it's good, you'll like it. Or don't drink it, I don't care what you do. And you can take white again if you want it, big winner."

"No, I take black this time, give you a chance. Your move. I hate root beer, Tommy, even when I was a dumb little kid I didn't like it—"

"And now you're a dumb old man you still don't like it, right? Go ahead and make a move, your clock's turned on, if you didn't notice."

"Okay, there you go. So would you drink a root beer? What'd you get for yourself, my friend?"

"I got nothing. I can't drink that kind of stuff no more, no bubbles for me now, baby. I can't even drink goddamn club soda, my stomach is so bad, and my wife is all the time trying to make me eat yogurt. You're sitting here whining about root beer, wait till somebody makes you eat some yogurt sometime."

"But I like yogurt, Tommy. Yogurt is good for you, you should eat more of it. You should eat it all the time. But you got my sympathy, really you do."

"Yeah? Yeah, and you got mine too if you're gonna play that. Let me tell you something, nobody plays the Alekhine any more, not for about twenty years."

"Yeah, and I seem to remember you said something like that about the English, last game."

"Hey, I was distracted. You don't want to get cocky, Sal, especially if you're gonna play the Alekhine. Because it loses, it always loses, there's book on every variation. Nobody plays it."

"I know nobody plays it, Tommy. That's why I play it. Because nobody remembers what to do. You know all the book lines on the Alekhine? You know half of them? You know any of them past five moves?"

"Ah, shut up and move a piece, Sally, you make my stomach hurt."

"The stomach not getting any better, Tommy? I thought it should have all healed up by now."

"It should have, maybe, but it didn't. I'm missing about a foot of it anyway, never get that back. Hey, you asked me why I was so hot for this Dellacroce, and I'm gonna tell you. I got my guts shot apart by a lousy goddamn dope dealer, for no reason at all, and now I can hardly take a drink, no beer at all, thank you, and I can't eat this and I can't eat that, can't eat practically anything except yogurt, let's not forget that, and I quit the force and lose about half the benefits I should have had, and I hate lousy goddamn dope dealers, whether I know them or not. And that is the bottom line, my friend."

"Yeah, and Stevie too. I can see where you kind of got a case, Tommy. You know, I bet Stevie comes back though. What I hear, a lot of these kids only stay with these things for a couple years or so, sort of like a phase or something."

"Sure, he might come back. Or somebody might tell him to drink some Kool-Aid with cyanide in it, and then he might not come back. Kool-Aid, now, I can drink that, all of it I want. But I hate it. I hate it like you hate root beer, maybe I hate it worse."

"Hey, I'm sorry I said anything about the root beer, okay? I'm drinking it. I'm not saying I like it, but I'm drinking it all right."

"And if Stevie does come back, you know what I'm gonna do? I'm gonna pop him right in the chops is the first thing, and then I give him exactly ten days to get a job, or out, and no more collect phone calls either. Been nothing but a pain in the ass since he turned twelve, that kid, jerking us around all the time, especially his mother."

"That's the way it is, huh? Well, maybe it does him some good if you tighten him up. Don't know if I'd hit him though, I were you. He's gonna be younger than you are, you know."

"Ah, but he's gonna be a Moonie too, they don't eat anything but rice. They're not strong, Sally, no."

"So what was this Dellacroce doing when you went up there?"

"He was sitting on a bench. Sitting there smoking a cigarette. You got to have some patience, Sally."

"You don't got to tell me that. You wouldn't say he spotted you, would you?"

"Why should he? I don't wear a sign says COP on it, do I?"

"Well, look, Tommy, I don't want to bug you or anything, but I really can't stay here all day, and it's one o'clock already. And I got my people standing by, but if I call them in here to watch this guy smoke a cigarette, they're gonna laugh at me, you know? I mean, I'm not saying anything against the tip, but there's not enough here, not yet. I think what you should do, you want to, watch him yourself for a few days maybe, try to put the pattern together, and call me back. Because I just don't see a collar here today."

"Okay, Sal, I guess you got a point. Maybe I was a little sudden with this, I admit."

"Hey, look, I know you get me good stuff. This one's just not quite there yet is all."

"Sure, sure. Gimme a week, I'll put it together and hand it to you with a ribbon on it. But you can stay long enough to finish the game, right?"

"Sure, I'm gonna finish the game. Let's see now, what does the book have to say about this?"

"Plenty. There you go."

"And what does it say about this?"

"Wait just a second."

"Ah, come on, Tommy, every time you get in a tight spot on the board it's 'wait a second.' And you still lose. The clock don't wait, you know."

"Shut up and take a look what's going on behind you."

"You going to try to steal some of my pieces? Come on, Tommy, sit back down and play the game."

"Look, there's something going down up there. I think I saw him in it too."

"Oh yeah? Hey, there is something going on at that. No, Tommy, but it's just a bunch of Rastas messing around up there."

"But I saw him in there. I saw his shirt."

"So maybe he wants to play soccer with the Rastas. His funeral. Let's play chess."

"Soccer hell, listen to the yelling. Follow me down, I want to see what's happening."

"I'm not leaving my clock here all by itself. Cost me plenty, that clock."

"So bring it with you, jerk, this is serious."

"Okay, I'm with you. Slow down a little, damn it, I'm no track star."

"Now what are you gonna say, still a soccer game?"

"Jeez, maybe I do need glasses, can't see a thing. But it don't look like a soccer game, I'll give you that."

"Christ Almighty, I think we got a riot here."

"I see him now, I see him. Look at all those niggers. Don't think you need to bust this Dellacroce, Tommy, these guys gonna bury him for you."

"Yeah, what are we gonna do? Wait, I think I saw him go down. No, there he is again. Christ, Sally, he's got chukka sticks, look at him go. He's gonna burn them, I think."

"You think we oughta go in after him? We could bust him for the sticks if we can get him outa there."

"Yeah, no, I don't know what to do, dammit. Goddamn the rubbernecks, I can't even see through these people."

"Just stay with me, Tommy, don't get separated. Excuse me, lady, could you please move your ass?"

"Well, excuse me, and who do you think *you* are?"

"I think I'm the police, will you get outa my way?"

"Sally, get to a phone and call your people in. We got to get some crowd control before some idiot gets himself hurt."

"Right, come on out of it, we can't do anything in this mess."

"Right behind you. Let me through here, you."

"Don't be calling me 'you', bro, I don't be no 'you.'"

"Just outa my way, okay? Goddamn stupid people, Sally, can you believe it?"

"When was it any different? Oh no, look at all those people all over the phones. Hey, move over, buddy, I gotta make an emergency call."

"Sure you do, but I'm calling the police, okay?"

"You're calling the police? I am the police. Get away from that goddamn phone right now."

"Hey, don't point that. Don't point it at me. Here, take the phone, take it. Look out, everybody, this guy's got a gun."

"You ought not to pulled the gun, Sally, somebody's gonna write you up for it."

"Who is, you? Tommy, do you see my clock anywhere? I dropped my clock somewhere."

"The hell with your goddamn clock. Make your goddamn call."

"I'm trying, I'm trying. Come on bastards, answer the phone."

"Hey, that guy's calling in about you now, Sally, listen to this, 'a crazy guy with a gun.' How you like that?"

"Beautiful. Leave me alone, go find my clock. Answer the phone already, what are they, asleep or what?"

"I told you I'd get you something, didn't I?"

"Hello, this is Brasi, Washington Square. Where the hell you *been*?"

"I told you something was going to happen. Didn't I tell you? And now something's happening, right?"

Porco

I wake up with a jar, clutching and afraid. And touch cool brass.
The saxophone is still here, all right, huddled in the center of my
body. But what am I doing here, and where is here? I stand up,
wobbling, pins and needles in my legs.

I feel terrible, what nightmare did I wake from? The sun has just
tilted west of the crack of sky between the buildings, throwing
sharp glare and harsh shadows. Not enough sleep is the problem, so
I'm still stuck in my ghastly dream. All of those things, they can't
have happened, and I breathe out in relief of sorts. Then I feel the
Stone sagging in my pocket, corroboration. Not to mention the
saxophone. It's all true, then, or some of it is.

I watch a crumpled sack come scuffing down the street. All on its
own, apparently, but then I feel the breeze hit my own face, the
dents printed there by the corrugated metal I've been lying on.
That's nice, it is, I'm hot and clammy. It's an oven there between
the dumpster and the wall, I've been baking myself like a casse-
role . . . this may account for my strange state of mind. I only
wish I could sort out whatever it was that happened from whatever
it was I dreamed. This evil forest of images inside my brain, I have
to find a way to work some sense into it.

Could always step up to the park and wait there for a sign. But
that is one thing I do remember clearly, he said no, they all said no,

no way. Ah, you bastards, that was the wrong thing to say to me, if you'd said maybe, then I could have stayed away. But as it stands . . .

As it stands, I'm rolling up West Broadway just as fast as I can move my little legs. It's a free country, by God and by Jesus, and if I cared if I get killed or not you wouldn't see me where I am today. I swing the horn around to one side and clamp my elbow over it to stop it clashing into my sore bones. My vision goes staccato, I'm bouncing along so jerkily. But now here comes the park. I cross Fourth Street and step up on the curb, feeling slightly tremulous now at the last minute. I've stepped over the line. Come on, go ahead and hit me, what are you waiting for?

And now I see him, Johnny B. propped into the fountain, fingers pressed onto the rim behind him. With the white shirt and the dark glasses he looks like a genteel blind man, out on a Sunday to feel some of the sun he can't see. I watch him push himself off the fountain, moving fast, like he has to meet someone and in a hurry too. I cut my eyes to the right and see that what he meets is a big fist in the midsection. My jaw tightens in sympathy. That connected, man. What's going on here, anyway? This makes no sense at all.

Johnny B. is hurt, I think, he's tumbling end over end like the proverbial rolling donut, and I'm moving in, to cover for him if I can or anyway get a better look. Johnny B. has got into it with the Rastas, that's what it is, and plenty of them too. Not a good idea, I wouldn't say, nor typical either. Wonder what brought this one on? Johnny B. finds his feet again, jackknifing erect with one hand coming up from the left boot with—nunchuks, yes. Well, trust him for a sense of style. He's going to ace everybody this time too. Only how much is it going to cost? I think that over briefly, but the sticks are whirring, hypnotic, and the hissing of the chain pulls me in even closer. A fight is a simple thing, after all, even I can understand what goes on in a fight.

Johnny B. spins the sticks, how light and effortless it looks, shaping the first three or four Rastas in a semicircle in front of him, holding them out of his range for the moment. Now he stops and holds the chuks out loosely, favors them all with a nice bright smile. Want to try to touch this, guys? And they all hang poised like dancers waiting for the music to begin. I let out one elephantine scream on the horn, causing one Rasta to look back to see what the hell I am, and now they all close in.

Can't see so well now, but I can hear the sticks tearing holes in the air, so Johnny B. is still all right. Except for this one Rasta moving in behind him, not so good. I step closer, tuck the sax into my armpit, and kick him sharply in the back of the knee, step out, and watch him fold up as neatly as an empty pair of pants, and now I can see the sticks again, reversing direction, off of someone's head, I think. A half second later comes a sound like the popping of a paper bag. The sticks whirl backward, right to left, you'd think to look at them they'd only kiss you lightly, fan your skin like an easy spring breeze, but in fact they can break stone, and that's one down, down and lying very still. And now I reach the fountain.

So I hop up on the edge of it, teeter and crouch. This is the place to be, I can see a lot better from up here. Also if anybody bothers me I can kick him in the face conveniently, also I can watch Johnny B.'s back for him. Where is the rest of the team? I wonder, something's very strange about all this. There's a pause in the action, and Johnny B.'s showboating a little, the sticks buzzing all around his head and shoulders faster than you can see, while the Rastas try to make up their minds to come in on him again.

I watch the motion of the sticks, there's a nice even pulse to it. It's even almost on the Beat. Almost, and here comes that blinding, whining itch at the very top of my brain (if it's exactly on the Beat I'm in big trouble) and now the instant of translucent clarity, the shocking flash which reveals everything together and whole, which also tells me that in one more second I will throw myself on the pavement and start trying my best to chew off my tongue, contorted with absolute and unspeakable hatred and rage. There's thunder in my diaphragm, and my tongue thickens as I remember the other time, the time I screamed the things I should have never even said, and therefore got my exile and my name, and it is not even a memory now because at such moments all times are fused together and the same. Now, the same, but *not this time,* this time I will not fall. This time, only the light.

And now I'm out of it, I made it through, and I can see that no real time has passed at all, because nobody has moved. Johnny B. and the Rastas still hang in suspension, like repelling magnets held at a certain distance. The doctors have a word for what just happened, and they can keep it too. *I know what I know.* And now I'm going to tell everybody about it.

Because we're getting a crowd, a nice little captive audience, being that there's no such tourist attraction as the prospect of somebody getting his head broken in. I touch the saxophone to my mouth and play a little something, not much, a talking blues. Johnny B. and the Rastas study each other for an opening, and I hear myself begin to talk.

"All right, my friends and my enemies, I know you're not listening. Even if you were listening you couldn't hear me, and even if you could hear me I'm probably not saying anything. *Do you think I care?*"

I blow a piece of any old thing, a blues in C, and Johnny B. gives me a period. One Rasta, the big one with the squashed nose, comes a hair too close and gets a slapshot to his upper arm, which may be broken from the looks of things. Stops the rest of them cold again. And the crowd is thickening, pressing against the walls of the fountain, rounding the full circle.

"Let me tell you why you are gathered here today. It's not because you're fond of each other, no. Check out your neighbor. Ever see him before? Ever want to see him again? No. The fact of the matter is that you all hate each other more than you can ever hope to understand, and you will all be trying to consume each other from the toes on up, from now even unto eternity. And do you know why? *And do you think I care?*"

Awonk awonk on the horn for emphasis. I see one of the Rastas has come out with a nice shiny belt knife, genuine Bowie knife, made in Japan. He slides forward, and Johnny B. stops the sticks and waits for him.

"Well, my friends and enemies, you also don't know that each and every one of you is in fact a bizarre hydra-headed monster, a physical body with its plexus of weaknesses and needs, which also includes both an unacknowledged demon and an unworshipped god, jerking your *self*, whatever that may be, back and forth between them like a doll on a string. And you are here watching this fight not because you have any stake in it, no, not if you are fighting it yourself, but only because it is here and you are too. And you can thank whoever or whatever you have to thank that while the fix you're in will never be any more than that, it will never be any less either. And now I'm going to tell you all about Moses."

The hand with the knife crosses an invisible barrier, and—*tok*—a stick touches it and the knife shimmers away, making a small momentary hole in the crowd, leaving another Rasta with a bruised or broken wrist. I find a new dissonance on the horn, *eee eee ork arak*, what's that? No matter.

"Yes, Moses, who lived most of his life as you or I live ours, all uncomprehending manipulanda in the hands of our sweet luck and fortune. Good luck Moses called it when Pharaoh's daughter fished him out of the river, or he would have called it that if he had been able to say anything more than *gaa-gaa* at the time. And bad luck, when he killed a man and was exiled, but not so bad as all that even then. For he got a wife in the land of Midian, and a son to be named after the fact of his exile. Then Moses was only on a business trip when he passed Horeb, the mountain of God, he was only looking for more luck good or bad, but there luck stopped, and God arrived.

"And that is what you are all waiting for, know it or not. But let me now tell you, my friends and enemies, what it will be like when and if it ever happens."

The Rastas have a few more knives out now, but they must be able to figure out by this time how far they can get with knives. A couple of words pass from head to head, and one of them ducks out through the crowd.

"What was it like for Moses? Well, first of all the bush was burning, and Moses had to put the shoes from off his feet and hide his face from the sight of God, all of which probably distracted him no little. Then God gave him a little task to perform, which was to deliver the nation of Israel out of Egypt as you may or may not recall, and Moses said, 'How am I gonna do that? What am I supposed to say when I get there? Assuming they don't just string me up the minute I cross the border, because I'm not supposed to go there any more, you know. Then God said, 'Well, my son, just tell them this from me—*I AM THAT I AM.*' "

It's getting so noisy around here I can hardly hear myself anymore, everybody shouting and stuff. I blow some more on the horn to clear air space, and keep talking.

"And Moses had it all, right there, because that was the best thing God was going to say to him ever, up to and including the whole rigmarole about the altar and the tabernacle and the shittimwood and everything else besides. He should have stuck with the hand he had, but he was a fool and took another hit. 'That's not good enough,' Moses says. 'I can't even understand it; nobody else will either. You got to do better than that. You got to give me a guy that can talk.' "

Now here comes the messenger back again, with a whole lot more just like him, and this bunch all's got baseball bats. A bright idea. With the bats they just might do something, if they all come in at once. Johnny B. can see that too. His shirt is pasted to his back he's running so much sweat, and I can look down and see all the muscles tightening down his back.

"So God did give Moses a guy that could talk, and do you know what happened? The guy that could talk made the biggest disaster out of the whole thing you can possibly imagine. It took a while for that to happen, and at first everything was very nice. Moses never had to open his mouth, all he had to do was point his rod at the river or the sky or whatever and wait for all hell to break loose, which it would, and then Aaron would tell everybody what it meant. And all this for the sake of publicizing the name of God. Now you may well ask which one of God's names was supposed to be making the headlines? Moses asked that too and got the same old answer: *I AM THAT I AM.*' "

Now they try it. I lose my breath and have to stop talking. All coming in with the bats at arm's length, what they want to do is tangle up the sticks for a second so they can get inside with the knives. Now what are you going to do, Johnny B.? And he breaks for the middle of the line, takes out one on the way, and comes out behind the rest. For a second I lose him in a blur, he's fast, faster than I would have thought. Then he comes back into focus, facing me. He's all right, only thing is he lost his glasses. He looks up and our eyes lock.

"Watch your back, you idiot," I say. And I go on with my sermon.

"So then what happened? Quite a bit, in fact. The sea parted and the nation of Israel split the hell out of the land of Egypt, and then they wandered homeless in the terrible burning desert and nothing much happened that was very much fun, not for a couple of decades. Then Moses climbed back up on the mountain of God, and the people wot not what had become of him."

Johnny B.'s not so good where he is now, not a good idea to let them come between him and the fountain. Because now he's stuck with his back to the crowd and anything could come from there. Here it comes, two new ones pushing through, but Johnny B. smells them before I can say anything, makes a neat turn, and whips a stick to the ribs of one, stopped him, and Johnny B. turns full circle and plunges back through the first line, making it back to the fountain. One Rasta, caught between the hammer and the anvil, flips over into the water to avoid the rush. Gets me all wet with his splash, also my horn. I watch him from the corner of my eye, but this one's had enough, he's splitting out the other side of the basin. And Johnny B. is right back where he started. How long is this going to go on? Does he know I'm here? He cuts his head a quarter turn toward me, but he can't afford to take his eyes off the action.

"Then Aaron, the guy that could talk, he was stuck holding the baby. The people came and said to him, 'Do something,' so Aaron did what he could do. Which was to set up an image, a graven image in fact, and advise the people to get down and worship it. Which they proceeded to do. It wasn't an unreasonable move for a good PR man, and you might say that the whole thing was really God's fault, since he certainly could have seen it coming and stopped it too, being omniscient and omnipotent and so forth and so on. But when Moses came down off the mountain he was mad as hell."

Six Rastas now, fanning out along the edge of the crowd. Two of them reach the edge of the fountain and start inching their way closer, along the rim. They're moving in sync, so Johnny B. can't cool them both at once. So he does what he has to—breaks to the left and pushes that one back into the crowd, then swings back into the center, clearing space. Nice, only now the safe spot in front of the fountain has been claimed by another Rasta. Johnny B. closes in on that one now, trying to will him out of the way. Fool, I think, watch your back, there's four of them behind you. Johnny B. backs his man another step toward me, and praying to keep my balance, I sink my toes into the hollow just below the base of his skull. He goes down, okay. I don't fall in the water either, but if this goes on I'm going to make myself unpopular with a whole new bunch of people. Johnny B. glances at me, expressionless, and pivots back into his position below me, not any too soon either. He holds the sticks out in front of him, not spinning them now.

"Moses knew that something had gone terribly and irrevocably wrong when he got back, not from the tablets he had brought with him, which were themselves graven images and which he promptly smashed as soon as he realized what had happened while he was out, but from his own inexorable knowledge of certain constants of life in the world, which, however, he was *still* unable to precisely define or clearly articulate. Then Moses knew what he had always suspected—he would never be able to speak his message and have it understood. And perhaps he turned to God and said, 'I told you this would happen.' "

The Rastas, they just won't give up. They're edging in again, trying the same number, and eventually it's going to work. Johnny B.'s tiring, it's too many guys. Somebody should come and cool this thing out. What the hell happened to Santa and Yusuf and Holy Mother? And by this time there should be cops here too. I look all around, and who do I see but Tommy Whelan down by the phone booths. I think I catch his eye, but he looks away like there's something on his conscience. A chill down my back, there's another thing I didn't dream. I talked to Whelan last night, talked way too much. It's all too complicated. And the Rastas explode toward Johnny B., making the first move this time, and this may be where they get him. He's in the middle of it now, but no, he's pulling it out after all. He's all over the place, and I think he's lost his temper, spinning in the center of the ring like a top. Finally, it looks like he's broken their nerve, the Rastas are scattering, they're churning up the crowd. And now here comes Yusuf Ali at last, head and shoulders over everybody, with Santa behind him too, clearing a path like Moses parting the sea. A day late and a dollar short is what I call it, but at least they made it in in time to catch the last of my brilliant remarks.

"And that is the reason, my friends and enemies, that no matter what you say or think or do, no matter how sweetly your luck may beguile you, you will sometimes or often wake up in the night in the chills and fever of the sudden knowledge that you know nothing, you understand nothing, and if you did you could never speak of it. Therefore you are alone, and you will always be alone. And despite whatever devices your crawling intelligence may contrive, whatever gods you may throw up in front of yourself, they or the great wide world itself will never say anything more to you than this—*I AM THAT I AM*. And that's it, that's the bottom line. *How do you like it?*"

I'd wait for an answer, but now I can see the cops coming in at last, not Whelan, but bluecoats with the hats and guns and everything. Which means that it's time for me to jump down off my soapbox and beat it out of here, if it's not too late already for that. It's not that I care about myself so much, but I wouldn't want anything to happen to my saxophone.

Johnny B.

I've had it now, I thought then. It's all over, all my planning, the careful lonely years, all gone and out the window, and for what? For nothing.

And I thought too, it doesn't matter how the fight turns out. It doesn't matter even a little bit, because win or lose, when the cops get here I will be stuck standing with the car keys in my pocket, and that will be the end. The absolute end, give it lawyers or anything else you want, on what's in the car I'll spend the next twenty years sitting in a cage somewhere, and if I ever come back I'll be an old man, my life broken and over.

It was the not caring that made it a better fight, at least a better and easier one for me. Because all this hungry heart business is a lot of crap. In the fight it's better not to care, not to have an interest. Better to rely only on the unmonitored reflexes, the chilly learned knowledge of where and when to strike.

So the fight, that part was easy. Porco and his voice behind me, that was not so easy. I couldn't hear whatever he was saying, had no time to listen to him preach. That voice, it was nothing more than a mumbling and muttering inside my own head, until the Rastas forced me out and around so that I had to look at him. Then I knew. I knew exactly what it is in him I hate, my own murdered conscience reincarnated in new flesh not my own, where I cannot command it. I made my run back to the fountain, and I could have killed him then. It would have been too easy, I could have broken his head like an eggshell. There was no reason not to either, except for this: I needed him to watch my back. A silly accident, but at the moment there was nobody else around who I could trust for that.

Then I was tired. Tired and there were always more of them to come at me, and every one I could take out would be replaced by two. And it had all gone on too long. Someone should have come, something should have happened to break it up. But no one was coming and I was alone and weakening and I was tempted to give it up and let them have me. I thought that might have been the better way, to take the clean and sudden death and miss out on all the trials and jails and prisons, to join Holy Mother maybe, wherever he is now. But would have been too easy too.

So then I got angry. I thought, I could let them have me, but not this way, not because I have weakened and failed. Let them kill me, that's all right, but never let them think they beat me. I was angry and I thought, They don't even know what's waiting for them, I haven't even hit my stride. Then I went on the attack, and there was a moment when I thought that they might take me after all, because it was hard and I had to move faster than I thought I could. It was not long though, and then came the next moment when I knew I had it over them, that for them it was no longer worth it. They had their own concerns, their own lives to protect. I didn't, not any more. I worked the sticks as hard as I knew how and I drove them back into the crowd. Then the fight was over and I had won it, not that there was anything for me to win at all. I had already blown all my bets when I got into it in the first place.

So I wiped the sticks and dropped them, not needing them anymore, and I stood there in the center of the crowd, the last one left in the middle of the ring the gawkers had made for me, and I waited for whatever was going to happen next. Then Yusuf Ali came, too late, but he came, and I looked at him and Santa was behind him, and I waited to see in their eyes some sign of what they surely must know (if only because I have taught them enough to recognize it), that I am finished and done with and nothing to bank on at all anymore. But there was no sign of anything like that.

In the circle, which was then beginning to close, there was only me

*and Yusuf and Santa, and one Rasta down, the first one, the one that
hit me, and I remembered thinking when I hit him back, That's too
much, too hard. Yusuf Ali bent over him and rose again to tell me
what I really knew already.*

"This one's dead, Johnny B.," Yusuf says. The crowd breaks its
lines and presses in all around us, and the cops are coming in too,
finally, from the south side. Now Yusuf raises his right hand and
pushes some of the people back, and I walk under his arm, I don't
even have to stoop to do it, and behind me Santa is blocking my line
of movement, and I can hear him making a new disturbance to
cover my departure.

Why are they doing this? I'm wondering. Don't they know that
there's no profit in it? Because there is no profit in it, no more than
in placing your bet on a dead horse. And they should know that, it's
what I trained them for. And I am getting even angrier than before,
am furious at them for helping me without any good reason, but
there is no time to spend explaining their mistake to them. I cut
through the crowd and never look back, never even see what's happening to them.

And the whole time I am waiting for the hand to fall on my shoulder, but it doesn't come. I get out at the back of the crowd and see a
burst of flames on my right, an orange column climbing the sky. It's
Tony the Fireman, who has just lit himself, and I watch him burning, and then the crowd reshapes itself around him, because my act
is finished and his has just begun.

So I am standing stupefied in front of the arch, all by myself and
in the open, when Eva the Swede comes up to me. She's still on her
skates, though not very steady, and she rolls up to me like she wants
to say something, but I don't give her the chance. I had forgotten all
about her, but it infuriates me even more having her turn up like
this, the audacity of her even dreaming that I would ever have done
anything for her.

"Get out of here," I say. "What are you doing still hanging
around. Go somewhere else and learn to be careful." And now I
start to move myself, not that I have anywhere to go but only that I
want to get out of the sight of Eva and the expression on her face,

with its ripening bruise. I want to get somewhere she and all of them will never cross my mind again, under any aspect or any name assumed or real. So I start walking, and Eva falls away behind me and I lose her.

And now I am under the trees in the north corner. It is quiet here, unchanged and unaltered, the three old ladies and the dog, the old man still cradling his cane. For them, nothing has happened, and none of them even looks up. But Porco is here too, and he is waiting for me.

I walk past him. I go out of the park and over to Sixth Avenue, and he comes along beside me, taking double steps because he's shorter. I don't want to talk to him, don't even look to the side to see if he's still with me. But he is with me, and I know it, because when we hit the avenue he starts to play the horn.

So we go up the avenue. I'll let him walk with me, so long as he doesn't talk and violate the beautiful emptiness inside my head. Sunday afternoon and the avenue is crowded, the people streaming down around us like stones falling through space, the blank faces arriving and then passing away, not noticing anything, so absorbed are they in business of their own. And I in mine, and I am thinking, You don't slip quietly away from a murder one when you're yoked to a maniac playing a saxophone. But no one is watching us after all, no one gives us even a glance, and now I know that it's the horn that's blinding their attention, and I begin to laugh. So we walk up the avenue, him playing, and me laughing like a loon.

Santa Barbara

Then it all be over and I coming home to myself again, hump down on my knees in the rain. Dont know nothing what I do. Only know I make my obligation and now it finish. So I getting up again on my feet, but weak like they nothing left of me at all.

I following Yusuf down the street. A long way west we going. Too long for me walking all of it. Somewhere middle of the island, I fall down. So Yusuf pick me up and carry me along like I an empty plate, don't got nothing inside no more. I go back in the dark and I waking up just one time more. One minute I wake up and see me rising up one wide stairs, coming up in a yard between buildings and up in the sky some stars still shine in the light of first morning.

Yusuf take me in his house and we sleep maybe four five hour. I sleeping like I drown in black water. Know no thing and have no dream, till Yusuf call me: "Santa, wake up, time we go back in park." So I opening my eyes and seeing the sun stand high at the windows of the house.

So Yusuf make food and I walking through the rooms of the house. All them empty and white walls, only in one a chair and table and in one a bed. And everywhere, books sitting. And on the walls, from bottom to top, the black marks Yusuf's allah making there. This in two rooms and half the third, and at the place the black marks stop, there Yusuf's brush and pen lying. So I see it a strong thing, to have the words of a god for the walls of the house. Then we eat the food and go out in the shining sun.

We walking up and across fast, because we already late this day. Now we come near the park, and it too much noise there, even for Sunday. Something happen, something not right. Come closer and see it one big fight that happen. So I go for the place where the people are, but I too short to see what really happening. Now Yusuf come and move the people to the side, so I go down in the path he make. So we come in the middle of the people and it Yanni-B and one dead man be there.

So many dying, I thinking to myself, such a day for dead men it be. Must be Oggun very hungry, so Eshu Oku Oro too much busy making death. I see Yanni-B standing like half asleep half dead so I know it Eshu Oku Oro who just leave him. And Yusuf Ali raise he hand and make the place for Yanni-B going away by, because this Yanni-B now have to do.

Now come police in the blue shirt. First one come and push me out the way, so I give him good push back. One good shove and slow him down some little.

"What for you push me, mon," I say. "I not doing anything, only standing here."

But still the cop try to pass me by, so I take him hold of the arm. Pull him back near me.

"What for you come and push people for," I say. "Only because you have blue shirt on?" And I hold him by the sleeve. Then coming two more cops and I push one so he fall over the other one.

Now I getting them good and mad. Last cop I push come and hold .45 gun right in my eye, so close I cant see he face around it. But I still saying some things, keep them mad and keep them standing there.

So now they taking one my arms and pull up over my head and down. They twist other arm up behind my back, and lock them there together with the chain. They move me down the south side of the park, to the place I see they park they car. They pushing me now pretty hard and with the way they put my arms it dont feel so good. But I knowing they dont keep me long, maybe for some hours but not more. And I know how Yanni-B going far away in the hours they keeping me, and that feel fine.

Yusuf Ali

So out of the night there comes the morning, and Santa and I go back to the park again, because that is what there is for us to do. And I arrive, and everywhere there is still more confusion. I stand higher than the heads of the people, so all of it is present to my eyes. I do not know what it is that has happened, or how there came to be this battle, nor can I find any reason for it. But I can see well enough that it is over now. Johnny B. stands still with his weapon hanging from his hand, and Porco stands over him on the lip of the fountain, crying out in a loud voice, and he is speaking of Moses. So I remember and silently recite:

> We gave Moses the Book, and appointed
> with him his brother Aaron as minister
> and We said, 'Go to the people
> who have cried lies to Our signs';
> then We destroyed them utterly.
> And the people of Noah, when they
> cried lies to the Messengers, We
> drowned them, and made them to be
> a sign to mankind; and We
> have prepared for the evildoers

a painful chastisement.
And Ad, and Thamood, and the men
of Er-Rass, and between that
generations a many—for each
We struck similitudes, and each
We ruined utterly.
Surely they have come by the city
that was rained on by an evil rain;
what, have they not seen it? Nay,
but they look for no uprising.
And when they see thee, they take thee
in mockery only: 'What, is this he
whom God sent forth as a Messenger?
Wellnigh he had led us astray
from our gods, but that we kept
steadfast to them.' Assuredly
they shall know, when they see
the chastisement, who is further
astray from the way.
Hast thou seen him who has taken
his caprice to be his god?
Wilt thou be a guardian over them?
Or deemest thou that most of them
hear or understand? They are but
as the cattle; nay, they are further
astray from the way.

But even as I am reciting to myself I am moving in closer, because if it is always well to recall the words of Allah the Most High, I think that now may be a time to do something too. So I come into the midst, and I see that a man is dead, and there is nothing to be spoken of this, except "This man is dead." So I make a hole among the people for Johnny B. to go into, and he goes behind my back, and I do not see him anymore. I look only in front of me, and I see Porco jump down from the fountain, and he too vanishes from my sight.

So now the police begin to come and I begin to push the people into one another and stir them all up together, so that the police cannot come too quickly. I keep my hands low so that no one will see what I am doing, but my head I lift high to watch for any police not in uniforms.

Now I see one such, and it is the same old white devil from last night. So I move toward him and let him look at me. He comes for me now, and another with him, with a darker skin but still another white devil, and behind them there are three more. So I stop and wait for them, and they reach me breathless. Now there is a gun in my stomach and also one in my back, so I stand very still, not wanting to frighten them into pulling their triggers. Some of them pull back their coats to show me the gold badges, and here is a pair of handcuffs too. So I hold out my hands for them, but they are much too small to close over my wrists.

One white devil police strains to lock his chains over my hands, but they will not fit on and that upsets him.

"What am I supposed to do?" he is saying. "They won't fit on the big mother, not at all." And the guns are pushed harder in my front and back, as if someone thinks that that will make my arms get smaller. Truly they are all mad, the unbelievers. I turn my head from side to side and see that Johnny B. is gone.

"You do not need the handcuffs," I tell them now. "I am not resisting you. I have not committed any crime either, but I will go with you and answer questions. You do not need the handcuffs."

Of course they cannot believe me, but neither can they fit the handcuffs on. So they tell me to put my hands on top of my head, and I do that to make them happy. Now they lead me out of the crowd with the guns still pressed against my back and sides. I could tell them that they do not need the guns, but they would not believe that either. So I hold my silence and allow them to put me in the back of a car. Santa is already there, but I do not look at him, because now and for however long it will be necessary, we are only two people who have never seen each other before in our lives.

Tommy/Sal

"So what do you think, Sally? What do you say?"

"What do *I* think? I say, out of this whole crazy thing there's just one thing happened I understand, and that is, I lost my good chess clock. Comes from Germany, cost me forty dollars, and that was ten years ago. Don't even want to think what it would be now."

"You ought to hung on to it better then is what I think. I'll split it with you though, you want me to."

"Forget it, all right? Sorry I brought it up. One thing and another, it hasn't been such a great day, you know? But one thing, Tommy, whatever you do, don't ever say I didn't give this one a damn good try. I mean, we been talking to these people for six or seven hours, and if nothing shakes out of it, it's not my fault."

"I still say we ought to be able to put something together. Maybe not the main dish, but something."

"I know you say that, but you're wrong. Want to count on your fingers and see what we got? Okay, we got one little spic, won't even give us his right name. We got one very big nigger, won't give his right name either. Then we got five of those jive niggers with the hair, and they're so stoned I think they don't even know their names. And one dead jive nigger, and he's not even saying hello. Just taking up room in the morgue. Now what can you put together out of that? A whole lot of nothing is what."

"What about the Perry Street detail, they pick up anybody?"

"You mean besides me? Very funny, oh sure, they picked up some kids that were standing around. Put them through the grinder over some pills and things they had in their pockets and let them out two hours ago. Right thing to do too, there's nothing coming from there."

"That was pretty good, when those guys tried to collar you."

"Good? It was a goddamn disaster."

"Hey, Sal, I'm just saying it was funny is all. What do you want, the guy you pulled on at the phones called in your description. So the Perry Street guys picked you up on the description, not bad in a crowd like that. You ought to be proud."

"Yeah, they should all get a medal. Tommy, that is my own goddamn precinct. I been there eight years, they should know what I look like. But no, punks outa the Police Academy, they come and hang guns in my face."

"Yeah, you know, Sally, it may be your home precinct and all, but it would have been better, those guys never showed up. Because all they did was get in their own way. You want to know what I think, they're the ones lost us the collar."

"Maybe. Maybe. I'm not saying you're right. No way to keep them out anyway. You got these people punching 911 and yelling riot, and they're the closest place."

"Still. No organization, that's the trouble with the whole department. Nobody ever knows what anybody else is doing. I mean, joking aside, Sally, you really ought not to be getting busted by your own guys."

"Please, Tommy, please. Don't rub it in. But you're right, those Perry Street guys, they should stick to oppressing the queers. I'm gonna put in for a real transfer, come down here full time."

"You like the Fifth? You like Chinatown?"

"I like it better than that. Tommy, it's getting late here, the wife'll be crawling the walls."

"Call her and tell her to wait. Let's go back a minute. We got to be able to think of something."

"Okay, I'm listening. Think of something."

"Well, what about those chukka sticks? I mean, we got a felony homicide here, and we got those sticks, we should put out a warrant on Dellacroce."

"Sure, only we got no way to put Dellacroce with those sticks."

"What are you talking about? You saw him, I saw him."

"Yeah, we saw him all right, Tommy, but we didn't see him kill the nigger, now did we?"

"So print the sticks."

"You know, Tommy, this Dellacroce guy of yours is not bad. He must have oiled those sticks, there's not a print on them anywhere."

"Wouldn't you know. Okay, the big nigger and the little spic."

"Yeah, them. They're no good to us either."

"Why the hell not? Chrissake, Sally, they're accessories after. They covered for him, they got him out of there. Probably know where he went too."

"Sure, you know that and I know that. You want to, you can call up the D.A. with it and listen to him laugh at you. Me, I been laughed at enough for one day."

"Seriously, Sal."

"Seriously, I tried it and it didn't work. I went in with both of them and gave them the accessory-after pitch. Told them the time they could pull if they didn't want to be helpful, the whole rap. And neither one of them even twitched."

"That big guy, what's his name, Yo-something, what'd he say his name was?"

"Yusuf Ali Muhammad Arafat Baraka Bulljive I Didn't Do Nothing Man. Something like that. What about him?"

"I saw him last night. He took my gun off me and broke it in half."

"Jesus. He must be as bad as he looks."

"You can take that to the bank. But what I'm thinking is, I could put in a charge on that and we could work from there. Hold him a little longer anyway."

"Maybe. Yeah, that could work. One thing though, Tommy, you got a license, right?"

"Yeah, of course, I got one through the snoop shop."

"And the gun you had last night, that's the one you have the license for? It was a bigger caliber or anything like that?"

"Okay, I guess that's out."

Tommy/Sal | 329

"Sorry, but it won't play. Tommy, you ought not to be doing things like that. You know what the laws are like now, somebody decides they don't like you, you could even pull some time for it. I hate to see you pull time for anything as stupid as that."

"So what do you want me to do, walk around with a BB gun? There's people don't like me in the street too, you know."

"Look, call me in the week, I'll fix it for you. I can fix you for anything you want short of a machine gun."

"Yeah, you're right. I'll do it, Sally, and thanks."

"Don't mention it."

"Only you sure I can't get a machine gun? No, but what about the little spic, what does he say to you?"

"Says his name is Santa Barbara, and he didn't do nothing either, man."

"Santa Barbara."

"Listen, this guy is fresh out of the jungle. I come across some guys like that before, and I don't like it. They all do voodoo, gives me the chills. They all got saint's names too."

"Anything we can get him on at all?"

"No. I mean, I bet he doesn't pay his taxes, but that's about it. These guys, the laws they're breaking are ones we never heard of anyway. And this one, he's only got about five words English, can't talk to him much at all."

"You tried them together?"

"Of course I did. They say they don't know each other and they act like they don't, and there's no way I can tie them up. Tell you the truth, I almost can buy that part of it, because I just don't feature those two guys getting along so well. And I don't see either one of them being in drugs either, while we're on the subject. The witch doctors, you know, they're past all that. They take some stuff, but what they take is plants and things, there's nothing on the books about it. And Black Muslims, I don't love them or anything, but they're not in dope, they never have been. Against the religion."

"So what are you trying to tell me? They didn't really cover for Dellacroce back there? The whole thing is just some kind of weird accident?"

"First of all, I can't prove any different. And I'm not so sure it is any different. Maybe they just got caught in the middle, like they say."

"But they were part of the tip."

"Oh yeah, the famous tip. You know, Tommy, I didn't know you for so long, I might be just a little annoyed with you. Because I go after this thing just as hard as I can, and it's mainly to do you a favor, and I end up with egg all over my face, and you're still not telling me everything."

"What? What am I not telling you?"

"You're not telling me enough about this tip."

"I told you, Sally, you don't want that guy."

"Yeah, you told me all right. But I'm beginning to think maybe I do want him. Because didn't I see him there today? Right in the big middle of everything? Little bum-looking guy with a great big horn? And where he goes nobody knows, except for maybe you, but I'm starting to think if anybody could tell me what's really going on with this thing, that's the guy. So you can play or pay, but quit complaining."

"I can't give him to you, Sally, I can't do that."

"Yeah, it's what you keep saying. Why not?"

"I couldn't give him to you if I wanted to, not now. I mean, the guy is not stupid or anything, after today I don't think he's gonna show up on Spring Street and buy me another drink."

"So. But if you want a warrant on Dellacroce, I want a warrant on him."

"Can't do it."

"Why? Tell me why, give me a goddamn reason."

"Sally, I don't even know his right name."

"You don't—Oh Jesus. Hey, Jerry, Jerry, come over here a minute, will you?"

"What can I do for you, boss?"

"Go downstairs, get those guys we brought in here two o'clock. Desk sergeant has their numbers. I want you to give them back what they had in their pockets and tell them to get out of here and never come back."

"Hey, Sally, wait a minute, you going to throw it all away?"

"Throw what? Tommy, what do you want?"

"Can't you keep them a couple of more days? Could be one of

them'll say something, you keep working on them."

"Are you joking? Tommy, you know how it is, we don't got room in the cooler for guys we do got cases on. Go on, Jerry, get them out of there."

"You got it, boss. You want I should tell them anything?"

"Tell them they're not good boys in the future, they're really gonna get it next time. I don't know. Tell them what you feel like, just get rid of them."

"You got it."

"All right, Sally, all right."

"I'm sorry, but you know that's how it's got to be."

"Ah, you don't have to say that, Sal. I screwed it up myself, I admit. I owe you one."

"Forget it. It was worth a shot. We missed, that's all. Next time. So let's get out of here. We'll go the Baxter Street place, have a drink, then I really got to get home."

"I'll buy you a new clock."

"You don't have to do that."

"No, I'm gonna do it. We should finish that game too, you know."

"Now you're gonna tell me you remember the position, right? Uh-uh. Better we should start another one sometime. And next time, Tommy, chess only."

"Whatever you say."

"Days like this, you know, they get me down. Lot of people start talking, and none of them can tell the same story the same way. Little bit of that and nothing at all makes sense anymore."

"Yeah, Sally, that's the trouble with this one, it's just too crazy all around, none of it makes any sense anywhere."

"I know. And a whole lot of nothing, that's what we end up with."

"I know. Come on, I'll buy you a drink."

"I'm not blaming you, understand. It's just how it was."

"Sure. I'll still buy you a drink."

"A whole lot of nothing. Okay, I'll take the drink."

Yusuf Ali

Now for a long time I must know nothing but my name: Yusuf Ali. How long it is I cannot tell, for I am kept in a room with no window, only a hot and unmeasurable electric light. And there I wait. It is impossible to know the time. The police talk to me, singly and in groups. They leave me alone and then they come back, and still I tell them nothing. They put me in a room with Santa and watch us together through a glass. This is the longest time. I do not look at Santa, or even at the mirrored glass, but only at a section of empty light some feet above my own reflection.

The police come back again to talk and then to scream at me and Santa. I do not answer them. I look only at the section of light and I try to make the words of Allah begin in my mind. But the words will not come and I cannot recall or recite them. Now it is no longer a matter of not saying anything. Truly, I know nothing. Of this I am afraid. But now the police stop the shouting. They take us apart from one another and lock us in the bars, and more time passes.

Still I am nothing but a vacancy. I stand, hold the bars, and think nothing, can no longer even imagine the progress of time. If I could remember anything to say, perhaps I would tell it to them now. The police return and I think now, now comes the question, and this time perhaps I will answer. There is no question, however. And now I am standing in the street, where the night has fallen, and my own world also has fallen back into its place around me.

I walk up Elizabeth Street, breathing in a heavy smell of Chinese cooking, but still it is gratefully free air. I move into the crowds of Chinatown Sunday night, and once among so many people, I slow down and wait. Now Santa passes me, not looking back, but I catch the words that fall from his mouth as he turns into a side street.

"Columbus Park," Santa says.

I do not follow him, even with my eyes. I walk up to Canal and turn down through the street market, letting the crowds carry me down the steep sidewalk. When the crowd has expelled me at the bottom I begin to walk more quickly through the small crooked streets, away from the lights and the people. I turn the last corner and walk along the dark border of the park. Santa is already waiting on a bench and I sit down beside him. From the habit grown in the hours of questioning, we still do not look at each other. Santa is the first to speak.

"You telling them something, Yusuf?"

"Nothing."

"Me, I don't either. Don't say nothing, only my name."

"Good."

"I scared some plenty, though," Santa says. I look at him. He is fingering his necklaces.

"I know," I say. "So was I. I think you were never in jail."

"No."

"I was. And I don't ever want to be again. Never."

"No," Santa says. "You don't want, and I don't want. But it okay now anyway. We make out. They don't call us back."

"No," I say. "They cannot. They do not even know who we are."

But now I see the two white devils, the one from last night together with the one who was asking most of the questions today. They are walking together on the other side of Bayard Street, and the second one looks up and straight at us, but it is a look which seems without curiosity or recognition. I watch the two white devils going into a door on the corner, wondering what they may do.

"They saw us," I say. "One of them saw us." Santa shrugs.

"I don't think they see us," says Santa. "We sitting in the dark. And if they do, they don't know how to tell us from the trees."

I say nothing. The wind rises to stir the branches of the trees in the park behind us. Now, with the night, it is cooler.

"Good idea maybe we don't stay here no more anyway," Santa says. But he does not move.

"Yanni-B, he speak to you?" Santa says.

"No."

"Not to me either," Santa says. "And Porco talking. Talking, talking, all the time. Yusuf, you hear what he say this time?"

"No," I say. I listen to the wind on the leaves behind us.

"Maybe I know what he was saying," I say, "even if I didn't hear it."

"Yes," Santa says. "But what you think, Yusuf, we seeing them ever again?"

"Maybe not," I say.

"But maybe so, Yusuf," Santa says. "Maybe one day, rings the phone. Or you turn a corner, there they are." He stands up.

"Can't stay here no more," Santa says. "But Yusuf, I like to talk to you some time."

"We can't go back to the Square," I tell him. "That is finished."

"This I know," Santa says. "But maybe one day I come your house."

"Come," I say. "The door is open to you." Santa moves a little away and then turns back.

"So what you think it be like, Yusuf, when Yanni-B and Porco they come back again?"

"What makes you think they are together?" I ask him. And he shrugs.

"I don't know," Santa says. "Maybe they not together, I don't know."

"What it will be like," I say. "It will be different, I think. Everything will have to change."

"Maybe," Santa says. "So I going now to my house to sleep."

"Sleep well," I say. Santa laughs.

"I sleeping well tonight I think. Tonight I think I sleep like stone."

I watch him cross the street and turn the corner, and now I am alone with the wind on the leaves, and truly I am very weary. But after some minutes I get up myself and go back into Chinatown, back to Canal Street and the noise of the market. There I surrender my emptiness to the sound of the many voices, which speak in several tongues which I do not understand and do not need to understand. The voices merge and the combined sound lingers with me as I walk down into the lower end of Canal Street, where all the doors are locked and darkened and silent. Here at last the words of God return to me, not now as the divided matter of recitation, but conformed into one single sign. So I go farther through the darkness of the night street, secure in my knowledge and my power, for God is very great, and there is no God but God, and God knows everything.

Johnny B. / Porco

So it turns out that it isn't over after all, that would have been just too much to ask for. I keep on up Sixth Avenue, with Porco playing the horn at my left side, and somewhere around Twenty-third Street I finally manage to stop laughing, which is a very good thing, because my stomach is starting to hurt something awful by this time. Only now I have to start thinking again. The good luck is that I have thought this one out before.

And we keep going and going up the avenue, me wearing myself out trying to keep up with him and play at the same time. Because I have to keep playing, it's a necessary thing. I preached a good sermon back there, all right, maybe it was one of my best, but I can't just fall over dead, now can I? My head is buzzing with what's going to happen now, what now? And finally I run out of breath altogether.

Now finally Porco shuts up with the horn, but almost immediately he starts talking again.

"Look," Porco says, "I don't want to follow you around or anything, but the fact is I have to go somewhere too."

"All right all right all right all right," I say. "I can't do anything about anything anymore. I don't care what you do, but why don't you just be quiet about it."

"Because the cops are going to be looking for me too," Porco says. "If they find me it's not going to be good for you either. Because I can't go through that one, I'm too old to do time."

"I don't want to hear about it," I say. "I do not want to hear about it. Come along if you want to, I really don't care, but just try to keep your mouth shut, okay? This one time, do that for me."

Deal, I say, and I don't even say it out loud. Because I'm about to pop a lung anyway, so just as well that I give my whole attention to moving my legs. Only thing I would like to ask is, are we going to try to get out of town by walking? But I don't ask that one either.

So Porco shuts up with his mouth too, which is a great relief to me at this time, but still I'm getting angrier and angrier, and I don't even know what I'm mad at unless it's the circumstances, or maybe my own incompetence. I just keep tearing up the blocks, with smoke pouring out of my ears, and I really don't care if Porco is keeping up or not, but I do notice that he is.

Now Johnny B. is cutting over to the west. I stay with him pretty well, but somewhere around Penn Station I get a horrible stitch in my side. Like I might lie down and die the next minute. I think that I would even trade off my horn for five minutes of sitting down, but of course no one is offering me that bargain. And just when I think it's really all over, the pain shuts off and now I feel only euphoria. I feel like I'm good for all the way over the George Washington Bridge. Which may be where we're going too. But Johnny B. turns off at the Port Authority and I follow him into the station. Thinking, ah, we're going to take a bus somewhere. But instead he stops at a locker.

————

I jam my key into the locker so hard I almost break it. This is where I keep my rainy-day arrangements, and right now it's raining bad luck so hard I can't see daylight. I open the locker, jerk out the briefcase, and open it to check the contents, all of which are there in place: a wallet with cash and credit cards and a driver's license all in a nice new name—I never used it before, this name—and traveler's checks and even a clean shirt and a toothbrush. Here is everything a citizen needs for a sudden unanticipated journey, so I snap the briefcase shut and discard the car keys into the locker for somebody else to find sometime. The keys clash against the back of the locker and I smash the door shut on them, luxuriating in my bad temper, and then I start moving again.

Oh, so we're not taking a bus after all. Just when I thought I could breathe again, Johnny B. moves out of the station double time. All the way across town now, and then on up some more. Once again I feel death knocking at my door, but now we end up in the lobby of Avis Rent-a-Car. Where they try harder. And Johnny B. walks up to the counter and suddenly becomes the incarnation of sweetness and light—yes, miss; no, miss; thank you so much. But while we are waiting for the car to come down to the street, he starts snapping and snarling again. Now the car comes down, it's a new car, a Dodge.

"You want to put that in the trunk or something?" I say, pointing at the horn. But he won't give it up. He won't even say anything, just shakes his head.

"All right, all right," I say. "I don't care if you're comfortable, get in the car already." And I get into the driver's seat.

So it's okay after all? Yes it is, I'm going to get out of here. And a good thing too, because if there's one thing I can't stand up to now it's a lot of cop questions and psychiatric examinations and things like that. So I jump in the passenger seat all ready to let out a great sigh of relief. But unfortunately there's no room for that, with the horn jammed into my midsection. I should have put it in the trunk, but I was too afraid he might ditch me.

I take the car over to the West Side and head down toward the Lincoln Tunnel, being careful to obey all the rules of the road. Then I take it through the tunnel and come out onto the Jersey Turnpike, picking up speed. The car handles well, probably because it's on its first hundred miles, but it does improve my mood to feel it doing what I tell it to. Finally, I've got a grip on myself and the world again. From the ramps I can look back over to the New York skyline. We're running parallel to the island, down toward the foot of the city. I'm beginning to relax as it all drops away behind me, and I think I'll turn Porco on again, he's better than the radio.

"All right," I say, "Talk to me."

But all I get is a nice long silence.

"I don't know," Porco says finally. "I don't think I have anything to say."

"Surely you jest," I tell him. "You always have something to say."

"So where are we going?"

"I don't know. Anywhere you want to go?"

Porco starts to laugh.

"So how about New Orleans?" he says. "Maybe I could get some sessions down there."

"Sure you can," I say, laughing myself at that. "When was the last time you had any sessions anywhere?"

"I never was in New Orleans though," Porco says. "They don't know what I'm like."

"They'll find out," I say, "soon enough." But Porco doesn't rise to that. In fact, he doesn't say anything at all. Unbelievable, the world must have come to an end, Porco doesn't have anything to say.

I keep driving, it gets dark, and we're somewhere in New Jersey, and Porco still hasn't opened his mouth.

"So all right, Porco," I say. "Let's hear from your talking rock. I'm ready. Get it out and let's hear what it's got to tell us."

———

And I start patting down my pockets. Hard to do, cramped up like this against the horn. I look everywhere, feel every pocket twice. But it's not here. It's not anywhere around here. The weight of it is gone. It's left me.

"I can't find it," Porco says. "I think I must have dropped it somewhere."

"You lost it?" I say. "How could you do that? Where did it go?"

"I don't know," Porco says. "I had it last night."

"I know you had it last night, my man," I say. "It would take me a lifetime to forget that, if not longer."

"It left me," Porco says.

"What do you mean, it *left* you? You dropped it somewhere, that's what happened. You weren't paying attention and you lost it."

"It left me," Porco says. He looks pretty dismal about it too.

"Well, that's the breaks," I say. "We can't go back and look for it, you know. Not practical, not now."

"Of course," Porco says. "I wouldn't ever find it anyway."

"So cheer up about it," I tell him. "You probably don't need it anymore. Probably you never did."

True enough, I think. It's a little sad, that's all. It was nice to have it around, while it was there. But also, on reflection, a lot of trouble too. And now it's done its business. And maybe I've done mine, for the present anyhow. So there's not even a reason to be sad for. I'm just tired, that's all. Oh lordy, lordy, yes, I'm tired.

"You will be going back though," Porco says. "Sometime."

"Of course I'm going back," I say, getting very suddenly angry again. "You think I wouldn't go back, after this? This is nothing, it will cool out in a month."

Which gets no comment from Porco.

"I have to think all these things over. I have to figure them all out. But one thing I already know is that there will be some people

Johnny B./Porco | 341

expecting to hear from me. And some that aren't expecting it might hear from me too, because I'm beginning to think I owe some people a few things."

Porco still doesn't say a word. This is an outrage, all summer long he gives me no peace, and now I can't get a word out of him.

"Can you hear me?" I say. "Can you?"

"I can hear you," Porco says. "I've already said my piece, that's all. If you want to talk you can do it yourself."

He works the horn up to his mouth and starts to play.